GUARDIANS OF THE FOUR SHIELDS

A Lost Origins Novel

A. D. DAVIES

www.addavies.com

ISBN: 978-1-913239-46-6

NOVELS BY A. D. DAVIES

Lost Origins Novels:

Tomb of the First Priest

Secret of the Reaper Seal

Curse of the Eagle Plague

Guardians of the Four Shields

Gold of the Lost Empire

Adam Park Thrillers:

The Dead and the Missing

A Desperate Paradise

The Shadows of Empty men

Night at the George Washington Diner

Master the Flame

Under the Long White Cloud

Alicia Friend Investigations:

His First His Second

In Black In White

With Courage With Fear

A Friend in Spirit

To Hide To Seek

A Flood of Bones

To Begin The End

Moses and Rock Novels:

Fractured Shadows

No New Purpose

Persecution of Lunacy

Standalone:

Three Years Dead

Rite to Justice

The Sublime Freedom

Co-Authored:

Project Return Fire – with Joe Dinicola

PART ONE

CHAPTER ONE

TLAXCALA REGION, EAST OF MEXICO CITY

The Cathedral of St Bernard rose out of the jungle surrounded by thousands of trees and shrubs, shadowed by the cliff beside which it was built. Its blackened stones, stained green with moss and wild grass, suggested it wasn't in the rudest of health. However, the Church kept the bulk of this building pristine, not least for the tourist revenue—a steady stream of the curious and the devout eager to behold the bust of St Bernard in the courtyard, which was rumored to glow depending on the time of year, the weather, and the angle of the sun.

There were three ways to access the cathedral: a helicopter for the visitor willing to pay top dollar, a winding but more direct trail accompanied by mules and workers who carried tourists' bags and lunch for a small fee, or picking your own route the long way around through a jungle trail that took the average person two hours to traverse.

It had taken Toby Smith almost three.

The trail brought the cheaper tourists to the opposite side of a hundred-foot-wide gorge which, frankly, Toby thought gave them the best view of the incredible building. If the trek with his friends, Dan Vincent and Charlie Locke, hadn't exhausted him, the scenery would have taken his breath away on its own. He noted, not for the first time since rising at four a.m., that he really needed to press on with the last twelve new year's resolutions and, finally, get into shape.

The trio rested, assessing the bridge that would take them to their destination.

"When the Roman Catholic Church first constructed St Bernard's, there was no need for the second approach." Toby wiped his brow with a red handkerchief. Although they'd set off at the literal crack of dawn, heat was building, even this high in the hills. "But they own the trail, and we can't afford the toll at the moment."

In his khaki outfit, including a wide-brimmed hat, Toby quite fancied himself as a rakish Indiana Jones type. However, considering his five-foot-six stature and a handful of gut flopping over his belt—combined with the typical fitness of a British man edging ever closer to the end of his sixth decade—he was perhaps somewhat optimistic in this vision.

Closer to the layperson's interpretation of what an intrepid explorer should look like was Dan Vincent. The former US Army Ranger had been scouting ahead at his own insistence. Whether this was to ensure Toby's and Charlie's safety or that Toby's slow pace frustrated him, he never said.

"Disappointing," Dan announced. "I was kinda hoping for a rickety rope bridge. Not that steel and glass thing. Hell of a walk, but I guess it's worth it."

Perched on a conveniently shaped rock, Charlie replaced the top of her water canteen. Like Dan, she was visibly tired and decked out in modern hiking attire, but nowhere near as sweaty as Toby despite the pack of equipment she carried on her back.

She said, "We could have afforded fifty dollars. But I'm not objecting. I enjoyed the walk."

"We don't know how much it will cost us to get out of here," Toby replied. "If we find anything like what I'm hoping for, we may need every penny available to us."

Dan scratched his chin, the hard stubble rasping under his fingernails. "If you hadn't insisted on paying so much for our fixer, you could have saved a couple of bucks."

"He's the best, though. And you know it. In fact, I think I see him."

Toby squinted to see across the gorge and waved. A figure waved back, dwarfed by the cathedral's fascia and the courtyard.

"Guess he must have taken the direct route," Dan said.

"He'll come back." Charlie rested a hand on Toby's shoulder and softened her tone. Her Welsh roots always came through stronger when she offered comfort like this. "Once we're properly funded again, he'll jump at the chance."

Dan strode on ahead. "Guess we best say hi then."

Although the bridge appeared steady, it swayed ever so slightly. Toby clung to the handrail as he crossed. Charlie remained behind him, charitably not commenting on his progress, or lack thereof, while Dan remained ten paces ahead, increasing that margin with every step.

On the other side, Harpal Singh greeted them. No sign of a handshake between the two men.

"Hey." Harpal's normally bubbly demeanor was absent, presumably because of the frosty reception he had received from the group's man-at-arms. "We were right to come early. The priest is alone in his quarters, but I got a message to him. He'll meet us in the entrance."

Toby clapped Harpal on both shoulders, beaming his way, which seemed to take the man back a little. "Thank you for arranging this. I know it can't be easy getting away."

Harpal shrugged and glanced at Charlie.

Toby dropped his hands, his smile stretched into a near-grimace.

Charlie skipped forward and offered a brief hug, which Harpal returned without meeting her eye.

"Good to see you, Harps," she said, but sounded less than good.

Harpal stepped back to take in all three. "You know I wouldn't have taken that job if I had any choice."

Dan sniffed. "Your boss okay with you helping us?"

"Gig economy." Harpal gave another shrug, clearly trying to hide his nerves. "I'm technically a freelancer. He can't stop me working for anyone else as long as there's no conflict of interest."

"There are no hard feelings here," Toby said. "But let's press on before the hordes arrive."

Harpal led the way towards the vast structure growing out of the jungle. Dan still barely looked at him, and Charlie's frown was unmistakable. Toby understood their sentiments, the pair having clung on for the past months of frugality. But he also recognized why Harpal needed to part ways. He was a young man with rent to pay and hobbies to pursue, not to mention parents back in Britain who relied on his presence from time to time. Toby couldn't deny Harpal's choice to work semi-regularly for Colin Waterston, Toby's former protégé, had squeezed his heart somewhat, but he was confident Harpal would return to the group once their financial situation improved.

"So," Harpal said with strained joviality, "is this another wild goose chase, or something important?"

"Not sure we should be sharing that information," Dan said.

"Client confidentiality extends to you guys, as well as Colin."

"Colin?" Charlie said. "Not 'that upper-class twit'?"

"You don't have to tell me." Harpal's eyes found the ground in front of them, a cobbled courtyard where several state employees were currently setting out ropes for the queueing system. "I understand. I just had to set this up and get you visas and an appointment."

"We got our own appointment," Dan said. "You just smoothed the way. Better hope no one else knows we're here."

"Locals are secure," Harpal said. "I made sure the cops know you're researchers approved by the Vatican. You won't get any grief from them."

"Great. Although, I doubt they're gonna like what we find. If we find it."

Charlie made a *hmm* sound, and said, "Think they'll hold up their end of the bargain? Or cover it up? If it points to something they don't like?"

"Don't care." Dan pointed at the cross over the yawning entrance. "As long as we're paid."

Their footfalls were loud on the hard surface, crunching with the dust that blew in from the jungle every night. The staff kept it clean, but nature tended to make a mockery of such efforts.

Striding to keep up with Dan, Toby glanced up at the big former soldier. He didn't believe for a second that Dan was motivated purely by money. He wouldn't have stuck around on the strength of an IOU if he was. "When Catholicism found its feet in this part of the world, there were still hundreds of temples dedicated to gods erected by the native populations."

Simultaneously, Dan and Harpal made an exaggerated snoring noise. They snapped their attention to one another, their eyes met, and they burst into laughter.

"Some things never change," Harpal said.

Dan grumbled, but could not kill his smile. "I guess."

Toby normally scolded them for making fun of his attempts to educate. The more knowledge, the better armed a person was for difficult situations.

He pressed on. "It was common for the Roman Catholic Church to suppress indigenous religions by incorporating their own buildings into existing architecture. As happened here."

The priest waited ten yards away, bathed in the rising sun under a doorway that was big enough to drive a bus through. He was dressed in black robes with the traditional Roman collar, and he clasped his hands before him as he rocked back and forth on his heels. He sported a silver-gray beard and black hair flecked with white. He was of Indian rather than Mexican descent, which Toby had guessed by his name already: Rajveer Pandi.

Toby said, "This site was once a temple dedicated to an Aztec god, although records of which one exactly were lost. It wouldn't do to remind the locals of what their ancestors used to worship. They converted the natives, demolished the ancient shrine, and built this in its place. Within a generation, the old ways were forgotten."

"Until the modern world came calling," Charlie said. She tapped her ear. "Phil is online and waiting."

"Will we need that?" Harpal asked. "Backup?"

"Let's hope not."

They arrived on the steps and ascended with small waves of greeting toward Father Pandi. He extended his hands in welcome. They each introduced themselves.

"Father Pandi, thank you for seeing us," Toby said. "I know this must be a frightful intrusion."

"Not at all." Rajveer Pandi spoke with one of the oddest accents

Toby had heard. Solid English, with a strong Indian inflection, tinted with Spanish flavor. It was quite delightful. "We always welcome researchers from the Vatican."

Father Pandi led them into the main building. Unlike the outer shell, the interior was underwhelming to say the least, reflecting people's ability to forge outstanding architecture so far from civilization. *Functional* was the byword here: the pillars were rounded rather than sculpted, the floor was plain flag stones without the ostentatious adornments that you find in European cathedrals, and the windows were slits instead of massive stained glass made up of storybook pictures.

"I am very happy to accommodate you," Father Pandi went on, "but perhaps I can help you more if you tell me what aspect of our cathedral you are interested in. Then, perhaps, we can get to the... other subject. I doubt very much it's the *miracle* my predecessor reported fifty years ago."

Toby didn't need to see Dan's face to guess his barely concealed smirk. It was in his bunching of the shoulders.

"No," Toby answered. "I believe that matter has been taken care of already."

They paused at the altar where the bust of St Bernard was housed in a respectful cabinet made completely of glass.

"Sadly, we had to encase it," Father Pandi said. "Too many people wished to touch it. I do not know where the rumor came from that stroking his smooth head brought good luck and a strong hairline, but many seem to believe it. We reserve that privilege for special guests." He cast his gaze over Toby's thinning pate. "I can arrange a private moment if you would like."

Toby paid less attention to his hairline than he did his ever-softening waist. But he was fully aware that he overtook his prime some time ago and demonstrated it in more physical ways than one. He didn't need reminding.

"Perhaps if there's time later," he said, diplomatically. "What we really want to see is any potential artwork, as depicted in this codex. I believe it will be found in the cavern that's closed to tourists."

Charlie had removed an aged leather-bound manuscript from her backpack and was holding it with cotton gloved hands. She opened the brittle, yellow pages to the section bookmarked with a static-free plastic strip.

The group halted, and Father Pandi reversed his last steps to examine the picture.

Like many of the discoveries from the Lost Origins Recovery Institute, Toby had stumbled across this by accident. He was researching a clue dredged up eighteen months earlier on the expedition that had sealed the team's fate, namely scrolls that predated known human writings. This had led him to a conclusion that more modern, educated humans had kept these secrets from the masses, fearing the suppression suffered by the indigenous populations of South America and beyond. He had tracked this codex to a collector which their benefactor purchased on their behalf—on the assumption it would lead to a greater reward and a return on the man's investment. All they had to do was prove their calculations were correct, and they'd soon be in possession of the next stage of their hunt.

This particular codex, of course, was not a part of the haul from Africa. It was only hundreds of years old, not millennia.

"Where did you get this?" Father Pandi asked. "It is exquisite."

"The author is unknown," Toby replied. "It's written in a Spanish dialect known to be common in the 1600s. We think it was a trader or merchant who worked on the original foundations for this very cathedral. He is clearly well-traveled because the rest of the codex reads like a journal of sorts. He would have traded with people responsible for building St Bernard's before it was called St Bernard's. He may well have had access to both what we think we will find here, and the item I am hoping you'll loan to us. Once we prove our credentials."

Father Pandi paused, thinking. "You are not the first people this month to ask about that item. But you are the first to come with an order from the Holy See to lend it to you. Under the assumption you are correct about this other exploration."

"Who else was asking?" Dan said, his eyes becoming slits, roving the interior.

"Oh, a Chinese pair." Father Pandi sounded relaxed. "Possibly Korean. I assumed a gay couple, not that this matters, of course."

"Of course," Toby said. "They inquired after a picture like this? Or about what we're here to borrow?"

"They mentioned the cavity beneath and asked if anything interesting remained from those days. I explained it wasn't open to the public. And I assured them there was nothing there. I was not lying to them, Mr. Smith. Or was I?"

Toby referred to the codex again. "The author describes the location, and the cavern, in detail. We are certain this is the correct place."

The page Father Pandi resumed examining featured a cross-legged godlike image, not dissimilar to one of the many Hindu gods. It was clearly not your average Aztec deity, but there was something about the design that suggested the same people crafted it. Depicted in brown ink, tiny human creatures toiled all around this unnamed God, farming, harvesting, and eating. It was the opposite page that had led them here, though. A map, and an illustration of a much larger church, which Toby guessed was gleaned from the original plans.

Charlie said, "We think it is some sort of benevolent blessing on the people here."

"It looks kind of Indian," Harpal remarked.

Dan made a *hmm*. "We've been over that, thanks."

Harpal shrank back. Toby would give the lad a slap on the back later and tell him not to worry about the attitude. They would come around soon enough.

Instead, he concentrated on the question of the author's identity. "The descendants of the conquistadores were often of mixed race. As I'm sure you are aware, Father, their ancestors married into native families and supplanted the religions and traditions observed for centuries."

"Supplanted?" Father Pandi said, glancing up at Toby. It was the first time his tone came across less than genial.

"Supplanted or adapted." Toby offered a pacifying smile. "It's undeniable that the spread of Christianity was so successful due to their willingness to bring local traditions into their own doctrines.

Even our most traditional Christian ceremonies have roots in other cultures. The cutting down of a tree, bringing it into your house, and decorating it—a fine Christmas activity in all our homes, I'm sure—is a Germanic pagan ritual, which was common throughout Western Europe and up into what we now call Scandinavia—"

Dan snored.

Harpal did not join in this time.

Charlie said, "Father, are you able to direct us to the part of your cathedral where we can view this?"

The priest frowned. "There is no such artwork here, I can assure you."

Harpal opened his mouth to speak but thought better of it.

"If we can view the room," Charlie said, "we'll determine if what we need is there."

"Please." Toby put his hands together, like an upside-down prayer. "We understood you would grant us access."

Father Pandi took in the four people whom the archbishop of Mexico City, by way of the Vatican, had requested he accommodate. He shuffled a few steps to his right and said, "Follow me."

They deviated from the original path, passing by the supposedly miraculous bust and out through a modern annex that housed the toilet block. Beyond the fire exit, Father Pandi hurried along the western edge of the building, and even Dan had to stride to keep up.

"I don't like this," Dan said.

Toby trotted to maintain the pace. "He just wants to see what we're searching for. He has to be sure it's genuine before granting us access to—"

"Not right now," Charlie said and tipped her head toward Harpal.

"You're my employer here, not Colin bloody Waterston," Harpal said. "Everything is confidential. What exactly *are* we looking for? It might help if I know."

Charlie pulled to a halt. "*We* are looking for whatever the author chose not to write in this book."

She handed the codex to Toby. He put on his own cotton gloves and eased the book closed before securing it in Dan's pack.

Charlie swung her own backpack off her shoulder and dug inside, pulling out two golf ball sized nodes. She slapped one on the wall beside the door next to which Father Pandi lingered, beckoning them inside.

"What is that?" the priest asked.

"It's to help with our comms," Charlie said. "Don't worry, it is completely harmless to the brickwork. The adhesive is temporary organic compound that'll evaporate an hour after I remove it."

Harpal's eyebrows popped. "Impressive. You've improved them again."

Charlie gave a sharp nod and followed Father Pandi in through a thick wooden door which he held open for her. She slapped the other node inside the frame.

"You're quite sure...?" Father Pandi started.

"We've tested them on older surfaces than these. I promise they won't leave a mark."

They progressed through what Toby thought of as a hovel, like a hobbit house, where they all had to duck to avoid rubbing their heads on the rough ceiling carved out of the bedrock. It was lit with electric lanterns designed to look like oil burners and got darker as they trailed into a narrow corridor. There was no room for lights, so they edged through on faith that the priest did not have a cadre of mercenaries waiting to ambush them.

Melodramatic?

Perhaps, but it wouldn't have been the first time. In fact, it was one reason LORI was down to bare bones here in Mexico.

They emerged into a gloomy bedroom which Toby had seen online, the former priest's quarters, recreated for modern tourists to gawk at and comment on how spartan the living conditions were back in the Cathedral's glory days.

Father Pandi faced them, his fingers tapping a handcrafted chest of drawers. "Are you really from the Vatican?"

"We are here with the blessing of the Vatican," Toby said. "I promise, this is nothing that will harm your congregation or the building itself. It is a curiosity that the church would like explored. They trust us with what you and your predecessors have been keeping safe all these years. Using us to investigate means they can distance themselves from any accusations of supporting unholy relics."

Father Pandi's fingers ceased dancing. "Unholy..."

"Nothing that would compromise you." Charlie placed another communication node just inside the corridor they had exited. "Just a painting you didn't know was there."

Again, Father Pandi frowned at the tech. "This seems... highly irregular."

"It daisy chains our comms so we can talk to the outside world when we're deep underground," Dan said. "Don't worry about it."

"The drawers." Toby gestured to the chest that the priest was touching. "Does this lovely piece of furniture hide what we are here to see?"

"It might." Father Pandi braced himself against the item, both hands ready to lift. "Perhaps your large friend could give me a hand?"

Dan gave Toby a *who me?* look, and Toby answered with a nod. Dan sighed and went to work, taking the other side of the chest of drawers, which was plainly weighted down with more than just underpants and dress shirts—presumably to prevent damage should a tourist bump into it with any degree of force. They dragged it with a screech across the smooth flagstone floor, revealing a plain plastered wall. Father Pandi insisted on pulling it farther away than Toby expected they would need.

At an appropriate distance, the holy man appeared as out of breath as Toby had been after his trek along the jungle path, and even Dan looked as if he'd just finished a gym workout.

"There's nothing there," Harpal said.

Father Pandi pointed at the ground. "Not up here."

Charlie crouched and examined the square stone tiles making up that part of the floor. Father Pandi joined her, then the other men crowded around.

Father Pandi rapped his knuckles on one tile. A faint echo came back at them.

"Hollow," Charlie said.

"Indeed, indeed." Father Pandi extended a hand towards Dan without glancing at him. "If you are as organized as I expect, you will have something to pry this up with."

"Ah-hem." Charlie again flipped the backpack off her shoulder and opened it, producing a foot long crowbar, and handing it to Father Pandi.

The priest accepted the tool and levered up the square of black slatelike stone. Cool air hissed out and Toby's breath caught in his throat.

"What you seek is down there," Father Pandi said.

CHAPTER TWO

The priest of St Bernard's Cathedral had revealed a hole with metal rungs sewn into the rock like staples that hadn't embedded fully. The meagre light only illuminated the first ten feet.

Harpal peered in. "Another day, another dark pit." He looked pointedly at Dan. "You know I miss this sort of thing."

"You'll be back," Toby said, tempted to engage his back slap now, but thought better of it.

"Don't we all get a say in that?" Dan asked.

"Of course, but—"

"We agreed," Charlie said. "He's welcome whenever he's ready. Just like Bridget will be back."

Dan tutted. "This is nothing like Bridget. *He* had a choice."

"Alright, I've taken your crap ever since I had to go freelance." Harpal squared up to Dan and jabbed a finger in his chest. "It wasn't my fault we lost our funding. It wasn't my fault I've got bills to pay that LORI can't meet. And it wasn't my fault Bridget got recalled by parents who don't understand what she's trying to achieve."

On the third jabbed finger, Dan caught the digit and squeezed. Harpal's knees buckled, and he yelped in pain.

Father Pandi leaped between the pair and shoved Dan, breaking his hold on Harpal. "This is still God's house. I will not have this. And I will remove you from these premises, refuse to give you what you are here for, and take whatever punishment the Vatican deems appropriate—if any. Which I doubt there will be."

Toby had regained his feet without realizing it. His face was hot. "For crying out loud, we are a *family*. That's why am trying to keep us together. Families argue. Families fall out and break away, and they come back. They always come back."

All held their ground. Toby's blood pulsed in his head as he took several deep breaths.

Dan ran his hands through his hair, bringing his temper under control. "I'm sorry." He pointed at Father Pandi while Harpal regained his feet, gripping his finger. "And I'm apologizing to the Reverend and Toby, not you, Harps. Don't lay your hands on me again."

Harpal steeled his jaw, scanning between Toby and Charlie. "Let's just get on with it."

Charlie's feet were already dangling over the hole's edge, finding purchase on the makeshift ladder. "Boys will be boys."

She commenced her descent, followed by Harpal, then Toby. Toby paused when he heard Dan say, "Wait, you're coming too?"

Father Pandi was indeed climbing over the side. "I am responsible for this property. No matter that the cardinal says you are allowed in, you do not strike me as holy people. I will not permit you to damage my home."

"It's fine," Toby said. "He'll need to see this."

Charlie dropped several glow sticks, showing the bottom was around thirty feet below. She, Harpal, and Dan wore head torches, while Toby kept a flashlight clipped to his belt, although he did not turn it on yet.

With the air growing hotter and more humid with every rung, it took less than five minutes to reach the bottom and group together in the halo of light from the glow sticks. Toby handed Father Pandi the torch from his belt as a courtesy.

Charlie placed another node on the wall at the base of the ladder and tapped her ear. "Comms check."

A second later, she nodded. The subvocal earpiece, which ran on bone conducting technology, was working. Due to a deficiency in funds they hoped would be resolved shortly, Charlie and Dan wore the only two currently available. Toby had volunteered to be the one to go without. Right now, Charlie's husband, Phil, was listening in, ready to send in the cavalry if anything untoward occurred.

It seemed to Toby that nobody else was interested in their bounty. Nobody except a couple of Chinese gentlemen. Possibly Korean. But they were no longer present, and Phil would spot any incursion.

They all followed Father Pandi again, although the trip was shorter.

"We have no lights down here," the priest said. "We do not usually accommodate people in this part of the structure. I have a stash of candles, though. Give me a moment."

"Don't worry," Charlie said. "I've got this."

She used her latest gadget, a ferociously bright spotlight on squat tripod legs, which she had christened *dwarf arc lights*. She could angle almost them like a satellite dish, so they didn't blind everyone surrounding them the way a lantern would. It reached to knee height, and cracked to life, lighting up half the wall of this cavern. Dan took another from his own pack, set it up, and lit it.

They were in what appeared to be a cave, part of a larger structure that stretched into the dark behind them. Toby wasn't interested in that area, though. He studied this blank wall, dusting the fingertips of both hands over the surface. Searching... "May I see the codex?"

"How big is this place?" Harpal asked.

Dan passed Toby the book and Charlie shone her head lamp as Toby creaked open the pages.

"It is half the footprint of the cathedral," Father Pandi replied. "But it does not sit directly beneath. There is little here. It got looted before the original architects took possession. After, care was taken to preserve what remained. No gold, no jewels, you understand. But other things that could be removed. There was no need to demolish this. The ruins above were already abandoned hundreds of years earlier. The church did not rampage through the natives' lives, nor 'supplant' their temple."

Charlie concentrated on the diagram on the page before the one they showed Father Pandi. "But they did use the traditions to indoctrinate the native people into a foreign religion."

Father Pandi responded without malice, taking no offence, although he may have been lost in thought as he, too, scanned the wall before them. "Bringing Jesus into their lives is hardly indoctrination."

Toby migrated to the right, Charlie alongside him.

Dan checked back up the pipe. "Hey, Phil, all clear?" He waited for an answer and seemed satisfied. "Toby, you need me? I should be up top, watching our six."

"No drone keeping watch?" Harpal asked.

"It's a small one. Store bought. Phil says all clear, but—"

"It will spot anyone entering the quarters," Toby said, still searching for what he was sure would be here. "Ah."

His fingers found the grooves he was looking for and poked inside, flicking out dust and tiny pebbles. In seconds, the shape was clear in the dwarf arc lights.

Father Pandi squinted closer. "Is that... a figure-eight?

At some point, Charlie had taken the gray metal case from Dan's pack, a container the size of a lunchbox. She unclipped it to reveal two stone bangles encased in protective foam rubber. Both were shaped like a tight letter C, the edges cut in opposite angles so they mirrored one another and could slot together magnetically.

"The Aradia bangle," Toby said. "And the Ruby Rock bangle."

He removed them both and balanced them in his hands as if attempting to discern which weighed the most. The green flecks in the Aradia bangle and the red ones in the Ruby Rock one were barely visible. If he didn't know they were there, he would think it was just a fine crystallization.

"Don't you need Sibeko?" Harpal asked.

"I'm hoping not," Toby said.

"No hard feelings about Sibeko either?"

Charlie answered for Toby. "Jules was never fully committed. And our phone calls and emails have gone unanswered. He's got his own life now. It's just us."

Father Pandi observed closely. "The bracelets match the pattern."

Toby said, "We recovered these some time ago. They are a key. When accessing the most ancient of places, yes, it needs a special type of person to activate them—possibly a DNA link which we are ill-equipped to investigate, even with proper funding. However, the codex is younger. It indicates no such requirement."

Toby slotted the two bangles together, the open ends coming together, snapping into place as securely as powerful electromagnets.

"To us, it looks like a number eight. But that is just our modern way of thinking about the shape. The people who crafted the bangles had their own language. I doubt they even thought of these objects as bangles. Certainly not jewelry."

Toby moved them toward the grooves he'd uncovered in the wall.

"Before she was recalled to... other business... our language expert, Bridget, had already determined that this shape was their word for *key*."

He slotted the assembled bangles into the grooves, grating at first, remnants of debris having built up over the centuries. It stopped inches inside.

They all waited, not a breath taken between them.

Father Pandi asked, "Is something supposed to happen?"

"Maybe you need Sibeko after all," Harpal said.

Toby examined the wall around the key, dusting it, wiping, blowing on the surface. "This was constructed less than five hundred years ago, not thousands. They can't have known about the genetic line needed to activate..." He found another groove.

"Careful, Toby." Charlie helped him with the shape, the depression forming a circle with an approximate two-foot radius. "It's literally a key in this case."

Toby brightened. His feet wanted to dance. "Hidden for all this time, just waiting for someone to reunite these and return."

"But what is it?" Father Pandi demanded.

"Everyone back," Toby said. "Film this, one of you."

"I've been filming since we got down here," Harpal said, indicating a Go-Pro type body cam that Toby hadn't noticed until now.

All backed away, leaving Toby alone at the wall. He grasped the bangles, half-inserted into the corresponding holes.

"Careful," Charlie urged.

Toby looked down at his feet. He recalled the time Charlie tried to a "pick" a lock similar to this one, which triggered a mechanism that caused the floor to fall away. This chamber had been mapped dozens of times, though, including by echolocation, which indicated no such cavities.

Toby's heart raced. "Okay. Let's see what you're hiding this time." He twisted the key clockwise.

It didn't budge. He tried counterclockwise.

A tiny shift.

He strained, and it budged only another half-inch. "Dan?"

"Sure." Dan strode forward and added his strength to the exercise.

The circle defined in the stone wall turned with a grinding scrape, resistance kicking in as an unseen mechanism engaged. Toby pictured cogs sculpted from stone or treated wood.

The wall before them cracked. Spiderwebs ruptured out from the center, the disc in which the bangles were inlaid.

"Back," Charlie said. "Now."

Toby didn't need telling twice. He snapped out of his reverie, rushing back with Dan, and retreating farther with the others. Father Pandi's eyes were wide, his mouth open in fear rather than amazement.

"It can't be a trap," Toby said. "It can't be—"

The wall before them juddered, then started to crumble. Parts of it turned to sand and pebbles, before the entire mass disintegrated in a fluidic cascade and dropped into a pile, like snow sliding from a rooftop. Dust clouded the air, a fine fog pluming in the dwarf arc lights.

All wafted their hands in front of their faces, the four better prepared people pulling the snoods up from their necks to filter the detritus, while the priest whipped out a handkerchief and pressed it over his mouth and nose.

It took several silent minutes for the air to clear.

When it did, the first noise might have been considered blasphemous were it not uttered by a man of God. "Holy mother of Jesus..."

The destruction had unveiled a fresco, a mural spanning an area the size of a double-decker bus. Faded by time and the fine layer of dirt, the images were of a landscape, a desert to the left, merging with fields in the center and jungles on the right. Only the disc in which the bangles rested remained from before.

Toby breathed, his words almost a gasp. "A journey..."

All were now standing in a row, unable to look away.

On the desert section, lines of 2-dimensional people marched from a point in the distance where a cross-legged god resembled the picture they'd shown Father Pandi up in the nave. The characters were big, led by a man in profile, carrying a curved, rectangular shield which he held horizontally behind him, sheltering those nearest from the sun. The man was far taller than those he protected, and a glowing ball seemed to descend from the sky towards him.

The desert section merged with the fields of green and crops where the larger human figure, a whole torso and head taller than the nearest people, again held out his shield. This time he was sheltering them from rain and lightning. One bolt struck the raised circle at the shield's center.

In the final third, the man stood before women and children, his shield outstretched, fending off an army of spear-wielding warriors.

"From the Codex," Toby said, "this giant offered his services to those who needed him most. His only fee was food and somewhere to sleep until the danger passed. He helped migrate people from one place to another, or deflect rocks hurled by the gods. He sheltered worthy communities from poison from the sky and from hordes of barbarians."

"Like the A-Team," Dan said in a way that suggested he thought he was offering a clarification.

Toby ignored him. He'd said the same thing as a joke back when he and Charlie interpreted the manuscript for Alfonse Luca, their benefactor who reluctantly agreed to fund this trip. They weren't only seeking a fresco, though.

"Does this guy have a name?" Harpal asked.

Toby approached the section of wall where he had unlocked the false facia. "We believe he may the forbearer of the Aztec god Huitzilopochtli."

Dan gave one of his customary frowns and leaned in as if Toby hadn't already explained this before. "Hoo-wetz-i-what-now?"

"It is pronounced Weetz-ee-loh-*posht*-lee," Father Pandi said. "I am a student of the history of the region. But Huitzilopochtli is always depicted as a birdlike deity. The patron god of the Aztecs, worshipped by warriors and citizens alike. He received much blood in the form of sacrifices." Father Pandi paused, as if he had made some sort of point. "Catholicism requires no such sacrifice, so perhaps we were more welcome than you realize."

"Yes, yes," Toby said. "Huitzilopochtli *was* the patron god of the Aztecs. During the great migration from Aztalan, he told the people where they should establish their capital city—Tenochtitlan. He even has a shrine on top of the pyramid of the Templo Mayor in Tenochtitlan. It's decorated with skulls and was originally painted red to represent blood. And please, nobody snore."

"I wasn't snoring," Dan said. "Were you?"

"Wasn't even thinking about it," Harpal said.

For a second it seemed as if the pair were about to commence bantering like they used to, but they lapsed into silence.

"So, where is it?" Charlie asked.

Toby again touched the disc in which the bangles were embedded, half-hoping for some sort of psychic revelation. "I don't know."

"If we come home with just a video of a painting, Alfonse won't be happy."

"That'll be three-for-three," Dan added.

Toby waved them off. "Yes, yes, I know. We have had little in the way of success lately."

"There are giants in the Bible," Father Pandi said. "Not just the one felled by David."

"There are giants everywhere in fables, legends, and myths," Toby said. "We see many hoaxes to that effect. Just twenty-five years ago, Texas excavators recovered bones supposedly from a thirty-foot human. They were shown to be a mix of bones from ice age creatures, a cache of bodies washed down here from the great melting period."

"Wait, are you saying this is real?" Harpal asked.

"Not literally," Charlie said. "But this shield... It features in more than just our codex."

"Is that what you are investigating?" Father Pandi demanded. "Some sort of treasure? Are you grave robbers?"

Toby rounded on him, swallowed back his annoyance. "We do not rob graves. We are interested only in the historical record. This shield may have its origins in legends that have made its way into classic literature. How much do you know about the voyages of Odysseus? The battle of Troy?"

"Children stories. I know of children's stories."

Toby gripped the pair of bangles that had formed the key. He tried to turn it further, with no luck. Dan added his own muscle again, with the same result. When Toby checked on Charlie, she was carefully leafing through other pages.

She said, "I wish Bridget was here. I can't make sense of the rest."

Father Pandi offered to look, and nobody objected. He read the new page, the browned ink slightly smudged, like the rest of the book. "It is a puzzle. 'Respect for the Guardian must be shown, or the place of rest will take its revenge. Leave your offering, in blood or stone, and gaze upon his magnificence.' This is very odd."

"Yes," Toby said. "We interpreted 'the Guardian' as being a proper noun or title, and offerings at the time were not necessarily sacrificial animals. But then we don't know who wrote the passage. It could have been the author of the book, or he may have transcribed it from an older source."

"So, it could have been an Aztec ritual," Harpal said. "It might be asking us to slaughter a virgin goat or something."

"Been over that," Dan answered.

"Leave your offering..." Charlie mused. "Blood *or* stone. Or."

She unsheathed the knife from her hip, a snub-bladed military weapon, a replica of the one she lost on the mission that bequeathed them the Aradia bangle. She used the point to nick a dot of blood on her fingertip.

"What are you doing?" Father Pandi asked. "You cannot believe a drop of blood will do anything."

"I've seen weirder stuff than this," Charlie replied, ushering Toby out of the way.

"This is like some pagan ritual."

"As we've established," Toby said, "just because something is pagan doesn't mean it is anti-Christian. Please, let us do our work."

Perhaps he was still stunned from the cascading wall, but the priest stayed quiet.

Charlie extended her hand, leaving a dot of blood on the disc that had triggered the wall's demise. Nothing happened. She smeared a little more on the pair of bangles embedded in the lock.

Again, nothing.

Charlie stepped away, brow furrowed, obviously considering the passage, and whether this had all been a waste of time.

"Maybe the blood should be on the inside," Dan suggested. "That way, it gets into the guts of the machinery."

Toby shook his head. "I doubt—"

Dan reached for the bangles.

Charlie lunged to tackle him. "No! Don't—"

But her warning came too late. Dan snatched the bangles and withdrew them from the grooves. Immediately, a shuddering groan sounded from behind the mural. Dust rained from above.

"Out, now," Charlie ordered.

Crunching surrounded them, the rending of stone. All five dashed for the base of the ladder.

"What is it?" Father Pandi demanded. "What have you done?"

"*Leave your offering in blood or stone*," Charlie repeated. "We should have left the bangles in place."

They urged the priest to ascend first. As more cracks and crunching grew louder, there was no time to argue. He scrambled up the initial rungs.

"Now you," Toby said, tapping Harpal on the shoulder.

"No way," Harpal replied. "I'm the one filming. If this place is coming down, we need as much footage as possible."

"If you're injured, Colin will sue the hell out of us," Charlie said.

"Glad you're worried about me. But look." He pointed.

Part of the fresco had fallen away, a slab large enough to carry an SUV through. Beyond was another room. The dwarf arc lights penetrated deeply enough to see through the falling debris, where Toby could just about make out the end of a sarcophagus of a simple design, square with a domed top.

"Oh my."

For several seconds, Toby forgot about the impending destruction, and trotted forward. Harpal joined him, although it was unclear whether he was urging Toby back or if he was desperate to film what Toby was viewing.

The new angle revealed the coffin to be at least fifteen feet long and six feet high, with plates of gold and electric blue metal adorning the perimeter. It was a coffin big enough for three men.

"You don't think...?" Harpal started.

Two hands grabbed them roughly from behind and dragged them backwards. The view they'd had died as more of the wall collapsed in front of them. The hands belonged to Dan, which shoved them both towards the ladder.

"Out. Now."

Toby was nearest, so with Charlie already racing upward, he gripped the cold metal, braced himself, and climbed. Behind him, the two men argued about who was next.

Harpal said, "I need to film this."

"There's nothing left," Dan said in a growl. "And if you're going to come back and work with Toby and the rest of us one day, you've got to be alive to do that. This is my job. Now get your ass up that damn hole."

They exchanged no more words, and Toby doubted he would have heard them anyway, as the crashing and banging of ancient stone rose in volume. Above, Charlie and Father Pandi were already at the surface, calling to the trio bringing up the rear.

Although his lungs burned with the exertion of rushing up a humid hole, Toby pressed on. The air grew cooler, and the two men behind him made enough noise to show they were still alive. At the top, Charlie helped Toby out, where he lay on his back, soaked in sweat.

Harpal came up next, followed quickly by Dan, standing aside from the hole in the floor. A final clap of thunder echoed from below, leaving only a fog of dust to chase them out.

Toby propped himself up on his elbows. They were all gray in the face and hair.

"This is your *job*?" Father Pandi said.

Panting, Dan answered, "Yeah, sometimes I question it myself."

The priest got to his feet, trembling with what may have been adrenaline, fury, or a mixture of both. "You people destroyed a piece of history today."

"We revealed a piece of history," Charlie corrected, rising to meet him. "You got the images, didn't you, Harpal?"

"The SD card is all yours," Harpal said. "Part of the service."

Toby sat up straight, cross-legged, still catching his breath. "Unfortunately, we aren't as well-equipped as your regular employer."

"You aren't suggesting he sends this to Colin, are you?" Dan said.

Toby sighed and considered getting to his feet but chose to rest a little longer. "He can excavate. Or arrange it. Hopefully, the sarcophagus is intact, and whatever is inside can be examined. That's not a task we can manage. Unless you know something I don't."

Charlie and Dan exchanged glances, sadly shaking their heads.

"We're *fine*," Charlie said. She indicated her ear. "Phil. He's been badgering me for an update since we evacced. I told him on the way up, but he wants us all to check in."

Father Pandi had been stewing in silence, but he made a decision. "All of you, get out. We must close this site until we can be sure the foundations are still intact. I will petition the Cardinal in Mexico City to complain most strongly to whoever issued the order from Rome. You are not welcome here."

Toby struggled to his feet, facing the priest as he offered calming hands. "We will be leaving without question. But the orders still stand. Our intent here was always twofold. The first was, as we showed you, an exploration of the Aztec cavern beneath your cathedral. The second is more delicate. But I believe you received this instruction in writing."

Father Pandi might have paled if he wasn't already covered in dirt. "You cannot expect me to just hand it over. Not after this."

"I'm afraid I must insist." While Toby hated strong-arming people, he was more than capable of it. He wasn't always a freelance archaeologist. "The order came from the Holy See. If you wish to argue, we will wait outside while you make that call."

Harpal asked, "There's more? What was this, a warm-up?"

"A second codex," Charlie said. "The conditions negotiated were that if we proved there was more in in the Aztec cavern than the church knew about, then they would lend us the other codex. The one Father Pandi guards in the safe under his own quarters. It'll lead to what Alfonse funded us to bring home."

Through gritted teeth, Father Pandi said, "I will abide by the terms. But first I will report what you have done and allow the Holy See to decide if the contract still stands." He tensed, smoothed his robes, which released a cloud of dust, and marched out, leaving them in the gloom of the fake oil burners and their head torches.

"What now?" Harpal asked.

"Well," Toby said. "If you're free for another week or so, I would very much like to retain your services."

"As long as Colin won't need me here, I'm all yours."

"In that case, we need fast, *budget* travel to the United States. And tourist visas for everyone except Dan."

"Anywhere in particular?"

"First, New York City, then we'll see." Toby nodded towards the interlaced bangles still in Dan's possession. "I have a feeling we might need someone else to come back into the fold if we're to locate what we promised."

CHAPTER THREE

With his gun drawn and pointed at the ground, Jules Sibeko peeked around the corner of Kwong-Luk Wholesale Storage. He jerked back. In the quarter-second he exposed his face, he had taken in enough to see there was, indeed, a robbery in progress—a 10-30, as they had reported it over the radio. He retreated to a distance where subdued voices wouldn't travel.

"Officer Sibeko, call it," Massey said.

Jules's training sergeant was a gruff veteran of the NYPD, and although it plainly irritated him that Jules remembered every teaching from the academy, he'd been patient with Jules in relation to his real-world weaknesses. Mainly, Jules's preference to solve a problem via his instincts rather than hold back and consider the procedures drilled into all new patrol officers. His brain still worked in a way that had kept him alive during far more dangerous encounters than what street-level criminals posed and tried to apply his lifelong intuition over measured thought.

"Three white men, one black," Jules replied. "The two with ski masks are armed for sure, others are loading boxes, but they're wearing jackets. One black suspect, one white, both with ski masks rolled up. Two potential hostages, face down, hands zip-tied."

"Let's assume they're all armed."

"Always."

"Next move?" Massey asked.

Scale the roof, Jules wanted to say. *Drop the one story to the floor behind the largest armed suspect. Disarm him and the other individual. Render the other two unconscious in case they're armed too, before returning to the first. Tackle them, check for other threats, then bind all four. Free the hostages.*

That wasn't something Massey, nor any internal investigation reviewing body cam footage, would appreciate.

Jules said, "Secure the area. Wait on backup. Watch for the suspects fleeing the crime. Intercept if necessary."

"What about the hostages?"

Jules had gotten that part of it wrong. The two red-capped and aproned employees were lying with their hands zip-tied behind their backs while the men loaded boxes into a pickup truck.

"There are cameras," Jules said. "Ample time to shoot the staff if that was the plan. The guys on the floor aren't in immediate danger."

"Can you be sure?"

Jules's mouth was dry. He didn't have Massey's experience in the city, but Jules had already determined several things that he was not allowed to assume without firm evidence. This meant the neural pathways honed over a decade outside the law, chasing high-level smugglers, scaling and traversing tall buildings, and accessing countries and cities impenetrable to most, were useless to him today. And probably would be for as long as he wore the uniform. Or at least until he rewired his brain to fit the job of an NYPD police officer rather than a vigilante-come-thief who operated on the fringes of society.

He concentrated on the options available to him.

"Backup is inbound," Jules said. "We should hold tight."

"Kid, I ain't ever seen a newbie stay as calm as you." Massey's teeth shone through his smile as he flicked his head towards the crime scene. "I'm guessing you can handle this."

"You mean..."

Massey thumbed his radio and asked the dispatcher for an ETA on a second unit which had to be pulled from its regular rotation. Jules cocked his head, listening through his earpiece to the answer: seven minutes.

Massey said, "Let's take them down before backup gets here. I'm judging the hostages are in danger. You ready for this?"

"Sure. You want me to go up?"

"Up?"

Jules indicated the roof.

Massey replied with one of his *don't be a dumbass* looks, then checked the slide on his SIG Sauer P226, a gun Jules also preferred to the Glocks on offer. Jules checked his again, although he'd already done so twice since drawing.

"Hard and fast," Massey said.

Jules nodded and made his way to the corner and checked the suspects again. They were still moving boxes—an action Jules needed to question. Not yet, though.

Officers approaching a robbery scene should be alert for escaping suspects and be aware of suitable places to take cover.

Between him and the loading dock was open ground, except for a metal trash can that might offer some respite from a bullet if it was full of sand or some other dense material. But not on its own. Massey was correct; hard and fast was the only option.

Massey silently counted them in.

Three... two... *one!*

Jules rounded the corner, his gun aimed. Massey advanced in a wider arc to cover the team of four without catching Jules or the hostages in a crossfire.

"NYPD!" Jules shouted. "Show me your hands. You reach for anythin', we open fire."

The four men snapped their attention to the cops, frozen in place. The two armed suspects with the masks down wielded handguns but did not raise them, while the other two kept their arms out to the side.

Massey moved fluidly on a diagonal trajectory, gun steady. "Weapons down, gents. On the floor and step away."

The first time Jules had ordered a suspect to drop a weapon, in that case a knife, he'd used a movie cliche ordering the young woman to kick it away. This was despite learning at the academy to move the suspect away from the danger, not risk them booting the blade at the cop or accidentally firing a round from a badly maintained gun. Massey had chewed him out, but Jules was more annoyed at himself.

The world he'd left behind followed different rules to the one he'd joined, and his brain kept kicking him back to the former.

The one he could no longer live in.

Jules kept his gun trained on the pair of armed individuals as they slowly bent at the knees, lowering their firearms to the ground. Once relinquished, Jules said, "Back up, to your left."

This grouped the suspects together, away from the hostages and their vehicle.

"No sudden moves, gents," Massey said.

He passed behind Jules, lifting his gun as he did so it didn't aim at his young charge, then returned his aim.

If anyone made a move, Jules had no doubt Massey would shoot to kill. A decision Jules had yet needed to make.

"You guys on the ground," Jules called to the two men tied up. "You okay? Need medical assistance?"

Top priority for a responding officer is to help the injured and protect physical evidence...

One employee replied in Cantonese, "Do not shoot. They are the bad guys."

Jules had learned Cantonese over a one-month period four years ago, in which he'd immersed himself as an intern in a Hong Kong museum. It was partly an education and partly his cover, as a younger man more willing to break the law, hoping to obtain a relic that was stolen from Japan during the second world war. The same ability that allowed him to learn and never forget complex subjects—a near-eidetic memory—often hampered him in his work as a cop. Today, he was happy that his former life aided his new one.

"Remain calm," Jules replied in Cantonese, his accent terrible, but they appeared to understand. "More police officers will arrive in minutes."

"You know Chinese?" Massey said. "Along with Spanish *and* Arabic?"

"I told you, I traveled a lot before coming home." Jules concentrated on the suspects before him. "We good here, Sarge? I ain't cuffing anyone 'til we got more hands."

"Three minutes."

His training sergeant advanced, providing cover as Jules took charge.

"Hands on heads," Jules ordered the four suspects. "You're all under arrest on suspicion of robbery. You have the right to remain silent—"

"Get down!" Massey suddenly yelled. "Gun!"

The four men before him hadn't moved. His sergeant was too experienced to panic. Meaning a fifth suspect was in play.

An *armed* fifth suspect.

After that split-second calculation, Jules ducked and rolled aside —again, not something he learned as a cop—heading for the pickup truck rather than the trash can. It offered a wide shooting gallery for an attacker emerging from the loading dock, but better cover.

Massey hadn't moved, but at least there were no gunshots.

Jules quickly reassessed where he was and found a man of Chinese appearance holding an old-looking revolver toward Massey. He'd positioned Massey between himself and Jules, approaching the older cop from behind. Massey had placed his weapon on the floor and now glared at Jules.

"Take the shot, kid," he said.

Jules was shielded from the newcomer, so kept his gun on the four men they'd just tried to arrest. They hadn't been searched.

Jules momentarily aimed at the Chinese man emerging from cover, ducking behind Massey. "I don't have a clean shot."

"I don't care," Massey said. "Ain't no graduate ever filed marksmanship like you."

"Everyone, go," the gunman shouted.

The four robbers shifted.

Jules said, "Nobody moves."

The Chinese man advanced to within touching distance of Massey and slung his arm around the man's chest and shoulder from behind, positioning his face in the crook of Massey's neck. No gun was visible, so Jules guessed it was poking in the sarge's back. The man backed them up toward the dock, stopping eight feet from the wall.

"Put gun down," he said.

Fluent English, accented, from the Chinese mainland. Beijing region, if not the city itself.

More info useless to the situation.

"All of you, keep both hands on your head," Jules ordered.

"They leaving," the man holding Massey said.

Jules needed to keep them occupied for two more minutes. "It's over. You're goin' nowhere. Release my partner, and we can forget this happened."

A lie, of course, but there was no law or regulation against promising a hostage-taker the world to preserve life.

Again, Massey said, "Take the shot."

Jules expected the gun in Massey's back was cocked. Any sudden movement meant it could go off. That close, even if it went into Massey's vest, it wasn't clear how much damage it would do.

A .22, he might be okay.

A .44, his innards would be mincemeat.

Jules held his gun one-handed as he unclipped his baton. Then he called in the situation over the radio, officer in need of immediate assistance. The jargon was easy enough to learn, and when one of their own was in trouble, a small army would descend.

"You got one chance," Jules said. "Put down your weapon and release the officer, and we will go easy. You keep this up, you got a dozen cops about to smoke your ass."

Massey glared at Jules. Eyes narrowed.

The hostage taker shifted. His gun came around Massey to point toward Jules. It was unlikely he'd be able to hit Jules from there, given he was maneuvering a larger man as his shield, but Jules needed to act.

He was certain at least one of the four on the dock was armed, and ready to use the gun to aid their escape. He stared hard at the black man who had reached for his waistline prior to the hands-on-head order. The man grinned. His white friend also smiled.

"I count to three," the man holding Massey said. "Then I shoot. One."

Jules fingered his baton out of its sleeve.

"Two."

Jules turned his head to Massey, roved his eyes to the floor where the Sig Sauer lay four feet ahead. Massey followed his gaze and nodded. The only part of the hostage taker Jules could see was his head, meaning that was the only target.

Yet another aspect of his former life was his absolute refusal to kill. He couldn't get away from the fact he had killed in the past, albeit by accident, so he was fairly confident he would not seize up should the need arise again.

It gets easier. Isn't that what they say?

He wasn't so sure. He'd talked about this with Massey, and although he'd never been in a situation where he'd *had* to shoot, there'd been two occasions where such force would have been justified. After both incidents, he'd assured his partner he'd have pulled the trigger if he had to.

If he had to.

Jules darted from cover. He slipped the baton from his belt and swung it toward the man he suspected was reaching for a weapon seconds earlier, flicking his wrist as he released it. The man dropped his hand to his waist.

Jules adopted a shooting crouch, aiming not at the person holding Massey, but past him. Calculations burst through his mind in a fraction of a second.

The baton flew straight into his target's forehead with a clunk.

Jules fired.

The wall behind Massey spat dust, then the hostage taker arced his back with a cry of pain.

Massey pulled himself away from the Chinese man's firearm, levered the gun-hand over, and as the man fell, Massey relieved him of the weapon, then slid the gun away before scooping up his own. He came up as the second of the four men on the dock was going for his waistband.

But Jules had already made it to Massey. He whipped the Sarge's baton from him, then flung it underarm to slam into the handgun emerging from its owner's belt.

The man dropped the weapon.

By the time it hit the floor, Jules obscured Massey's shot. He leaped onto the loading dock where he first launched a ferocious jeet-kun-do-style side-kick that slammed the white man back into the roller-door mechanics, then shouldered into the black man he hit with the first baton. He simultaneously swept his opponent's feet and snagged the small revolver from his belt, flipped the cylinder, and shook the bullets free, then tossed it out of reach.

The two with the ski masks scrambled for the guns they'd discarded, but as the air filled with sirens, cars screeching to a halt, they froze. Massey was back in position too, holding fast on the danger zone.

Jules holstered his Sig and cuffed the white suspect he'd floored, before holding out his hand for more handcuffs. Massey tossed them and Jules bound the black suspect too.

As the remaining pair in ski masks sunk to their knees, hands on their heads, Jules read them all their rights, and looked over to his training officer.

As three pairs of cops swarmed the area, Massey kept his face slack, but his jaw remained tense—a sure sign he was not pleased. But they had a job to do, and Massey reverted to checking the man Jules had shot with the ricochet.

Jules was not looking forward to explaining that one.

While not every rookie who messed up on the job got hauled into the captain's office, Jules had previously been dressed down by his watch commander, the senior detective on many a shift, and his own training officer. These were all minor issues compared with some officers' first months on the force, but ones that needed ironing out. Jules had been assured plenty of times—by the same people who occasionally admonished him—that he had the potential to be an outstanding cop, and they were hard on him because they need guys like him to reach that potential.

Massey had come to terms with Jules's introverted approach to socializing and his almost robotic precision for memorizing rules and regulations, but he had never been happy with the way Jules dealt with confrontation. Memorizing regs were not the same as employing them during a shift.

It seemed the captain had taken note.

Most had considered Carla Demetriou a veteran for the past ten years, and there were few cops Jules had met that didn't respect the hell out of her. She had participated in some of the biggest busts of the city's history, not to mention handling riots, politics, and two divorces. But there was another case that Jules suspected guaranteed him additional attention from this particular captain.

"Sit down, Sibeko." She motioned with her hand as if she was about to slap a file on the desk, but all reports were digital at this stage. A printout would come along in due course, and her muscle memory could slap it onto whatever surface she chose once it was in her hands.

"May I stand?" Jules asked.

"No. I'm your captain. Sit. That's an order."

Asserting her authority.

Jules couldn't blame her. She was shorter than Jules when they first met twelve years earlier, and she seemed slightly shorter now.

Jules sank into the seat opposite Demetriou.

She remained standing. "That's three. Massey tells me you refused to discharge your weapon, despite there being grounds to do so."

"Ma'am, I did discharge my weapon." Jules kept his tone even, respectful, and concentrated on ensuring Massey stood on a pedestal, someone he looked up to. "I missed. I got lucky with the ricochet."

"Massey ordered you to shoot someone who was holding a hostage. From your body cam, that was a very small target. But your training officer thought you could make it."

"He knows I had the highest marksmanship scores in the history of the Academy. Not to show off, ma'am, but if the target wasn't moving, I would have had no problem." Jules didn't want to lie, but the world of the cops differed from the world of a civilian. "Like I said, I got lucky with the ricochet."

Demetriou sat, her fingers laced before her on the desk. "Sibeko, being a cop is about more than doing the job. You do almost everything well. But after 'getting lucky' you *threw your baton* when you should have shot the suspect. Can you refer me to the class at the Academy where you learned that maneuver?"

Jules said nothing.

"Seriously, this is the one thing your T.O. can't teach you. If your partner can't rely on you, you can't be a cop. You only have a couple of months to meet the grade. All the memorizing of regs, all the advice you give to the detectives—which, by the way, is another conversation we need to have—and your techniques for subduing suspects when a... *more robust* approach would have been appropriate, it's all for nothing if you don't have your partner's back."

"I do have my partner's back," Jules said.

Demetriou assessed him, the lines at the corners of her eyes softening. "You're still that little kid. Still searching for something you can't find."

"Ma'am?"

"How many times did I arrest you back then? Four?"

"Six. Although, you only booked me four times. The others you sent me straight back to the foster home. So, yeah, technically four."

"Do you understand how lucky you were that it was me, not some jacked up guy looking to make a name for himself by being tough on crime?"

This was not the correct setting to reveal to Demetriou that Jules committed his juvenile crimes during times he knew she would be on a shift. As a child, he read people, and used them when needed. And he needed someone to be kind to him, even when they shouldn't be. It wasn't luck. It was a calculated risk. After the first couple of arrests involving her, he'd guessed she'd slipped the reference "Jules Sibeko" to the dispatcher's desk, so she'd get the call whenever his name came up.

He said, "I appreciate all you did for me back then. But I've experienced a lot. I've grown up." Jules flashed the kind of practiced wry grin that he'd seen many cops aim at their superior after a minor snafu. "I even carry a gun now, ma'am."

Demetriou slapped the desk lightly. Not in rage, but in mild frustration. "You never told me if you found that damn bracelet."

"It was a bangle, ma'am. And the matter was resolved."

She shook her head with a joyless smirk. "And you were always good at that, too. Answering a question without answering it."

Again, Jules found no suitable reply, so remained silent.

"If you can get through this and convince Massey you'll do what it takes to keep your partner safe, you will be a fine cop. I assume you want to be a detective since you seem intent on solving the crimes for them?"

"I only offered my observations. As the responding officer, it's my duty to inform the detectives what I saw, and explain—"

"You don't need to draw conclusions for them. In fact, you shouldn't."

"Was I wrong?"

Demetriou sat back in her chair, her fingers interlacing again, resting on her stomach. "No. They *were* stealing bottles of whiskey and other booze. Imported illegally. If they got away, it wouldn't even have been reported to us. The two hostages were also in on it. You concluded that by one line?"

"They thought I was going to shoot them. Guilty conscience. Adding to the fact that they did not appear scared when I first observed the scene and two of the robbers were happy to reveal their faces during the crime, it was pretty obvious to anyone with half a brain."

He regretted the last ten words. He could have been more subtle.

"And the CCTV?" the captain said.

"If the low-level workers, and the supervisor who took Massey hostage, were all in on it, it stands to reason they would have to switch off the cameras. I believe the plan was for the suspects to remove the disc before fleeing the scene, so it looked like a planned operation. But of course, that's up to the detectives to prove."

"Oh, good." Demetriou pointed at him. "Do you think you could remember that next time?"

Jules didn't really understand what he'd done wrong. "I will, ma'am. Wouldn't want to bruise a detective's ego."

"It isn't just an ego thing. Uniformed officers coloring their cases or giving them absolutes—which they can't prove immediately—could lead to confirmation bias. And that's a gift to a savvy defense lawyer."

Jules wanted to argue, but there was logic in what she said. "I'll do my best to keep future observations neutral and not draw conclusions for the detectives."

"Thank you, Officer Sibeko." She paused, a typical delaying tactic for most people when they had something uncomfortable to say. Unusual for her. "You are on mandatory leave for a few days, while the department investigates the weapon discharge. I don't need to explain it to you, since you seem to remember everything anyway, but you are not in trouble over the shooting. It is standard procedure when an officer fires his weapon. Normally, I would put you on desk duty, but you have some things to sort out."

"Such as?"

"Such as whether this is really for you. I'm not so worried about you stepping on detectives' toes. It's what Massey has been speculating in his reports. Nothing obvious. It's clear between the lines, though. And today, using your baton instead of your sidearm... Do you want to be a cop? Can you show your training officer you won't let him or any future partner down in a similar situation?"

"You're saying I need to kill someone when there's a better alternative?"

"I'm saying get your head straight. Objectively speaking, if you'd missed with your non-lethal approach, are you certain you and your partner would still be alive?"

A few years ago, Jules would have answered with a resounding *yes*. Since interacting with more people, getting to know them on a personal level, he had learned this sort of response made him appear arrogant. That wasn't good in social situations, and it was even worse before your captain.

He said, "I understand. But I don't need to be on leave."

"It's your choice, of course. But you and Massey are grounded until the police shooting investigation is complete. Consider taking some time out, though."

She dismissed him with a nod and Jules stood. He remained straight for a moment, then took the formal march out. He paused at the door, and turned to her, seeing the woman who had been stern but understanding with him as a youth. She deserved the truth.

He said, "I found my former life unsatisfying, even though it did a lot of good for people who'll never know it happened. Being a cop, with rules and firm regulations, feels like the right fit for me. I'll work on it."

"See you do, Sibeko."

Jules exited the office and returned to the watch captain who'd already received the paperwork for the early end to Jules's shift, and had dismissed Massey in anticipation. He'd also called in the pairing of Laszlo and Whittington to cover.

"No big deal," the watch captain said. "Couple of hours overtime won't break the bank. See you back here in the morning. Bring your favorite pen."

Jules showered and changed in the locker room, gathered his personal items, and left the building in his civilian clothes. Unlike many of his colleagues, he chose not to carry a firearm off-duty. Some worried about retribution after a shift, but Jules had not witnessed enough yet to warrant such a precaution.

He had walked sixty-seven yards toward the subway when three men and a woman approached him. He'd clocked them ten yards earlier but hadn't slowed. Now, they impeded his path, leaving him no option but to confront them.

"No," he said without a pause.

The men blocking him were Harpal Singh and Dan Vincent. He halted rather than cause an incident.

To the side, Charlie Locke said, "Give us ten minutes. Then kick us out if you have to."

"I don't have to give you ten minutes." Jules twitched toward the precinct sixty-seven yards away. "One shout, and you guys are face-down, getting your fake IDs examined. I assume you ain't here legally."

"It's important," Toby Smith said, next to Charlie. "Ten minutes."

Jules stared, not budging. His heartbeat slowed to a sluggish *clump... clump... clump*.

"We might need Bridget, too," Toby added. "Please. Give us ten minutes."

Jules scanned his old friends' faces. He shook his head. "I can't get involved again."

Charlie was holding a box, a small metal case. "We thought we'd return these to their rightful owner."

She opened the clips and lifted the lid, showing him the two bangles that had brought him into these people's orbit a couple of years earlier.

"Ten minutes," Jules said. "Then I'm done."

CHAPTER FOUR

Jules didn't drink, but sometimes he wished he did. The medicinal benefits of a swift shot of whiskey from the dilapidated room's minibar might have shifted the ache in the back of his throat and relaxed him somewhat. He accepted the offer of water from Harpal, a fresh bottle on the side of one of the single beds.

He was evidently sharing the room with Toby, a significant step down from what Jules would have picked, even when traveling incognito. The beds were made, although one was littered with clothing, which Jules pegged as Harpal's. He perched on the edge of this one, undid the clasps on the case he now placed in his lap, and opened the lid.

The two bangles were nestled in protective foam rubber. Jules ran his finger over the one on his left, making the tiny green flecks in the stone body glow. He touched the other, activating the red stones, dull in the harsh lights of the hotel room. He went back to the first bangle, selected it with his finger and thumb, and slid it out. Holding it before his face, he let it glitter, absorbing the minuscule vibrations through his fingertips.

The Aradia bangle was the object that had brought him into contact with both Toby Smith's group of unconventional archaeologists and Captain Demetriou. Or *Detective* Demetriou as she was back then. Demetriou was the cop who, with her partner, arrested the men who'd killed Jules's mother and father in a botched pizza restaurant robbery, and snatched the stone jewelry from his mother's wrist. It held no street value, and Jules had subsequently learned they pawned it along with the rest of the items taken that day for a bulk payment of a hundred dollars. Since the police were not interested in pursuing the trail of a trinket of only emotional worth, it was up to Jules to track it down himself. As a fourteen-year-old boy with nothing but an exceptional brain and a near-supernatural memory in both his head and his muscles, he faced more obstacles than an adult would have. Such as foster parents being reluctant to let him out after dark.

He'd learned far more skills than anyone that age should be capable of, and by the time he turned seventeen he was an expert in parkour, burglary, and possessed the level of knowledge of antiquities and black-market trading that the average university professor and FBI agent would be jealous of. Once he came of age, he was free to access the insurance payment from his parents' deaths and continued to pursue the phantom trail of his mother's bangle. Already skilled in more than one martial art, Jules set about educating himself further, in whatever discipline might aid his hunt, a hunt that extended to retrieving stolen artefacts for reward—since he still needed money to live on—and several pro-bono cases where it was morally right to relieve the current owner of an object of cultural interest and return it to where it belonged.

A little over two years ago, his single-minded obsession led him to the Lost Origins Recovery Institute, a warped, sociopathic billionaire called Valerio Conchin, and several expeditions that revealed to Jules a history dating back thousands of years before conventional wisdom said human intelligence begun. It also made him believe he was capable of genuine friendship for the first time in his life, but it wasn't to be.

Jules no longer had any interest in that. He gave a heavy sigh and replaced the Aradia bangle in its slot.

"Why are you here?"

Toby and Harpal adjusted their stances, having been polite enough to wait in silence while Jules reminisced about the items before him. Dan and Charlie had remained outside, apparently to find something to eat, but Jules had picked up on more tension than hunger. He didn't care to inquire, though.

Toby said, "For you."

"You can't believe I'm gonna say yes, can you?" Jules said.

Harpal opened his hands. "It's worth a try. And you said you'd listen."

"I can't leave right away. I gotta work out a few things."

"Such as what?" Toby asked. "Can we help?"

"Such as how to make life work in the real world."

"How does one do that?"

Jules didn't answer. When no one else spoke, he figured he was being manipulated in some mind game. Besides circumventing official channels to aid travel and diplomatic issues, Harpal was a former MI6 officer, skilled at getting assets to do what he needed.

Jules shook it off. "It's been almost ten minutes already, so you better be quick. You got some story I never heard or cared to learn? A legend made real? What is it this time?"

Toby lowered himself to the edge of his own bed, leaned his elbows on his knees, and let his mouth hang open for a moment before speaking. "Yes, it starts with a legend. But it ends with me being here in New York, asking you to take a few days to visit an old friend. In the real world."

Jules snapped the lid shut. "Bridget."

"Getting the band back together," Harpal said.

Jules was vaguely aware that was probably a pop culture reference, new or old. Figured he might look it up later, if he was still curious. "Is this to do with the Witnesses? You need me to open some dangerous doorway? Shut down some ancient device that runs on... Whatever's generated when I touch these rocks?"

"No, no," Toby said, as if it was the most ridiculous thing anyone had ever suggested. "This is something much more recent. It may have stemmed from our mysterious pre-ice age friends, but we are on an entirely fresh path."

"You're doing it again."

"Doing what?"

"You know what," Harpal said.

"Very well." Toby put his hands together, flat, pointing towards

Jules. "This is about a shield. Or possibly more than one. I assume you've heard of Achilles, and the battle of Troy."

Toby was used to the younger LORI members mocking him for his erudite recitals of facts and theories which they might find useful. Jules, whom he still stubbornly considered part of the team, rarely joked about being bored, instead stating outright that he had no time for useless small talk. The lad could walk out of here if Toby didn't snag his attention right away. Mention of the Battle of Troy seemed to have done that.

He went on. "Homer's epic story depicts Achilles as the greatest warrior in the world. In the Trojan War, he donned his father's magic armor, but after the gods took away his lover, he chose to give up fighting and loaned the armor to a friend, Patroclus. Although Patroclus fights almost as well as Achilles, the hero of the Trojan army, the man known as Hector strips Patroclus of the armor and defeats him. Hector parades the armor in his triumph, which triggers Achilles to return to the fray.

"This time, Achilles' suit of armor includes a spectacular shield. When Achilles meets Hector on the battlefield, Achilles is victorious. The Iliad ends with Hector's funeral, not Achilles'."

Jules twirled his hand in a "get on with it" manner.

"Yes, yes, I'm getting to that." Toby felt under the mattress, and slipped out one of Charlie's computer tablets, similar to an iPad but with the functionality of a satellite phone. He called up a screen but did not show it to Jules yet. "I'm sure you know the legend of how Achilles died."

"The poisoned arrow through his heel." Jules spoke in a monotone. "The only vulnerable part of his armor."

"That is correct," Toby said. "But it's what happened afterwards that we are interested in. After Achilles died, there was a power struggle, a disagreement over who would inherit the armor and, more importantly, the shield." He turned the tablet to show Jules the mural they had discovered in Mexico, a screenshot of the footage from Harpal's chest cam taken before the room collapsed around them. "This, we believe, is the shield Achilles carried into battle."

Jules squinted to look at the pictures. "Who's the big dude?"

"We don't know. But we have a fair idea that the artist, at least, considered him a giant among men. Or a 'king of man' as we have seen it phrased."

"King? Giant? Literally?"

"If Toby's research is close to accurate, yes," Harpal answered. "I think it's nuts, but hey, I'm just the hired help."

Jules lingered on Harpal a moment, then returned to the screen.

Toby flicked to another picture, a document scan of the Codex procured before entering Mexico, the clues that led them to the Cathedral of Saint Bernard. "Alfonse funded our project to obtain this record made during the time of the conquistadors, or rather in the peaceful decades when they lived in the region after supplanting the natives. We assured Alfonse that the shield depicted in not only this book, but several frescoes, Greek records, and Roman texts known to the Vatican, could be real."

Jules's brow had gained a few lines, sparking hope in Toby that the story actually intrigued him.

"To date, all we have found are more clues." Toby swiped to another photograph, this one featuring the Codex that Father Pandi loaned them. "Recognize this?"

"Is that...?" Jules pointed at the screen.

"We believe so."

The cover of the tome, much thinner than the one they transported from Europe, depicted a symbol similar to an elongated figure eight. It differed from the number by the two loops not crossing over. It was far closer to the shape made when someone connected the Aradia and Ruby Rock bangles together.

"This book," Toby said, "is of course far younger than anything we have dealt with in relation to the Witnesses." He swiped to more pictures, taking his time, narrating each one. "Back when I was in the employ of Her Majesty, we were interested in a cache stolen by industrialists during the heyday of the slave trade, delivering people to America and Europe—"

"Delivering?" Jules said.

Toby had long come to terms with the fact men of his age and background often minimized the impact of slavery, treating it as they would any aspect of history. It was easy to forget, for him and academics like him, that it was a dark chapter in humanity's past that occurred far more recently than many could do well to remember.

"Bad choice of words, I apologize. I of course meant people who were kidnapped and transported to America and Europe against their will, where they were forced to work with no renumeration under the threat of death."

Toby paused, aware that he sometimes sounded sarcastic when he meant to be contrite. With no further objection from Jules, he continued by showing a painting of what appeared to be black men in rags carrying a shield over their heads.

"This is what intrigued me thirty years ago. I only rekindled my interest when I found the codex that Alfonse funded. Now, I see this picture currently hangs in a museum funded by the Carson Corporation."

"Bridget's parents." Jules gave nothing away, as if it were just another dull presentation in an office environment. "What do they have to do with it?"

"We can't be sure. Let me rewind a moment." Toby switched back to the book obtained from Father Pandi. One of the earlier pages showed a map of the world. "You will see, much like the manuscripts we've encountered before, we believe this was transcribed rather than the original penmanship of the author. Or artist. These continents are accurate, but not in the current day. They show the plates as they were over a hundred thousand years ago, but later..."

Toby swiped to more faded, hand-drawn pictures, narrating their importance.

"Through the ages, legends feature in this purely visual journal. I believe whoever penned this was much like us, following a trail to the truth. Here, we see a knight deflecting fire from a dragon using a shield similar to that in the fresco. Here we see a Poseidon-like character, rising out of the sea, armed not with a trident but with a shield, defending those small people on the shore from a fanged sea creature. Note the similarity in the shield's design."

"Noted." Jules had returned to his disinterested tone, but his eyes were glued to the screen.

Toby showed another. "Here, we have a warrior dressed much like a Roman gladiator, deflecting a rock flung from a catapult, defending this small village."

Jules glanced at Harpal, then rested on Toby. "I know there's a point to this. Are you gettin' to it? You've rewound from your slave trade clues, made me listen to observations I could have worked out for myself, and now you're gonna deliver the main event. Or I walk."

Toby believed he was getting better at this, since he was about to arrive at the finale. "I won't bore you with the rest of my research, suffice it to say there is a lot of it. But this shield is known in many formats. Sometimes a single giant warrior or guardian lording over a people in need, or—like the painting hanging in the Alabama Freedom Museum—as four people and four shields."

"So, it could be a collection of shields, or one remaining relic, used as a symbol of... What? Freedom? You mentioned that museum."

"Exactly. Alfonse has funded our trip, under strict budgetary guidelines, but—as much as I hate to make this about money—he will reward us if we bring back the shield shown by the codex. Which, by the way, he arranged to be loaned to us by the Vatican."

Toby returned to the original document scan of the codex that led them to Saint Bernard's.

"Scholars are of the belief that such a shield, or series of shields, was a cover for a mercenary army. A fighting force without a homeland, dedicated to the betterment of humanity. One of greater stature than the average person, but far from a single giant. Known invariably as 'The Giant Ones' and 'The Mighty', but most commonly, it seems, as 'The Guardians,' they offered their services to those with the ability and resources to feed and shelter them and who made the best case for needing them. Not money or wealth, but the worthiest who lived up to the army's ideals."

Harpal gave a single barked laugh. "Yeah, you know, like the A-Team."

"Who's the A-Team?" Jules asked.

"Everyone knows the A-Team. You don't have to remember the series from the first time round."

Toby had lost his flow of thoughts and couldn't help an annoyed grunt. "Don't worry, Jules. I was aware of the term but had never watched the show. It's from the eighties."

"Right. A TV show." Jules returned to the tablet screen and swiped the screen himself, stopping on the train of black men in rags, sheltering beneath the large shield as they trekked a dirt road. "Back to this. I'm guessin' it's why you need Bridget."

"Ah, that's where it gets tricky. Her family dates back to the bad old days." Toby swallowed, regretting the levity in his tone. "That is to say, they have ancestry that profited from slave owners. The museum receives generous grants from the Carson Corporation, and we would appreciate access to the land on which it is built."

Jules considered what Toby was asking. "This ain't about my friendship with Bridget. Hell, you and Dan are probably closer. You need an African-American person to make the request, not some pasty white Brit academic. You're hopin' it adds some sorta weight to poking around on their land."

Toby nodded. "That, and your affinity with the bangles, which seems to tie in somewhat. At least tangentially. Many of these references pre-date Sumerian culture, like the continental drift of the map. We might need your more... esoteric gifts too, but initially... yes, your race may help sway things."

Harpal pulled up a seat and sat on it backwards, leaning against the chair's back, presumably to sit at the same eye level as Jules. "We use what we've got. My parents are Indian, but I can pass for any number of ethnicities in that region, and frequently do. At a push, I fit in around the Middle East, too."

Jules faced him. "I don't got a problem with that. My problem is *why* you want access. Why here?"

"It's the final reference," Toby said. "Chronologically, it seems to me this was the last time the shield, or collection of shields, was identified. After Bridget's ancestor, Jacob Carr, freed his slaves—years ahead of emancipation—the shield trail goes cold."

Jules again fell silent, considering what Toby had said. He lay the case with the Aradia and Ruby Rock bangles on the bed and paced to the window where he looked out onto the street three stories below.

"You guys, you think I'm gonna swallow any of this?"

Toby stood, opened his hands, and approached. He halted halfway as Jules turned to him.

He said, "I would have thought that after all we'd seen, the notion of an army of extremely strong mercenaries protecting the innocent wouldn't be such a tremendous leap."

Jules shook his head. "Ancient machines hidden beneath the earth, quantum physics tapped into by people who didn't really understand it, crazy billionaires who think they're entitled to take what they want. Now giants. Shields that can deflect meteors and sea monsters. We are gettin' into children's stories. Where's the actual evidence?"

Like the other two, Harpal stood. "That's where the fun begins. Have you ever heard of a You Tube kook called Sally Garcia?"

Jules threw up his arms and blew out his cheeks. "Yeah, I've heard of her. And if you think I'm doing anything based on her ridiculous notions, you've just wasted a bunch more of Alfonse's money."

Jules had had enough. He marched to the door, snatching the case containing the bangles.

"Professor Garcia has a plethora of documentaries out on the web," Toby said. "Including the theory floated in her previous book. About two civilizations that thrived before modern humans evolved? Ancient technology, and the like?"

"Yeah, yeah." Jules reached the door but made his point more sternly. "She's got mad stuff on there, too. Hollow Earth theory? You go with that too?"

"To be fair," Harpal said, "she doesn't promote hollow Earth crap. She investigates it, finds nothing conclusive, and leaves it open."

Toby kept up the last-minute pressure, his speech pattern speeding up, his hands open. "Phil and Charlie performed a scrub-search of her cloud accounts and laptop. They found a lot of references to giants and shields, but only a couple featuring both, starting with a video saying she has found the resting place of the Giant's Shield. Giant singular or giants' plural, we can't tell from the dialogue. But we see the video in which Sally cannot enter the land on which she believes the site to be based, because of it being private property."

"Phil geo-pinged the video," Harpal added. "It's in Alabama."

"The museum's land." Jules now understood the need to involve Bridget. "A bit coincidental, ain't it?"

Toby licked his top lip. "Not entirely. I was... I stumbled across references to the Carson family history and back traced a couple of interesting leads. That sent us to the codex at the Vatican and whetting Alfonse's interest—"

Jules cut him off. "So, you went searching for something to make Bridget's folks see the value of the work you do? Hopin' they'd release her out of her contract?"

"Indeed. And it sent us on a wider than expected arc. But here we are. With both evidence of an almighty archaeological discovery and a chance to reunite our team."

"Still," Jules replied, "it's not grounds for—"

"We believe modern humans slaughtered the guardians," Toby said.

Jules squeezed the door handle, but left it closed. "Modern humans?"

"If this Guardian army were descended from the Witnesses, or a group protecting that knowledge, it's possible they came across a force that could subdue them."

"In pre-Civil War era United States."

"Seems that way," Harpal said. "If the kook is right about even a couple of things."

Jules turned fully to view the two men. "And that's where the big issue is. You're askin' me to hang out with Bridget, tell her there's a big deal ancient artefact that needs unearthing, and it might all be for nothing. It's even less clear than those orbs, or the tomb in India."

Toby strained as if lifting a heavy object, his fingers curled as if massaging that item. Jules read it as frustration, but it might have been anger. "Don't you want to get back to it? Deep down? A regular job, an apartment, frozen yogurt, and bagels? Is this really for you?"

It wasn't lost on Jules that Demetrio had posed a similar question.

He said, "This ain't anything to do with Valerio, is it?"

"We've heard nothing from him," Toby replied. "Remember Prihya Sibal?"

"Sure. Clever girl. No formal qualifications. Hoodwinked into thinking we were the bad guys."

"Correct. She went dark a few months ago." Toby again seemed cautious to talk about this. "She'd sent some updates my way, mainly that they were struggling to get into the scrolls, just like we were. And those they accessed were not readable. Some had run due to the age and whatever they used for ink. Others simply impenetrable. There were no references for the language. No Rosetta Stone. I doubt even Bridget would have been able to decipher them."

"You didn't slip her a few texts on the down low?" Jules asked.

"A couple of times," Harpal said. "But she asked us to stop."

"Why?"

Harpal turned away, hands in his pockets, head down.

Toby just looked sad. "I think... Perhaps she didn't want reminding of our work. She could only dip in and out, while she concentrated on fulfilling the promise to her parents. If they caught her, what little crumbs they threw our way would be rescinded."

"And Prihya?" Jules said.

"The final coded message she sent said she was through with Valerio's craziness. Sounded like he was getting more manic. She had fled the town in India that he had made his base and assured us she was safe."

Jules aimed his next question at Harpal. "You sure it was her? Did you verify it?"

Harpal raised his hands. "I'm not officially with the Institute anymore. This is the first I'm hearing of it."

Jules frowned, hoping his confusion came through without words.

Toby said, "We have had a few funding issues. Not all of our missions following Kenya paid off. We have the Château, courtesy of Bridget's parents, but we travel coach at the moment. Can't afford fuel for the Learjet. And we all have living expenses."

He cast a brief glance toward Harpal.

"I've had to find other work," Harpal said with the sort of finality Jules understood meant not to probe deeper. "But on this job, we have put out feelers. No chatter about Valerio Conchin."

If this were simply an exploration, following a historical trail to either a wild goose chase or physical objects used by benevolent fighting force, Jules might've been tempted.

Last year.

Not now.

"Two teams," Toby said. "You and Dan work on accessing that site. Harpal, Charlie and I will head out to California and see what research Sally Garcia has kept hidden. I'm 99% positive she hasn't made everything public. Perhaps if we can penetrate her fantastical conspiracy theories and oddball notions, we can confirm the truth. Access the full depth of her research."

Although Jules had no intention of taking up the offer, the involvement of a kook like Garcia compelled him to ask, "If she's so crazy, how come you're certain she's right about Alabama?"

Toby seemed hesitant to answer. "Her notion of giants—literal giants—is only one conclusion. It seems to be her favorite, and the hypothesis she is most eager to prove. Her public comments on the matter are restricted to the idea that nobody knows for sure. And she wants to investigate the possibilities. But, as far as we can see, she has made up her mind."

"Why's she holding back?"

"Tenure," Toby replied. "She's up for tenure at the University of SoCal. If she embarrasses the institution before then, they can withdraw it. After, she can publish pretty much what she likes. As long as it isn't immoral or dangerous, she keeps her status."

Jules saw where this was going. "And as a tenured professor, she gets better funding, and more leeway for her own fields of study."

"Exactly."

"And you're goin' along with this?"

"We are interested in all the legwork she has done. She has facts, locations. More than we have. Just because she has jumped to a literal conclusion instead of an allegorical one—which is what *our* research indicates—doesn't change the fact she has made more progress on the ground."

Jules thought about it.

"I don't expect you to decide on the spot this minute." Toby approached Jules, who had remained in place next to the exit. The smaller man put both hands on Jules's right forearm and stared up at him. "Imagine what this could mean. Either an artefact so old and grand that we can fund the Lost Origins Recovery Institute for the next five years, or we uncover more of the Witnesses' technology, something that has the potential to protect mankind from the scale of meteor that wiped out the dinosaurs."

"Because we're overdue a strike," Harpal said. "You know that, right?"

"What a find it will be to prove an epic like the Iliad has more truth to it than the milieu." There was a wet fire in Toby's eyes. "It would be incredible."

Jules turned the handle and stepped out, his head hanging low, as something tugged at him, urging him to stick around. But he couldn't. "You don't need me to get Bridget to help, or her parents. I got a life here. I gotta concentrate on not screwing that up."

Jules left them to it, unsure exactly why his stomach felt tight or the pressure behind his eyes had grown. He figured he should give alcohol one more try.

CHAPTER FIVE

Jules wasn't necessarily hoping to bump into his T.O. but was oddly glad that Massey was sitting at the bar, nursing a Guinness, when he walked through the door. The dimly lit Irish pub was filling without being overwhelmingly busy, and Massey was alone. Jules realized this was because the pair had finished their shift early. The regular rotation would not pile out of the precinct for another half an hour.

He sidled up next to Massey and waited for the older man to spot him.

"Sibeko," Massey said with an air of surprise. "Didn't think you enjoyed hanging with us ordinary cops."

"What does that mean?"

"You know, people who don't see things with their psychic powers. Can't fling a truncheon like a spear at the Olympic Games. We just use our guns and our common sense."

"You don't need your gun that often."

Massey shrugged and returned to his drink. "You should have used it today."

Jules leaned both elbows on the bar and signaled the bartender as he'd seen people do on the rare occasion he'd attended this place. The man in the apron lifted his chin and held up a finger to say he'd be just a minute.

Jules said, "I'll work on that. You're right. It was a dumb thing to do."

Massey twisted on his stool again, his mouth pulled into a big grin. "You really mean that?"

Jules had made a concession, bringing the man onside. It worked better than his previous attempts to explain or excuse his actions.

The bartender came over.

"I'll take a whiskey," Jules said.

"Anything in that?" the bartender asked.

"Ice."

"One for me too," Massey said. "Make 'em doubles. And they're on me."

As the bartender poured the drinks, Jules took his seat, laying the bangles case on the top of the bar. He met Massey's eyes in a mirror laden with drinks and the name of the establishment—Riley's Retreat.

"You don't come here much," Massey said.

"No," Jules replied. "I'm not a big drinker. And I find the type of conversations here are... I dunno. I'm never sure how to join in."

Massey waved an open hand, a friendly dismissal. "The boys and gals here are good people. I know they go a bit hard on the protesters and whining types—the civil rights lot, the gay marches, whatever. But it's a tough job. Difficult to know what's right sometimes. All we can do is our best. And that's all you can do, too."

Jules had understood that, had made a point of being friendly to even those who dismissed the racial equality movement out of hand based on a handful of bad actors who hijacked such occasions to destroy property and loot shops. He was no expert in how to handle such conflict, but after much reflection alone in his apartment and walking in the park, he figured it was better to engage, to help his fellow cops understand no one was saying blue lives, or any other life, held less value than black lives. Of course, it didn't help when many of the most vocal allies lumped all cops into the same deplorable hand basket, or that the minority of violent protesters received the lion's share of the publicity across the mainstream media, and blanket coverage from the far-right outlets.

He didn't want to get into it here.

"It's not politics," Jules said. "It's..."

What was it, exactly? He couldn't label his reasoning, his hesitancy to indulge with his colleagues.

The whiskeys arrived and Massey plucked his off the bar right away. Jules mirrored him and Massey clinked his glass into Jules's. The ice tinkled and the amber liquid swirled, pretty in the dim lighting, an inviting tendril of melting ice tracing the movement.

Unfortunately, as Jules brought it to his lips, it didn't *smell* tempting. The odor traveled up his nostrils and burned the back of his eyes. He gave nothing away but set it down in front of him.

"We're on desk duty tomorrow," Jules said, rotating the glass on its wet spot.

"Standard procedure." Massey sipped his and made a deep *aah* sound. "I fired my weapon twice in five years. They cleared me both times within forty-eight hours. Don't sweat it. We'll be out there again soon enough."

The ice was melting, which diluted the foul liquor somewhat.

Jules had read that this was the correct way to drink whiskey. In Scotland, it was common for pubs to supply a small jug of water alongside their single malt. Diluting it a little at a time, rather than the macho practice of downing it, sounded similar to how much salt a person added to their soup—it varied depending on individual taste.

Jules said, "The captain thinks I might benefit from a few days' vacation."

Massey weighed it up. "You don't get many. You want to use your time off for quiet contemplation, get your head straight, that's your lookout. Personally, I wouldn't."

"No, I don't think I will."

Massey assessed Jules's whiskey. "You not drinking?"

"In a minute." Jules held up the glass to one of the spotlights.

The halo around the ice cubes was clearer, the water seeping into the whiskey. Jules gave the glass a shake to mix the two liquids and brought it up to his lips. Still too strong. He sipped it anyway. The burning behind his eyes that he'd experienced when sniffing it was nothing compared to swallowing the alcohol. He held in the cough that his body demanded.

Once it settled, he had to admit the afterglow was not unpleasant.

"I got some friends askin' for help."

Massey laughed. "Didn't know you had friends."

Jules watched his drink.

"Sorry," Massey said. "Wasn't being mean or nothing. You just never talk about people."

"It's okay. I haven't seen 'em in over a year."

"Coming back when they need something? Don't need friends like that."

Jules angled his drink so he could calculate when another twenty percent of the ice had mixed with the liquor. "Ain't like that. It's my fault. I haven't replied to them. Got tied up with the Academy and gettin' used to this job. Now they got something goin' on that they think I'll wanna join in with."

He considered his conversations with Bridget and Toby. They had believed his idea of joining the police was a way of sheltering himself from the stresses of living on the run—from both bad people who wished him harm and several law enforcement agencies around the world. Luckily, America was not one of those where he was a wanted man.

Jules said, "I was into archaeology before."

"Thought you were a volunteer for NGOs," Massey answered with the tone he used addressing a witness who'd made suspicious statement.

"It was a side thing. A hobby." Jules positioned his mouth into another of those wry smiles that he had attempted to use on Demetriou. "I enjoyed it. I was good at it."

Why those words felt awkward falling out of his mouth, Jules couldn't say. It was almost like confessing a secret. The only other people he knew in the city were participants in his outdoor yoga class, various shopkeepers, and the occasional regular patron of his preferred coffee shop. He hadn't yearned for more human contact, happier in his own company, so he couldn't call any of them true friends. None of them people who would come to his aid, risk their lives for his or put their lives in his hands.

"You're thinking about it," Massey said. "Taking some days."

Jules gave the glass another turn, brought it to his mouth, and sipped again. It went down smoother, less of an ordeal, but not pleasant. The afterglow repeated the one reason to feel good about drinking it.

"Not really."

Massey downed the rest of his whiskey. "I don't know. Scrabbling about in the dirt, brushing off stegosaurus bones... If you're into that sort of thing, maybe you'll come back refreshed."

Jules stared at the case.

"What's that?" Massey said.

"Something to remind me of the good times." Jules stumbled over the word *good*. He took a deeper sip of the whiskey, finding the hit smoother to swallow and actively enjoying the sensation. "And they're right about one thing."

"What's that?"

"It'll be easier with me on board."

The outer doors opened, and a rabble of cops Jules recognized from his precinct hustled in. Both he and Massey twisted to greet them. The group was eight strong and six of them made their way to a horseshoe-shaped booth which would accommodate them all and then some.

"You joining us?" Massey asked as he nodded to Jenson and Butler, who were getting the first round in.

Jules, likewise, acknowledged the pair. They reacted the same way Massey had—pleasantly surprised to see him.

"Hey, Sibeko," Butler called. "Get you a pint?"

Jules tilted his whiskey in Butler's direction and replied, "I'm good, thanks. Rain check. I gotta go in a minute."

Butler nodded towards Massey.

Massey held up his Guinness glass and waggled it to say yes, please.

"Good luck with it," Massey said.

"Good luck with what?" Jules asked.

"Whatever it is your friends want you to do."

Jules threw back the whiskey, the remnants of the ice cubes clacking against his teeth. It was too much too soon, and Jules coughed and spluttered, getting most of it back in the glass.

Jenson, Butler, and the other cops all clocked the failed attempt at a macho exit and hooted with laughter.

Massey slapped him on the back. "Wrong hole?"

Jules nodded, making mental notes for the next time he attempted to consume strong liquor this way—because he was sure there would be a next time. He'd quite liked it. Most of it.

"Did this near-death experience help make up your mind?" Massey asked.

Jules stood, wiped his mouth, and laughed at himself, his motions broad enough for the other officers to see he found his own fall amusing. That would be vital to camaraderie; joshing one another seemed to be the way these people expressed friendship. In time, Jules was sure he would get it.

He shook Massey's hand. "Thanks for the drink." He took the case from the bar.

"You leaving me to push paperwork alone, then?"

"I'll think about it. Need to check something first."

Two hours later, Jules was risking his job by scaling the down-market hotel roof. He had donned his midnight blue all in one suit, which incorporated a belt full of useful items, such as the grappling hook attached to a bungee cord. For this outing, he had added a balaclava and nonslip gloves but left behind the usual mini flashbangs, smoke grenades, and throwing knives, bringing only what he expected he would need.

Hidden in the shadows of the rooftop cornices, he watched Toby, Harpal, and Charlie catch a yellow cab. Dan waved them off and returned inside.

Jules jammed the grappling hook into a suitable nook and measured out enough tight cord to crab down the outer wall. Having identified the room in which Toby had made his presentation, he landed silently on the fire escape, used a thin, pointed slice of metal to slip through the wooden frame, and knock the flimsy lock off the window. Then he climbed inside.

The light from the street was enough to navigate by, and he located a laptop under the bed next to a suitcase that had not yet been moved. He figured he had about three minutes before Dan returned.

He opened the laptop and hit the power button.

Nothing happened.

Jules frowned. "What are you doing?"

This was ridiculous. He had no business being here. The computer was a dummy, something to hand over to robbers or nefarious agents who were competing for the prize.

That meant Harpal had lied. There *were* other people interested. That implied danger—the kind of thing Jules had left behind.

He closed the laptop, unconcerned to alert Dan that there had been an intruder.

Halfway to the window, intending to go home and text Massey that he would see him in the morning, a white rectangular piece of card lying at the foot of the second bed gave Jules pause.

A plane ticket. No wallet.

If they were being so careful as to provide would-be enemies with a fake computer, why leave a plane ticket out advertising their destination?

Because they intended it to be seen.

Jules picked it up at the corner using his thumb and forefinger, as if it were a piece of soiled underwear he didn't recognize. He angled it towards the window, a streetlight offering enough illumination to read the name on it.

Julian Sibeko.

"Arrogance, much?"

From outside the door, Dan's deep voice reverberated. "You're getting sloppy."

Jules sagged, disappointed in himself. "Cameras?"

"And mics." Dan tapped on the door. "Hey, listen, if I come in there, you're not going to jump me and start throwing me around, are you?"

"Nah, I was just leaving."

As Dan entered, Jules flicked the plane ticket onto the bed. Dan turned on the lights. He was holding a small firearm. It didn't look like a conventional gun.

"I'm a cop now," Jules said. "You got a concealed carry permit for that?"

"It's a tranq gun," Dan answered.

"Pretty sure you still need a permit. Planning to use it on me?"

"Like BA Baracus? Wake up in Alabama and hope you play along?"

"Who's BA Baracus?"

"You know, like the A-Team?"

"Why is everyone suddenly into an 80s TV show?"

Dan closed the door behind him and tossed the tranq gun onto the other bed. "Harpal brought it up when Toby first came out with this theory of a gang of fighters helping out the oppressed. I just want to get back to normal. If finding this shield means we get Harpal back, maybe Bridget too, I'm all for it."

"And me?" Jules asked.

Dan slumped in a worn-looking armchair, propping his feet on the bed without removing his shoes. "I don't think anything I say will matter. Bridget had to go start on some college degree that her parents approved of. Economics, I think. Harpal abandoned us because his share of the take wasn't enough to live on, so he ended up taking Colin Waterston's offer of a retainer. Charlie sold a couple of patents to the British communications industry to tide us over for a while, but we've hit too many goose eggs lately. Toby is usually right, but then he normally has Bridget backing him up and talking through any gaps in his thinking."

Jules's throat had gone dry, accompanied by that harsh ache that he'd felt earlier. "And I chose to leave."

"Guilt does that to people. But I get it. You didn't mean to kill that man, but it happens when they choose to sign up with the bad guys."

"Who's to say we aren't the bad guys sometimes?"

"Killing doesn't automatically make us the villains. You might have to do it again someday. If you have no choice."

"Yeah, that's pretty much what my T.O. and captain are telling me."

"I guess we all have to work out how to deal with it for ourselves." Dan placed his feet on the floor and sat upright. "If this doesn't pay off, I'm not sure how long I can stick around either. I figured if you and Harpal had stayed, we might've made it work. But you were never fully committed. Harpal has other priorities. And I think Phil is pressuring Charlie into quitting too."

Jules glanced at the laptop. Then at the plane ticket. "He never wanted her to join up in the first place."

"He was happy for her to help. He just wanted her out of the field."

"Now she's flying to California to dig up evidence on a tribe of giant warriors."

Dan shrugged and leaned back again. "It's not exactly heading to war."

Jules shifted himself to the laptop and closed the lid. "If it's not dangerous, why the decoy?"

"This is New York. You don't need a team of ninjas descending on you to worry about getting robbed."

Jules saw his point.

"You're still here," Dan said.

"Yeah."

"Are you coming?"

"Do you think it's real?"

"The shield? Yeah. Whether some Greek warrior used it, or it's just sitting in a museum or under some burial mound... I think it's out there, sure. In Alabama?" Dan gave a simultaneous shrug and sigh. "So far, Toby's calculations have paid off. He asked Alfonse for a bit more cash and learned that old flaky book was holed up at the Vatican. Alfonse called in a couple of other favors, then we were on our way to sunny England. That's where we found out Harpal had teamed up with Colin."

"Doesn't sound like a team up," Jules said. "Sounds like necessity."

"Whatever. Colin was a real ass about it, but we explained some old trading company's records and ended up in Central America. Then it's the usual story: dark holes, ancient legends being brought up to date, collapsing caves, escaping by the skin of our teeth..."

"Yep, that sounds like the usual. The priest gave you the other book?"

"It confirmed what Toby was hoping for. A connection to the Carson family. Something that might bring us a bit of financial relief, and maybe even Bridget back into the fold."

"If it's there."

"Yeah, if."

Neither man spoke, the traffic outside loud through the open window.

Jules picked up plane ticket. "And you haven't had to fight your way out of any jungles or confront some other... interested party?"

Dan gripped the arms of the chair and shook his head tightly. "Nope. Not a sniff."

Jules could not put his finger on it, but Dan emanated the same indistinct deception as Harpal had when asked the same question. He didn't think they would lie about this, but there was something they weren't telling him.

Jules said, "Just talking to her?"

"Can't hurt." Dan relaxed. "I'm about to leave for the Yellowhammer State." He nodded towards the plane ticket Jules now gripped. "You joining me, or do I get some decent elbow room?"

Jules could not deny it would be good to see Bridget again, but he was still skeptical as to Toby's motivations for involving him. Sure, having a black friend of Bridget's might help sway the Carsons to investigate an artefact linked to the slavery era. They funded a museum dedicated to recognizing individuals who played a role in fighting to end the practice in a part of the country where it was embedded into the DNA. That alone was curious enough.

Jules brandished the plane ticket towards Dan. "If I find out you're lying, I walk. No questions, no second chances. Understand?"

Dan stood and pulled his bag out from under the bed. "Glad to have you on board. We're wheels up in three hours."

PART TWO

CHAPTER SIX

ANISTON, ALABAMA

With a minor delay, it turned out to be four hours until Jules was airborne, sharing an armrest with Dan on the redeye to their connecting airport, then onward to Anniston, Alabama—the nearest hub to the Carson estate. There was a private airport a short car journey from where Bridget was living, but they agreed it would be better to surprise her than announce their intentions too far in advance.

It was morning when they picked up the hire car, and the southern heat was already building. Anyone foolish enough to venture out found themselves wrapped in a cocoon of humidity. When Dan insisted on driving, Jules did not compete, preferring to doze for the first hour on highway 78. After the snooze, Dan grew bored with the radio, and engaged Jules in conversation, mostly relating to how they would approach Bridget.

Once they pulled off the highway and traveled the road stretching in-country, they found a town to refuel both themselves and the car and called Bridget from the diner parking lot while they ate sandwiches in the blistering late morning.

"You're here?" Bridget said.

Jules had made the call but kept it on speaker. Her southern belle inflection was more pronounced than it had been the last time she and Jules spoke, and it sunk into his brain the way feet enjoyed slipping on a familiar pair of comfortable shoes.

"Oh, yes," Dan said when Jules failed to expand on his announcement that he was in the state and would like to drop by for a visit.

"Dan? Is that you?" Her voice rose an octave at hearing Dan Vincent speak.

Jules narrowed his eyes at him, annoyed at the deviation from the plan to let Jules do the talking initially.

Bridget said, "How did you know where I am?"

"Toby gave us the address," Jules said.

"That's not what I mean. I—" She cut herself off. "It doesn't matter. It's great to hear from you. How soon will you be here?"

"About an hour," Dan said.

They said their goodbyes and Jules said nothing to Dan as they got in the car and headed back out onto the road. Jules could tell Bridget knew something was up. He got the impression this excursion hadn't been planned as intricately as he would have insisted upon.

One hour and five minutes later, they pulled off onto a narrow approach road, bordered on both sides by railings—a road that may have been nothing but dirt had this been a conventional farm. Halfway up, they faced a double gate made from wrought iron and guarded by two cameras and several boxes that Jules knew emitted an infrared beam. He also noted the railings appeared ornate, cotton-thin strands weaving between the spires—more than likely electrifying the entire length.

Dan lowered the window at the speaker, but before he could announce himself or press any buttons, Bridget's voice sang through.

"Drive right on up. If there are any dogs running loose, ignore them, but don't get out of the car until I say so."

There was a static squelch, and the gates swung open.

Dan drove through and up the road, the hot air shimmering as it rose, which was where the house came into view. It was a mock colonial mansion, bright white in the fierce sunlight, with a lower annex off to the left. The fields to two sides spanned the landscape to the horizon, rising out of view, while the east side ended in woodland.

Bridget stood on the top of three redbrick stairs under the colonnaded awning. The only thing that looked odd, from memory of such houses on TV and cinema screens, was that she was not surrounded by servants or gun-toting bodyguards. It reminded Jules of Alfonse Luca's villa on Sicily, only this was three stories instead of one, and the heat was damp, not dry.

He checked for dogs then climbed out at the same time as Dan. They were dressed for New York—jeans and loose tops, although Jules had removed his hoodie as soon as they landed and ventured outdoors.

Had it been so long since he experienced a tropical climate?

Rusty, perhaps.

That attracted another worry: if he had been so slack as to dress inappropriately, what else was he going to screw up today? Sure, he'd packed all his usual kit before departing, but he did not expect to need his throwing knives, mini flashbangs, or his bungee cord baton. They were more of a security blanket.

Bridget bounded down the stairs and threw her arms around Jules in the kind of ostentatious hug he expected from a giggly cheerleader. It wasn't like her. Nor was her greeting.

"Oh my gosh, it's so great to see you both!"

She transferred her affections to Dan with identical over the top enthusiasm.

Once she disengaged, she stood back, her floaty dress billowing with the motion, and raised her hands as if beholding the two men for the first time. "Walk with me. I'll show you around."

"Kinda hoping I could change," Jules said.

"Oh, you'll be fine." Bridget gritted her teeth and narrowed her eyes, clearly demanding he shut up and do as he was told. "I'll have some lemonade ready when we get back."

Jules trusted her to explain herself once out of earshot of whoever was waiting inside the large house. He and Dan flanked her as she trotted off towards a path that appeared to lead to the woodland. The sun warmed the back of Jules's neck and the top of his head.

Bridget chatted in a way that Jules was not used to. "Sorry we're not fully prepared. I forgot to tell my parents you might be coming by. I know it was all loose arrangements, but they understandably get upset when plans change. We were going to do some virtual tours of more colleges this afternoon, but this is much better."

Jules and Dan played along, but Jules didn't want to open his mouth and say something wrong. Dan appeared to feel the same way. They gave "uh huh" answers and nodded occasionally. Although it was only twenty seconds, the prattling felt like it had gone on too long. But once Bridget dropped the act, she could speak freely.

"Okay, what the hell is Toby playing at?"

Dan held up his surrender hands. "What on earth do you mean, Bridge?"

"Don't call me *Bridge*. Tell me what's going on."

"Sorry, Miss Carson, I won't do it again."

Bridget jabbed a finger towards his face. "You know that's not what I mean. Why are you here? My parents don't bluff."

"They never said we couldn't visit," Dan said.

Bridget gave a frustrated sigh.

Jules said, "Toby shouldn't have known she was here. Right, Bridget?"

"Miss Carson," Dan corrected.

Bridget punched him in the arm, and he feigned pain.

She said, "He's right, as usual. I'm supposed to be at Harvard. The last time Toby and I emailed, that's where I was. I didn't drop out until last month. Which means he's been keeping tabs on me without my permission."

"Right." Dan rubbed the back of his neck, perspiration beading on his forehead. "We kind of didn't have time to ask. Charlie just double-checked your location, made sure there were no eavesdroppers on your comms, then we came out here to say hi."

They were approaching the woodland, a small atoll in a sea of scorched grass. Jules couldn't understand why anyone would need so much land if they weren't using it for anything more useful than bragging about how much acreage they owned.

"What's the set up here?" Jules asked. "It's like a governor's mansion."

Bridget sighed and tensed. "I dropped out of the economics degree after flunking the first year. I was hoping that would get me a bit of leeway in choosing a better course. My dad reminded me that my friends needed the Château and the hangar at the airport, even if they weren't using the plane. He let me take a couple of months off so I could, in his words, 'procrastinate on my future a while'."

"Failing intentionally," Dan said. "That's not like you."

"Not intentionally. I just didn't do much to arrest the decline."

Jules stared off toward the house. "So, your dad's blackmailing you into obeying him? That don't sound right."

"I wouldn't call it blackmail." They reached the shade of the trees and Bridget leaned against one, a hazy light around her bright copper hair making her green eyes stand out as if she had been photoshopped. The warmer climate had also brought out the freckles over her nose and under her eyes. "Economics wasn't for me. Too much left to chance. Mom and Dad said they understood, but, in Dad's words again, he 'won't allow me to sabotage my future.' I've agreed to try a new path, and he's pushing me towards a business degree, something solid and foundational. If I go with a science, I can't choose a 'wishy-washy' one."

"With definitive answers?" Jules said. "Something you know you're getting right or wrong?"

"Exactly. Whatever I like, as long as it isn't 'language stuff.' No humanities, no liberal arts. The impression they have is that I'm trying to put it off until they cave and let me go back to the Institute. They won't cave. I know that. But I don't want to commit to wasting four more years without studying something that... Something I know I can be passionate about. I've slipped Toby a few things on the sly, but I just can't get into a flow state. And that's what I need when I'm working out the most complex language and codes."

Jules had witnessed Bridget's "flow state" before, and it was a sight to behold. When she was younger, the Guardian newspaper in the UK wrote a brief article in which they dubbed her "the Human Rosetta Stone." It was a gift Jules hadn't seen demonstrated by anyone else, not even himself. He had an affinity for learning, retaining information, and applying it to the world around him. Once he had adapted to something, a new skill or academic practice, he never forgot it, but it took learning and practice to instill it inside him. Bridget learned on the hoof, and it was a shame she was being stifled by parents who didn't see the value in something that hadn't been paid for.

"He's forcing you to do something you don't want to," Jules said. "Using threats to control your behavior. I'm pretty sure that's a felony in most states. If you were past retirement age in New York, it'd definitely be elder abuse."

Bridget shook her head and pushed away from the tree. "This isn't New York. And even if it was, he's right."

Once more, Dan and Jules followed as she led them back towards the house.

Dan said, "Perhaps someone needs to have a quiet word with your father."

"Oh, put your chest away," Bridget replied. "I said he was right. Doing what we did in Austria and Monaco, I breached our agreement. If I use you strapping fellows to strong-arm him into letting me out of the contract, what am I gonna do next time he needs to trust me to follow-through on a deal?"

"It's still controlling behavior," Jules said. "If you're obeying out of fear that he'll ruin your life, you shouldn't have to be held to the letter of that contract."

They were halfway back to the house and Bridget had folded in on herself somewhat, her shoulders stiff as she walked, focusing on the white house ahead of them. "It isn't illegal to withdraw a favor. And that's what they're doing letting you guys occupy the Château and use the hangar. So, I'm sorry. As much as I want to help, you'll have to treat this as a social visit."

"Then we should be clear right now." Jules pulled up level with her and waited for Dan to join them. "It ain't you we need. We're hopin' you can give us access to your parents. Persuade 'em to help us."

"My *parents*?" Bridget almost shrieked the words in surprise.

"Yeah," Dan said. "Let's explain before we get inside. Then maybe we can all enjoy that lemonade together."

CHAPTER SEVEN

ARNOLD, SOUTHERN CALIFORNIA

Arnold was a quintessential college town. It started as a mining municipality which died decades ago and was reborn when the University of Southern California opened a satellite campus nearby. Driving the hire car from the airport, Charlie hadn't decided whether she adored the kitsch nature of Arnold's facsimile of an olden days historic borough or if it annoyed her. Annoyed her, because her hometown back in Wales swelled with genuine mining history of which she and her fellow citizens were rightfully proud.

Like the town, the college's design exuded a legacy that famous institutions like Harvard and Princeton oozed from their every brick, even though it was only a couple of decades old. Not that the students seemed bothered. They swarmed the grounds, lugging books and backpacks, holding hands and kissing, and throwing footballs. It reminded her of the backdrop in many a movie as people tramped through a campus to reach their destination.

The LORI trio had called ahead, so it only took a couple of queries of the security guards to find the correct building. Charlie, Harpal, and Toby signed in, then followed the brass plaques to reach the lecture hall where Professor Sally Garcia was finishing her second lesson of the day.

The three took empty seats at the back and waited in silence, looking down to the teaching platform over the heads of maybe twenty students, where Professor Sally Garcia held their attention. She was in her fifties and wore natural linen trousers and a rainbow blouse, her wild, gray, bird's nest hair mostly tied back with multicolored beads. Projected on the expansive white wall, the photo of a grassy mound popped up. A swollen mass of earth had grassed over but formed the unambiguously man-made shape of a serpent.

"Adams County, Ohio. That's in the United States, for the geographically challenged." Garcia paused for a polite ripple of laughs. "A curious mound of earth rises from the land. A snake winding for over thirteen-hundred feet, up to five feet high, and starts and ends with an open mouth and coiled tail. Understandably, it's called, 'the Serpent Mound.' Although it is not an isolated case, it is the largest effigy mound in the world. What makes it mysterious? Well, I'm glad you asked."

She was an engaging presence, Charlie thought. More so than her dear friend Toby's occasionally dry delivery—not that she'd ever put him down that way, of course.

"The Serpent Mound lies near the impact zone of an ancient meteor. In fact, the curve follows the crater for a while. We know little more about it now than we did back in the 1800s. One of its legends, which I'm sure you expected since you're in my class, is the giant skeletons allegedly found there."

The professor cut off the brief guffaw that seeped into the auditorium with a self-deprecating laugh.

"Please remember, we are learning about the *mysteries*, the *questions* of legends in the modern day. Do not take this as firm evidence. But pay attention, this might be on a test."

When quiet returned, she went on.

"We generally think the Serpent Mound was built by the Early Woodland Adena people, who inhabited the area between 500 BCE and 200 CE, with the structure most likely dating to about 300 BCE."

Charlie noted she was using BCE instead of BC and CE instead of AD, presumably because "Before Common Era" and "Common Era" had no religious intonations that might be lost on students who used non-Christian calendars or those from atheistic societies.

"It is thought that they constructed the serpent as a protector of graves, as serpents and snakes were often attributed magical powers by the Native peoples. Another idea points to how the head and the tail align with sunset during the summer solstice and sunrise for the winter solstice, much like Stonehenge in the UK. But..."

She paced, flipping to wider shots of the landscape, which showed more obvious contours that denoted the impact crater.

"Added to this is that the meteor crater has produced gravitational and magnetic anomalies, it's not unreasonable to speculate that it may have been constructed here for this reason."

Charlie caught Toby and Harpal shifting in their chairs, plainly snagging on the déjà vu of a meteor site giving way to more benefits than additional static in the air. But the site in Canada that this brought to mind was now inaccessible to them and guarded fiercely by the Canadian government.

"But why are we talking about this place? Well, simply put... The remains of three skeletons were *reportedly* recovered from this site. Their size would show they measured in life at least eight feet in height. The most remarkable feature was the double teeth growing in the front and back of the mouth."

The students all sat forward, no scribbling or clacking of laptop keys. Like Charlie, they were probably waiting for a new photograph.

Professor Garcia left the aerial shot of the Serpent Mound in place. "Unfortunately, upon exposure to the atmosphere the skeletons disintegrated, leaving nothing but dust and fragments."

The room groaned with disappointment.

"But this is not the only report from the Serpent Mound. Another stems from 1891 by none other than Professor Frederic Ward Putnam, who you may remember from our lecture two weeks ago. Whilst excavating of one of the outer burial mounds that surround the site, he came across a skeleton of a relatively smaller size. Putnam would write here..."

Now the photograph did change, this time to the scan of an article.

She narrated: "Several peculiarities of this skeleton are worthy of notice. It was that of a well-developed man, about twenty-five or thirty years of age. He never had any wisdom teeth, and a search in the maxillary bone of one side showed there was no wisdom tooth forming in the jaw. With this exception, he had a fine set of teeth..."

Garcia seemed to sense this section was a little dry, so summarized instead.

"Basically, it's suggestive of their being persistent first teeth. Putnam suggests it is the seven-foot-tall body of an adolescent which would have grown far taller had it not died. He went on, according to his papers, to discover several more skeletons who would've stood seven or eight feet tall, blessed with skulls twice their usual thickness.

"But he wasn't the only one. Farmers have discovered other burials in the area and there are at least seventeen reports listed in Smithsonian ethnology of remains over seven feet tall found in the areas surrounding the Serpent Mound. It has led people to speculate that some race of giant people could have shared this land with the people we currently think of as Native Americans."

She paused for effect. When no one gasped or fainted in shock, she continued to a modern picture of a man next to a measuring stick, showing him to be over seven feet tall. He leaned on a cane.

"Of course, this is nothing new. We have people in the modern era with gigantism who stand, literally, head and shoulders above even the most imposing of movie stars. But they come with health problems. Their bodies cannot cope with the rate of growth, and they end up weak, and, sadly, do not tend to live as long as the average person."

The visuals switched to a snowy tundra where a gaggle of orange-coated men surrounded a block of ice at least twelve feet long.

"Here we see what purports to be the bones of a human, recovered in the Arctic in 1982."

Charlie was recording the session on a camera that looked like a pen. It fed through the satellite phone in her small backpack, transmitted back to her husband in Greenwich, London, where he manned their hub of operations. Although Charlie was the tech expert when it came to computing and engineering, Phil was no slouch. She could hear him in her subvocal earpiece when he spoke, but he remained on mute for now, observing only.

"These bones, however," Professor Garcia went on, "disappeared into thin air before they could be examined in a suitable environment. Initial inspection suggested they were the correct shape for a human, but were, in fact, deformed and much larger than they should have been."

A hand went up. When Garcia nodded to the student, he asked, "Couldn't this have been some sort of primate?"

"Or Gravettian Man?" another asked.

"Good observation," the professor said, pointing her marker at him. "It's a wonderful question." She gave an exaggerated shrug, her bottom lip popping out. "Gravettian Man's existence is not in doubt. He was, indeed, a tall hunter in prehistoric times, averaging just over six feet, not the seven or eight feet of legend. Indications are that this offshoot—which, by the way, predates Neanderthals by tens of thousands of years—might even be responsible for the fact that certain ethnic groups tend to be taller than average. Those genealogical lines who kept this part of human DNA active may well be descended from real life *frost giants*."

The ripple of laughter this time felt genuine.

"And there would be a definitive answer," Garcia said, cutting off the fun, "were it not for the clumsiness of those who were supposed to transport this particular frost giant to Norway. In fact, by the time qualified professionals could access this site, the ship carrying them had experienced a fire, and all records were destroyed. And although the crew were thankfully unharmed, the boat sank and there was not enough money for a salvage operation. All that remains of this expedition..."

She slapped her hand against the wall where the projection shimmered.

"Is this photograph and the accounts of a young student who was later expelled from his university for drug possession. Which he denies to this day."

"Professor," a girl said without waiting to be asked, "this sounds like some mad conspiracy theory. Why would anybody cover up something like this? It's not like it threatens a powerful government or anything. If you're suggesting giants were real, and that knowledge somehow threatens the modern world, where is the *actual* evidence?"

"Now we're getting to it!" The professor trotted about the floor like an excited teen about to meet a popstar. "While the question of *why* is still a mystery, the question of *if* cannot be denied. But as so often happens in these cases, the evidence..."

Professor Garcia held a fist to her mouth, blew into it, and mimicked her hand exploding.

"Disappears."

She stared wide-eyed at the students, a few of them murmuring. It wasn't clear if they were impressed or wondering if it was worth getting into so much debt over such fantastical theories. Charlie wondered how Garcia got this curriculum past the board. It certainly wasn't the sort of mainstream learning taught at these places, so she guessed this was an extra credit class.

"But then," Garcia said, killing the projector and turning up the lights, "if there was firm archaeological evidence for such creatures, we could drop the word 'legends' from this class, couldn't we?"

Garcia ended the lesson on a static smile, and the students hustled out, some in silence, others already moving on to the next conversation. Once the auditorium emptied, Charlie led Toby and Harpal down the stairs, calling to the professor as she went.

Sally Garcia looked up from gathering her items and books. She beamed their way and poked her round spectacles up her nose. "Oh, hi. You're the visiting professors from Oxford? So brilliant to meet you."

Harpal had arranged for visas based on the three of them entering the United States for academic reasons. Colin Waterston, an alum of both Oxford and Eton, had rubber-stamped their credentials in exchange for Toby relaying all he had unearthed regarding the chamber beneath St Bernard's.

"That's right," Charlie said, arriving at ground level. "I'm Charlie Locke, this is Toby Smith and Harpal Singh."

As Professor Garcia shook their hands in turn, a new face showed itself. It was clean-shaven, borne atop a smart suit and tie, and was attached to a six-foot man with broad shoulders, thick black hair, and a facial tattoo that marked him as a native of the South Pacific—either born there or culturally immersed. As he wandered closer, Charlie pegged him as Maori rather than Polynesian or Hawaiian. The tattoo was etched in the lines of his face, representative of who he was, and of his life to date. He was older than the typical student here, too, but difficult to pin down, anything from early twenties to early thirties, although Charlie erred toward the middle.

"My teaching assistant," Professor Garcia said. "Tane Wiremu. Incredible asset." Her eyebrows bobbed at Charlie and she stage-whispered, "Just need to get an excuse to teach my class on the beach and insist on Speedos as mandatory. Am I right?"

She held up a hand for a high-five, which Charlie stared at for a moment, before Harpal slapped it.

"I'm down for that," Harpal said.

"Oh, yeah." Garcia aimed a finger-gun at Harpal, then winked at Tane, who had started working his phone as if a social media emergency had suddenly taken priority.

Without looking up, Tane chuckled and said, "Come on, Professor. You know that sexism works both ways these days."

It was a strong Kiwi accent; Charlie had been correct.

Garcia laughed at him and patted his arm. "Oh, really. You kids and your notions." She snapped out of *flirty-drunk-aunt* mode and reverted so quickly to *serious academic* that it was like she'd woken from a dream. "Right, you're interested in some of my research, yes?"

"Indeed," Toby said. "Specifically, the intriguing possibility that the Alabama Freedom Museum may be host to more evidence that points towards something that conventional wisdom posits is very unlikely."

Charlie had heard much of Toby's verbal diarrhea over the years and was never surprised when he outdid himself. Nor was Phil.

In her ear, Phil said, "Listen, as much as I would love to let Toby regale me with his intentions, I think my mom is pulling up outside with the kids."

Charlie didn't want him to go yet. "Tane Wiremu. That's an interesting name and even more interesting tats. Maori?"

The well-built teaching assistant finished whatever he was typing and smiled bashfully. "Got me. Student visa. Internship. Extra credit."

He gazed at Sally Garcia, an affectionate look that with less of an age gap Charlie would have assumed romantic. Then again, perhaps she shouldn't be so judgmental. Was it beyond the realm of possibility that they could be an item? Fiftyish mad hippie prof seducing a strapping mid-twenties buck? Unlikely but not impossible.

"Already running the background check," Phil told her. "Not sure why he didn't come up when we vetted Professor Garcia last week, though."

Phil went silent then, as he tended to their three children returning from Nana's house for the few days that Charlie and Phil took care of Toby's project in South and Central America. They hadn't expected it to extend to the United States right away, so they couldn't impose upon Phil's mother any longer.

"Is this a new thing?" Charlie asked Tane, hoping to glean a little info before Phil returned. "You working here?"

"He simply fell into my life," Garcia gushed. She opened her arms to the sky like an overdramatic Hollywood starlet auditioning for an epic. "Very open-minded, if you get what I mean."

"What she means is," Tane said, "I've done my own research, and found her theories intriguing. Of course, she won't tell me what she's holding back."

Garcia wagged the finger at her teaching assistant. "Well, well, well. Maybe today I should pull back the curtain a little more. These fine people have come all the way from England."

She picked up her bag, while Tane scooped up the heavy books in a practiced manner, keeping his phone out and turned on. Both turned for the door. The professor looked back over her shoulder, her glasses slipping down her nose half an inch. She looked over at them.

"That is, of course, if you're not spies from the university board."

Harpal held up two hands, the surrender signal again. "We are not spies." He narrowed his eyes and gave a cheeky smile. "Although, that's what spies would say, isn't it?"

Both Sally Garcia and Tane Wiremu stared, assessing them as they might a disturbed grave.

The professor laughed. "Okay, right this way, spies."

She flounced out of the room, with Tane chuckling at her back. Toby indicated the rest of them should follow, and Charlie was looking forward to what the woman might say.

It was a quick jaunt down three corridors in which Tane received a couple of alerts that he simply had to answer, resulting in eye rolls from both Toby and Garcia.

Kids and their phones, eh?

The walk ended at a neat and tidy office. End to end shelves lined the far wall, straining with the weight of books, while a modern computer setup gave the sturdy-looking desk a twist towards the 21st century. A second desk facing this one possessed only a laptop and a Bluetooth keyboard and mouse. The rest of the office comprised higgledy-piggledy bookcases containing smaller volumes, various awards, and photographs of Sally Garcia in exotic locations, on digs, and meeting several liberal politicians who Charlie recognized, and other dignitaries she didn't.

"So," Garcia said, slumping into her creaky leather chair. "Any reason you think you have more info about the Alabama site than I do?"

Toby took a tablet computer from his satchel and woke up the screen, which was already geared up with one of Sally's videos. They had scrutinized this footage, Sally Garcia presenting to the camera while the picture remained static.

Tane ceased working his phone and circled around her side of the desk where he leaned closer to the tablet than she did, frowning. "These are the landowners who wouldn't let you excavate, aren't they?"

Sally nodded and indicated Toby should lower the tablet. "There's a rich cultural history on that land, a violent and sad crime that lasted way too long. I hated to push the matter, but I think there's an even older injustice."

"Meaning?" Charlie asked. She heard her own voice coming across as accusatory, and added, "Professor Smith has his own ideas, so it would be interesting to see how they gel."

"Honey?" Phil said in Charlie's ear.

Charlie coughed once, drawing Tane's attention. She covered her mouth and coughed more forcefully, excusing herself and stepping aside.

"What can you bring to this?" Sally Garcia asked Toby.

"We may be able to negotiate access to this site," Toby replied. "Others from our institute are out there now. But we would need to understand why you are certain there's something to find. And what coordinates you have calculated."

"Hmm." The professor steepled her fingers and slung her legs up on the desk, crossing one leg over the other. "You want me to show you what's up my skirt, but you don't want to drop your trousers first."

Phil asked, "What the hell is she talking about?"

"I wouldn't put it like that," Toby said. "But I'll happily show you something."

He passed the tablet to Harpal and rummaged in his satchel again, producing the smaller codex loaned by Father Pandi in Mexico.

Garcia put her feet on the floor and reached for the trade paperback-sized journal. Exaggerated wonder elongated her features. "I've seen that symbol before."

She meant the figure eight made up of the two bangles' shape embossed on the front.

"You have more?" Charlie asked. She pretended she was asking Garcia, but Phil would know she had directed it at him.

He said, "It's about the T.A."

Charlie couldn't help flitting her eyes towards Tane, which drew his attention back to her. She returned to the object everyone else was watching, the leather-bound journal with an anonymous author.

She said, "The dates in there suggest it was written in the early 1800s, although it may have been later if it was a retrospective. The paper is consistent with 19th-century work."

Tane did not take his eyes off Charlie. "Who is the author?"

"As near as we can tell," Toby said, "it looks like a man named Jacob Carr. He was an Irish chap, wealthy landowner, who—"

"Freed his slaves, but kept a few as paid employees," Sally Garcia finished for him. "I know the man. Sudden hit of conscience. Is it a coincidence that land records show his farm covered the area now occupied by the Alabama Freedom Museum?"

"Do you want to hear this?" Phil asked.

Again, so she could come across as speaking to both those in the room and the man in her ear, Charlie said, "Go ahead."

While Toby recounted their expedition, minus some elements like collapsing walls and ancient bangles, Charlie listened.

"He seems clean," Phil said. "Everything he has said makes sense. And his records back it up. New Zealand national, graduate of Christchurch University, BA honors in history, focusing on prehistoric human society. There's a gap of a couple of years in terms of official documentation, but his social media gives us a lot of travel pictures and a bunch of motivational memes. Then he pops up here, student visa fast tracked, which is unusual for the United States, but I guess New Zealand is a friendly place. Immigration has him arriving four months ago, and social media shows he hooked up with Sally Garcia two weeks later."

Charlie had been nodding along as she listened, but Toby had stopped talking and all eyes were on her.

"Yes," she said, hoping to front it out, whatever she'd been asked.

"Good, good," Toby said. "So, Professor. You've seen what's under my trousers. How about a glimpse up your skirt?"

Garcia opened her mouth wide, her eyes bulging. "How *dare* you? What on earth do you think this is?"

Tane put her hand on her shoulder and squeezed. "Professor, you did it again. You... kind of started the analogy."

Professor Garcia leaned her head back in thought, then returned to Toby. "Of course. My skirt."

Phil said, "The thing is, this just feels a bit wrong."

Charlie made a discreet *hmm* noise, which again drew Tane's attention.

"It's the timing." Phil paused, but Charlie didn't dare make a sound to encourage him, especially as the professor was recounting her path to finding the Alabama site. Finally, Phil continued. "You might think I'm paranoid. But the end of Tane's official documentation gap, where he is mostly on social media, it's about one week after Toby started talking to Alfonse about tapping up his contacts at the Vatican. I know it may be nothing, but security was my job before Dan's."

Charlie sensed Tane's gaze upon her again. She'd been staring at nothing, focused on the desk.

Tane stood to his full height, unbuttoned his jacket, and marched towards Charlie. Harpal evidently read it as aggressive, gliding to cut him off. Charlie was briefly offended, since she could kick Harpal's ass six ways from Sunday, but her annoyance dissipated as Tane diverted and landed an open hand solidly in Harpal's chest. The blow sent him backwards, stumbling into Toby, who released the journal.

Charlie had less than a second to decide: fight or flight.

"Charlie?" Phil said. "Charlie, what's going on?"

She firmed up her stance and readied herself for a kick at the incoming man's nuts. Or maybe his knee. She misread his approach, though, and he shot out his other hand, which grasped her by the scruff of the neck and dragged her forward.

His strength was impressive, and she couldn't resist. He bent her forward over the desk and pinned her down, but she was already thinking through how she needed to squirm only slightly to get an angle on that knee.

Instead of beating her, he leaned over her and flicked the hair away from her ear.

"Thought so," Tane said. "There's a bug in her ear."

Sally Garcia stood sharply, pressing herself back against the bookcase. "You *are* spies from the University board. You don't want me to get my tenure. Who put you up to it? Was it that bitch Veronica Hardcastle? She's always had it in for me."

As Toby and Harpal found their feet, Harpal readying a fighting stance, Tane drew a compact Glock from his jacket and pressed it against Charlie's forehead. This froze everyone, and Charlie's heart stepped up the pace, thundering adrenaline through her.

"Don't shoot," Charlie said.

"Shoot?" Phil repeated. "I'm calling 911 on your behalf."

"Who are you people?" Tane demanded. "That's a micro transmitter, bone conducting technology, probably linked to a sat phone. Am I right?"

"Play along," Phil said. "Don't deceive them. This guy knows what he's talking about. That gap in his CV, it's probably time with some intelligence service or another."

Charlie fought with the rising fear, the likelihood that they had walked into a trap ramping up. She attempted to engage the man. "New Zealand has intelligence services operating in the US?"

"How do you know who I'm working for?" Tane asked.

Still pinned to the desk, Charlie forced a smile. "You just told me."

Tane gave a single laugh and pulled her upright without wrenching her. He kept the gun out of reach, backed away and gestured for her to join Toby and Harpal. “Clever. Take out the bug.”

“I’ll get someone there in minutes,” Phil said.

Charlie shook her head. “The police are already on their way. Let us go and you’ll have a head start.”

“Don’t be ridiculous,” Professor Garcia said. “You’re the ones going to jail. Tane isn’t just my teaching assistant. He’s my *bodyguard*.”

CHAPTER EIGHT

CARSON ESTATE, ALABAMA

The lemonade tasted like actual lemons, which stimulated Jules's saliva glands and enhanced both the sweetness and sourness inside his mouth. He assumed it was freshly squeezed, laced with lashings of sugar. This time, it was indeed a member of staff that brought it, and the young woman disappeared after leaving the tray on the glass-topped table where Bridget's father, Roger Carson, hosted the gathering. They were outside, albeit under a shadowed patio umbrella. It was more bearable than in the sunlight, but Jules still wished he was wearing shorts and a vest, or else ensconced behind a wall with powerful air conditioning.

Again, he wondered when he got soft in regards climate. He chose to accept it, a practice he'd lost since attempting a "normal" life, and immediately felt better, more focused.

As Jules, Dan, and Bridget helped themselves to the drink, Roger Carson left his alone, condensation pouring down the sides. Bridget had already explained that Roger and his wife had taken time out of their busy schedule to supervise and facilitate her choice of academic options, their billion-dollar oil and securities empire able to cope without them for a couple of days. Still, Roger maintained a vigil over two cell phones, and his laptop remained open at all times. Bridget's mom, Audrey, was in town shopping. Apparently, Bridget had no taste in formalwear.

"My daughter tells me you're here to ask a favor of us." Roger Carson spoke with a deeper southern drawl than Bridget. He was in good shape, at least for a man his age, and filled out his open shirt well. He wore tan slacks and brown loafers, his only concession to an oil baron stereotype being his bushy mustache. He'd kept his hair thick and dark, although the copper pigmentation that he'd passed to his daughter was clear. "Something to do with the museum over the way."

"That's right, sir," Dan said. It was the politest Jules had ever heard him address someone. He sounded almost nervous. "We think there are items of significant cultural value to the United States lying undiscovered."

It was an approach they agreed upon earlier, appealing to the man's patriotic duty, to his pride in his roots here in the South.

"What sort of significance?" Roger Carson asked.

"It's about Jacob Carr," Bridget said.

Roger held a hand towards his daughter and smiled at Jules. "Thank you, dear, but I'd like the gentleman to explain it." He angled towards Bridget. "You know what a soft touch I am when it comes to you." Back to Jules. "Now, what can you possibly reveal that we don't already know? The Alabama Freedom Museum has done some terrific work regarding our ancestors. And maybe yours, too."

Jules wasn't entirely sure about his lineage, having never met his grandparents on either side, and never curious enough to ask. He'd only ever been told they were all deceased, passing before he was born.

"I've learned a bit about Jacob Carr," Jules said. "He's Bridget's... Great great great... What is it? Fifth or sixth great?"

"Fifth," Bridget replied.

"Right. Great grandfather the fifth. Fifth-great grandfather. He was a slave owner before switching sides, helping the Union folks, right?"

"Yes." Roger picked up his lemonade, glass sweating, moisture pooling above his fingers. "He kept slaves in the late 1700s, and into the early 1800s. My understanding is he treated them well. He even collaborated with the on-site preacher over their health and faith needs. Hoped to keep them safe on his land. He even established renumeration for them to be used once they were freed. Accounts show he was instrumental in aiding slaves forced into labor to escape, and his farms were a common stop off on the Underground Railroad to the North."

"His first wife died before emancipation," Bridget said. "He married a black lady after that."

Dan showed them his palm and smiled as he sipped the lemonade. "Nobody is going to deny he was a hero. No wonder you want to fund places like the Alabama Freedom Museum."

"That said," Jules added before he could stop himself, "your family's wealth is still built on the back of the slave trade."

Roger halted mid-sip. He said nothing.

Jules might not have been the best at social cues, but he didn't consider this a social visit. His brain was tuned into deception indicators and anything that could turn aggressive. "I just mean, there's still a way to go before the country can say the legacy is done."

"Jules," Bridget said. She sounded shocked, almost offended. "It's the 21st-century. Our generation can't be held responsible for the evil perpetrated by previous ones."

"But with the repercussions still hurtin' folk, can we really move on?"

"We have to."

"Then when *is* it time to move on?"

Dan shifted in his seat. "Isn't this a discussion for another day? It's not what we're here for."

Jules switched his gaze to Dan. "Then I guess we'll move on from 9/11, too. How about we forget the world wars?"

"Make no mistake," Roger said, keeping his voice even and calm, "it *was* evil. What was done to your ancestors."

Roger then held Jules's eye, as if assessing whether to fling him off the property. Jules refrained from pointing out not every black person in the United States was descended from slaves.

Dan was correct, though, and Jules was screwing this up. He rarely got emotional, but with so much going on in the world, from the people who tried to unleash the Eagle Plague through to law enforcement and elected officials in his own country, even someone as disconnected as Jules found such subjects difficult to treat without anger and a drive to put right. At that moment, though, the man before him was not a bad person. Jules was certain of that. He could even be an ally.

"You do a lotta good work," Jules said. "Not just here, but around the world. I heard you invested in some South American projects, renewables in Africa, philanthropic projects in China." Jules sensed his own accent was ebbing, losing the New York twang, and adopting a more formal tone. He relaxed his shoulders and tried to return to his own voice. "The China thing? That helps smooth the way for business?"

Roger barely altered his expression, placing the glass down without additional movement. He licked the remnants on his lip and crossed his legs.

Jules sensed he had maybe thawed the ice that he had set over proceedings. "You're funding restoration work of the terracotta dudes, right?"

Roger nodded, still focused on Jules rather than Dan. "It's not too famous at this point, but... I assume I can trust my daughter's friends to be discreet?"

"Absolutely, sir," Dan said, almost as if addressing a senior officer.

"Yes," Jules said.

"This isn't an additional find alongside the terracotta warriors that are well known around the world. This is more than a hundred miles north of there, and the people on the ground are eager to explore further. Bridget even asked if she could intern out there, possibly part of a PHD."

Bridget cast her eyes into her lap.

"It's something we will consider," Roger went on. "As long as we see progress in other academic fields. Maybe we'll allow her to accompany you to the museum land, help smooth the way if needed. But first you need to convince me it's worth putting off her future."

It was an impressive about turn. Yet, the controlling nature of Roger's instructions still sat heavy with Jules. Bridget was a twenty-five-year-old woman, not a prepubescent child. She was only here, obedient and pliant, because of the deal she'd made with them regarding LORI; going back on it would diminish her in her parents' eyes and—possibly—her own too. Now Roger was tempted to ease the conditions he'd been strict about enforcing. Perhaps the thought of enhancing the family's heritage was a worthy pursuit in his mind.

"We are looking for a shield," Dan said. "There's a group, soldiers, not written about in history books, but we found several references to them. Stuff written at the time. They'd engage with people who needed help. Villages under siege, preventing the genocide of smaller groups, anything they could handle. Mostly small scale but significant on a regional level."

"Like the A-Team," Bridget said.

Roger sat up, his eyebrows popping. "We have a full set of Blu-rays." He quickly resumed his stoic poise, the hit of nostalgia for this TV show yet again prodding someone in a way Jules did not understand. Perhaps he should ask for a loan of the series once they concluded the shield business. "But go on. You think they were involved with Jacob Carr?"

"It's possible," Jules said. "Toby Smith has the bulk of the research. They had this reputation as fierce warriors, to the point where their enemies made legends out of 'em. The Lost Origins guys found accounts dating back to the times of the conquistadors. Sounds like your great, great, great, et cetera, grandpappy was in touch with 'em. But this was the last place they were heard of. Jacob Carr's journal."

Dan took over. "Actually, sometime before the Civil War broke out. After that, Jacob moved on to aiding the North wherever he could. There's not much mention of the shields or the Guardians after that. As far as we can tell, Jacob Carr is where the trail goes cold."

Roger considered it. "Seems a little far-fetched, don't you think?"

"Not really," Bridget said. "It's no more far-fetched than a dozen other things we found."

"Yes, yes, I've heard your stories." He adopted the kind of expression parents take with children who have an overactive imagination regarding monsters in the closet. "But can you honestly tell me nothing was exaggerated?"

"If anything, dad, I held more back than I gave you."

Jules suspected she would have omitted the life-threatening situations they had encountered. He knew she'd lied about how she got part of her leg burned; no way she revealed it was a glob of burning oil spat out of an imploding pyramid. Otherwise, there would be no way to change their minds about stifling her ambitions.

"Sir," Jules said, "if you were to grant us permission—"

"I can't grant permission," Roger replied. "It's not my land. I just make generous donations. I can't force them to do anything. I won't threaten them, either. I want to keep funding their work."

The four waited in silence, each expecting someone else to speak. Jules sensed the day slipping away and expected it would fall to him to infiltrate their target in the near future. Perhaps that was another reason for his involvement.

He hadn't yet decided whether he would go along with it.

As it happened, Roger had made a decision. "Okay, it seems you have a certain amount of luck and success with this sort of thing. If there's more to be found on that land, go for it. You'll get credit for the find, but the museum keeps anything you unearth—both cultural and financial. Clear?"

Jules held back the notion that LORI was in dire straits. Would the obligatory finder's fee be enough, rather than selling it to Alfonse, who would likely donate it to the Vatican?

"We'll need to document it," Bridget said. "We'll get time to study it, won't we?"

"We?" Roger said. "Who's we? All I see is they."

Bridget slapped her hands on her thighs, firing the brightest smile in the world at her father. "Oh, come on, daddy. This is the chance of a lifetime. It's not some trinkets in a jungle a thousand miles away. This is about family."

"It means that much to you?"

"It does. What will it take?"

Roger thought for a moment, then held his daughter's hands. "A contract. Your re-commitment to your own future. Once this matter is over, you commit within forty-eight hours to a specific course. Business related or hard science, something useful in the real world. And you give it maximum effort. No dropping out, no slacking. After, if you still think this type of work is important, it'll be up to you to fund it. For now, as long as you abide by the terms of our agreement, we will allow your friends to continue working from our property in Brittany. Nothing changes there. But you will commit. Clear?"

"You want it in writing?" Bridget asked.

"This time, yes."

Jules wondered if he had maybe overheard him and Dan suggesting Bridget should go back on the original agreement.

Bridget didn't even hesitate. "Fine, draw it up. I'll sign it. But I get free rein until this over, and full access to the family's pretty much unlimited resources. Okay?"

Roger gave a low, appreciative whistle, impressed with the negotiation. "Sounds good."

"Then we need to get going." Bridget stood and checked on Dan and Jules. "If I'm right, Toby is out pulling up new data, and we need to be in position when he delivers it."

"Something like that," Dan said.

Jules stood as well, downing the rest of his lemonade. "Thanks for the drinks, sir. Would it be okay if I changed before headin' out?"

Roger got to his feet, so they were all standing. "Just look after my baby girl."

"One hundred percent, I will," Dan said, shaking the older man's hand firmly. "Although how much trouble can we get into in a museum?"

CHAPTER NINE

ARNOLD, SOUTHERN CALIFORNIA

"I knew it!" Sally Garcia pointed vigorously at Harpal, Toby, and Charlie in turn. "They call it paranoia, but I was right all along."

Toby never wanted it to go this way. He wanted to bring her onside first, then slowly reveal that they had more knowledge than they should have. He'd hoped to be a friendly colleague.

He said, "It's not like that. We're not here to do you harm. We need to—"

"I know what you need to do. People have tried to silence me before."

"She's right," Tane said.

"What does SIS want with a cuckoo professor?" Harpal asked.

"NZSIS is on the professor's side," Tane insisted. "And she is *eccentric*. Not cuckoo. People have tried to smear her, in more ways than mocking or sabotaging her research."

"Such as?" Charlie said.

Toby barely wanted to hear the answer. "Just because others are interested, doesn't mean there's a threat. We certainly are no threat."

Tane shored up his grip on the snub-nosed Glock. Although compact and less accurate than the model with a full-length barrel, it was perfect for concealed carry—and more than sufficient for short range combat. Not that there would be much combat if he opened fire in the office.

The intelligence officer said, "Then why have we chased the last hack of Sally's equipment back to Greenwich? A coincidence that that's where your tech angel lives?"

"How did you trace it there?" Charlie demanded. "There are military grade encryptions—"

Tane flashed a grin. "You just told me."

Charlie blushed, then ground her teeth in annoyance at herself. "My background shows my address, but not my IP info. Very nice."

"Seriously," Harpal said, "what is NZSIS's interest in this?"

Silence.

"You haven't shot us," Toby said. "You haven't called the police yet. If you deem us a threat, why have you done neither of those things?"

Tane tilted his head towards Sally Garcia. "It's her call. She's the boss."

Professor Garcia twitched, life blooming in her face as if the notion was a revelation to her. "Oh yes, I am the boss, aren't I?" She placed her hands on her hips and raised her chin to appear somewhat imperious. She also adjusted her tone to that of a child playing a monarch in a school play. "I am in charge, and you will do as I say."

"And what do you say we do?" Charlie asked.

Garcia looked over to Tane. "Did they find out anything we haven't planted?"

"Doesn't seem like it," Tane replied.

"Good. Then, should we send them on their way? I mean, if you want to kick some ass a little bit, I won't tell anyone."

"I'm not sure kicking little bit of ass is in anyone's interests. But I would like to know what they want before setting them loose." Tane lifted the gun a quarter of the way, emphasizing it without bearing down on anyone.

"A plant?" Toby said. "Leaving information around that looks intriguing but doesn't give away the real secrets. Marvelous."

Harpal took a step forward, but reversed path as the gun twitched. "And how the hell does an intelligence service embed itself as a personal bodyguard in the United States?"

Toby was glad Harpal was here and not in Alabama. Although Toby was no stranger to the antics of international espionage, Harpal was far more up to date with the machinations of various intelligence agencies.

Tane looked to Garcia, receiving a nod to go ahead. "We have our own networks. Our own interests. Sally's name comes up more often than any other person studying this field."

"NZSIS is interested in the cover-up of giants existing?" Charlie said, dripping with sarcasm.

"The *legends* of giants," Toby said. "Am I correct?"

"That," Tane said, "and the fact that so many undesirable people have hacked Sally's work. They've taken the spoof intel and stepped up their activities. When they snag on the bait, we watch to see who shows up. In person."

"In other words," the professor said, "you swallowed the tidbits, but the important stuff can't be hacked. Because it's in here." She tapped her head with two fingers. "In my brain."

"Okay," Charlie said, "let's recap. You work for NZSIS, New Zealand's intelligence service, and you pop up here four months ago, claiming to be ready to protect and serve the professor."

Garcia nodded along. "Exactly what I needed."

"You sweet-talked her, delivered the paranoid conclusions that she'd been harboring—"

"Just wait a minute," Tane said.

But Charlie didn't wait a minute. "Informing her of foreign governments' interest, plus any number of additional morsels of potential confirmation bias, the university board trying to block her tenure, the computer hacks, the disappearing evidence. You needed to get close to her, because if everything is up in her brain, I'm guessing the NZSIS couldn't get what they wanted from her computer. Which means..." Charlie held firm on Garcia, addressing Tane. "It means you want something she hasn't given you yet."

Tane shook his head. "No."

"Oh yes," Toby said. "She even told us she had to pull the curtain back a little more for you. You're playing her."

"Classic recruitment," Harpal said. "Gain her trust, take what you need."

Professor Garcia scratched her head, took one step away from Tane. "That's not how it is."

"No," Tane said. "It isn't. There are bigger things at stake than any single government."

"And if you're a friendly foreign power," Harpal put in, "why are you undercover? Why not take this to the United States authorities? You mentioned Korea. I'm guessing it isn't South Korea. An ally."

"No, no," Garcia said. "We're sure it's the North. The bad guys."

Toby inched to his left, bringing himself closer to Garcia but not a threat to Tane. "If you've investigated us, you know we aren't here to do harm or steal anything from you. You know we're not assassins or murderers, otherwise I'm fairly certain the gentleman with the gun would be proficient enough to frame this as an attempt on your life. So, if he hasn't gone to the authorities either, the question is: why not?"

"Could it be because he hasn't been honest with you, Sally?" Charlie asked.

"New Zealand might be a friendly foreign power," Harpal said, "but they're still a foreign power."

Garcia was staring at Tane, her mouth turned down and her hands working, forming claws, slackening off, forming fists, slackening. "Tane?"

But Tane had already moved towards Charlie again. He held out his arm, so she remained too far away to reach his gun, but this time he pointed it at her, positioned near his hip. "Take out the earpiece."

"Not so amateurish when we're figuring things out in real time." Charlie raised her hands to her shoulders but did not put her fingers near her ear.

"Don't make me." Tane swallowed.

The motion made Charlie smile. "You're not going to. So, answer the professor's question. Why are you undercover instead of going to the authorities here? If you have her best interests at heart, and you aren't working against the United States, why the subterfuge?"

Tane backed away, the gun remaining where it was. But his drooping shoulders and resigned, sad chuckle said he was unable to make good on his threat of lethal force. He looked over to Garcia, who had now put the length of her desk between them. "I never lied.

We are completely in sync with you, and what you are trying to achieve. More than that. We know about the offers that the Koreans made to you when you were in Iran, and that you turned them down flat."

At another mention of Koreans, Toby wanted to butt in, to ask the others if they recalled Father Pandi's reference to two Korean men asking after the room with the fresco. He resisted speaking, reluctant to interrupt Tane's flow.

"There are people in our country doing similar research, but they are miles behind. We just want to be sure you are not in more danger than you need to be."

"Danger?" Charlie said. She had lowered her hands, but now touched her ear. It seemed Phil was getting worried.

"We know certain people have been following the same trail as you." Tane looked directly at Toby. "Saint Bernard's, London, Alabama. We noted your particular interest in Sally's work on the museum's grounds."

Tane's phone rang. All eyes fell on the handset. Tane once again moved his gun so everybody could see it, then picked up the call, receiver to his ear. He nodded at whatever was said, then replied, "Thank you." He hung up. "Okay, you check out. We find no connection to our North Korean friends. Or any private individuals."

"Private individuals" could be many people, from the reclusive Valerio Conchin to Colin Waterston or even Jules Sibeko himself—if the lad had checked out Toby's proposal, he may have flagged on NZSIS's background checks.

"Are the North Koreans looking for the shield?" Toby asked. "If they are, they may want to reverse engineer the technology." The implications gave him pause to consider a potentially wider conflict. "If they are able to take the kind of kinetic energy absorbing technology used in protecting the orbs we found in Scotland, and apply it to—"

"Should we be talking about this openly?" Charlie said.

Toby felt tired, exhausted at these types of stilted conversations. "If we can't trust New Zealand over North Korea, then the world really is upside down."

"Thank you, brah," Tane said, slipping into a more casual dialect.

Harpal smiled at that. “We don’t have any evidence that the shields are anything but symbolic. Functional.”

“But there is some distant connection between the Guardians and the Witnesses.” Toby caught Professor Garcia’s look of confusion. “You don’t know about that, do you?”

“The shield,” Garcia said. “I’ve heard things. But it’s never been my focus.”

Toby’s brow scrunched as he tried to think back to what else they may have missed. “You’re not looking for the shield?”

“What’s up with her?” Tane asked, gesturing towards Charlie.

Charlie had turned away, looking out the window, coming back to the group, focused on Toby and Harpal. She held up a finger to Tane.

“You know, I still have this.” Tane tapped the Glock’s trigger guard.

“Yes,” Charlie said. “It’s very nice. But my *amateur* husband is inside the school mainframe. The security system. There’s activity on the roof.”

“What’s wrong?” Harpal asked, seeing the same urgency in Charlie as Toby had.

“I can barely hear him.” Charlie pointed at Tane’s mobile phone. “Check it.”

Tane paused, then seemed to twig and snatched it up. “No reception. Sally, the phone.”

Garcia, who had almost faded into the background in the past few minutes, picked up a desk phone, held it to her ear, and reported, “Dead.”

“He’s gone,” Charlie said. “They’re using a jammer.”

“In broad daylight?” Harpal said.

“Must have an old-school listening device in here.” Tane bustled towards Professor Garcia. When she leaned away from him, he held up a placating hand. “I am a trained bodyguard. Close protection. I wasn’t lying. The only reason for this kind of cut-off is ahead of a breach. They are on their way. Do everything I say. If you can, we’ll all get to live.”

CHAPTER TEN

ALABAMA FREEDOM MUSEUM, ALABAMA

"Are you certain we aren't being monitored or followed?" Bridget asked.

"Positive." Dan Vincent was never one for panicking the people around him. He remained on constant alert for tails, for eyes lingering longer than they should, or odd behavior from vehicles and passers-by, but especially since Phil delivered the news of gremlins playing havoc with the comms. He had asked Jules to drive so he could concentrate on the world around them. "We're in the middle of nowhere. We'd see them coming a mile off."

Bridget stood in the entrance to the main house that made up the Alabama freedom Museum, a sprawling mansion, far larger than her own home. Spanning three hundred acres, consisting of fields and dozens of structures, and Dan had not expected to be impacted by the history of the place. It leached up through his feet and spread through his body, forcing him to think about what went on here. It was a similar sensation to entering Auschwitz as a teenaged soldier on an R&R break. What had once been a distant history lesson turned into a solemn education in human evil.

Jules said, "See who coming?"

"No one," Dan replied. "There's no one we know of."

"And the gun on your leg is just a comfort blanket, is it?"

Dan tapped his left shin with his right toe. "We're in Alabama. Isn't being armed at all times mandatory?"

Bridget tutted. "Stereotyping. Let's go."

She led the way into the main entrance, the original door having been widened to allow more people to queue at once, although it was currently empty. They waltzed up to the reception and paid their fee to the elderly black lady behind the glass whose name badge said *Telah Willis*.

"There's a school party in today," Telah said in the ubiquitous Alabama drawl. "Either avoid 'em, or tag along if you wanna learn something."

They had clearly renovated the inside to accommodate foot traffic, and signs informed everyone that the tourist dollar was invested directly into the upkeep of the museum and poverty projects in the surrounding region. The first display of note was a gilded framed portrait of a white man in a light-colored suit with the bearing of a nobleman, the plaque beneath stating the figure in question was Jacob Carr, and the portrait was donated by Roger and Audrey Carson.

The next portrait along presented a weathered, gray-haired black gentleman in long tails, a suit that wouldn't have looked out of place at the Oscars.

"Denbe Willis," Bridget said. "The first black landowner in these parts. Jacob sold him the farm for a dollar."

Jules stared at the man, hands in pockets. He said nothing. It was the sort of background information he normally scoffed at, but maybe—like Dan—he felt a duty to hear this.

"Dan, you there?" Phil said in Dan's ear.

As the three of them moved on, Dan fell back, holding up a finger to his ear to show he was listening. Jules and Bridget stood by the painting of bedraggled black men carrying a shield which they'd seen in the codex, while Dan listened to Phil.

"I have eyes on the college. But I'm struggling to get a visual on our guys. There are no alerts, so no one else has dialed 911. Which is good because it probably means there've been no gunshots yet."

"But comms are still down?" Dan said.

"Affirmative. And I think it's being jammed. Could be college kids screwing with the faculty, but we'd have bypassed that."

"Okay, keep us informed."

Dan continued on, hiding his concern. Despite the lack of exterior input, no 911 call, or visual confirmation, his gut told him the California branch of the excursion had not gone to plan. How severe the issues were, only Phil could find that out.

He said, "They're still dark, but no evidence of problems."

"What would count as evidence?" Jules asked.

He repeated what Phil told him, and that seemed to appease Jules. But not Bridget. She remained quiet as they toured the house. The route led outdoors onto a narrow concrete path with more arrows suggesting the route. It funneled them to bungalow-like buildings that a sign informed them had been restored to their original specs, a place where slaves would have eaten, slept, and bathed. Here, they caught up with the party of twenty schoolchildren, a near equal mix of white and children of color, the latter encompassing Hispanic and black kids alike. They wore uniforms, and all listened to the guide in silence. The 70ish man's oversized name badge on his blazer read *Andre Willis*.

Jules came between Dan and Bridget, put his arms around them on the shoulders, which freaked Dan out a little. Jules was not the most tactile of people.

He said, "Let's get on with this. If things are going south in SoCal, we need to be ready. Bridget? Which way?"

Bridget hesitated a moment. "The library. It isn't open to the public, but we need a way in. It's a family business and they won't say yes without a good reason."

Inside the main house, Bridget appeared to know the layout, taking them up a set of stairs that seemed to be part of the regular route.

"Can't you demand access?" Jules said.

Bridget gave a smile. "That's a bit rude, don't you think?"

They veered away from another room, full of what appeared to be items owned by wealthy people, towards a dark alcove barred by a velvet rope. Dan didn't realize they used these anymore but was happy to see it rather than a locked door.

Jules said, "Is demanded access ruder than sneaking in?"

"I don't think so," Bridget said. "Dan?"

"No," Dan answered. "Sneaky is better than demanding stuff."

They stepped over into the kind of area Dan would expect to see in a British university like Oxford or Cambridge—all dark wood fittings, desks, and small gooseneck lamps, surrounded by bookshelves. It wasn't a huge space, a fraction larger than Dan's last studio apartment. Lights flickered on and Dan ducked into a crouch, ready to go for his ankle holster.

"Relax," Bridget said. "The lights are on motion sensors."

"You've been here before." Jules turned a full circle, taking in the room. "Once or twice?"

"Closer to twice." Bridget wandered the aisle to her left, the floor-to-ceiling shelves forming a horseshoe around the study tables. "I always enjoyed being here, as well as the larger museums and libraries in the cities. This was the closest to my house growing up."

Dan took in the scene, standing back. "I suppose every nerd needs an origin story."

"What are you doing in here?" said a deep voice from the entrance.

Dan spun, backtracking towards the wall, assessing the scene for a threat. His adrenaline didn't spike, experience telling him it was more than likely benign.

The newcomer was a black man somewhat older than Jules, who looked to be in his thirties, wearing a smart pinstripe suit, hands behind his back, feet parted. The way he held himself made Dan reconsider how harmless this man might be, his legs bent in a subtle ready stance—a military bearing.

"Darkeen!" Bridget said, her southern Belle lilt front and center.

"Bridget?" Darkeen said. "Been a few years."

Bridget swept forward and stopped next to Dan. This told him although she recognized the man, she was not a hundred percent sure about him.

"You can't be in here," Darkeen said. "Who are these people?"

"Friends of mine. I'm sorry, we should have called ahead. We are looking for information down on your southern spike. Who owned it back in the late 1700s, that kind of thing."

"We did. The Willises."

Darkeen Willis. Andre Willis. Telah Willis. A family business.

"Any more Willises we need to know about?" Dan asked.

Darkeen faced Dan. "Why would you *need* to know anything?"

Jules stepped up next to Bridget, probably reading the same military bearing that Dan had. "Hey. We're just lookin' for some books. And your family didn't own this place back then. We're assuming Jacob Carr or his family did, but we need to find out."

"Why?"

"Because we want to excavate part of it."

"Right. Well, at least you didn't just trespass."

The direct approach had not been part of the plan, but Darkeen appeared to appreciate that.

"Darkeen," Bridget said. "There's something there. We're sure of it. If we can locate it, it may be a significant find connected to the railroad that Jacob and your family organized. Something... spectacular."

Darkeen shook his head. "We've had archaeologists poking around the southern spike before. There's nothing but rocks and caves big enough for snakes and a small colony of bats."

"Our Intel says otherwise," Jules said.

This time the direct approach did not go down so well. Darkeen unhooked the velvet rope and held it to one side pointedly. "If you wouldn't mind, this area is closed to the public."

Dan waited for Bridget to lead them out as she had led them in, but she remained fixed to the spot. Her usual bright demeanor had dulled, and she sighed heavily.

"I'm sorry," she said. "But I must insist." She spoke these words with exaggerated southern-belle-ness, like a bad actor doing Blanche Dubois, even though they were in the wrong state.

Darkeen angled his head and narrowed his eyes. "Insist on what?"

"On access. You can throw me out, but do you really want my father to reassess his grant following a lack of... good, southern hospitality?"

Darkeen considered that. "I know your father better than I know you. And I very much doubt he would withdraw funding just because his spoiled princess of a daughter turned up and... *impolitely*... demanded we accommodate her."

"Then call him."

"Okay, have it your way." Darkeen fished a cell phone from his inside pocket.

This was not going to go their way. Dan wasn't sure how long they should persist with the bluff, given Roger Carson's reluctance to play ball.

"What's going on here?" a woman asked as she entered.

It was Telah Willis from the reception desk. Although she was clearly over seventy and moved stiffly, there was a strength to her, an aura that demanded attention.

"I'm dealing with it, Nana." Darkeen showed her his cell phone, on which he was yet to hit dial.

"I heard how you were dealing with it." She roved from Jules to Bridget to Dan, then back to Bridget. "I thought that was you on the way in, but my eyesight isn't what it was. You think you've got something worth our time?"

"I do." Bridget fixed her with a firm stare, meeting the old lady as equals. She appeared to intimidate Bridget less than she did Darkeen. "We just need some clues about where to look. About who owned the land, and who might have had access."

Telah Willis considered it for longer than Darkeen had, a loud humming accompanying her thoughts.

"Nana," Darkeen said, "this isn't right. They can't just—"

"What can't they just do?" Telah asked.

"Come in here and start pushing us around."

"Oh, just hear yourself. If little Bridget wants to do some research with her friends, I don't see any harm in it." The old lady faced Bridget, glanced at Dan and Jules, but nothing more. "Knock yourself out, honey. Do let us know what you find, won't you?"

"I will." Bridget beamed a big smile, nodded towards Darkeen, and backed away, placing her bag on the nearest workstation. "I promise, I'll come to you before we do anything."

Darkeen sighed and put his phone away, rolling his eyes as he stepped out.

"Umm," Dan said. "Can we order pizza in here?"

Darkeen ducked back in. "You can order it. But you can't eat it near the books."

"No problem."

Darkeen and Telah left them alone, and Jules asked, "Where do we start?"

"I'll be over here," Dan said, pulling a chair up to the window on the sole wall with no books.

"Still not worried about anything?" Jules asked.

Dan tapped his ear to show he was on it. "Phil, any news?"

For a moment Dan thought Phil wasn't going to answer. Then, he came through. "I'm busy dealing with it. I'll get in touch soon."

Dan read the tension between Bridget and Jules, clearly hoping for confirmation all was okay. "No change. But that means nothing. Now, I'm planning to sit over here and play some old-school Tetris on my phone while admiring the view."

But as soon as he sat, his feet and shoulders shivered, his leg muscles restless, his body demanding he act. Do Something. He could not remain static.

"Actually, I'm gonna take a walk, keep a wider scope on things. Unless you need me to lug some books around."

Bridget and Jules accepted the plan, such as it was, and nobody voiced what must have been on all their minds: that if they heard nothing from Toby's group soon, they would all start to fear the worst, and this quick research trip might require more than an ankle piece to get them safe.

For now, Dan had to trust that Phil had the matter in hand. But something told him being "busy dealing with it" had more of an undercurrent than the words themselves. It told Dan there had been progress.

Positive or negative, they would soon learn.

CHAPTER ELEVEN

ARNOLD, SOUTHERN CALIFORNIA

Harpal cracked the door. The corridor to his left appeared empty. He risked opening it all the way. Checking to the right, he spotted only a man in his fifties reading a stapled sheaf of papers as he walked. Balding, short, and mostly round in body shape, he wore brown cords and a sport coat with leather elbow patches. If a director had cast him as "stuffy professor" in a movie, Harpal would have thought it a lazy piece of work. But, he supposed, certain stereotypes existed because they were real.

Mr. Stuffy Professor diverted through a doorway without glancing up.

Harpal slid into the passageway and Tane followed. Neither knew which way to go, so they headed toward the nearest stairwell. Harpal reasoned it was a sensible escape route to monitor, along with the stairs near the lecture hall and the elevators. Anyone posing a threat would cover each ingress and, manpower permitting, the exits too. Phil had said he'd spotted four on the roof, but that was before he could perform a full sweep. Then he got cut off.

"Hiding your employer in a loft, eh?" Harpal said. "Did they teach you that in close protection school?"

"Protect the principle," Tane replied. "And since you might be useful to her, protecting you, too. Unless you think dragging four unarmed people around with me is better than just the one."

"You didn't have an emergency plan?"

"Yeah, but four suspicious individuals who get seen on camera means at least four others I can't see. Lying low is the best tactic at this stage. Until we know the landscape."

At the stairwell doors, Harpal lowered his voice and pressed himself against the wall. "Any idea who they are?"

"If it's the North Koreans, they're working for Ryom Jung-Hwan."

"Who's that? One of those crazy generals?"

"Private businessman. But loyal. Very loyal. They have contractors who're former soldiers, and our intelligence says a fellow called Ah Dae-Sung is running the squad."

Harpal searched his memory but could find no mention of that in any dispatches or briefings. "Okay, ready?"

Tane nodded and advanced on the doorway, gun tight to his chest. He counted down by dipping his chin three times, then gradually turned the handle and eased the door open. He listened.

Harpal cocked his ear that way, hearing nothing.

Tane widened the crack enough to blade his body through, weapon ready.

Harpal held the door, checking left and right as the big Kiwi intelligence officer craned his neck to view upward, then sidestepped to check down. He then backed up into the hallway and indicated Harpal should follow, shutting off the would-be escape route.

Once they were several strides away, Tane spoke in a low but urgent tone. "I couldn't see exactly, but there were shadows. At least two people."

"Could be students snogging."

"Kids don't need to hide when they make out. It was someone who shouldn't be there. I don't think I alerted them, but let's check the other way out."

Unarmed, Harpal felt exposed. Yes, he could shoot and handle physical confrontation better than the average man in the street, but he was in no position to question Tane leading this exit strategy.

Tane chopped the air with one straight hand, approaching the vestibule with two elevators. "If we get comms back up with your man, do you think you can reconfigure the satellites to map a way off the grounds?"

"I doubt it," Harpal replied. "For one thing, by the time we get comms back up, we should be out of here. For another, we don't have any satellites."

Tane sighed at this, seemingly expecting LORI to have been as well-resourced as the FBI or Homeland Security. "Watch our backs."

He flattened himself against the wall, gun close to his leg, and switched to a casual "leaning" pose as a kid of around twenty exited an elevator car and walked with a bobbing motion, ear pods buzzing. With his thumbs hooked into his backpack straps, he gave Tane and Harpal a cursory glance, before bobbing on his way. He hadn't seen the pistol.

Tane resumed his military frame and peered around the corner. "Clear."

Harpal followed him along the passageway beyond the lobby, approaching the lecture hall where they had first encountered Professor Garcia. The door was closed.

Harpal said, "The way we came in, the back of the hall?"

"It takes us straight out into the main quad. Plenty of people. If we'll have a clear line from the janitorial closet, I think we have a better chance of getting Sally clear."

"You're sure they want her alive? Not a kill-squad?"

"If they wanted that, they could have jumped her anytime. Nah, this is an abduction. They want what she hasn't left lying around on her laptop or YouTube."

"And what's that? Because it sounds—"

"Help me get her out of here, and *then* we'll discuss it."

Harpal repeated the process used when accessing the stairwell: palm on the door handle, squeeze, depress the lever, crack the door... Eye to the vertical gap running from the floor to the top of the frame.

Not in complete darkness, but very little light.

Harpal eased it closed. "We left the lights on. Are they motion activated?"

"They are. Guessing that means nobody is moving around in there."

"Also makes us immediate targets if someone is lying in wait."

"Then I guess we'd better be clever about it. We're students looking for the prof."

Without waiting for Harpal to agree, Tane opened the door fully and called out, "Professor Garcia?"

Harpal came in beside him. Cementing the ruse, he employed an American accent. "Yeah, Professor Garcia, I wanted to ask about that coffin in the ice."

Both men wandered farther in, activating the nearest lights. They flickered on in turn, starting in their corner and spreading along the front. Nothing in the auditorium lit up.

Tane stared at the darker areas, dim rather than pitch black. He hefted his gun from the blind side of his right leg in a two-handed grip. He signaled with two fingers that Harpal should go past him towards the teaching station, then resumed his double hold.

"Come on, man," Harpal said, retaining his American accent as he followed Tane's directions. "She ain't here. Let's check out her office."

"Nah, brah, I heard she sleeps in here sometimes." He chuckled. "Crazy kook."

Harpal laughed, reaching the heavy-looking desk, and wondering why he was here instead of retreating to the safety of the corridor. When Tane made a scooping shape with his free hand, Harpal slowly moved the chair and found a bundle of tape stuck to the underside of the desk.

"Professor?" Tane called.

As he adopted a shooting crouch, covering the seating arrangement, Harpal picked at the tape. He clamped the end between his thumb and forefinger and pulled as slowly as he could manage.

A barely audible rip sounded.

Both men froze, straining to see beyond the first ten rows. Nothing moved. No shadows. But the lights had plainly spooked Tane into initiating a more thorough search.

Once Tane recommenced moving, Harpal gave the tape another tug, this time eliciting a longer rip as gum disconnected from wood.

Again, they turned into statues, ears and eyes tuned for any sign of life.

When life failed to materialize, Tane twisted toward Harpal and raised a finger to his lips. Harpal braced two hands on the slack tongue of electrical tape, a pistol's butt visible. He wondered how long it had been here, and what would have happened if a cleaner or other teacher searching for a dropped pen had spotted it. Maybe Tane removed it each evening and reinstalled it before class, giving him—and Sally Garcia—access to a firearm he couldn't conceal in a shoulder holster.

What had made him risk the backup piece today?

"It's a bust, brah," Tane said, winding his hand to say, hurry. "Let's go."

Harpal managed to dislodge another inch of tape without transmitting it around the lecture hall, then got his hand around the grip. It was very sticky on one side. He waggled it but could not release it. He gave it a firm twist, which tore off several inches more tape and made the desk move, scraping on the floor as the gun pulled free. It was very loud.

The first of the men in janitorial overalls pounced from behind a white board that someone had wheeled to the right. He barreled forwards. The man of Southeast Asian appearance was built like he had been chiseled from stone in anticipation of worship by those who valued strength.

Harpal whipped up the gun at the same time as Tane drew on the charging man. Before either could fire, their target halted, hands in the air, eyes wide as if startled by the weapons. Neither opened fire.

Mistake.

Two gunshots cracked in quick succession, but Tane had already thrown himself to the floor. The slugs impacted the closest wall, making Harpal duck lower. He brought the gun back up and fired in the general direction of the attackers.

Tane rolled and snapped onto one knee, but his target had fled behind the second row of seats and the barrel of a gun snaked around to fire blindly. He joined Harpal at the desk which was only hiding their exact position rather than bestowing a bulletproof nest from which to shoot.

Tane checked himself for bullet wounds, then returned fire. "Damn it. I knew it couldn't be that easy. At least this will bring the cops."

They only had moments until their attackers shredded the wooden desk. To have any chance of surviving, they had to keep the gunmen pinned down.

"And if I know Charlie," Harpal said, "she won't be hanging around if she hears this."

Charlie pulled up the loft hatch, ignoring Toby's instruction to remain where she was. "We can't just hang around. Those are gunshots."

"And we don't know where they're coming from," Toby said.

Charlie hung her legs out and braced against the hatch's frame. This was amateur hour, and it made her want to scream, but this group needed a level head. All the signs were there, all the tiny signals that someone was onto them, but they'd ignored them. Having faced only two regular competitors in recent years—Valerio Conchin and Colin Waterston—they could have grown sloppy about others. Even Toby, better versed in international subterfuge than perhaps any of them, ignored the fact two Korean men were asking about an obscure relic the same week they had discovered its whereabouts.

He was so desperate to pull LORI back together, it was hardly surprising that they'd sleepwalked into the facility where the foremost expert on the subject was based. But having toured extensively with the Royal Signals, learned her trade, and expanded that knowledge in Civvie Street, Charlie was no slouch in these predicaments. She rarely volunteered, but when backed into a corner with no other choice, she acted. And looking at the options available, she chose to move.

She said, "We'll know where the fighting is in a moment."

Sat in the dark loft, Professor Garcia held her head in her hands. "And people say I'm crazy."

Toby reached for Charlie. "No, wait—"

Charlie swung down before he could say more, landing deftly before peeking out. There was no one to be seen, but another grouping of gunshots told her the firefight was going down to her right, and some distance away. To her left, the stairwell door was still closing after someone had used it.

Then, footsteps rushing from the direction of fire. A dozen or more students and faculty members hustled this way, a university security guard ushering them to evacuate, a handheld radio up high.

Charlie withdrew and called up, "Let's get going, we can blend in with the evac."

Toby fussed and wrestled with the ladder they'd pulled up after ascending to the hidey-hole, and Charlie helped him and the professor down. Sally Garcia moved sprightlier than her age suggested she would, and she even slapped Charlie's helping hands away.

"I can manage, thank you."

Swinging open the door, they latched onto the tail end of the evacuees, many asking if it was an active shooter situation or just some idiots letting off firecrackers. The guard herding them said, "I don't know, but we're treating it as a live event. Follow the drills, you'll be fine."

Charlie noticed him thumbing the radio and listening. As with her comms linking them to Phil back in England, it looked like local airwaves were also dead. Meaning LORI hadn't been hacked; it was a blanket attack.

"Go, go," Charlie said, pushing Toby to the stairwell. It was sweet the way the older man tried to be protective of her despite both knowing she was far more capable, physically, then he was. "Professor, do you have a car?"

Their voices echoed as they descended.

"Yes," Professor Garcia replied. "But it's the other side of the campus."

"Any other vehicles?" Charlie asked.

"Some security personnel, maybe."

"Then we go that way."

Mingling with the students and staff, they broke out into sunlight. The people fleeing the noise that had lessened to the occasional *pop, pop-pop* stuck close to the walls in their rush to a predesignated safe area. Cowering under desks, it seemed, was no longer the standard practice.

God, how weird it must be to live in a country where "active shooter" drills were both commonplace and accepted as a way of life.

Static crackled in her ear.

"Phil?"

Toby and Garcia looked at her.

Charlie pressed a finger into her naked ear to amplify the bud in her other. More static. She asked, "Which way to the security car lot?"

The professor pointed and Charlie led them away from the line of well-drilled personnel toward the next building, actually more a collection of cabins. As soon as they got close, she saw the three saloons painted to look kind-of-but-not-quite like police cars.

"*Ch—lie?*" came Phil's stuttering voice.

"I'm here." Charlie had her phone out, checking every direction as she guided Toby and Garcia along. She snapped the nearest car's number plate. "Sending you a reg. Can you see if it's remote activated?"

"What's happening?" Phil demanded.

"Just open the boot."

While Toby didn't exactly need mollycoddling, Charlie made sure he stayed ahead of her as they approached the security vehicle. The lights flashed to show it was unlocked.

Phil had come through for her, accessing the car's computer by way of the manufacturing company's anti-theft technology. Ironically, it made things easier for people like Charlie and Phil to break into them, providing they had an up-to-date back door to the firewalls. Which they did, for any number of companies—mainly security systems but auto firms were useful too.

With all security personnel distracted, Charlie popped the boot.

"Why are you opening the trunk?" Professor Garcia asked.

"To hide you two," Charlie said. "Get in."

"No chance."

"Is this necessary?" Toby asked.

"Look, if those people are looking for us, or her, they're not going to think about checking the back of one of these cars. And I'm needed."

"You are not needed near any gunfight," Phil said, likely tuned in to the police bands which must have lit up with the news.

Toby's thin lips and narrowing eyes reflected the same sentiment.

"I won't get involved," Charlie assured them. "I'll hunker down and wait for Harpal and our Kiwi He-Man to get clear. Then we all leave. Okay?"

Silence from everyone.

"I'll take that as a yes." Charlie prodded Toby, making him climb into the trunk, followed by an even more reticent Sally Garcia.

She closed the lid, jogged back to the trickle of people evacuating the building, and approached the security guard who had now exited and was directing stragglers onto the safe route. Charlie skirted close to the wall, hearing the static kick in, meaning Phil couldn't hear, then sidled up to the guard.

She said, "Can you help me? I'm new here and I'm not sure which—"

"Follow the crowd, miss," the beefy guard said.

"I will." Charlie leaned into him, swiped his gun from his holster, and shoved him back. "Sorry."

To the cries of, "Hey, come back with that," Charlie sprinted toward the action, the guard having hesitated just long enough to give her too much of a head start to worry about him catching her.

There were four of them, opting for potshots, keeping Harpal and Tane pinned. Tane had already made a dash for the door through which they entered, but their new friends dissuaded him from that course within two steps.

"Why don't they finish us off?" Harpal said.

"They're getting in position." Tane had clearly taken more notice of their opponents' movements than Harpal.

Mostly, both of them had been glad no one seemed to have a machine gun that could have shredded the desk to pieces. That they were still alive felt like a miracle in itself.

Tane had a hypothesis for that, too. "I'm guessing they want us to lead them to Sally."

That made sense. And was scarier than attempted murder.

"Listen," Harpal said. "If I unload this around the chairs, do you think you can make it to the door?"

"Sure, but then you're pretty much dead."

"Or I'm the only bargaining chip they'll have."

"You think they'll take you captive, then you get to hold out until the cavalry arrives?"

Something like that, Harpal thought, but didn't want to vocalize. He said, "Just do it. The professor is your chief concern, isn't she?"

Tane bit down, his face a solid mass. "That's—" A gunshot cut him off, and another coin sized section of desk splintered near his shoulder. "That's true. How do you think you'll hold out with a bullet in the knee?"

Harpal was thinking on the fly. He had never endured actual torture before, although he had been roughed up plenty.

"Long enough for you to get them out," Harpal said. "My friends are there too. Let's get on with it. Before I change my mind."

Tane nodded once, his jaw still set with movie star grit.

Harpal placed one firm foot on the floor, checked the gun's slide, which moved smoothly despite the bits of glue clinging to parts of it. "Count of three. One."

Harpal risked a peek over the desk and pinpointed two of the four men.

The massive assailant who'd first shown his face had found cover behind the wall that ran alongside the far column of chairs, while a different janitorial impersonator took a post ten yards up the auditorium, using the natural V between two seats to shore up his aim. The others remained hidden.

Harpal ducked back down and said, "Two...?"

Tane adopted a sprinter's position, his ankles braced in invisible stocks, ready to run the hundred-meter dash.

"Three." Harpal sprang up, centered on the guy ten yards away, and fired three shots.

There was no cry of pain, no flying through the air, just a would-be killer slumping in place.

Tane launched himself for the door, bent almost at right angles, but his speed was that of an Exocet missile homing in on its target.

The man with the muscles poked his arm around the divide and blasted in earnest, but Harpal was quick to switch directions and fire once. He needed to conserve ammo. By his count, the fifteen-strong magazine was now down to six bullets.

As if bonded in psychic harmony, the other two assailants exposed themselves and fired on Harpal, forcing him flat to the floor as wood shattered and flew, and bullets raked the wall behind.

A quick flit to the door showed Tane had exited as planned.

Good.

Harpal snaked over the ground, switching his head with his feet so he could look out from the other side of the desk. It kept the muscle head out of sight.

He aimed up at the perches from where the second two gunmen had attacked. They were frantically shuffling towards the stairs at the auditorium's edge, which would bring them down towards the muscle head, grouping on their leader.

It still bothered Harpal that they hadn't destroyed the desk in order to kill him. Tane was right. There was torture in his future.

Four, maybe five bullets remained. He hadn't asked Tane for his weapon, as he might need it later.

So, he could gamble. Hold his ground and hope for the cavalry or make a run for it the way Tane had gone, then flee in a different direction.

There was still no way he would allow these men to get close to Toby and Charlie.

Okay, this is it.

Harpal crouched in the same position as Tane, an Olympic sprinter prepping for the race of his life. With the desk still obscuring him from view, he held the gun one-handed, on its side the way idiots on TV did, but angled slightly up. He was planning to run, firing backwards. The odd stance would steady the recoil while maximizing his foot speed.

Or should he run backwards, firing two-handed, giving him a better aim?

Stop thinking.

Go.

Harpal took off. He fired once. Twice. A glance over his shoulder.

The three attackers must have been more experienced than he had hoped, as they were now out in the open. His shooting position was awful, posing little threat.

Gunfire rained in. It missed, but the only way it hadn't cut him down was because their aim was intentional. The bullets raked the wall ahead, pocking the door.

Harpal fired back, but the gun's slide snapped open, signaling he'd spent the final slug.

"Stop!" shouted one of the men.

Harpal was less than two meters from freedom. He kept going.

A single gunshot rang out.

Harpal ducked, as if he could evade a projectile moving faster than the speed of sound. Something had already bitten his upper arm —the outside, a line of blood slashing the skin.

He lumbered to a halt. It was over for him. Trapped. Nowhere to go.

Then the door whipped open.

Charlie said, "Get down, numbskull." She held a pistol two-handed, a Barretta if Harpal wasn't mistaken, and opened fire repeatedly.

He stayed low, crouch-running for the exit, glancing back as he went.

The muscle head had grabbed a colleague and used him as a shield. The shield's chest had blooded as the muscle head retreated behind the cover of the aisle leading up the stairs. The other minion had fallen.

Harpal dove out of the room, and Charlie was seconds behind, guiding him along the passageway, the opposite direction to where they had hidden. It was a winding route, and Harpal saw little. He concentrated on holding his arm together, putting pressure on the wound which already throbbed and burned.

Charlie pushed out into daylight and continued to lead Harpal by touching his good elbow. Only when they were hurrying down a path with their backs skirting a wall did Charlie enquire if he was okay.

"Fine, thanks," Harpal said. "The others?"

"Alive." Charlie snapped her head around at the sound of sirens. She looked at the gun in her hand, then hurried towards a trash can, wiping prints from it, and dumped it in there.

"What are you doing? We might need that."

"You know which country we're in. They see me with you,

carrying a gun, they won't ask questions. It might still have some DNA, but I'm not in any database. We should be okay."

"Fine, which way?"

Charlie answered by leading him toward a block of what appeared to be temporary cabins, out of place in what he'd seen as a traditional-looking American college campus. She went for a car, opened the boot, and it surprised Harpal to find Toby and Sally Garcia curled up inside.

Toby sat upright, his legs hanging out, and drew his attention directly to Harpal's arm. "Good Lord, are you okay?"

"I don't know," Harpal said. "Feels like a couple of stitches will fix it, but they weren't aiming to kill."

"Good job," Charlie said. "You're welcome, by the way."

Harpal smiled at her, his heart slowing. "Couldn't have made it a few minutes earlier? Tane Wiremu is out looking for you."

"He's found us," Professor Garcia said, unfolding and climbing out with Toby.

Sure enough, Tane approached from the same exit they had explored first, checking back constantly, gun by his leg. He hadn't taken Charlie's precaution.

He reached them, and all retreated behind the two security cars, obscured from view in case the gunmen found their way here.

Charlie opened the driver's door. "We should use these to get out. You know the way?"

"I'll drive, you follow." Tane muscled past her and she went to work on the next car.

"Phil, you there? We need your automobile magic again." She paused, then the second car unlocked. "I'll explain on the way."

Before she could get behind the wheel, Toby said, "I think it's safe to say those gentlemen who visited Father Pandi in Mexico were not tourists. One hundred percent caution from here on out."

Harpal winced against the pain spreading from his minor wound. "Any idea how they're doing in Alabama?"

Charlie put the question to Phil, then answered, "They've made some progress."

"Alabama?" Professor Garcia said. "You're really pushing for the shield? Even I'm not positive it exists."

"We need to know what you know," Toby said. "I expect the men who attacked the building are desperate to speak to you too. They need your knowledge."

Tane was already behind the wheel, beckoning for people to get in. "Stop talking. Let's move."

"If they want what she has," Charlie said, "it has to be valuable."

Tane slapped the wheel in exasperation. "Then it's a damn good job she doesn't know everything, isn't it?"

Even Sally looked surprised.

"Just get in. We can talk on the way."

"On the way?" Toby said.

"Alabama," Tane said. "At least, we will if you can stop jabbering and start running. *Now*."

CHAPTER TWELVE

ALABAMA FREEDOM MUSEUM, ALABAMA

Jules closed the latest land registry record, having double- and triple-checked what he thought they needed, which he'd discovered a half-hour after the museum closed and all but Darkeen Willis went home. Bridget, though, had her nose in what appeared to be a handwritten manuscript, another she hadn't deemed fit to share with them. All she'd done was hold up a finger and said, "One minute." That was twelve minutes earlier.

"Okay, I'm done." Jules stood and stretched. "If all we're doin' is getting colorful background, maybe I can leave you to it. I gotta get back to New York."

Bridget glanced up, sagged, and sighed. "New York? But we've barely gotten anywhere. Haven't even persuaded the Willises to grant us permission to explore."

"Wasn't my brief. All they needed me for was to help get your dad on side. I did that."

"You know that wasn't Toby's main reason for wanting you involved." She tapped her finger on the pages. "You might want to stick around for this."

"All clear," Dan said, turning back to face them. He had been muttering with Phil in the corner near the window, having returned from his post outside to offer them news of the other team's escape from what Jules had feared was chasing them. "They made it to the airport without being detained. Stitches for Harpal and they've picked up a couple of passengers. Someone who might be useful in a scrape, and another for this book stuff."

It had been over two hours since they learned of the gunplay in California. That point signaled the first time Jules announced he was leaving, explaining that he couldn't get involved in anything that might lose him his job. Just now was the third time, but something kept pulling him back.

In his civilian life, he'd been quite the expert at scraping out of arrests on either technicalities or pointing out a lack of evidence and the likelihood of local courts being able to prove beyond reasonable doubt that he had done what they'd accused him of—even though he was guilty almost every time. It had been a badge of honor for him.

"What's so interesting?" Jules asked Bridget, coming back to the question prior to Dan's interruption.

"Your official federal records and my local agreements differ up to a point," she replied. "You found the Southern Spike was owned by the state, not Jacob Carr, right up until the same date he sold his own properties to the people who'd worked the land."

"For a dollar, yeah. Got that. Then he married a black lady and disappeared into retirement. We covered this."

"Yes, but it all builds. Let me get it straight, and don't forget..." Bridget tilted her head toward Dan. "Not everyone was around for all of that."

"Don't mind me," Dan said. "I'll hear it when you repeat it to Toby later."

"That settles it." Jules made for the main body of the museum. "Let's head out. I'll catch another red-eye home. You wait on Toby and the newbies."

"Then let *me* get it straight." Bridget thumped the table. "Unless you want to take a two-hundred-dollar cab ride."

Jules glanced at Dan.

Dan shrugged. "I'm hoping to stay at her place. Can't afford a hotel, so she's in charge of transport."

"I could steal it," Jules said.

"Thought you were worried about getting fired for associating with criminals. How's grand theft auto gonna go down?"

Defeated, Jules leaned on the arch's frame, his back to the darkened exhibits. "Fine. Jacob Carr sells his farm and property for a dollar, remarries once his kids are all grown up, and retires. The land our new friend from LA thinks contains a deep, dark secret is the Southern Spike we've been talkin' about, which was federal land for a time."

"This is what reverted to Native ownership?" Dan said.

"Correct." Bridget brightened as they dug back in. "Jacob's property line abuts the Southern Spike, and right along there, it's documented a number of figures in the underground railroad lived and worked. After the civil war, the land was carved up, and the Spike returned to... it says the Cherokee but doesn't go into which band."

"And it was never populated," Jules said, boredom stretching his patience.

"Ah, yeah, that rings a bell." Dan hopped up onto a desk, sitting there with his legs dangling. "If I remember from school, places like the Southern Spike were subject to land surveys as part of the Indian Termination Policy between the 1940s and 60s."

Bridget frowned up at him. "Umm, yes. How did you—"

"And in 1956, they passed the Native Relocation Act which encouraged Native Americans to move to more urban areas." Dan screwed up his face in concentration. "It's coming back to me. Around 750,000 Native Americans headed for cities before they expected to be evicted. But, oddly, the land we're calling the Southern Spike was gifted to none other than Telah and Andre Willis in January of 1956, several months before the act passed."

Bridget checked the documents and notes she'd taken so far, blinking fast before settling on Dan again. "Impressive. You remembered all that from high school?"

Dan tapped the side of his head. "Oh yeah, all up here. The natives knew the act was coming, and rather than risk it falling into federal hands, they donated it to the museum."

"Yes. Dan, are you—"

"He has Phillip Locke in his ear," Jules said. Watching Bridget flounder at Dan's encyclopedic knowledge had amused him for a short while, but it was getting late, and he really intended to be on the next plane home. "It's public record, backing up what I dug out. Just the timings that are different."

Dan appeared more amused than annoyed at Jules selling him out. "Point remains. Jacob Carr passes his land on to the people who'd worked it and made him rich, he takes his wealth and retires with a hot new wife, and the property passes from generation to generation of the Willis clan."

Jules wound his hand in the air. "Yeah, yeah, then they sell off bits and pieces along the way, endin' up with this plot of land for the museum. Plus, the Southern Spike, which stays untouched. It's odd, but not worth the attention of a group who specialize in the kinda things we've seen."

Bridget fingered a section in her latest manuscript. "It's only just gotten interesting. That finger of land passed to the Willis family, same as the museum. But that's simply the official contract. Here's the one signed *in*formally, but one infinitely more important to the Cherokee... and this other signatory."

Dan leaned over to look.

Jules considered holding his ground but ambled over and read what Bridget had found.

"Okay, fine," he said. "Guess we got one more stop to make after all."

Bridget had started the day excited to see her friends, then disappointed that they'd visited only to recruit her for a mission. Well, an errand. But it was becoming something more. Now she was ending it with a buzz in her rib cage, in her fingers and toes, her knees both weak and strong as they pressed home the need to hurry.

Even Jules had come along willingly, swatting at mosquitos in the early evening dusk.

Jules.

Why couldn't he admit that he loved this type of work as much as she did? Why deny himself the chance to explore the planet, to explore history, and even rewrite chunks the world thought it had known?

A *cop* of all things?

She understood he'd been through an ordeal back in Austria. His actions had led to him accidentally killing a man—a dangerous man, who'd have murdered Jules in a heartbeat and smiled while he did so. But Jules had this code, something to do with all life being precious. One of the martial arts he'd studied meant he had to respect all life, and to always seek a different way to end conflict. Perhaps joining the police was his way of giving back. To help others, to protect and serve.

Still, carrying a gun for a living was an unusual way of hoping never to kill again.

"You do the honors," Dan said.

Bridget rang the bell.

The Willises' house stood alone on the eastern edge of the museum. It had been constructed at least thirty years earlier and looked its age. While they were land-rich, probably millionaires, technically, it seemed unlikely they could unlock that wealth and translate it into ready cash.

When the door opened, Andre Willis—the tour guide they'd seen with the schoolkids—greeted them as a fog of spicy aromas, mingled with something cabbage-like, wafted out. "Hello. What can we do for you? It's late."

"May we come in, please?" Bridget asked in her most polite voice. "We won't inconvenience you long, I promise."

Andre looked to his left, received an answer, and stood aside for them to enter.

The door led directly into the lounge without encountering a hallway or reception room, two doors besides the outer one. The first opened to a kitchen, dishes on the side of a sink the only sign of mess in the house, the other a passage running out of the lounge which presumably contained the bedrooms and bathroom.

Before Bridget, Telah Willis sat in a sturdy armchair with a purple flower pattern. She faced them, as if she'd been expecting visitors, the TV directly to her right. It wasn't until she raised a hand, appraising Bridget as she approached, that Bridget noted the chair swiveled side to side as well as back and forth.

Telah asked, "You found what you need?"

"We found something," Bridget said.

The door closed. Jules removed his shoes and padded over, halting behind Bridget. Dan had remained outside, still concerned about the possibility of being jumped as Toby's group had been.

"It's small," Andre said, finding his own armchair—a twin of Telah's in shape, only a leather design. "But it sees us well."

Telah hadn't taken her eyes off Bridget. "What did you find, child?"

"I don't mean to accuse you of anything—"

Telah's lips parted wide, the approximation of a smile, but lacking warmth or humor. "I'm sure I've heard worse in my time. Speak. Candid-like."

Bridget did so, recapping the official records and the more personal accounts of deal-making, until she found herself on the precipice of being shut down. "The land you took over from the Cherokee... It was a deal on paper, and in fact. But there was another facet that didn't make it into the federal records."

Telah hummed, nodding gently, although it made the chair wobble more than it should have.

"What you mean another facet?" Andre asked.

Jules finally gave in, having had to relive the research for a third time. "Are you part of a super-secret inter-generational group of people dedicated to helping those in need, providin' they meet your strict moral standards?"

Both Telah and Andre stared at him.

"Inter-gener-what-now?" Telah said.

"The Guardians," Bridget answered. "Are you, or are you not, descended from the Guardians who protected people through the centuries? And are you still doing your bit by taking on the responsibility of protecting both African American and Native American culture by refusing development and—"

Andre said, "Girl, what are you smoking?" He laughed and slapped his knee. "Whatever it is, can I get some?"

"We know it's true," Jules said. "Come on, Bridget, we can wait for the others. Then publish our findings."

Bridget had suggested they use that as a threat, but only as a last resort. She gave him a shove and addressed Andre. "I'm so sorry about my associate's bad manners, sir. We don't want to impose or suggest any impropriety, but the evidence is quite clear. You took on the Southern Spike to—"

"You're a decent child," Telah said. "I know you wouldn't go public with anything just to spite us."

"Telah, honey," Andre said, reaching for her hand.

Telah pulled out of his reach. "They want the shield. Don't you?"

Bridget literally gasped. She hadn't expected anyone to be so forthright.

"It's okay," Telah went on. "They said someone would come, eventually. Didn't know whether we'd still be around or if our grandchildren'd be the ones to send 'em on their way."

"Telah." Andre took on a grave tone. Not quite a warning but urging caution.

"It don't matter. They know. They figured it out." She fixed Bridget with a serious glare. What had been a somewhat irreverent old lady before was now as firm and immovable as a sentry guarding a palace. "But you can't have it. We swore to protect it, and we will not reveal its whereabouts. I'll give you this warning, too. Even if you figure out where to look, it's well-protected. Oh, yes, you won't be leaving our property with nothing we don't give you."

Bridget crouched to Telah's eye level. "Ma'am, we really need to see—"

"You got a nice house, right?" The old lady's crows' feet crinkled deeper.

"It's... nice, yes."

"Your family is rich because of mine, child. Because of the sweat off my ancestors' backs. I'm old enough that my grandmother remembered her father working the fields under the whip, so please don't give me that hogwash about it being a long, long time ago."

Bridget lowered her gaze to the floor. Couldn't summon the words from the pit of her stomach.

"But don't think I hold that against you. We got plenty these days. We need money, we can get it. Thing is, what we promised to do, what Jacob Carr wrote into that dollar contract, it's more than a business deal. It's an oath."

Andre again pawed at his wife. "Telah, please, they—"

"Oh, who they gonna tell? Who'll believe them?" Telah leaned forward, her purple, flowery chair squeaking as the springs holding it in place stretched and contracted. She lifted Bridget's chin, so they were face-to-face. "What we agreed to, it's more important than wealth. More important than fancy houses and helicopters and jewels. We protect a heritage—our own, and those like us who've had it ripped away." She sat back, the springs protesting, and held her husband's hand. "We might not be warriors, but we know our job. And we do it well. If you have any respect for that whatsoever, please go. And do not tell anyone about this."

"There are others," Jules said. "People who won't ask nicely like we are."

"We can protect it," Bridget added. "Let us help. Because they *are* coming. These others."

Telah gave a sad shake of the head. "Then they will be disappointed too."

Silence descended, the two older people watching Bridget and Jules.

Bridget straightened tightly. "Ma'am, if we could—"

Telah turned her chair to face the blank TV. Andre did likewise, searching for the remote. The conversation, it seemed, was over.

"Come on." Jules touched Bridget's elbow. "We're done here."

As she accompanied him out, pausing only to put their shoes back on, Bridget asked herself why she was feeling like absolute dirt. The imposition she'd caused, the fact she'd been left to run around seeking facts hidden in the museum, or the crack about how she lived in luxury while the Willises resided here... or simply that Telah Willis had dismissed her as a nuisance, the way one might a cold-calling insurance salesman, rather than a seeker of knowledge.

Outside, she couldn't face Jules or Dan. It wasn't until they got to the car that she pinpointed why she'd experienced such a sensation of nausea, of guilt and shame.

She said, "You know we have to ignore what they told us."

"Can't just respect their wishes?" Jules asked.

"With those other people coming after it, after *us*, do you think they're going to ease off?"

"So, we're stealing it to protect it?" Dan said.

"First we find it," Jules said. "Then we figure out how to stop those other folks from getting it. If I'm stickin' around for this, that's the mission. That's the goal. No stealing, no donatin' it to the Pope. It belongs here. And it'll stay here. Clear?"

Bridget thought it'd be a tough sell to Toby, given all Alfonse had invested, but theft wasn't LORI's reason for existing. It was knowledge. Understanding.

Truth.

And the truth was, if someone really hid this shield on the Southern Spike of the Willises' land, it wasn't anyone else's to take. Bridget would make sure everyone understood that.

"Deal," she said.

CHAPTER THIRTEEN

SOUTHERN CALIFORNIA

Ah Dae-Sung allowed one of the American-Korean personnel to drive the RV that had been his home for the past two weeks, conversing with Pang Pyong-Ho in his mother tongue regarding the report their employer, Ryom Jung-Hwan—or rather *Executive Ryom*—demanded. Although the American and his co-pilot came recommended by people back in the Democratic People's Republic of Korea, Dae-Sung did not trust them. Especially now three of their colleagues had perished during the botched extraction.

While the surviving Americans made excuses for their failure, Pang Pyong-Ho had offered to resign and return home in disgrace. There, he and his family would undergo extensive debriefing before a qualified expert assessed his worthiness to the country and whether his dip in performance might affect his sons' potential in the military.

Dae-Sung had said no. He would not condemn his compatriot—a man who had become his friend—over a failure of intelligence. Not one report suggested the crusty English archaeologist would have firepower with him. Nor that the mongrel New Zealander was anything but a foreigner on a student visa.

Certainly, missing the New Zealander's true status could be laid at the door of the Americans. Vetting had been their job.

Their loyalty to Dae-Sung's people, Executive Ryom had assured him, was not in question, having delivered many favors over the past ten years. From information to assassination, they hated the United States, despite reveling in the money doled out in their direction in return for their services.

Information to assassination.

It sort of rhymed in English, but Dae-Sung had no time for frivolity. He cared only for the urgent business of protecting his country, under threat yet again from outside forces, as it had been since his birth.

"Are we secure?" he asked his second-in-command.

"Yes." Pyong-Ho set up the laptop, which mimicked an American brand, but the guts were pure Korean workmanship. "If they intercept our signal, it will look like we are pirating a movie from 1992 starring Clint Eastwood."

Dae-Sung smiled. The movie star was Pyong-Ho's one weakness for western culture. Cowboy movies were a banned luxury in Korea, but as men whom the authorities trusted to venture beyond the country in order to strengthen its borders, Dae-Sung and Pyong-Ho had permitted themselves that taboo. Dae-Sung was less enamored with the genre, and its leading man, but he tolerated it. And he was glad it made his friend happy for a couple of hours, especially in such dark times. In times when their very survival was in question.

The laptop screen remained blank while the speakers trilled, and then a box appeared in one corner showing Ah Dae-Sung's angular face.

When did he get so old?

Not old like an old man, but at fifty he was no longer *young*. He was only ten years Pyong-Ho's senior, but while he was fitter than most Americans half his age, that was damning with faint praise. After all, what Koreans weren't fitter than the average American? That wasn't his concern. Dae-Sung could see the lines creeping into the corners, the cheek bones that had once charmed many a lady now less prominent, while his eyes had sunk slightly.

Perhaps, should he find success here, he might permit himself to turn his attention to his own happiness. If he found a suitable woman, it wasn't too late to start a family, to bring life into the new world that awaited them, and finally relax and cease thinking about how to defend from the next assault on Korea's freedom.

The screen flickered and turned gray. "I'm here."

Executive Ryom's voice flowed thick and steady, as it always did. The man was both a genius and a true patriot, and his standing in both business and the Party was as high as anyone outside the military or the leaders' family DNA could ascend. His calm, measured tone projected assurance in himself, and hearing it imbibed that same confidence. But it also hid those times his anger boiled over, making it difficult to assess his mood.

"Executive Ryom, please forgive us," Dae-Sung commenced. "I should have monitored the Americans more closely. We had not expected such resistance from a college—"

"Do not make excuses." This was the same timbre he used to order coffee or close a business deal. Not robotic or absent emotion, just complete truth. "You are the only agents in the field, so I cannot replace you. As long as I can be sure you have learned from the experience."

"I will not fail again." Ah Dae-Sung bowed his head, unsure if the Executive could see him. He met the inbuilt webcam's unblinking eye. "Now we know who Tane Wiremu really is, we will not underestimate our quarry. You have my word."

"Update, then. What is your current status?"

Pang Pyong-Ho sat off-camera, his face as unemotional as the Executive's voice.

"We are still using the recreational vehicle," Dae-Sung said. "We altered the license plates as a precaution, but this is excellent camouflage."

It wasn't quite a laugh, but Executive Ryom's voice seemed to shave a sliver of humor into its tone. "Only in a country like America could a giant rolling house be considered 'camouflage.' What are your next steps?"

"We have determined the Englishman and his people have other associates working in a different state. Because of their presence here, we are convinced we are on the correct path, and will dedicate all resources to Alabama."

Alabama. Dae-Sung had played with the word several times,

tossing it around his mouth like a rubber ball. He and Pyong-Ho found it amusing, almost ticklish the way the English syllables seemed to bounce.

Al-a-bam-*ah*!

"There's only one site in Alabama on Professor Sally's computer," Dae-Sung said. "They must have intelligence we lack. As they did in Mexico."

No reply from the laptop, but an audible shifting of weight told Dae-Sung the Executive was considering his response. After uncountable numbers of conversations like this, he knew when to keep his mouth shut.

"This is sensible," came the answer at last. "Do you need more resources?"

"We will require transport from the same airfield in Nevada. We are on our way there now."

Dae-Sung glanced at the RV's cockpit. The driver held his eyes on the road but the man beside him, who had shown himself to be shaky and irritable, quick to anger and eager to use lethal force, kept glancing back.

Perhaps he spoke more of his genetic homeland's tongue than he'd let on.

Dae-Sung used a code instead. "We have two adequate men, but we would like additional hands, plus a bonus package."

Adequate men meant *liabilities*. *Additional hands* translated as *replacement personnel*. And *bonus package* was code for *disposal of bodies*.

"Are there additional obstacles?" Executive Ryom asked. "Police?"

Dae-Sung looked to Pyong-Ho who continued to monitor law enforcement transmissions. He shook his head.

"Negative," Dae-Sung said. "They are sweeping for what they call an 'active shooter' in the area. We left Mohammedan leaflets in the vicinity as planned, but they have not released details of who they are hunting yet."

"'Active shooter'," Executive Ryom repeated. "Americans and their phrases. No matter. I will arrange what you asked. But time is running out, Commander Ah. You must acquire either the woman and her research, or the item itself. Am I clear?"

Ah Dae-Sung braced against the shiver cascading down his back.

Despite the volume and manner of the Executive's voice remaining constant, he rarely used Dae-Sung's official title.

Commander Ah.

"We will track her via satellite," Dae-Sung said.

"And if you cannot take her without bloodshed, do not await orders from me. Move immediately to the next phase."

"Of course. If necessary, blood will be spilled. As much as it takes."

CHAPTER FOURTEEN

THE SOUTHERN SPIKE, ALABAMA

Having utilized another favor from the Carson household to borrow a flatbed truck and some essential equipment stashed on the rear, Jules, Bridget, and Dan rumbled up to the dirt track rendezvous and parked on the grassy lay-by somewhat later than Charlie and her group. Toby had flown them all in the previous night and opted for a hotel midway between the Alabama Freedom Museum and the airport, while Dan and Jules bedded down at Bridget's place. Better to remain separate in case the Koreans tracked one or the other.

Jules and Dan got the shiny side of that deal.

Excited at having houseguests, Bridget's mom, Audrey—as instrumental a part of the corporation as Roger—dismissed the small number of staff in order to cook up a feast herself, one comprising fried chicken, pulled pork, spicy vegetables, and various carbohydrates, followed by a ton of dessert. Bloated in the cooling evening, when offered alcohol, Dan and Bridget had opted for beer while Jules surprised them both by accepting a fine whisky—a single malt that Mr. Carson was delighted to share. "Don't get many opportunities to indulge with a fellow aficionado of the Scottish liquor. It's mostly bourbon around these parts, which is fulfilling on the right occasions..."

Jules had pretended not to be bored by the man's enthusiasm as he added the desirable amount of ice and found the drink smoother and more pleasing than the spirit back in New York. He was sensible enough to turn down a second, too, given the early start—and the day's heat.

Seemingly unaffected by either the rising temperature or the dawn alarm call, Charlie manned a portable workstation alongside Harpal out the back of a hired 4x4 while Toby and a gray-haired woman dressed like someone cosplaying a Victorian archaeologist shielded their eyes from the rising sun as they looked over acres of fields. Once Dan parked and the trio disembarked, Toby strode over to the truck, shadowed by the woman.

Bridget called, "Hey, Harps, how's your arm?"

Harpal rotated his shoulder. "Good to see you, Bridge. It's stiff, but Charlie's patched it tight. Full movement. She makes a cracking nurse."

"It was a scratch," Charlie said. "I've dealt with worse injuries when Alexander fell off his first bike."

A door opened at the front of the 4x4 and a figure as tall as Dan stepped out—bigger than Dan too, although a lot of his bulk appeared natural rather than ripped via a gym.

"Well, well!" the woman exclaimed. "Two more strapping men to help find our prize."

"Let me introduce you," Toby said with the enthusiasm of a drunk uncle at a wedding, hoping to pair Jules off with his single daughter. "This is—"

"Tane Wiremu," Jules said, pointing lazily at the Maori in his short-sleeved top and linen shirt that half-covered the gun in his shoulder holster. "And Professor Sally Garcia. I ain't deaf and I can read the updates Phil sends through."

"Right, right." Toby faked amusement at Jules's intentional rudeness. "Everyone, this is Jules, he's our... expert in..." He was lost for a label to pin on Jules.

"I'm the one who works stuff out and memorizes whatever's needed. Oh yeah, and my magic DNA can make rocks sparkle and activate magnetic orbs."

Tane either already knew all about Jules or he took it as sarcasm. Jules assumed the latter but wouldn't write off the former. The man surveyed the landscape with concentration, as someone who knew what he was looking for, not simply for something to do. "And not a bad thief, by all accounts."

"But that ain't why I'm here."

"No? Because from what we've talked about since flying in, we don't have permission to step over that boundary."

"Sure." Jules brushed past the security agent, preferring Dan and Bridget performed the time-wasting but necessary *getting to know you* nonsense, and watched Charlie work instead.

"You got a drone up there?" Jules asked.

"Correct." Charlie was working the controls using haptic gloves, the image on the screen split between real-time imaging rolling beneath the camera and a globular overlay lit up in greens, reds, and blues.

"Before I left, you customized that from some games console." Jules watched as she guided the camera with movements akin to playing piano in midair. "It works now?"

Charlie concentrated on the task, unable to draw away from the computer screen. "Games console uses gestures rather than a hand-held controller. I haven't got that far yet, but yes. It's better than our old joystick model. And I minimized the puck, too."

The puck was the radar-like node that emitted a signal, penetrated the earth below, and read the data as it bounced back, transforming into images on her bespoke computer. It was similar to the Li-Dar tech used in aerial archaeology which had led institutions around the world to discover the walls of Biblical cities buried under centuries of sand, massive constructions eaten and supplanted by jungles, and pre-historic burial sites beneath fields where no one would have thought to dig. Charlie, though, aimed for smaller variations, and had redesigned them for lightweight drones—something that helped bypass troublesome questions in airspace laws, and matched LORI's current budget.

Jules sensed the others nearby.

All but Dan and Tane crowded behind, the two tactical guys now sentries should anyone approach, which seemed unlikely since the view swept around almost uninterrupted for dozens of miles.

"Hey," Jules said. "How's it going?"

Toby attempted to draw a smile his way, still eager to please, eager to keep Jules on side. "Charlie found a wrinkle she needs to concentrate on. It might lead to something not on any official survey."

"Yes, yes, it's wonderful news," Garcia said.

Jules watched the pictures on the screen. Charlie squinted as she pulled the drone into a slow descent, zooming in on a particular point.

Harpal sidestepped for a better view. "What's the betting it isn't another pyramid disguised as a hill?"

"A what?" Garcia said. "Are you mad, young man?"

"Let's hope this one don't collapse on us." Jules couldn't stop his mouth pulling into a smile. "Gets kinda old kinda fast."

Garcia switched her gaze to Toby. "Are they making fun of me? Because I really don't appreciate the past twenty-four hours. Guns. Stuffed in the trunk of a car. Dragged across the country. Barely five hours sleep. The university was terribly worried about me, and they don't even know where I am. And here you are making jokes about pyramids in America."

Jules sniffed and checked on the imagery. "Ain't a joke."

"Won't be a pyramid," Charlie said. "Or an ancient temple in disguise." Through her jibe, Charlie's attention remained locked on her work, hands forming claws frozen in midair, her thumbs twitching to adjust the angle. "Seriously, though, the earth is too dense. Too rocky. If it's a small chamber quarried out, I'd say they sealed it up. If it was ever there."

"Nothing?" Toby said.

"Something. But might be nothing. Okay, battery's low, I'm bringing it home." Charlie performed some high-tech tai-chi, and the camera banked away from its target.

"So, it *might* be there?" Harpal asked.

Charlie blew out her cheeks. "Could be a cave formation. But it matches what Sally said to look for."

Jules glanced at Harpal, who had often come across as the most sensible of this bunch.

In this case, Harpal gave an exasperated shrug and nodded toward Toby. "He says the prof knows her stuff. And it's all in her head, not on something Charlie can access."

"Access," Professor Garcia scoffed. "You mean *steal.* Spy on. Invade my privacy. No. You can't steal it using the cloud or internet tricks."

"Right," Jules said. "You're kooky. I get it. Wanna tell us what this shield is, then? Why some hostile country's interested in it?"

Garcia tramped a half circle back to where she was standing when Jules arrived. "Who truly knows? The tribes who remained in this part of Alabama lived alongside the landowners for decades. Even during the civil war, both sides avoided it. Before then it was a vital stop-off point on the railroad getting escaped slaves to the north."

Bridget stepped forward, having been uncharacteristically quiet. "You think they were stationed here while Jacob Carr smuggled supplies and food?"

The professor snagged on something in the sky, the drone most likely, and tracked its progress. "I was mapping other routes when I learned about the railroad and Jacob Carr."

"Other routes?" Toby said, perking up as he did whenever additional information came about. "Like what?"

"Like..." Sally Garcia faced them and wiped her brow, leaning against the fence delineating the Willises' boundary. She sounded weary, as if an interrogation had broken her resistance. "Like, there are tribes of people who we deny existed."

Tane Wiremu apparently possessed the hearing of a bat, wandering closer to listen in. Dan kept his distance.

Garcia said, "Pretty much every single culture in existence talks about giants."

"Are we back onto the notion of literal giants?" Bridget asked.

"Always literal." The professor's face flashed with the sort of enthusiasm Jules was used to from Toby and Bridget. "Otherwise, where's the fun?"

Jules groaned internally. Not out loud. He'd learned that set folk on the defensive, especially in this world, where exacting science was performed in reverse—state a theory and challenge people to prove it *wasn't* true instead of offering evidence that it *was*. Still, he'd also come to understand there was sometimes a kernel of truth wrapped deep in the shell of a myth.

"From Native Americans to the indigenous people of New

Zealand," Garcia went on. "Europeans have their own legends, too, not to mention Africans, the Middle East. Giants. Colossus. Kings of men."

"I haven't heard 'kings of men' before," Harpal said. "Is that new?"

"Old. Probably older than David and Goliath. Oh! Goliath. That's another noun used frequently today."

"My grandparents told me stories about them," Tane said. "I always like Kiharoa."

Garcia nodded along. "Of the Ngati-Raukawa and Ngati-Whakatere tribes in the Tokanui Pa region."

Tane closed his mouth and arched an eyebrow. Dipped his chin to tell Garcia to carry on.

"As for mainland USA, the Apache had Big Owl Man, the Ice Giants came from the Algonquian, and in this region the Cherokee passed down stories of Stoneclad."

"Stoneclad," Charlie said. "Sounds like the ground all around here."

Garcia again watched the drone coming in, the hum becoming a buzz as the six-foot-wing-spanned device swooped in on the makeshift runway that made up the dirt road. Jules was surprised; he'd been expecting a quadcopter, as LORI normally used. This looked more expensive, although still below military grade. Charlie began unhooking herself from the haptic gloves.

Garcia said, "Versions of the Stoneclad folklore vary. Some say it's one creature. Others that it's an entire race. In others still, Stoneclad is the size of a man but can turn himself into an invulnerable... super-hero, I guess. Or demon if that's your thing. But the ones I've found that gel best with the notions you've given me—of this band of warriors guarding the downtrodden—Stoneclad becomes a giant humanoid with rocklike plates of armor that fend off fire and ice and weapons of all kinds. He could be defeated only through sapping his magical powers, destroying his symbols, or... and you'll like this... exposing him to a menstruating woman."

Toby, Harpal, and Tane looked aghast, while Jules predicted a quip from Bridget or Charlie. As it happened, Charlie spoke first.

"Okay, sounds like a good time to compare wild and crazy theories. Before the men lock us womenfolk in a shed for a few days."

Jules caught Garcia's grin and that Bridget was about to speak, but he referred to Charlie's screen. "The darker greens?"

"Irregular. Fairly deep. But there are these stringy bits too." She used the mouse as a pointer on the screen, Sally Garcia at the head of the group observing. "I think they're tunnels. Manmade or formed through water run-off, I can't say from this."

"Sounds about right." Professor Garcia made an earnest face, taking in everyone who was paying attention. "The races we're talking about were nature's children. They would know how to use the caves and natural contours. If they are one and the same as your Guardians, they'd need to be close to supply routes. It makes sense that this would be the staging post."

"It's two kilometers in that direction." Charlie chopped her hand through the air. "Give or take."

Sally straightened and faced Toby. "While you work out the specifics, I have to call the university and update them on my safety. May I?"

Toby thought about it and nodded. Harpal gave her a blocky phone—an encrypted satellite device. While Garcia returned to the 4x4 for privacy, Toby called Dan over to consult.

"She never answered the question," Jules pointed out. "What *is* this shield?"

Dan grunted. "I'm more interested in why a hostile nation wants it. Sounds like they know more than us. I'm guessing it isn't entirely a defensive thing."

Jules, again, needed no reminding of the report he'd read, how Ah Dae-Sung was a dedicated veteran, privately employed by a state-approved computing firm which both British and New Zealand intelligence suspected of being a front for various espionage projects. "I want to know how we handle the artifact. That's if it turns out to be literal and not some symbolic myth that got mangled over the years."

"We secure it," Toby said. "We ensure it is safe from other parties and reveal to the owners that we have it."

"And we'll be givin' it back?"

"Of course. Once we understand what it is."

Bridget must have picked up on Jules's discomfort. "We're here for a reason. The truth. That's all. And we could've walked away before Toby and Charlie and Harpal got attacked. But we're on their radar now. They know about the shield, and if they tracked Sally and the others, they probably know about you and Dan coming here."

Jules met their eyes one by one. Toby wanted more.

"What is it?" Jules asked.

"I'll authenticate it," Toby said. "At the bare minimum. I can't let Alfonse down again. I need to verify its existence, its provenance, and document it. Give me that, at least."

Jules replayed the previous day's interaction with Andre and Telah Willis, how the elderly couple espoused such determination to carry out their duty. It mixed badly with LORI's current position. About to prove to them their mission, noble as it was, could be doomed by the right—or wrong—people learning it existed.

"We drew these guys in," Dan said. "We have to be the ones to end it. If giving Alfonse what he wants helps keep it out of the bad guys' hands, isn't that worth it?"

Jules had already reached the same conclusion. But there was one more factor Jules could not account for. "Tane Wiremu. Where do you come in? Why're you even here? Ain't to keep things a secret, that's for sure."

"They were willing to kill to get hold of the prof," Tane said. "I'm not. I hoped she'd give us what she knew in exchange for protection. Because we'll look after the secret better than the Americans would. And we can't let Ah Dae-Sung or his people have it either."

"You screw us," Jules said. "I'll come find it. I'll take it back and make you pay. I'm good at that kinda thing."

Tane didn't quite smirk but wasn't far from it. "Okay, deal. But I thought you were a cop."

"I am. And just because I'm outta my jurisdiction, don't think I won't bust your ass if you don't keep your word. I bet it don't say NZSIS officer on your student visa, meaning you're here illegally." Jules indicated the British contingent too. "So are you folks if you're able to travel freely after that shooting yesterday. That makes you mine."

"Understood," Toby said. "You have my word."

Sally Garcia closed the door and trotted toward them, carrying a motorcycle helmet, and cleaning her glasses. "Okay, everyone, good news. They've given the students and faculty a few days off to recover from the traumatic events." She put her glasses on, followed by the helmet. "Okay, I'm ready. Who am I riding with?"

Jules hurtled over the fields on one of the ATVs that Bridget's parents arranged—those "unlimited resources" she'd negotiated—following the directions from Charlie's drone mapping. Their target was a gentle rise in the topography, barely worthy of the word *hill*, hoping to locate one tentacle the ground-penetrating radar had detected.

They'd doubled up on the vehicles, Jules riding with Bridget behind, Charlie piloting Toby's transport, and Tane leading Sally Garcia. That had left Dan and Harpal to argue over who got to be the alpha up front and who "spooned." Charlie had been the one to crack their heads together, saying Dan should ride out and Harpal could lead them back. Neither seemed pleased with the outcome, but at such a childish stalemate there wasn't much choice.

It took less than five minutes to start ascending and then another five to circle around to the first potential entry point, where they stopped for water and to assess whether it was a viable spot. The ground was predominantly scrubland, dry grass with cracked dirt serving as its bed. It was rocky, inhospitable, nothing of note would grow here. Even the trees were mostly gnarled and old. It was definitely not land that human hands had tended.

They stopped at the point Charlie directed, but what they had expected to be a small cave entrance was little more than a sewer hole-sized depression between stony plateaus. Then when Harpal and Dan probed closer, hoping for a weak spot, they retreated with the speed of someone fleeing an avalanche.

"Rattlesnake nest," Dan reported as they slowed. "Diamondbacks."

Harpal was breathing heavily, likely from the adrenaline more than the dash away from danger. "It was just there, shaking its tail."

"More than one nest." Dan ran his hand over his close-cropped hair. "Pretty hairy, if you ask me."

"Bit of a coincidence, don't you think?" Toby said. "The entrance to a supposed cave? Somewhere a pair of Guardians have sworn to protect? But without high-tech resources?"

"Oh, my, you might be right." Sally Garcia opened her arms towards the danger zone. "Rattlesnakes are not native to this part of Alabama."

"How do you know about rattlesnakes?" Tane asked.

"I'm very careful about where I put my feet. After being bitten for the third time, I thought maybe I should bone up on the local wildlife wherever I head out on my explorations. It'd save a fortune in antivenin, at the very least. The only way you would get *that* species out here would be to introduce it and feed it for a while, then let it colonize."

Like Garcia, Jules had never liked the idea of heading into the wild unprepared, so he'd made a point of reading all he could get his hands on about snakes, spiders, scorpions, and other venomous creatures. Since he was virtually incapable of forgetting anything, he concurred.

"The prof ain't wrong," he said. "And if those *are* tunnels up there, you can bet there'll be more wildlife to play with."

"We can expect all the entrances to have a similar welcome," Toby said.

"Not necessarily." Charlie swung her legs over the ATV and slipped the laptop out of a saddlebag. She opened it and the screen lit up, a magnification of the faint rise they were on. "Several of those fractures branching out like tunnels don't make it to the surface. Rather than waste time wrangling the snakes, we should try blasting a new door."

Jules didn't need to look. He remembered many of the vein-like cracks stopped short of the membrane of dried earth.

Tane said, "Won't explosions alert people?"

"We're at least ten klicks away from that museum," Dan answered.

"Sound travels," Bridget corrected him. "I've heard blasting going on from over ten miles away before. Open land. They'll hear."

"Then we'd better move quickly." Toby saddled himself up on the ATV again, leaving room for Charlie. "This is the closest we've been."

Harpal said, "I thought we wanted to get it out covertly."

"We just need to prove it exists," Jules replied. "When the genie's outta the bottle, we politely explain why it needs to be secured someplace else."

Toby looked dejected at this, then perked right up. "Right. The point remains. Time is wasting."

They gave the rattlesnake nest a wide berth, coming back in at an angle towards the eastern side of the rough rise in the land, which was steeper down the far side than the original approach suggested, before parking up and giving the area a thorough sweep for anything that might slither or sting.

Charlie pinpointed the location to within a few feet and called over to Dan, "You're up."

Dan hustled over with his pack and removed several chunks of packing foam, each one swaddling a brick of plastic explosive. He did not source this through the Carsons, for obvious reasons, but through his own black-market contacts. Jules didn't ask how it arrived in the locker at the bus station where they stopped on the way, and he doubted Dan would have told him, anyway.

Harpal offered to help, but Dan said no, instead waiting for Charlie to double-check the coordinates.

Jules loitered nearby in case Dan needed a hand, since setting explosives was labor intensive and required meticulous attention to detail. It left Sally Garcia, Bridget, and Toby to hypothesize about further security measures, and for Tane to scan the horizon using binoculars. Jules considered approaching Tane and making nice, but he didn't expect the New Zealander to remain long enough for any friendship to be worth either of their time.

The target for Dan's explosives was a grass-free section of hard-packed mud, only a couple of surface pebbles on top. He used a small pick to break the surface, then caught Jules's eye and tossed him a folding spade. Jules said nothing and went to work, digging out three feet of earth. Soft earth. Softer than the surrounding strata.

"That's enough, I think," Dan said.

He sliced off six inches of plastic, inserted a detonator, and retreated a suitable distance. He then returned and packed the earth around the half-brick and advised everyone to get as far back as the ATVs, best if they ducked down behind them. They all obeyed.

Dan joined them with the detonator switch. "Fingers in the ears, people."

Again, they did as they were told. Dan dispensed with the usual countdown and hit the button.

The eruption tore through the sky, sending a plume of dirt upward at least twenty feet, which descended in a pebble-rich cloud and expanded over the bikes. Everyone stood, ears ringing, coated in a fine film of dust.

Harpal was the first to advance. "Next time, we check the wind direction."

There was a time when Jules would have pointed out that he'd assessed the wind direction and would have said something if they were lying in the fallout zone. That the explosion sent the dirt towards them, and without much wind to speak of, it suggested there had been a change in the structure where they'd set the explosives, meaning the energy expanded outwards equally in all directions. When it slammed against an immovable object like bedrock, it reversed direction and added power to the upward drive.

Either that, or Dan used too much plastic.

They all dusted themselves off and followed Harpal to examine the results. Although still swirling with debris, it was clear there was more than rocks under the original hardscrabble layer.

Dan said, "They'll be out to investigate soon. Best we have something to show for it when they arrive."

"And if it's the cops who arrive?" Jules said.

"Then we're trespassing, and we'll leave." Professor Garcia counted off four fingers. "Trust me, I've been moved on plenty. No one wants to waste time on that kind of piddling paperwork."

"And my parents can spring for a decent lawyer," Bridget added then looked embarrassed as if she'd been bragging to the underprivileged.

Jules set about checking the hole. "Let's just get on with it."

The breach was wide enough to accommodate Jules, Dan, and Harpal all at once, with room to spare for Bridget if she wanted to squish up. Not necessary, of course, as they'd go single file. The particulate debris swirled and danced, obscuring more than four or five feet down, but a breeze funneling from below revealed they had broken through to somewhere hollow. Hollow, and deep.

Aided by Harpal, Bridget, and Dan, Jules hammered spikes into the ground and used them as a fulcrum to wrap around one of those old tree trunks, diverted at angles to avoid tangling with each other. As they slipped into harnesses, Tane remained at his post, ever watchful.

"Okay," Charlie said after testing the comms. She handed Dan and Harpal the spare earbuds and kept one for herself. "Action dudes go first and check we're in business. Then the brains can follow."

"Which group am I in?" Jules asked. "Since I'm pretty much top of my class in both departments."

"You keep Dan and Harpal company. Make sure they don't screw up through bickering."

Harpal was already testing his line. "I know that should offend me, but it's fair."

"Harsh," Dan said. "But fair."

With the lineup agreed, and the order sorted out, Jules, Dan, and Harpal equipped themselves with cramps, carabiners, head torches, gloves, and helmets. Charlie handed Jules the comms nodes that would allow them to remain in contact. They then made final checks before Jules donned a breathing mask like those used on a building site and crabbed backwards into the opening to descend first.

For the initial four feet, he was blind, glad of the filtered mask as the dust wafted and danced all around, making him blink the itch from his eyeballs. Six feet down, he set the first comms node here, ensuring a clear signal with the surface. The deeper he went, the clearer the air became, but also the darker it got.

After another ten feet, it would have been pitch-black if not for the flashlight. From what Jules could make out, the tunnel was more a fissure than a planned borehole. It looked natural to him, although it could have been hacked out using rudimentary tools over several decades. The intervening couple of centuries could have hidden the fingerprints of artificial construction. Lower, the passage narrowed so much, Jules had to turn sideways to squeeze through. The obstruction bent only inches, but it was enough.

On the other side, Jules examined what had delayed him and

shone his lamp up at Dan's incoming body. "Hey, big guy, you got a big knife or something?"

"Machete and a K-bar," he answered. "Why?"

"Tree root. You're gonna have to hack through."

"Okay, wait up."

"Nah, I'll set up down below. Careful of the node."

He inserted another of Charlie's comms relays and went on, ignoring Dan. He didn't work for LORI and didn't take orders. Besides, time was of the essence, so waiting for Dan to move the root was out of the question.

After a further ten feet, he touched floor.

Only, it wasn't the end of the shaft, but a sudden change in the angle of approach. Jules let the rope's slack out and tossed it around to let it drop farther. It was no good. It coiled around near his feet.

"Hey," Jules called back up the shaft as he fitted another comms node. "It evens out here. Gotta walk." He dropped a couple of glow sticks but didn't wait for an answer.

The tunnel was still steep, but he negotiated it simply. While he had let his free running and gymnastic practice lapse since settling down into a regular-person life, the muscle memory of balance and the reaching out with his senses, feeling his way, swept back to him. Like his ability to retain any and all academic learning, once he'd mastered a physical skill, it was only ever dulled, never extinguished.

The light strapped to his head showed the walls smoothing out, growing more regular. Like a mine shaft.

We're onto something. Might be a shield, might be digging out ore. Could be the foundations of a building they never built.

He drove onward. Blood flowed faster through his veins, thumping in his chest and his head, and he found himself speeding up. He could control this, if he chose, but he chose not. He was the first human being to walk this path in centuries. And if Toby or the kook were even half-right, there was something to discover. Something denied by the landowners. Something a foreign power believed could benefit them...

The tunnel ended. A vast openness engulfed him. Even though he couldn't see much farther than the flashlight beam, it was obviously a cavern, spanning several hundred feet if not more.

Jules emitted a hoot which echoed back at him.

"Ha!"

He pulled off his pack and took out one of Charlie's dwarf arc lights. She had allocated them one each, partly because of the bulk and partly in case one person fell and damaged them all.

As he extended the legs and found a suitable spot to wedge it, Jules again couldn't fail to be impressed with Charlie's aptitude for improving on existing technology. She'd make a fortune if she entered a more commercial field. But from what Jules could gather without indulging in quid pro quo heart-to-hearts, she lived with a healthy family of three children and earned enough to maintain a nice house in Greenwich and keep her wheelchair-bound husband mobile and pretty much independent. It was only the lure of what they were searching for today that clenched around her and dragged her on these jaunts.

With the scrabbling footfalls getting closer, Dan and Harpal having surmounted the offending tree root, Jules braced himself. He cracked on the arc light and took in the sight.

From dusting off a two-inch piece of porcelain buried for a thousand years in a desert, to breaking through ancient doors powered by his mother's DNA-activated bangle and confronting a millennia-old acropolis the size of a city, those represented the two extremes of Jules's treasure-hunting-come-archaeology life to date. Not forgetting perpetual motion orbs, volcanic networks linked around the world, or the discovery of ancient humans who pre-dated Australopithecus. But not every revelation in archaeology needed to be extreme to be spectacular.

What Jules now gazed upon in the glow of a single arc light made him question why he could have thought a "normal" life was right for him.

CHAPTER FIFTEEN

Toby Smith had long resigned himself to the fact his finest physical days were behind him. All he could do was present himself with dignity and purpose and emphasize his assets. He'd always brought value to the institute he founded after learning several of the most long-held beliefs about ancient man were misunderstood at best, intentionally withheld at worst.

But key to this was dignity.

He loved this work, although he loved *having finished* this work more than the act of detecting such discoveries, precisely because of the position in which he now found himself: dangling from a rope twenty-some feet below the woman who co-founded LORI as she offered gentle encouragement regarding the application of the descender.

It was all well and good knowing how to do something, but lack of practice rendered Toby into a gibbering infant. He could scuba dive and abseil, but the technique of squeezing that stiff piece of metal in the pulley system, the ropes under his bum shooting by as he dropped in increments, took several minutes to grasp once more.

Below, Sally Garcia descended with an aptitude he envied, while above, Bridget only made a couple of disparaging grunts of impatience before her manners kicked in.

"Easy," Charlie said again. "Use your feet too."

"Yes, thank you." Toby had been half-walking, half-falling with each depression of the release lever, and now regretted accepting the remaining ear-bud unit.

But after Dan exclaimed that everyone had to get down there right that minute and see what they'd found, Toby got swept up in Bridget's whirlwind of forward motion. She'd been the one to push them, fumbling the grips and pulleys in her haste. That was the main reason Charlie insisted she go down last; the girl needed to calm herself lest she make a mistake.

By the time Toby touched down on the angled shaft, Sally was already gone. He disentangled himself and unclipped the carabiner but kept the leg harness on. He didn't relish the climb out, but Charlie would set up a pulley system so it wouldn't be like urchins climbing out of a chimney.

He picked his way through the steep tunnel, holding the rope between his hands as he went. He just hoped what they found was neither physically huge nor symbolic. He'd considered the possibility it was an affectation, a monument to the Guardians or a sigil, something to carry before them like a Roman aquila. If they'd been in the thrall of larger-than-average humans, or pushed the notion that giants of folklore marched beside them in spirit, their prize might still turn out to be too big to extract the way they came in.

It was a significant downside to this type of fringe science.

"Oh, my golly gosh!" Sally exclaimed up ahead.

Toby sped up, his legs feeling like a windup toy let loose. This was the culmination of months of work, of three failed expeditions, and the most important find he could remember. Even more so than those history redefining moments he'd experienced with this team, or even the world-threatening use of ancient machines, this would decide the future of the Lost Origins Recovery Institute. Toby needed to satisfy Alfonse that his investment bore fruit, or it would be the last such funding he extended them.

He reached the end of the tunnel.

Bridget hadn't been this jazzed in years. Yes, she got most of her thrills through the deciphering of language, of codes and maps. The action dudes explored the physical, she analyzed what they brought her, and sent them on their way. Yet, there was nothing quite like being there. Getting her hands and feet and face filthy as she trod the path others had walked.

She could *feel* the history.

As her feet touched solid ground and she progressed a couple of car lengths behind Toby and his unsteady flashlight, the walls vibrated. They all but spoke to her.

Perhaps it was through being cooped up so long, trying to learn economics at a higher level than she was ready for, or cared for, that resulted in her heightened senses. Sat in a classroom, a dorm room, or a lecture theater, listening to someone drone on about the nebulous ways countries attempted to drive their GDP and how much of it was guesswork based on historical analysis of markets...

Not real history, she'd once opined after a few too many beers.

Her fellow students, either the offspring of some financial master of the universe, like her, or an aspiring financial master of the universe desperate for daddy's approval, looked at her like she was a moron. Her alternative notions—based on genuine history, on real civilizations that had thrived and bloomed for centuries longer than the United States or the British Empire had existed—found her labeled a socialist or a communist, sometimes interchangeably. That no one could make up their mind about what her ideas made her, she despaired at their stupidity and ceased trying to explain that she was neither of those things. And nor were the economic models of various stages of the Roman Empire (they had several over the centuries), nor Alexander the Great, nor Cleopatra's Egypt. They were just different from the systems used broadly across the West today. But, in the pocket universe of ivy-league schools, it seemed anything other than strict adherence to free market capitalism, and the notion it was individual mistakes that led to boom-and-bust cycles, got a person labeled as an *other*.

Socialist.

Communist.

And even explaining the true meaning of those words fell on deaf ears.

Not modern capitalism = socialist. Or communist. Or something bad. Because, like, who cares?

Yet, since Bridget was only ever interested in facts and evidence, she refused to back down. And that made her life miserable, despite acing her classes.

Her begging to quit had made Dad angry, but Mom had been insightful enough to see the truth. Their daughter was being destroyed by the culture at the college, by attitudes encouraged by the institution's curriculum. Dad, in the end, agreed to give her time. Bridget would find her way, eventually.

"Oh, my golly gosh!" came Sally's delighted cry, barreling up the passage.

As Toby's light bobbed and pulled ahead, Bridget adopted the same pace. Her momentum made her steadier, her feet finding the fastest path. Within seconds, she'd caught up to Toby, but neither slowed. Toby actually sped up, the bright portal ahead glowing brighter, the three dwarf arc lights illuminating what lay beyond as if the sun had descended below ground.

"It's incredible, come on!" the professor shouted.

The glare from the arc lights filled Bridget's vision. She blinked spots away as she stepped out into what appeared to be a cave. Stalactites hung from a roof maybe fifteen feet over her head, a virtual dome of rock and seeping mosslike vegetation. The ground was strewn with rocks, the far wall about an average swimming pool length away, and the action dudes were exploring what Bridget could only think of as—

"It's a graveyard." Professor Garcia could hardly breathe, her panting like a marathon runner being interviewed after breaking the finishing line tape, overawed to have won. "It's everything I need to justify my work. Every asshole who ever made fun of me online or to my face or in peer review..." She faced Bridget with her expression as bright as the arc lights. "They can suck it!"

Toby was equally stunned, and she'd never seen Jules flowing from one feature to another so swiftly. He even seemed to be smiling. Dan and Harpal, too, raced from one find to the next.

Bridget had to see more.

She followed the faint slope of the floor up to her left, checking the first plinth—what looked like a rectangular stone box the size of a socialite family's dining table. Upon this, the sculpture of a giant human skeleton was carved into the surface, a 3D bas-relief that would have been nine or ten feet stood upright.

"The detail is extraordinary," Bridget said.

Garcia swung one leg up, pushed with her hands and one knee, and climbed onto it. She braced on the flat surface and her palms hovered over the statue in repose.

"Here," Toby called.

Bridget switched attention to him. He'd located an alcove in the wall, a horizontal cut-away where another carved skeleton lay. This one was smaller than the figure Garcia was fussing over, but a good eight feet long, armed with a real sword and a dull, metal shield.

Toby, with gloved hands, probed the shield, then came away with a shake of the head.

"Who carved these?" Bridget mused.

"They weren't carved." Garcia brushed the statue's femur with her fingertips, the leg bone three times thicker as well as longer than an equivalent human. "They're fossilized."

Bridget squinted closer. "That's not how fossilization works. You need to die in mud, then as the flesh and bones rot, minerals seep in to replace the gap where the bones were. That's why it's so hard to find them—"

"I know how fossilization works, young lady," Garcia said. "But I also know the difference between a carving and a bone."

Bridget examined the join between the arm and the surface on which it lay.

Jules said, "She's right." He'd come up beside Bridget without her noticing. "It's like someone pulled the fossils outta the ground along with a chunk of the rock they were fused into. These days, we can separate dinosaur bones from the surroundin' hard stuff, but I bet back then they couldn't."

"So they hauled it out complete," Toby picked up from him, lost in wonder. "They sculpted the base into a grave plate of sorts."

Sally Garcia scrambled about, wide-eyed, and jittery. "Yes, yes. That's what this is!" She mounted the giant skeleton as if she planned to ride it out of there and leaned over so she drew face-to-face with it. The skull was at least twice the size of hers, maybe more. "Hello, my friend. I've been looking for you for a long time."

"Doesn't make it actual giants," Bridget said. "Like, the legends or anything like that. The bones could be animals, then a malformed skull fell or placed alongside." She hated to be the only one showing an iota of scientific analysis, but having been out of the game so long, she was determined to cling to every rung of this ladder. She couldn't simply accept the fantastical without firm proof. "These could just be mutated humans, too. Jules... you're the logical one. Can you please apply your brain to what we're seeing?"

"This way." Jules took Bridget by the shoulder, his arm around her, guiding her on past a similar box to the one Garcia was examining in minute detail. He smiled all the way, urging her toward a pool of water in the middle of the cavern. "Here."

In the water lay a glimmering plate in bronze or gold with red trim. A straight top, curved only slightly, pulling down like it was about to form a rectangle, then shaved to a point. She could make out grooves, possibly slashes, or maybe they were ornamental, or some form of writing on the surface, but under twenty inches of water, she couldn't tell. She estimated it to be as long as she was tall.

"It's..." Bridget couldn't get her breath.

"The shield," Toby finished for her. He was braced on the opposite side, his skin reflecting the pool and the shining yellow light. "Good grief, we've actually found it!"

Nervous laughter rippled among them.

Harpal nodded, a finger to one ear. "Yes, Charlie, it's here. Just need to get it out. Our access tunnel is too small."

"There are more tunnels," Jules said, pointing one direction, then another, then a third. Two of the dark passageways appeared large enough for the shield. "Guessin' they sealed 'em up some time ago. We gotta figure out which way, then blow the—"

"Guys?" Dan said, an urgent inflection catching everyone's attention. He stood over a semi-circular rim of stones set off in one corner, the highest point in what Bridget had started to think of as a tomb. "These aren't fossils."

"Nor are these." Toby referred to the bones of people set into the wall in graves cut away like bunk beds. "They're more... mummified. More recently than our friends on that side."

"These aren't mummies," Dan said. "Take a look."

Jules bounded up there first, Bridget right behind, then Harpal came up to the scene. Toby and Sally remained where they were, listening in.

Dan had indeed found skeletal remains, but these looked far less ancient. Rotted rather than fossilized or even mummified. Clothing still stuck to them. Some still had hair. Bridget couldn't count how many, but it was at least five.

"How long have they been here?" she asked.

"Hard to tell." Dan crouched by the nearest one, its head pointed toward him. "Conditions down here, could be ten years, could be a hundred."

Jules poked the skull with his toe. "Wasn't natural causes, either."

It fell aside, revealing a jagged gap in the front.

"That's a bullet hole," Harpal said. Presumably bringing Charlie in on the conversation, he added, "No, they're old. But not old-old, if you get what I mean."

By now, Toby and Professor Garcia had joined them.

Garcia said, "I wonder what they did to deserve that."

"Same as you." The new voice came from behind, a deep baritone spoken with purpose. "Grave robbers."

They all rotated slowly, following Dan and Jules's lead with their hands to the sides. Bridget already knew who it was, the voice distinctive in both tone and timbre.

"Darkeen..."

"Hello, Bridget." Darkeen Willis aimed a submachine gun, stock to his shoulder, a suppressor on the barrel. The two others with him, both men about the same age whom Bridget did not recognize, wielded identical weapons—one man black, the other appeared to be Hispanic or Native-American. "My nana said to trust you'd do the right thing. I'm glad I didn't listen to her."

"Just wait a second," Bridget said.

Jules showed his hands were still empty and took a half-step forward. "Yeah, this is bigger than you realize. Let us explain."

"Actually, it's bigger than *you* realize." Darkeen took his own half-step toward Jules, firming up the gun to halt any progress. "Now, all of you, on your knees. I won't ask again."

CHAPTER SIXTEEN

Jules assessed all three armed men in farmhand-style working attire as well-trained, organized, and deadly serious about their task. Only Darkeen spoke, the other two flanking him awaiting orders as they covered their targets who had conveniently grouped together.

"Ah, I got it," Jules said. "You were already here. Waitin' for the best time to show yourselves. We're bunched up here, so this is it."

One side of Darkeen's mouth turned up. "Smart kid. Be smarter."

All but Jules were on their knees, hands on their heads.

Jules joined them. "I'm a cop. New York, but still a cop. I go missing, they'll find you. Plus, we got other people who know where we are."

"You mean Tane Wiremu and Charlie Locke up top?" Darkeen said. "Phillip Locke in London? Yeah, we know about them, thanks. Charlie and Tane got crosshairs on 'em right now. Y'all have had since you showed up by our field. We were curious to see how far you'd take it. Guess we know now. You're thieves. And we'll be treating you accordingly."

"He's a cop?" the Native-American gunman said, concentration never wavering.

"Cops don't get to break-and-enter sacred tombs just because they carry a badge." Like his companion, Darkeen remained focused. "I'm gonna zip-tie you now. Then you'll be blindfolded and taken out, where we'll bring in the cops." A deviation to Jules. "You can sort this out with your brothers in blue. See how they feel about a trespasser on the force."

Toby said, "You're descended from the Guardians."

This drew all three to him. Briefly. Only Darkeen held on Toby as he came forward, sighting on his head. The black and Native men spread out for an angle that wouldn't catch Darkeen in a crossfire.

Toby closed his eyes, trembling but upright. "That's why you inherited this land. The Indians couldn't hold on to it. But even in the fifties, the government couldn't touch it if you owned it."

"No more talking. Move."

Darkeen stowed his submachine gun on his back. He zip-tied Toby first, cinching the plastic cuffs tight, moving to Dan and Harpal, then Bridget, before ending on Jules.

"Unclench those fists, kiddo," Darkeen told him. "This ain't my first rodeo."

Jules saw four different ways he could get out of this, but that would mean another crime to add to his list. Instead of assaulting a person legitimately defending his property, Jules had been pumping his fists tight, a means of expanding the muscle and ligaments around the lower arm so a zip-tie could only bind the expanded limb. When the prisoner relaxed, this allowed a few millimeters of give—plenty for Jules to have squirmed out of several times in his low-level criminal days.

He acquiesced to Darkeen's demands and received an additional squeeze of the cuff for his trouble.

"Up, now." Darkeen backed off, allowing Sally Garcia's hands to remain free.

"What did I do?" the professor asked.

"I'm out of ties," Darkeen said simply. "No offence, but you strike me as the least threatening."

"Oh?" She put her dukes up like Scrappy-Doo in cartoons Jules used to watch as a kid.

"Not the time, Sally," Toby said. "But talk to them. Explain it."

Professor Garcia hesitated as she considered the situation. Jules tried to put himself in the eccentric woman's shoes: her life's work either embodied as fossils or an elaborate hoax; a fabled shield a pool of water away; the team who'd dropped out of nowhere and turned her life upside down before becoming her savior, now captured and helpless; her proof slipping through her grasp…

"We don't want the shield," Garcia said.

Jules nudged Toby before he replied with what would probably exacerbate things.

Darkeen's men lined the group up with concise gestures, while Darkeen faced Sally Garcia. "You've been poking around here before. We've warned you before."

"This is the same as lying," she replied, her chin high. "You're concealing truth from people who deserve to know."

"Who *deserves* anything in this life? Your YouTube followers? Your Maori bodyguard?"

At mention of Tane, Dan tensed. That was odd, and the shuffle of feet and lips moving like a bad ventriloquist alerted Jules that something was off. Charlie would comprehend the situation.

"Who else?" Darkeen pushed. "Who *deserves* to know things that are none of their business? Who are you to decide what the world needs?"

"I'm a scientist," Garcia said. "I see people like you, like governments and private investors, concealing this, and I have to ask why."

"But you haven't asked why, have you? None of you have. You broke in, ready to take it. Like so many before you, you think you're entitled to—"

"Hey, Darkeen, man," Jules said. "Something's up."

"Don't even bother." Darkeen pointed at Jules before resuming with Garcia. "You called this place a graveyard, but that's not quite right. They're killing fields… they're what you see after a massacre. After a genocide."

He pointed at the nearest fossilized remains.

"The truth is lost. They pre-date Horace's people by a long way." A half-gesture to the Native American suggested he was Horace. "Lived alongside them for a time. But they died out, mostly, because of low breeding. Then, when populations from across the sea arrived—long, long before Europeans 'discovered' America—they were taken. Bred for labor. At least that's what the oral histories say."

Jules said, "And the Guardians helped them."

"In some ways, yes." Darkeen's eyes flared with passion and anger.

"But the Guardians weren't a single race. They were individuals who amassed knowledge over centuries. Scholars as well as warriors. Folk who understood both who they defended and who they were fighting. They incorporated those they fought for into their ranks, training them, educating them—"

"They took the best from the communities they helped," Jules said.

"Those people *volunteered.*" Darkeen seemed to struggle to hold his anger in check, something Jules thought of as misplaced. This was *history*, not a personal attack. "If the Guardians saved a town under siege, and that town wanted to give thanks, yes, they could offer their brightest and most capable to join the fight."

Bridget said, "The ultimate pay-it-forward."

"If you want to boil it down to childish nonsense, sure." Darkeen fished in his cargo pants pocket and retrieved a fistful of black lengths of cloth. "Time to go."

As Darkeen applied the blindfold to him, Toby said, "The giants received the Guardians' help, then some of them joined the ranks."

Bridget was next. As if using the blindfolds as cues to speak, she said, "And because they were the most distinctive, they were the ones that got talked about and painted most. The ones that drove the legend."

Darkeen said nothing as he tied her off and moved on to Jules.

Jules picked up the narrative baton. "And the weapons got bigger. The tech got more useful. Not tech like we see it, right?" He caught Dan's lowered head, his tense jaw, flexing shoulders. *Definitely something going on in his ear*. "Like my bangles. Like the Witnesses' vaults and their transmitters. They didn't have a clue how it worked, but they knew it did. I'm bettin' that shield in there's got some properties or function you can't explain."

"Bet all you like, my friend." Darkeen approached Dan with the next blindfold. "You'll get to explain it to the cops."

Harpal jumped the queue and asked, "What happens when they ask to see the tomb you caught us in?"

"They'll need a warrant. And what judge would sign off on something as silly as a child's fairytale? All we need is to show you were trespassing, using explosives without a permit, and—"

"Others are coming," Dan said.

Darkeen laughed, sharing the joke with his two comrades. "Okay, now it happens."

Dan looked wearily at Jules. "I didn't think they'd believe me."

"Predictable play," Horace said. "Pretend there's worse than you on its way. Old as time itself."

Jules absorbed the factors—Dan's concern, Harpal's attempts to conceal it, the fact Darkeen had eyes up top watching for activity, and that no one had contacted him yet. "Okay, no messin' around. You lost contact with the guys on the surface, right?"

"We're underground," Darkeen replied, as if that was the most obvious thing in the world.

Ordinarily it would have been.

"We got that covered," Jules said.

Dan tapped his ear. Harpal did likewise.

"Look, it's true," Jules admitted. "The little guy wanted the shield. He's desperate to keep funding his archaeology club. And that chunk of metal would've pulled him out of a hole with his investor."

"Hey. I don't recognize that as entirely accurate." Toby moved his head around as if searching for something in the dark.

Jules went on as if he hadn't spoken. "In California, our guys got attacked. People who want the shield. People who shouldn't have it."

"You think it's magic?" Darkeen asked. "It isn't magic."

"No, but it can do stuff if the right person's using it, right?"

Darkeen's eyes narrowed. He was holding the blindfold, clearly eager to strap it to Jules. "I never touch it. No one does. That's our mission."

Bridget said, "But you've heard of things it can do, haven't you?"

"I got the bangles with me," Jules said. "In my pack. I put it down, over there. Lemme show you. There's things going on I can't explain, but you need to see it."

Darkeen chuckled without humor. "You think you're one of the Guardian Warriors?"

"I don't think I'm anythin' but a guy trying to leave all this behind. I got some ancestral blood or DNA that means I connect to certain rocks or metals inside those rocks. And if that's true, you gotta believe what I'm saying."

Darkeen watched Jules's bag for a long moment, then faced Sally Garcia. "Is this true, Mrs. Scientist? Is the cop brother special?"

Garcia flitted between Jules and the blindfolded Toby.

"The truth," Jules said.

"I haven't seen anything," the professor confessed.

"Take them out." Darkeen gestured to one of the pitch-black tunnels and approached Jules with the blindfold.

"In my car," Harpal said, twitching his head closer to his shoulder. "You don't believe me, speak with the people up top. Our contact in England. It runs through packs designed to move signals through tunnels like the one we came through. Just listen. If you don't believe me—"

Darkeen rushed forward and punched Harpal in the kidney, doubling him over, winded.

"You came here to rob this place. One of the few places that some other culture or religion has not usurped. People lie here in state..."

Darkeen gestured to the row of fossilized remains.

"We honor others for their service in the defense of the needy."

He swept an arm toward the wall of armed skeletons.

"You think I'll believe you just want to prevent other people getting it? Sorry, but our mission here is to *stop* you. Now get out. Stay close to the person in front, shuffle your feet. Any attempt at escape and we will shoot you. Clear?"

The reply came in the form of clenched teeth, of Harpal standing gingerly, and of Jules sighing, ready for the blindfold.

Sally Garcia shook her head in resignation with one last gaze toward the submerged shield. "Then you're handing this over to the North Koreans without even understanding what it does."

Darkeen's hands hovered in midair, the blindfold above Jules's head, about to apply it. "Did you say Koreans?"

"Yeah, she did," Dan said, picking up on Darkeen's surprised manner. "What was that name?"

"Name?" Darkeen said.

"He's not talking to you," Jules answered. "He's talking to the surface."

"Ah Dae-Sung," Dan said. "You know him?"

Darkeen's two men spread out farther, the Native American checking the exit they were aiming for.

They know that name.

Harpal said, "There's at least six incoming."

That didn't sit right with Jules. "How'd they get so close without Charlie or Wiremu seeing?"

"Parachute," Dan said. "We have to move! They're dropping out of the damn sky."

Darkeen consulted with his comrades.

Jules took the initiative. "You don't believe us, fine. Let's take it outta here and you can talk to whoever's keepin' watch. We'll cooperate. Just, please... If they're coming, they won't take prisoners."

Charlie was sick to the back teeth of trying to understand what the hell was going on. She had Tane on one side of her, urging her to get the hell out of there, while Dan and Harpal were struggling to convey events from below. So far, it had swung from wonderment and disbelief to the disagreeable confrontation they'd been hoping to avoid.

Find the object, with bonus points for fossilized giant human remains.

Get expelled for violating someone's sacred resting place.

Now, mercenaries dropping out of the sky.

"Great."

"No, not great." Tane fussed around the hole, nodded to himself, then helped pack up the comms equipment, the laptop controlling the drone on autopilot. He prioritized pulling out spare ammo for his handgun. "Listen, Charlie, I have to tell you something. I have backup."

"Backup? What backup? You never mentioned backup."

"No time to explain exactly, but they had to stay loose. They're based a long way out. They'll be here, but not in time. Those guys above us? Three minutes, max. That leaves us two choices. Run on the bikes or head down." He waggled a rope. "I don't fancy down."

Charlie scanned the horizon, then used her hand to shield from the sun as she checked the sky.

Six 'chutes incoming.

"They're not my people," Tane said. "And I doubt the guys

guarding this place are using a plane so high up we can't see it. Whatever way, I'm moving out."

Charlie took out her stubby knife and slashed through the first rope. "We toss these in, pack up, and seal the entrance."

As Charlie sliced the second rope and tossed it in the hole with the other, Tane took her by the shoulders and got in her face. "We don't have time to cover our tracks. We can't let them get what's down there. We have to block it up and leave."

Charlie was about to object and deliver a message in putting their friends and the secrets below ahead of personal concerns, when Phil came through her ear firmly and clearly.

"Charlie, go." He had a quiver in his voice. The one he couldn't hide when Charlie was facing death. "Think about me. The kids. Get to cover. Show the Koreans you aren't a threat, and hopefully they'll leave you alone."

"Well?" Tane asked. "I have the detonators ready."

Charlie sensed something more to Tane's eagerness. But closing the entrance wasn't enough. She had to ensure they left nothing obvious that would help them capture her or her friends. She cut the final rope and threw it in. "Fine, but we're not making it easy for them."

Tane breathed out in relief, scooped up a pack for the laptop, and stuffed it an already half-full one, heading for an ATV. "They say we're under crosshairs, so let's head that way. Strength in numbers. Can you ask them which direction to—"

"There's a low ridge half-a-mile south east," Phil said. "The drone picked up movement there. And it's the best vantage."

Charlie conveyed that to Tane as she rummaged in the pack Toby had left, checking there was nothing of value, but hoping for a particular item. "Found it." She pulled out a white handkerchief. "Corny, but effective. Hopefully, they won't shoot if we're waving this."

Tane nodded and climbed on his ATV.

Having salvaged all she could from the bits the others didn't take with them, Charlie kicked the remaining backpacks and detritus down the hole, hoping it either concealed their identities a little longer, or stripped their opponents of vital clues. She got on her ATV and consulted the tablet computer one last time.

"This way." She pulled on her goggles and set off, circling back around the route they came.

The sound of the ropes dropping from above visibly caused Darkeen concern. His probing eyes reached Dan, but of course Dan couldn't see them. Jules translated it as frustration and confusion, starting to realize Dan and Harpal might not have been lying after all.

Jules said, "I wouldn't trust us either. But come on. Charlie's up top, leaving us here. You know anything about these guys, and it sounds like you do, you know she don't do that. Ever."

"A trick," Darkeen said.

Jules had marked him as military earlier, and Dan had mentioned something similar, but even if he had been trained by a branch of the armed forces, he couldn't have seen much combat. Dithering was not a part of an experienced soldier's repertoire.

"Need to decide," Dan said. "Take us out or send one of your guys here for reinforcements while we make a stand."

The black guy who'd left the Native American to check the way out took his eye off his target for a second. "Willis, we need a decision, man."

"I know that, Blake," Darkeen snapped.

Then the *thump-thump-thump* of heavy cloth echoed down the entrance Jules had used.

"That's everything they can't carry," Jules said. "They know they can't hold off what's comin'. We gotta cut loose now, or fight. And we can fight if you let us."

"I'm armed," Dan admitted. "Ankle."

Darkeen winced, an embarrassing oversight. More proof he had undergone training but had little experience in these matters.

"These people are crazy," Garcia said. "One minute they want to take the shield to the Vatican, the next they say they can't do that because of you people and what it means to you, and now all they want to do is help you defend it from the bad guys chasing me. Chasing *us*. But you won't let them, which is even crazier if you ask me—"

Darkeen cut her off. "Okay!" He waved hard at the exit. "Horace, get them out. Me and Blake'll hold off anyone coming this way."

"That's a mistake," Jules said. "Let us help."

But his mind was made up. No more discussion. No more arguing. Darkeen just pulled the blindfolds, but not the cuffs, off the group in turn and said, "Go. This isn't your fight."

Ah Dae-Sung touched down seconds behind Pang Pyong-Ho, accompanying the hired guns to oversee the retrieval himself. He also might be needed if the radio message they intercepted was anything to go by.

They knew the approximate area they'd be approaching, but it had taken the accumulation of activity below to trigger their attack. The bikes, the explosion, and various scurrying figures were enough for Dae-Sung to give the go-ahead.

The four new soldiers were former Republican Guard Special Forces who came to America following the fall of Saddam Hussein, where they entered under assumed identities and attempted to start fresh lives with their families. They'd been no fan of Saddam, but the commercialism, the racism, and the lies about the American dream had soured any prospect of them falling in love with their new country. It was now just a place to exist, a base from which to raise families or find different ones. They rebranded themselves and hired their skills out to whoever could pay enough. Usually more accustomed to single assassinations to silence witnesses or bullets to the knee to dissuade suitors from certain people's precious daughters, they'd seemed positively eager to join Ah Dae-Sung's mission.

Or, rather, the mission Dae-Sung sold them.

Acquire a work of art wanted by a businessman in the Far East. Kill anyone who tries to stop them.

The kill order was a big relief. They'd been hobbled back in the college, unwilling to finish anyone off in case they had information the Koreans needed. There'd be no such caution here.

In truth, Ah Dae-Sung could barely contain his excitement. Not for the high-altitude jump, of which he'd performed too many to count, but that his two-year quest was almost at an end.

Back in California, he'd assumed it was another bend in the road, another rung on the ladder toward their goal, but it seemed this group had proven more resourceful than they'd imagined. Zeroing in on the clues it had taken the Executive years to accumulate and decode, they had done so in mere months.

It was almost as if they had prior knowledge.

No matter the reasons for their unlikely success, Dae-Sung held the solution to his country's woes in his grasp.

One of the Iraqi dogs of war approached. They didn't speak Korean, and Dae-Sung knew no Arabic, so they conducted all exchanges in English.

"Commander, we can pursue using the vehicles they left behind."

Dae-Sung and Pyong-Ho had discussed the people below, scattering as they'd descended. Even considered cutting their cables and dropping faster, pulling their backup 'chutes at the last minute to take them out. But they were not his concern. He didn't care who went free and who didn't. He cared only about what lay beneath his feet, now he was on the ground.

"Can you shoot them from here?" Dae-Sung asked.

The dog sighted on the pair receding down the slope on their quad bikes. They were using H&K submachine guns, imported by the group for their ease of use, anonymous supply, and plentiful replacement of ammunition. Unfortunately, even with the folding stock, they were not long-range weapons. A master marksman might make this shot, but Ah Dae-Sung saw the impracticality of opening fire.

"Save your ammo," he said.

The man lowered the gun, stoic but disappointed in himself. Good. Dae-Sung liked a perfectionist.

"Commander!" called Pyong-Ho.

He'd been examining the hole the English and Americans had made. It was interesting watching them through the detailed camera lens designed for low-orbit applications, seeing them in cinema quality high definition as they assessed the ground before blowing up a piece of it.

They hadn't seen them plant the secondary devices, though.

Pyong-Ho didn't need to explain, just backed their men away. Someone had laid several bricks of plastic explosive in the entrance at different levels and on opposite sides. Dae-Sung counted four, two stuffed in the topsoil, the others jammed between imperfections in the rocky tube below. The detonators were linked, meaning they only needed to fire a signal at a single receiver to blow the access hole, and that receiver appeared to be dangling below the lowest brick.

"Why haven't they set it off yet?" Pyong-Ho asked.

Dae-Sung retreated with him, checking between the entry point and the fleeing bikes. "They have. But the angles are wrong. They must have left in a hurry." He laughed. "They cannot seal the hole."

One of the Iraqis came forward, having listened in. "If they are transmitting a signal, when we lift the receiver into the open, it'll detonate."

"It is a good thing that we can jam such signals, then." Dae-Sung could do that with a command on his sat-phone, which he enacted right away. "Deactivate the explosives. Then prepare to breach."

Darkeen directed Blake to the cave's right flank while he took up the left. Both drew down on the sounds of incoming people.

This had never been Darkeen's preferred method of defending their oath, but Telah refused to skimp on stories of myth and legend, digging up their history and the heroism of their near ancestors. They knew little of the route taken by the original prisoners transported from their African homeland, although DNA sites in the modern era had suggested Darkeen's ancestry stretched back to the area now known as Somalia.

Since discharging from the army, he had pledged to uphold the duty his family had beaten into him since he was a toddler, a duty he had hoped he'd never have to act upon. Blake and Horace were in a similar predicament. Although they'd learned this place existed as young men, that the shield lay in its perpetual watery grave without rotting or tarnishing, they had never believed someone might attempt to steal it.

Professor Sally Garcia was the first person Darkeen had encountered who showed anything more than a passing interest. From that moment on, the Guardians had been on high alert.

The Guardians.

A melodramatic title for what was essentially a glorified janitor, some way below the people he'd trained to defend wildlife preserves in Africa and Asia during his army days, local volunteers who armed themselves and patrolled areas where poachers picked off endangered species.

"You ready, man?" Blake asked.

"Of course I'm ready."

Their approach from outside was not silent, but nor was it a racket like those from the Lost Origins Institute had made. But then, Toby Smith and his advance party had not expected a welcoming committee. No doubt, the men descending would be well-armed and well-prepared.

A light several yards up the tunnel shone, then was quickly doused.

"Here they come," Darkeen hissed.

Blake firmed his grip and readjusted his position to hunker down more between the natural V in the rocks that he had made his den. He had seen more action than Darkeen, but it was Darkeen's responsibility to lead their group.

It wasn't a noise that alerted them to the fact intruders had made it to the mouth of their tomb. It was more of a shift in the air, perhaps a minuscule click of a firearms mechanism slotting into place, but nothing Darkeen could put his finger on. All he could do was brace himself.

Sweat dotted his top lip. Electricity shot through his spine and down his arms.

This was not just his duty. According to Telah and Andre, and his beloved grandparents, it was his destiny.

A *clink clink clack*, followed by a metallic noise rolling forwards, disturbed the silence.

"Flashbang!" Blake cried.

They both ducked right down.

A crack rang out, the entire chamber flaring white. Darkeen's eardrums burst, the confined space enhancing the grenade's potency. Even with his hands over his ears, the flesh and bone had been insufficient to defend himself.

Adapt.

Wasn't that what soldiers did?

He braced again, blinked hard to clear his vision, which hadn't been as badly compromised as his hearing.

Two men in pseudo-combat gear rushed out of the tunnel, firing blindly into the chamber. Darkeen returned the favor, cutting one of them down, while the other pirouetted behind a stalagmite.

Blake picked him off with ease.

They were bottlenecked. Darkeen could defend like this all day long.

Then another *clink clink clack* of a metal canister tumbling inside alerted him. A second and third.

"Grenade!" Blake shouted.

Not flashbangs. But grenades.

Darkeen pressed himself hard to the floor, and half a second later, a triple-layered explosion ripped through the tomb, and the entire world turned to pain.

CHAPTER SEVENTEEN

The passageway Darkeen ordered them through, by typical standards, appeared plain and simple. But to Jules, it represented a feat of engineering he couldn't help but admire. Yes, it looked like a mineshaft to the untrained eye, the passages down which miners would transport trolleys and equipment to hollow out a seam of coal, gold, or other commodity. But every ten feet, alcoves led to dull rooms, visible in the flashes of lights, dorms where people fleeing oppression could rest before commencing their onward journeys.

They were about to break into daylight when the first explosion sounded. A flashbang if he wasn't mistaken. Then gunfire. Then an enormous boom that shook the entire structure, showering them in dust.

Everybody, including their captor, Horace, ducked and set themselves ready to sprint.

"Let us help, dammit," Dan said for what felt like the fiftieth time.

"They're gonna get your shield," Jules warned.

Horace glanced back into the darkness, then up ahead to freedom. "Keep going."

He kept his distance, sensibly out of arm's reach from both Dan and Jules, although Harpal had shifted close enough to strike if his hands had been free.

They proceeded outside, expecting to find a unit of Guardians waiting for them. And they were right.

Sort of.

There were two men dressed similarly to Horace and Blake, currently on their knees as Darkeen had demanded of Jules and his friends. Using an outcropping of rock as cover, Tane Wiremu held his Baretta on the pair. Charlie was holding an AR-15 rifle she must've taken from them, a second propped up to the side. She pointed it at Horace, who removed his finger from the trigger guard and lifted his free hand above his head.

"Okay, easy." Horace pointed the gun down, and Jules collected it from him.

It caused Horace a moment of confusion. Jules showed him the cuffs' pieces and the two-inch throwing knife he'd used to free himself. "I keep a small blade in my belt all the time." He shrugged. "Old habits die hard."

"You couldn't have done that sooner?" Dan asked.

With the three men under control, Jules cut Dan free and handed him the submachine gun. "Figured they deserved a chance. It's their gig after all."

As Jules slashed through Harpal's binding, Sally moved out from cover. The crosshairs must have been on the blindside. If the presence of a sniper was not a bluff.

Charlie said, "Get back here. They'll see you."

Garcia pointed, her other hand shielding her eyes from the sun. "That doesn't look right to me."

"What are you going to do with us?" Horace demanded.

Dan had collected a second AR-15 as well as the submachine gun Jules gave him. "Gonna help you. Whether you like it or not."

"The big guy here has backup," Charlie said, hooking a thumb towards Tane.

"They're still fifteen minutes out, minimum." Tane pointed up at the area where Jules calculated they had entered the ground. "Our new arrivals are getting busy."

"You need to see this," Garcia insisted, fixed on something beyond the hillside.

Jules risked a peek out from behind the boulders, but couldn't describe what the professor was pointing at, other than he had witnessed nothing quite like it before. "Okay, yeah. Check this out. I don't think a sniper's gonna be too worried about us."

With everybody free, they took it in turns to study the incoming sight.

With the wide-open spaces, it was easy to observe the fat-bellied plane skimming the ground a couple of miles away, rising slowly while —for some reason—trailing a line behind it. It reminded Jules of an old troop carrier, but it wasn't quite distinct at this distance. As the engines whined ever closer, the cable whipped up a dust storm in its wake.

"What on earth is that?" Toby said.

"I don't know for certain, but I can guess." Jules rushed for an ATV, his mind performing somersaults, unsure if what he was imagining was even possible. But he could think of no other explanation. "Someone get back in there and stop what's happening. The shooting's ended, which is bad news for someone. I'm gonna try to change that."

Without waiting for permission or for anyone to join him, Jules sped away, hoping against hope that nobody had to die today.

Since meeting the kid in Prague a couple of years ago, Dan had oscillated between hating Jules's guts, to begrudging respect, to eventually kind of liking him. It was when he took decisions on his own, which impacted the wider team, that Dan veered away from the "like" side of his feelings. He doubted he could drop all the way into hatred, but when Jules chose not to free himself out of some misguided sense of respect, leaving them all in a predicament with amateurish militia holding them at gunpoint, it made Dan want to punch him.

"Do we back him up?" Harpal asked.

"We could have men down inside," Dan said. "Plus, that's where the bad guys are headed."

"He'll need help." Bridget snatched the AR-15 from Dan and racked the slide to check a bullet was chambered. While she'd never be confused for a soldier, and stayed clear of guns generally, Dan had seen that she knew how to shoot. "Anyone coming?"

"We'll back him up," Harpal said, the pair moving for the remaining ATV.

Tane had either read Dan's mind or possessed the same attitude toward a battle zone gone quiet. He was already ducking through the aperture Dan had come through. "Looks like we're on recon."

Dan might not have trusted him with regards to information, but he'd handled himself well so far. "Charlie, Toby, you good here?"

Toby nodded, keeping close to Professor Garcia.

"Do it." Charlie motioned to Horace and his friends, still on the floor. "You won't give me trouble, will you?"

Horace glared Dan's way, as if Charlie didn't bother him. "You can't have the shield. Darkeen will see to it."

"You and Darkeen can keep your damn shield." Dan hustled behind Tane for the passageway, "But only if we stop those assholes first."

Tane had taken a flashlight from somewhere, and Dan still had his own on his head, so they made good time up the tunnel. It wasn't a warren either, only a couple of forks Dan needed to remember. As the sounds of people moving around grew louder, they doused their bulbs.

The shield's chambers lay only a few feet ahead. Dan should have been able to see the fierce illumination from Charlie's arc lights, but there was only a faint glow. And not much talking, either. What he did hear wasn't English.

Working in sync, Dan and Tane stalked to the doorway.

Every fiber of Dan's experience told him nothing good lurked there, but he had to go on. If they'd come across a wounded man—Darkeen or Blake—they could have turned back and then joined Harpal, Bridget, and Jules up top, where they stood a better chance of stopping Ah Dae-Sung and his pals. But there'd been shooting and at least one explosion. And no one had emerged.

At the chamber entrance, Tane paused, bobbed his head to look inside, then retreated to safety. His startled face told the story. His military sign language conveyed two men down.

Not good.

Dan pointed fingers at his own eyes and then at the opposite side of the opening. Tane nodded. He then checked inside again. One fist in the air. When he judged it safe, he chopped ahead.

Dan glided over to the other side, glancing in as he went.

He only saw one injured man—Darkeen, splayed on his back, breathing rapidly, his skin and clothes bloodied—before making it to cover. He also spotted two Koreans who fitted Harpal's description from the college. One was positioned at the access tunnel through which LORI had entered, the other holding fast by the shield. They were working with the light from glow sticks, meaning Charlie's contraptions had been damaged.

Dan hadn't had time to analyze the scene in that brief glimpse, but he suspected they'd used a grenade or similar ordnance. Even Phil had gone quiet. Whatever took out the arc lights must have damaged the nearest comms node, too.

Dan held up two fingers.

Tane nodded agreement. Pointed at himself, then to the right, and held up one finger, leveling it at Dan first, then back inside.

Tane will go in first, draw their fire to the right while Dan takes out the first shooter—both, if possible.

Although Dan would have preferred to go first, they lacked the capacity for a debate. He counted Tane down.

Three...

Two...

ONE.

Jules was completely exposed. The rise they'd traversed originally barely looked like a hill, but the opposite side—where they'd come out of the shaft—fell lower on the land. Here, from the rattlesnake cluster to the entry point they'd failed to seal, it was open ground, with only a few boulders and dried grass to conceal him.

He'd parked the vehicle out of earshot, then advanced on foot, keeping low. The airplane remained on an approach vector, dragging that line, banking aside and back again—a near-zigzag to time its intercept for...

What?

Jules considered several possibilities, but only one seemed right.

Gathered at the hole, four men patrolled, spread out in a square. Military fatigues, well-armed, and possessing the bearing of former soldiers. Definitely former, as they weren't as crisp as someone who lived that life daily, but far more precise than a wannabe civilian exercising his Second Amendment rights. And they were not Korean.

Another bike revved from behind.

Damn it. Who the hell is that?

From his point amid a cluster of chest-high boulders, Jules searched behind him and waved the incoming ATV down.

Stop!

Harpal and Bridget veered aside, following Jules's frantic gestures to go wide. But it was too late.

The gunman closest mounted his assault rifle and loosed off a burst of three, pocking the ground beyond the vehicle. One other came to join him, still unaware that Jules was crouching ten yards away.

A howl of engines came directly across the landscape, the plane nearing for its final run, that cable kicking up dirt behind. It showed why only half the contingent of goons had engaged Harpal's approach.

Harpal?

Where was Bridget?

Jules surveyed the stretch, unable to see her. Was that a good thing or had she been hit?

No, Harpal wouldn't have left her.

Checking back to the men hunting them, Jules held still as they progressed closer to his hiding place. They had the angle on Harpal, but it'd be steadier with a platform, and they appeared to be heading for the rocks to do it.

Hunkering lower robbed Jules of his vantage point, leaving only a sliver of view on the main activity. The other pair were readying what looked like a cross between a grappling hook and a clamp the size of a trash can lid.

He was right. *These guys mean business.*

In a rare stroke of luck, the airplane was almost upon them, a deafening whine of engines from a vehicle not designed for this type of maneuver forcing hands over the ears for the approaching gunmen, and ear defenders donned by those intercepting the cable.

The hook snagged the steel line as it cut along with the plane less than fifty feet overhead, and the other guy slammed the clamshell device around it, trapping the cable in place. Rather than whipping them off the ground, it remained in situ, a tremendous amount of slack playing out from its housing on the aircraft, which soared onward. Jules pictured a winch feeding out hundreds of meters of line.

If he was correct about their intentions, they had seconds to act.

As did he.

One gun barrel pointed over Jules's head, the owner having not spotted him. That wouldn't last long, though.

As the first shot clattered, aimed at Harpal's now-winding ATV, Jules popped up to the side, yanked down on the machine gun, and took a blink to enjoy the look of shock on his enemy's face, before slamming an open hand into his throat. The man gagged, and Jules used his own bodyweight to lever him up, employed him as a temporary barrier, then spun him over his hip.

By the time the guy's face hit the dirt, Jules had disarmed him and repositioned them both behind the boulder where he applied a choke until the bad guy lost consciousness.

Bullets pinged off the rock, the other gunner getting closer with every heartbeat.

Six-two, a hundred and eighty pounds.

Counter-attacking a surprise opponent.

Near to zero winds as you can get.

Stymied by both caution and adrenaline.

70% chance of success.

"Close enough."

Jules sprinted from cover, the gun in one hand, his two-inch throwing knife in the other, palmed and prepped.

He'd miscalculated.

The hired gun was almost upon him. All that prevented the man from killing him was the surprise of Jules dashing out.

Jules launched his blade, which whizzed past the guy's face, taking a nick out of his cheek, but nothing else. He found himself running backwards, aiming the gun he'd taken, but hesitating. His brain hurled calculations at him, from hitting the shoulder to the leg, or even the gut.

It took less than a quarter of a second to calculate the guy was too well built, too well trained, and in a better position. Nothing except a kill-shot would prevent him from doing the same to Jules.

A gun fired.

But it wasn't the mercenary. His head snapped to the side, a jet of blood splintering out toward Jules. As he dropped to the ground, Bridget held the AR-15 to her shoulder, frozen in place.

The gun drooped. Her face was aghast at what she'd done.

Jules spun to the left, remembering the activity up the hill, ready to kill, ready to do what Bridget did for him, if it meant saving her, saving himself.

There was no need. The men were preoccupied with following orders. Handling the cable took two of them.

Keeping the machine gun in ready position, Jules ran to Bridget as she rose to her feet, still stunned with the shock of killing for the first time. Harpal—who'd obviously served as a distraction for Bridget—pulled up beside them.

Now they had to finish up with the men who were left, those feeding the line from the plane looping to the north. Jules only hoped Dan succeeded in his part, or nothing they did next would matter a jot.

Dan fired twice, the MP5a working like a charm as Tane swept inside. The guy at the pool shot at Dan, as expected, then took on Tane right away. This meant Dan doubled down on his target, forcing the man back.

As the gunfire from within receded, Dan advanced through, moving left where Tane had darted right. The cavern was bathed an eerie green, enough light to see both Darkeen and Blake lying injured and untreated.

Tane fired his Baretta from behind one of the larger casket-shaped rocks upon which lay the bones of a giant. Or so Sally Garcia believed. Dan had had little time to reflect on it, and he'd picked up plenty of that science stuff since growing attached to the Institute. He knew fossilized bones were just stone representations, not bones themselves, so he couldn't comprehend how someone could tell the difference between that and a statue.

It also made it bullet resistant, so Tane had made a wise choice.

The two Koreans fired back but appeared cowed by the flanking motion Dan instigated. Pulling around, gaining a better angle, forcing them back from the shield.

"Go! Go!" Dan cried above the din.

Tane read the scene and pelted over to the pool, before continuing onward to complete the second point of their pincer.

Dan remained wary of the ammo situation, but he soon reached Darkeen's spot, where he had dropped an identical gun to the one taken from Horace. Plus, there were two spare magazines in his belt.

"Hey, hang in there."

He then let loose, blasting several bursts at once, driving back the men who were finding it so difficult against a former Army Ranger and... whatever Tane Wiremu was.

"You..." Darkeen croaked.

As the submachine gun clicked empty, Dan swapped it out for Darkeen's weapon, unsure how many rounds were left. "Stick with us. We'll get you out." Then he called over, "Tane, you got our other guy?"

"Yeah," Tane replied between shots. "He's in a bad way but says he can walk."

Dan assessed Darkeen: blood at his mouth, a ragged tear in his thigh, slashes across his face, all indicative of shrapnel injuries. And if Dan could see all this in what little light the glow sticks gave off, he was almost certain there'd be worse damage underneath.

Dan said, "We'll get you home."

Then he popped up to shoot at the retreating men.

"The shield..." Darkeen stained to talk, struggling to move. "Get the..."

"Yeah, I told you, we got this. They're gone."

The pair of Koreans moved back fully into the hole, concealed from sight. Their lights danced in the tube, getting darker as they drifted away. Not that Dan would assume they'd fled. It seemed too easy already, but there were other priorities.

"Okay, let's get you up." With the gun ready in one hand, he pulled Darkeen's arm up and around the back of his own neck to lift him. He paused before doing so, leaning in to Darkeen's bloodied face. "This is gonna hurt, but I gotta do it."

"The... *shield.*"

The shield remained in the pool. Ah Dae-Sung hadn't had time to retrieve it.

Tane staggered up alongside. "Triage. You take him, brah. I'll hold them here in case they come back."

Blake was conscious, one of his legs shot to bits, but he'd applied his own tourniquet and functioned freely from the waist up. Cuts showed, but he wasn't struggling to move the way Darkeen was.

"Good call." Dan heaved Darkeen up, eliciting a cry of pain from the Guardian.

The mangled cry evolved into, "The shield," again.

"Would you quit it with the shield stuff? The bad guys are out of here—"

A mechanical shriek rang out. Everyone drew their eyes to where their enemies had fled, and then skipped to the pool containing the shield. A flume of water erupted as the treasured item burst out and flew into the air. It clattered on the roof, slammed to the floor, and shot into the access tunnel, leaving a fine mist behind.

Dan could not look away. "Well... I've never seen that before."

Jules was usually right, and this was no exception. From the moment the two pseudo-soldiers clamped the cable trailing from the airplane, the smooth winch feeding out hundreds of yards of slack, and the operators sending it into the hole, he'd known what was next. After seconds of well-rehearsed, repeated, and perfected activity, the result was inevitable. And even though they'd secured the pair under the guns Jules and Bridget carried, they were—as Jules had predicted—too late.

First, a man in a helmet, hooked up to the steel line, shot out of the ground like a champagne cork. Must have been a gradual tightening of the cable so it didn't tear him apart as the harness he'd attached himself to pulled him straight out. A second man followed, again connected to the line. Just when the end appeared, suggesting it was all an elaborate method of bugging out, a thinner rope became clear. Attached to this, a net containing the shield that may once have belonged to a mighty Greek warrior flew high into the air.

While Harpal and Bridget gawked at the sight, bewildered and forlorn as their prize receded into the distance, Jules bore down on the surrendering mercenaries. He rarely fell back on firearms, preferring to utilize years of training in subduing his enemies with non-lethal means.

"Where are they going?" he demanded.

The pair just laughed. There was nowhere to run, no way for them to escape if Jules gunned them down.

Harpal said, "Jules."

"*What?*"

Harpal rested one hand on Jules's shoulder, easing the rising anger in him. He needed to tell Jules something, and it didn't sound good.

"They got Darkeen and Blake out," he said, glancing at Bridget, who fretted nearby.

"What..." She stumbled over her words, the next ones stuck in her throat. "Are they...?"

Harpal, too, couldn't quite get to it, distracted by incoming helicopters. They sounded like gunships rather than medical or civilian vehicles, but Jules needed to hear the news.

"Darkeen didn't make it," Harpal said. "He's dead."

CHAPTER EIGHTEEN

The Beast had been procured from a US military auction by one of the Executive's shell companies based in Canada and had served them well during their mission in and around the Americas. They had successfully registered the airplane as part of a charitable mission, granting wishes to disadvantaged and terminally ill children. Their flight plan with the FAA had included several tandem skydives, so any radar operators seeing them circling much higher than most civilian aircraft ventured would not grow suspicious.

Since retrieving Ah Dae-Sung and Pang Pyong-Ho along with the Guardians' last shield, the Beast had kept below radar for several miles, before ascending and switching on a spoofed transponder. As far as anyone monitoring their movements was concerned, they were now a Gulfstream jet transporting a Saudi oil representative to a very important meeting with a local senator. This would allow them to set down at the airport where the real sheik was due to fly in to, switch out their transport for a different shell-owned plane, and be on their way home.

With the mission a success and the pilot leveling out for a smooth approach, Ah Dae-Sung needed to report in. There was only a bench seat and no table, so Pyong-Ho set up the same rig as they'd called from the RV—which was now a burned-out husk containing the corpses of the Americans who'd botched the college raid—and Dae-

Sung found himself standing, smiling up at a gray screen on the wall dividing them from the pilots.

"Executive Ryom, thank you for your patience."

"You have the item?" Ryom Jung-Hwan said.

"Yes. We return within a day."

Silence for a few seconds. Then, "Are there any loose ends?"

"We lost our contractors," Dae-Sung replied. "Regrettably, they will be captured. But even if they are tortured, all they know will be insignificant in less than thirty minutes. Americans will not arrange an interrogation in that time, let alone break their own laws to extract that information."

"Did you neutralize the Guardians?"

"Not all of them, Executive. I prioritized retrieval of the artifact."

Again, silence. Ah Dae-Sung understood they'd missed the full parameters of their mission, but the key ingredient was in place.

"Very well," Executive Ryom said. "But you are now under kill-on-sight orders. Do you understand?"

"Of course." Dae-Sung gave a shallow bow toward the screen before righting himself. "Do you wish to examine it, or should we transport it directly to the Dragon's Pit?"

"Commander Ah, your mission is evolving. Are you in good physical shape?"

Good physical shape?

Meaning the evolution could lead to more violence, more bloodshed.

"Your mission," Executive Ryom went on, "is not simply about bringing artefacts to the People's Republic. It is about what we found beneath the Dragon's Pit. About holding our country dear and ensuring the West cannot take from us what is rightfully ours."

"Yes, Executive Ryom. I understand."

"Because there are spies everywhere. Not only the satellites, but even in our country. They will learn what we have. And, like our nuclear program, they will seek to steal it. We cannot allow that to happen."

Although he wasn't privy to every detail, Ah Dae-Sung had been clear about the consequences from the very start. Like the Executive, he knew an invasion was unavoidable, and that they needed all the pieces in place if they were to defend against it.

"Our latest experiments did not produce the results we hoped for," Executive Ryom continued. "You must pursue the people you failed to kill. You may eliminate Tane Wiremu on sight. Along with his new friends. I want two people alive: the professor who knows so much about the items we have acquired, and the ones you must collect next. And, if possible, the negro. Julian Sibeko."

"Why him?" Dae-Sung asked.

"I understand he carries objects with him that may be of interest. Which only he can use. You saw the effects of the green rocks two years ago? Before our Striovian friends were neutralized?"

Ah Dae-Sung showed assent with another bow. "Yes, of course. It is rare to find someone who commands their properties."

"I believe we will need him for the other power source too. Along with your next mission. Details will follow."

"I will not fail."

He signed off and waited for instructions.

"They do not want us home yet?" Pyong-Ho said.

"One more mission." Dae-Sung read the revised orders streaming before him. "This is... daunting. Our own people will meet us soon. It is the final phase. We cannot fail, or this will all be for nothing. Either Korea will fall into the hands of the Americans, or we will all perish."

CHAPTER NINETEEN

While the rescue party comprised one Apache gunship, a squad of heavily armed Department of Homeland Security agents, a starched and hair-gelled FBI liaison who Tane's superiors had tipped off, and a medevac helicopter, it was too little too late. It took four hours of debriefing before they released Jules from the scene, and they supplied the team with an armed escort as they headed back to Bridget's estate. While it sounded like a long time, Jules found the ease with which the authorities discharged them highly suspicious. He'd voice that later, though.

Jules drove the truck they'd used for the ATVs, Bridget in the passenger seat, staring out the window, pinching her lip. They were alone, the others opting to use the Humvee from the backup contingent and the SUV hire car from the airport.

"It's tough," he told her.

"I don't want to talk about it."

The last time he ventured out in search of lost knowledge, Jules had accidentally killed a man. While Dan, Harpal, Charlie, and even Toby viewed those people as having dug their own grave by standing shoulder-to-shoulder with evil, Jules had found peace in devoting his philosophy to every life being worth something. After a tumultuous childhood seeking the artifacts stolen from his dying mother, he was angry and violent, and it took mastery of aikido, and the mentorship of one of the world's foremost teachers, to quell the rage and reveal to him a clear path.

While Bridget agreed with Toby and the others that she would not mourn the death of someone willing to do an evil man's bidding, it was different when you snuffed out that life with your own hands. Jules had understood that life as a cop might mean killing someone one day, but he'd hoped it would strike him as urgent, necessary, not a sad, inevitable shadow encroaching from within. If he carried on helping Toby with his shield quest, given the nature of their competitors, he expected that shadow would darken his soul sooner rather than later.

Jules drove in silence the rest of the way, the gates opening thanks to Bridget's key fob, and they allowed the two vehicles behind through too.

Once parked, Bridget said, "Not a word to Mom and Dad about what happened. Y'know, with the gun."

"Sure." Jules wouldn't have said anything, even without being asked, but he added, "It's your business, Bridget. You wanna talk about it, just talk about it. Okay?"

She nodded and climbed out, confronted by both Roger and Audrey Carson bursting out the door, demanding to know why their daughter was being accompanied by DHS after the reported death of someone she visited not twenty-four hours earlier.

"Darkeen," she said, folding into her father's arms with a sob. "They killed Darkeen."

Instead of fury dominating, Roger and Audrey embraced Bridget, Roger with one beady eye on Jules, drawing across to the others disembarking their vehicles.

"Let's go inside." Roger led Bridget toward the house. "The rest of you, get cleaned up, then meet me on the patio. I want an explanation, and I want it directly."

Half an hour later, all but Sally Garcia waited for Roger, a member of staff having served sandwiches and soft drinks. Jules hadn't realized how hungry he was until the first bite, then he could hardly stop.

Tane said, "We have to go soon. I have people waiting—"

"Just a minute," Dan interrupted. "As far as we knew, you were a spy, sent by the New Zealand government to get information out of the prof."

"Right." Charlie paced behind Tane. "Then suddenly, you're ordering around DHS guys and calling in Apaches."

They all glanced toward one of two armed agents, kitted out in full tactical gear, sweating in the afternoon sun.

"Yeah, and let's not forget how easy they let us go," Jules said. "I mean, *I* can predict what you got coming up, but I don't know if everyone else is there yet."

"What do you mean, easy?" Harpal asked.

"I mean, you and Toby and Charlie, you're in the country on either illegal passports or something false on your visas. They'll know that by now. They'll also've connected you with the shootings on the west coast. Not to mention the comms tech that ain't exactly standard spec, and Dan pulling in explosives without a license or planning. That's before we get onto several deaths..." Jules was careful to not even glance Bridget's way. "No chance we walk outta there without some serious pull."

"He's right." Toby was sweating in the heat, not having yet acclimatized. "I hadn't had time to think it through, but yes. We should be in custody. Why aren't we?"

"Fine, fine, look..." Tane paused as Roger came outside with Audrey.

"Don't let me stop you." Roger gestured stiffly toward Tane. "I'd like to hear all about the people my daughter was nearly killed alongside. Perhaps I'd even understand why I was under the impression this was an archeological expedition, not fighting foreigners who also knew of this lost item on the Museum's grounds."

Dan withered under the man's gaze. "Sorry, sir. We... didn't have a full picture."

"But you're about to." Roger again indicated Tane was up. "Please continue."

Tane spread his hands. "I wasn't here in my official capacity as a New Zealand SIS agent. I was here because I'm a damn good undercover operative, and we believed Sally was being targeted by the North Koreans. We couldn't let what they were chasing end up with them, so..."

"You were to protect her and run interference," Toby said. "Until such time as the threat eased and you could obtain the things she knew about. Under the radar."

Tane nodded. A nervous lick of the lips. "And now the Koreans have the shield, we *must* get it back."

Jules said, "We?"

"We." Tane leveled on Jules. "We can protect your status as a cop, to a degree, but obviously this is voluntary."

"Okay, I'm out, don't worry about it."

"I hope this isn't blackmail," Charlie said. "Cooperate or that chap with the gun and armor takes us somewhere to rot."

Dan's shoulders seemed to expand, the muscles in his neck swelling. "Let's hope that isn't the case. Because it won't go well."

Toby extended his hand, appealing for calm. "Let's hear what he has to say first."

Jules could have thrown a barb concerning how he was in the hole with Alfonse in a big way. The ex-mafioso had funded Toby and issued an ultimatum on results. Losing it to a competitor, regardless of their intentions, was not acceptable. But Jules could do without igniting an argument like that, so he kept to himself.

Tane said, "I don't have as much pull as you think. I'm sorry. I need you to volunteer, or we can't make you part of the task force. The DHS will do what they want with you."

They all let out a resigned groan. While some of those at the table would have happily put themselves forward, the fact they had little choice weighed heavily.

Harpal got to his feet, stretching. "Let's hear the big problem. The thing no one wants to ask."

"What might that be?" Roger asked.

Bridget sat forward. "What *is* the shield? What does it *do*, and why do they *want* it? Is it connected to the other three? Do they have the other three?"

Tane set himself and took a breath, a nervous student delivering a dissertation. "Okay, here's what we're facing—"

Sally Garcia burst out of the house with an e-tablet carried in one hand. She was white, almost gray. "Was it one of you?"

"One of us, what?" Jules said.

"What's happened?" Toby asked, rising from his seat.

As Garcia approached, she held up the tablet so they could see a video playing. "It's everywhere. YouTube, Vimeo, Twitter, Instagram, probably more."

All craned to look.

All except Jules. "I'm waitin' to hear what he thinks we've gotta do to help get his shield back. And why."

"But I didn't put this here." Sally marched over and stuck the screen in Jules's face. "It's my more esoteric video journals. A lot of them I've debunked myself, but now every single one of them is out there."

Tane watched the footage, currently silenced. "They were all on an air-gapped portable hard-drive in your safe."

She lowered the device. "How do you know that?"

"You told me."

"Oh, right, yes, of course." She resumed waggling the screen at everyone nearby. "So, who did it? They make me look like a crazy loon."

"I'm sure it's not that bad," Toby said. "We have software that can wipe all sorts from these sites. We use it to keep ourselves hidden, too. Charlie, can't you—"

"It's *too late*." The professor lifted a hand to her face. "The university already saw it. They called me, just now. It's how I discovered it. They've been up for almost a whole day." A couple of tears brimmed and spilled. "They won't give me a chance to explain. They say I've brought the university into disrepute. No way I'll make tenure. And I have to endure a board hearing when I go back." She dropped the tablet on the table, making the lemonade glasses shake. "I'm finished."

"Maybe not," Tane said.

"Okay, great," Jules said. "You get another recruit for your mission. Let's hear it. No more stalling."

Tane reset himself, taking that breath again. "Sally can be comforted that the giants thing may pan out. The secret history of the Guardians and their allies can be documented. But only once we secure the shield and neutralize the threat from Ah Dae-Sung and his bosses.

The other stuff, things she recorded and then refuted herself, she'll prove them false with the analysis she's also recorded, and denounce any thought of aliens landing, the connectedness of pyramids on different continents, the magnetic flips of the Earth, whatever."

"There's a great deal of evidence for magnetic flips," Toby said. "Mostly thought to be brought on by solar flares, but they are often accompanied by large-scale extinction events. The last one was around 42,000 years ago, which would have been—"

"Around the peak of the Witnesses' civilization," Jules interrupted. "Let's hear what's really going on here. Now. In the twenty-first century. History lessons can wait."

Toby reluctantly agreed.

"I only kept the films for posterity," Garcia said, almost in a squeak. "Giants and ancient civilizations, sure, we can prove them true in time... But will it wipe out the other stuff?"

"We'll get the truth," Bridget said. "If we can hear it."

"First thing you need to understand and accept," Tane said, "is that Darkeen Willis, Telah and the others here... They are *not* direct descendants of the Guardians. Sure, they know about the warriors who protected endangered people, knew the legends of the shield and the giant humanoids who carried this particular one. But they took up the mantle to honor them. To keep the secrets and guard the entrance."

"Then the Guardians are gone?" Toby asked.

"No."

"No," Jules said. "It's him."

Tane slowly nodded again. "That's why I have the authority I showed you today. I *am* one of the Guardians. Or, as it's known in black-ops government departments around the world... The Guardian Protocols."

"And you're one of them?" Bridget said.

"We're officially an NGO. A non-government organization. Multinational, with scope to do as we need. Anything connected to our history, and the need to suppress that knowledge from hostile agencies or private individuals."

"Private individuals," Dan said. "Like our old pal, Valerio."

"Yes." Tane had clearly heard the name. "We took steps to keep him in the dark, and it seems to be working."

"He knows about the Witnesses," Bridget pointed out. "He still has a ton of scrolls that we couldn't take ourselves."

"That doesn't concern us. Once we enacted our jurisdiction here, generals with top level security clearance activated the Homeland Security and ordered them to deal with this the same as any domestic threat."

"With command conferred to your good self," Toby said.

"Correct," Tane confirmed. "We know about what you call the Witnesses, of course, and there is a connection. They're just too obscure to get a firm read on them. But, that connection, the similarities in the materials, how they interact on a quantum level and tap the subconscious in order to activate... I think it's what caused us to cross paths."

"Please don't start talkin' about destiny," Jules said. "I'll throw up."

Tane chuckled. "We have our own agenda. The Lost Origins Institute has theirs. It simply happens that they've aligned. Belatedly. Unfortunately, what we're facing has little to do with ancient pre-history. It's chronicled. More recently."

"The shields." Jules heard the impatience in his voice as much as feeling it in his limbs. In recent times, he'd learned to temper this side of him, which could come across as obnoxious, but today felt like a good day for obnoxious to speed things along. "Tell us about the four shields. Now. Or I walk."

"Me too," Dan said. "Get on with it."

Tane sighed, unable to put off his confession much longer. "Ah Dae-Sung and Pang Pyong-Ho—the two guys who rabbited and left behind their subcontractors—work for a guy in North Korea called Ryom Jung-Hwan. He is known as the Executive. In Korean culture, they use important job titles the way we often use ranks and qualifications, like Professor, Doctor, Colonel. He is Executive Ryom, and he is very well respected in the North Korean government."

"Why?" Bridget asked. "What's his deal?"

"His deal," Roger Carson answered for Tane, "is that he is a multi-billionaire in a deeply socialist country. He swans around the world under assumed names, using numbered bank accounts, and about a hundred companies. His main firm is Dragon Teeth Enterprise, a tech company. He has almost as many contacts in the Middle East and China as the Carson Corporation."

"Thank you, sir," Tane said. "I have to add, though, that he does all of this under the gaze of his government. They approve of it because he ships his hardware to them, to their military, for free."

"What hardware?" Charlie asked.

"Chips, processors, phones cloned from the best in the world. You want the latest iPhone or Samsung in North Korea? Sorry, no. But you can get one of Dragon's Teeth's knockoffs with software backdoors approved by the ruling family, and it's a damn fine copy. He has a strip-mine up in the mountains and is channeling a river to a nearby dam where he seems to be moving into hydroelectric power."

Tane appeared to sense Jules was about to move him along again which he did with a rapid delivery of a line that made them all hush.

"They need the capacity to contain an orb. Much like those you've encountered before." Tane paused in the thick silence. "The mine is only a mine on paper. It's more of a Gulag. It's set in a remote mountain range near the Chinese border. A valley which, in English, translates as 'Dragon's Teeth.' Hence his company name, I guess. They discovered the object purely by chance when Gulag prisoners fell through a pocket of air during a fresh mining operation. They're now experimenting with metals and other minerals that have produced some troubling signals."

Jules recalled two encounters with spheres, linked to the Witnesses, that ancient order of hyper-intelligent humans that seemed to disappear on the cusp of the last ice age. From Bridget's translations, and Toby's understanding of pre-history, plus a significant contribution from Jules, they'd worked out this branch of humanity evolved in isolation, separate from the hominids and Neanderthals, and even shepherded the dumber side of the family to survive the climate catastrophe that almost eradicated the species. They hadn't been able to determine if they'd selected the brightest of the dumb apes or simply interbred, passing on their intelligence. Did they evolve, or did they die out?

What Jules did know was that part of their legacy contained these mysterious orbs.

Tane said, "You've encountered orbs left by this prehistoric culture. You know there's something powerful there, but—"

"They're magnetically charged," Jules said. "Takes a genetically attuned someone to control 'em properly." He waggled his fingers. "But hook 'em up in a certain way and they activate other rocks and stuff. They even kinda communicate with each other in different parts of the world."

"Communicate isn't quite right," Charlie put in. "There are signals. It's like they're linking up. A kind of circuit. They use neutrinos, which pass through solid matter without detection. As you say, it's ancient tech, only it's working on a quantum level."

"We think it's a natural occurrence," Jules said. "Like dark matter. Our Witness friends might not have understood what it was, but they worked out how to use it."

"But they built it?" Tane said. "The machines or equipment that tapped into this energy?"

"Not exactly," Toby answered. "We haven't been able to discern, empirically, if this is the case but Jules here—"

"They found it," Jules said. "Like we found their stuff, their accounts of pre-history, they found a bunch of these things, these places they took over. There might've been another race, older than them."

Dan clicked his tongue, winked, and shot a finger-gun at Jules. "Aliens, dude. I'm telling you."

Jules angled his face, lopsided toward Dan with the usual tired exasperation when the subject came up. To Tane, he said, "Dan and I have a hundred-dollar bet. If the final answer to these old machines is aliens, I pay up. If it's something else, he does."

Bridget picked up the thread, getting them back on track. "But the orbs. They're normally activated for something big. They're powerful, and when connected they seem to tap into energy we can't detect—"

"Energy?" Audrey Carson said. "What sort of energy?"

Jules sensed there was more interest here than simple curiosity or concern for her daughter. The Carson Corporation was, mainly, an oil company, after all.

"What are they powering?" Jules asked. "Something to do with the metal these shields are made of."

"Ah, the shields!" With his hands together in prayer, Dan gazed to the sky. "We've arrived."

Tane didn't falter at the sarcasm. "We didn't know what it was for a long time, but over the years we've concluded that Executive Ryom knows most, but not all, of the truth. They know of the existence of giant humanoids, dating back a few hundred years to the point they were enslaved and hunted to extinction. It seems they evolved much like other human species, like Neanderthals, who ran out of the ability to interbreed. That, and they were often kidnapped and pressed into becoming warriors."

"Like the Guardians," Jules said.

"The Guardians didn't enslave people. It was always a choice." Tane left no room for debate in his delivery. "The discovery of this extinct species and the weapons they carried, has led them to understand the legend of the Four Shields. Just as we do."

"But *is* it a legend?" Sally Garcia asked with a tremble of excitement.

Again, Tane needed a moment to steel himself before speaking. "We believe the 'Four Shields' isn't necessarily four individual shields gathered in one place, but they could be. They could also be one sample of the metal that works four-fold: First, protection and shelter using one device, a gifted individual—such as Mr. Sibeko here—generating an energy field that can hide those under its dome from sight, and physically repel attackers."

"Are you talking about a cloaking device?" Harpal asked. "Like a Klingon Bird of Prey in Star Trek?"

"Yes, like that. Two, you could set up a circuit. Four in a square, or maybe six in a ring around a larger mass. Say, a village. Or even a small country."

"Presumably, you'd need an orb to power that," Charlie said.

"Correct. Three is where it gets into the neutrino side of it, of these objects communicating through the Earth. Imagine a planet-circling cocoon. It could protect us from meteors, solar flares—"

"Aliens," Dan said.

Jules wasn't clear if he was joking, so offered a laugh out of politeness. A ripple of amusement passed over everyone except Tane and the senior Carsons.

The big Kiwi said, "Or four: it could, if hooked up correctly, become a weapon. It starts small, concealing an area the size of a town, then expands outward, wiping out everything from a few meters into the earth and above. We think they can encase an active ring around a bigger land mass, with enough samples, and essentially send a massive tsunami out from the center."

Jules pictured it like a wave, expanding from a small dam high in the mountains. "But wouldn't that take out the country they were in?"

"That's why they need the giant's shield. You see, the other metal samples—let's call them all shields for simplicity's sake—are blended with other materials. This one, the shield wielded by Achilles during the Trojan was... is pure. Whatever this element is, Executive Ryom seems to believe it will solve that problem. Perhaps it's a stabilizing agent, or improves the direction or range, or—"

"There are no accounts of Achilles being a giant," Toby said.

Jules groaned at the interruption. "Clearly a metaphor, Professor Smith."

"No," Tane replied. "Just in a different form. His armor, his sword, his regular sized shield. All melted down after his death, brought together in the form of the shield we lost today. And offered to the Guardians to aid their cause."

"I don't even care how you know that," Jules said. "What's the bottom line?"

"From one single device..." Tane held up a finger. "Expanding out to the next active ring, in the south-Asian land-mass, then all the way across to Eastern Europe. An energy wave powerful enough to deflect asteroids. Millions could die. But a government like that isn't bothered by death. They, and brainwashed soldiers like Ah Dae-Sung, care only for the Korean people, and defending them against an apocalypse they believe is inevitable."

"Us," Dan said.

"America," Bridget added.

Roger Carson shook his head. "Crazy-ass Koreans, eh? Don't they know we're the good guys and they're the bad guys?"

"Probably not," Jules said. "They're raised to believe we're evil.

From birth. In schools. Through military service. And they ain't got access to information outside of that country, so they're pretty much stuck."

"Where do we come in?" Bridget asked.

"Yes, how on earth do you expect me to allow my daughter to continue with—"

"We signed a contract, Dad. It's my decision." Bridget smiled sweetly at Tane. "Tell us."

"The US can't be involved," Tane said. "For obvious political reasons. They stand to lose too much if they interfere. Not everyone in the US hierarchy supports the Guardian Protocol... not enough authority on the US side... and they will pressure the President to employ a more conventional solution."

"War?" Dan said.

"If the shield can't be retrieved, or the Koreans' plan neutralized, yeah, war." Tane paused to allow it to sink in. "But mostly... the Lost Origins Institute, and Professor Garcia of course, has a ton of knowledge and experience."

"The whole group?" Jules asked. "Or my magic fingers?"

"That's a part of it," Tane said. "But we had no idea about that until Toby briefed me. It's an advantage, I can't deny it. But will we absolutely need you? Hard to say."

Jules replayed all he'd heard. "You really think this'll mean millions dead? If they succeed?"

"Maybe into the billions." Tane held Jules's eye. "You'll be formally seconded to the Department of Homeland Security. Your boss'll think it's because you witnessed something and they're using you for leverage and intel. Once this is over, your job's waiting for you."

Jules looked around the table. As far as he could discern, the others were already sold. Even Professor Garcia was nodding absently, a subconscious tic that Jules read like a newspaper.

Jules said, "If I agree, what's next?"

"We all fly out to New Zealand," Tane replied. "It's closer to Korea, we have equipment and personnel on-hand, and there's something else there you need to examine. An essential part of this whole thing."

"Something?" Charlie said. "What something?"

"Something I can't go into without formal approval," Tane told her. "An orb and its origins, and a little bonus. Rest assured, you'll be useful. And so will you." He gestured to Bridget. "And especially *you*."

"Wait a minute." Roger Carson's voice rose, his face reddening.

"No, Dad." Bridget matched his tone, but her skin remained unblemished. "Our contract says I see this out to the end. You'll support me. Keep an eye on me. Use your contacts in... the Middle East and China or wherever. Employ spies if you want. I'm sure you will, anyway. But if we're all agreed, I'm going with them."

"Well?" Toby said. "I think we all know I'm up for the challenge. With or without the threat of robust incarceration by the US government."

Harpal nodded. "Likewise."

"Yes," Garcia said.

They voiced agreement one at a time. All except Jules. Which meant they were all staring at him for a long stretch of silence, one he was sure was less comfortable for them than it was for him.

He eventually put them out of their misery. "Okay, I'm in. When do we leave?"

"Two hours," Tane said. "And pack light."

PART THREE

CHAPTER TWENTY

Jules had been to New Zealand twice before, and only once was on business. That excursion ended without conflict and during the other he'd learned to snowboard so, all in all, his experiences there had been largely positive. That didn't stop him from taking some precautions, though.

He had packed the regular gear he would take on jobs where he expected he'd require his more basic skills, namely being sneaky and —where necessary—using his physical assets to evade capture. Tane had not disabused him of this notion, so his baggage contained several of his mini flashbangs, a belt full of two-inch throwing knives, and his bespoke grappling gear—a baton that housed a strong bungee cord topped with a grappling hook, which he used frequently to drop from buildings to either escape or to infiltrate them.

That Tane did not prevent him from bringing this stuff wasn't particularly telling. New Zealand's intelligence service was perfectly capable of doing more than he or the Lost Origins Institute could. The only factor that resonated true with Jules was that he could interact with the two artefacts in his pack—the Aradia bangle and the Ruby Rock bangle, neither of which he was prepared to relinquish into the hands of *any* government.

Whenever they quizzed him about the specifics, Tane fell back on that old chestnut, national security. Confidentiality. All that nonsense seemed to Jules to be a pathetic example of the *in*security that all politicians harbored. It also gave them a warm, cozy feeling of power.

Information is power.

Whilst that was true in many circumstances, this was simply about the truth of history. The North Koreans already knew about the offensive capabilities—make that *alleged* offensive capabilities—of the shield supposedly used during the battle of Troy. That only left the idea that giants once roamed the land, evidence for which was sketchy and which Jules had not yet accepted as fact. Underground, it had seemed all too plausible. But while there was a world of difference between fossils and intricate carvings, no one had had time to examine them closely enough to make such a determination.

After only a few hours, they gave up trying to pry information from the intelligence officer and got some sleep instead. Jules was way ahead of them, having snoozed on and off, then refreshed himself with four straight hours of slumber before his ears started to pop during the descent.

They disembarked into cool sunshine, the airfield standing at an altitude of at least 5000 feet above sea level. It was certainly remote, with grassland on one side and mountains hazy in the distance on the other. It wasn't military, but it wasn't civilian either. Highly efficient, cheap-suited agents ushered Tane's guests from the tarmac as soon as they set foot upon it, hurrying them into a hangar. The personnel were pitched at them as a courtesy, but Jules got the distinct impression it was to prevent the team from deviating elsewhere on the property.

The metal doors closed behind them, their escorts remaining outside, and Tane led them towards the small grouping beneath the wing of a fat bellied transport aircraft. Three people. Two of them women, one a man.

"Oh, what the hell?" Dan said upon recognizing the man.

Jules had spotted him, too, but kept his face neutral. If there was one thing this person enjoyed, it was surprising his opposition.

Another petty power play.

Tane made the introductions as happily as if he were presenting new employees to the office team. "I believe you fellas already know Mr. Waterston."

If Dan had been annoyed, Toby was apoplectic. "You never told me *he* was here. You should have disclosed he was a part of this."

"Toby, Toby, Toby," Colin Waterston said. "I thought we were past this silly rivalry. After all, didn't I lend you a hand the last time you poked your nose into ancient matters of international interest?"

"You mean we saved your ass when you were too cowardly to do it yourself," Dan said.

"We're still waiting for that thank you," Charlie added.

"Indeed, indeed." Colin clasped his hands together. He had the bearing of a hawk crossed with a jellyfish, his haughty manner clashing with his lack of spine. Jules had found him to be useful and resourceful, but very much inclined towards decisions that ingratiated him with his superiors and to promote his own station. "But this matter is of rather greater importance than a few trinkets or a terrorist attempt to reawaken an old virus or excavate a cathedral in Mexico."

"That's why we keep asking about our involvement," Jules said. "We're not commandos. I sure as hell ain't some special forces super soldier. If the North Koreans are gonna use this tech to attack their enemies, isn't diplomacy the first step?"

"Absolutely. Your presence here is not without conditions. And I am yet to be convinced that your slapdash attitude towards protocol and caution will reap rewards."

"But let's not be hasty," Tane said, playing peacemaker. "It isn't Colin you need to impress."

"It's me." One of the women stepped forward, the older of the pair, a tall woman with a no-nonsense bob and a skirt suit Jules would expect to see on an accountant or—yes—a politician.

"I ain't here for a job interview," Jules said. "Someone needs to start tellin' us what our job is gonna be, or I walk."

"I'm Julia Grainger," the woman said. "I'm the Minister for environmental protection."

"I'm real sorry, Mrs. Grainger," Bridget interjected. "But we must insist on you being candid with us."

Tane again adjusted his position, gesturing towards Julia Grainger. "There's expertise required, and I am sure you can help. Minister, declassify the Ahua project and we can move along."

Grainger turned to the younger woman, dressed in a cheaper version of the Minister's suit, carrying a binder and a soft leather briefcase. Her demeanor screamed *assistant*. "Anything to add to your report from ten hours ago?"

The assistant passed a sheaf of papers from within the binder.

"No, ma'am," Tane replied. "It's all in there. All except certain things I haven't observed." He looked pointedly at Colin. "But he can confirm they have resourcefulness." He then turned to Jules. "And something a bit extra."

Jules chose not to elaborate for him. If they wanted to know anything specific, they should ask.

"Okay," Dan said. "Let's get it all on the table. You discovered some sort of ancient tech under one of your mountains. Or some inland sea. Or you mined an orb that you can't explain?"

Grainger stared at him with the pinched annoyance of a schoolteacher staring down an immature and troublesome brat.

"If it is," Toby added, "you don't need to play games like this. We have a plethora of information, knowledge, and experience that could be of use. We are happy to advise anyone who is seeking to stop an aggressive country from taking advantage of it."

"But we don't fully understand it," Charlie said. "We kind of know how it works, not why. We get the connections, the quantum nature of how these orbs throw molecules and neutrinos through the earth at one another, but that doesn't mean we can control it. It doesn't make us experts. We're archaeologists, not detectives. Not spies or scientists."

"It makes us more expert than them." Dan stuffed his hands in his pockets and pulled a smug expression aimed at Colin. "Isn't that right, Bertie Wooster?"

Colin took a moment to realize Dan was talking to him. "I can attest they have meddled with powers they do not understand. So far, they have been lucky. I cannot say if you can trust them with the Ahua project. They tend to go their own way rather than following the correct order of things."

"What is he doing here, anyway?" Jules asked, unable to play nice much longer. "He's British. This is New Zealand. Most of this went down in America. North Korea seems to be the bigger threat. Someone wanna come clean on this arrangement?"

Colin cleared his throat and folded his arms, smiling as he usually did when he had a point to make. "This is a multinational operation. And we cannot risk loose cannons making it worse."

"I'll tell them the basics," Tane said to Julia Grainger. "We'll fly them out, and if at any point I reckon they'll be a hazard, I'll dump them, and you can run them home." He glanced around the Lost Origins folks, settling on Professor Garcia. "At our expense, of course."

Grainger flicked through the brief but didn't seem to read anything, then let it flop onto her side and addressed Colin. "There have been developments."

"What sort of developments?" Toby asked.

Colin opened his mouth and made an *aah* sound. "American developments."

Harpal edged through the small throng of newcomers. "They know about the threat?"

"Our transatlantic cousins are cooperative with the Guardian Protocols when it comes to internal security warnings, but when it comes to foreign affairs they get a little... tetchy." Colin straightened his jacket, a condescending glance between Dan and Bridget. "They turned their fleet around in the Pacific and are heading back to the Korean peninsula. They're ready to strike at the first hint that the North Koreans are about to launch." Grainger accepted another piece of paper from her assistant. "We have assured them the threat is minimal because they do not have a vital component."

"Me." Jules didn't want to be the center of attention but having experienced being hunted for certain tasks associated with the materials used by the Guardians and others, there was no point in being modest. He took the bangles from his pack and held them together, hunched over them to offer a little shadow. As usual, the flecks inside the rock lit up—green for the Aradia bangle, red for the Ruby rock. "If they want me, being out in the open might not be a good idea. Surely you just stick me in the ground somewhere until the threat goes away."

"Were that it was so simple," Colin said. "Unfortunately, you are not the goose with the golden egg in this scenario. Or maybe you are. We haven't tested you yet."

Jules let the bangles go dull and replace them in his rucksack. "Tested?"

"We aren't certain what form their attack will take," Grainger admitted. "We know about the shield they took. We know they have three more. And we know they are not interested in finding any more of them. It seems they are ready."

Colin opened his arms and faced Toby. "How far have you gotten with the fact-versus-fiction around Achilles and the end of the Trojan war?"

"That family and allies fought over his magical armor, and it eventually ended up in the hands of the Guardians." Toby frowned and paced to the left before putting his finger to his lips. "But the conflict between who would inherit the armor afterwards... Are you saying they split it into four?"

"Exactly. And when... whatever it is made from is brought together by these odd spheres, placed at strategic points, and blasted with that magnetic energy given off by the meteor rocks..." Colin pointed at Jules, or more specifically the items hidden in his bag. "We can only speculate. But there are other people here. Sensitive to—"

"Are you saying you trust them now?" Grainger asked.

Colin chewed his tongue, plainly annoyed at himself for getting carried away. "They, particularly the boy here with the glowing bracelets, do have certain qualities that may be useful. A way of looking at things that perhaps we haven't thought of yet."

Dan patted Colin on the shoulder. "There you go. It wasn't that hard, was it?"

"This is no time for joking." Grainger displayed a somber expression that got everyone's attention. "Things we know. A private contractor with connections to the North Korean military and widespread international protection from the government has got his hands on unstable elements that are likely to consist of a weaponized use. It is somehow connected with a project we have been working on at a top-secret facility on the South Island ten miles from here. Without intervention, they will switch it on. Which means—"

"Without intervention," Jules said, "the US military are going to bomb the hell out of wherever they're keeping those shields. I'm guessing that dam in the Dragon's Teeth valley?"

"We believe so," Colin replied. "But we hope to disable it or render it neutral before the US warships arrive. If we can't do that, and diplomacy cannot assure the US and its NATO partners of a peaceful solution, several cruise missiles will eradicate that part of North Korea. And if that happens, I don't think we need to exaggerate the consequences."

The air had grown heavy. Jules found his lungs needed extra effort to work.

It was Tane who voiced what they were all thinking. "World War Three."

"How long do we have?" Toby asked.

"Unclear right now," Grainger replied. "A few days at best. Maybe less. We're working around the clock."

"Our experience might fill in the blanks," Charlie said.

Bridget nodded her agreement, her gaze passing over Jules first, and ending on the New Zealanders. "Or take a new tack. If we see something you thought wasn't important."

"Yeah," Jules conceded. "We got a habit of doing that."

Grainger closed her eyes briefly before focusing on Tane. "Take them to Ahua. Assess how much use they can be before exposing them to the inner workings. Then report in. I'm working to a forty-eight-hour launch window. After that, anything goes."

Tane beamed back at the group, more akin to someone who had won a bet than who carried the weight of a world war on his shoulders. "This is something else. Prepare to be amazed."

CHAPTER TWENTY-ONE

The helicopter was a civilian transport, a once-luxurious model stripped bare to the essentials to minimize weight and cost. Bridget wasn't fussy at this stage, though. She was just glad to be on the trail of another mystery. While that might have sounded naïve, or even cold and in bad taste given the prospect of war if they didn't solve this, she put it down to the same rush soldiers felt after months of training, months of waiting on deployment orders. No one wanted to be in that situation, but it was what they were best at. Plus, it made killing that man feel like it happened to someone else, a surreal act she observed rather than perpetrated.

And Bridget was good at this. Not economics, business, or politics. Digging deep into codes and languages, brain-taxing puzzles her contemporaries couldn't grasp, had given her a purpose. And buzzing the beautiful New Zealand landscape in a helicopter with her friends? There were worse ways to begin a new project.

It wasn't a straight line between the low-key base and their destination, taking in valleys and low-lying mountain ranges. Harpal commented at one point, through the scratchy earphones and mics, that the route was likely to mask the destination from the group. Bridget glanced at Jules, his smirk telling her he was already mapping their twists and turns in his photographic memory. As long as he knew where they started, they'd be able to find their way back here should their hosts betray them.

"We're coming up on Taone Pukepuke," Tane said. "It means Hilltop Town. This is for the people who staff the lab, and the workers for our other projects up here."

They passed over the town as promised, although Bridget interpreted it as smaller than she would label something a "town." It was more of a village or township, with low-rise accommodation, hard-packed but not tarmac streets, suitable for a few hundred people. There was a road leading out of the town limits into a lush green forest spreading across the hillside.

They didn't follow the road, instead trailing over a river. The waters below switched from serene flowing courses to being squeezed tight into rapids that frothed and broiled, then back into wider, calmer waterways.

"Next up on our magical mystery tour of Ahua," Tane announced, "we have Kainga Pukepuke."

They soared higher, showing how deep they were in this valley, carved out by the river that Bridget assumed came from a lake or meltwater, or both, up in the mountains. Those mountains extended ahead of them, farther than she could see, blanketed in cloud, and dusted with snow. The smaller mountains nearby were mostly green, tipped with the gray of cooler climates that would struggle to support the larger flora of the surrounding area. Below, a pier and jetty were equipped with what looked like traditional Maori longboats—*wakas*—alongside more modern contraptions, including Jet Skis. There was no lingering here, though, cresting the hill and banking to the right. It was enough to view Kainga Pukepuke without disturbing the activity going on there.

Bridget said, "Oh, I get it. Taone means town, Kainga means village."

"Spot on," Tane replied.

All on board craned to view the village. And this one really *was* a village. A working reconstruction of a Maori settlement, albeit somewhat mechanical and laid out more like a western town planning council made up the plans. They were low enough to see people milling around, some dressed in regular fashions, others in tribal getups. As they veered away, about a quarter of a mile beyond the village, a parking lot came into view, hidden from the staged setting by yet more trees.

"It brings in some cash, and it's great camouflage," Tane said. "We ship workers in and out disguised as people running this tourist trap. It's run by Maori, so they get an authentic experience and a bit of education about our history. We're not conmen. But it's a stop off for the coach tours and gives the tourists a good feed and an 'authentic' experience for folk who want to see the real New Zealand. Lots of arseholes, but mostly decent people, so we put on a show."

"We?" Dan said. "I don't see you getting all dressed up in native gear and dancing."

"I put in my time as a kid." Tane waved his arms to the side in what Bridget guessed was part of the show.

"I assume *that's* where we are going?" Toby pointed ahead, over the pilot's shoulder and out the front window at a conical mound.

Its distance was impossible for Bridget to gauge, but it looked different to the valley sides and the mountains encompassing the region.

She said, "Is that a volcano?"

Harpal and Dan groaned in unison.

Harpal said, "I had enough of volcanoes before I had to go freelance."

"Don't worry," Tane answered. "It's long extinct. And as far as any tourists are concerned, it's sacred to my people. No one can set foot on it without express permission from the chieftain, who needs to get permission from the gods."

Jules laughed and sat forward in his seat to get a better view. "They buy that?"

Tane laughed in response. "Hey, you've got to play certain cards when it's for a greater good."

Charlie had been quiet throughout, having spoken with Phil back in England before takeoff—in the middle of the night his time. Bridget had picked up that she promised this wasn't like fieldwork, although Phil was concerned. Bridget wasn't sure about the dynamics of Phil and Charlie's relationship currently, only that with Phil having been injured in the line of duty—whilst performing the same role Dan now carried out—he treated Charlie more tenderly than the others. Although Charlie was ex-military, her expertise and her stated function in the group was that of an engineer. She wasn't supposed to get her hands dirty in the field when violence threatened.

"This is all great," Charlie scoffed, "but we're not tourists. You can drop the bubbly demeanor and the useless facts. The Koreans have the Four Shields of Achilles. You have your own shield, I take it. As well as the power source. Why don't you fill us in before we walk into your lair?"

"I hardly think they are James Bond villains," Toby remarked.

"They still aren't being straight with us." Charlie waved her hand around the cabin. "You're all playing along like this is just another trip to a dig. It isn't. There are forces at work clashing with an immovable object." Her pointed gaze landed on Dan. "Your friends in the US military will not take any chances. That's going to bring other countries into it. If they bomb these things into oblivion, there will be no evidence they acted rationally. That Grainger woman was not exaggerating."

"It isn't about who used the Shields in the past," Tane said. "The Achilles legend is simply what drew people out to locate them. The ones Ryom has in his gulag are one example."

"You have others?" Toby asked.

"Of course they do," Jules said. "And they have the means to activate them, too. Right?"

Tane nodded. "Okay, I was going to save this until we got there, but if it makes you more comfortable..."

"I'm not sure 'comfortable' is the right word," Dan said. "But let's hear it."

Tane shored himself up. "You already know about the obscure language surrounding the Shields' properties. They don't only protect the bearer from physical objects. They can hide the persecuted from being detected. At least, that's what we believe the Guardians did. They only fought when absolutely necessary."

"You're talking about cloaking technology," Charlie said. "Science fiction."

"We can already cloak from radar," Dan said. "And I saw tech that hid equipment from human eyes and satellite way better than any camo net."

"This is closer to what Charlie said," Tane replied. "It's cloaking tech that corrupt nations would love to have. Only, this device works by tapping into the natural make-up of the surrounding genetic structures. We could hide Kainga Pukepuke if needed. From above, it would look like unbroken forests and fields."

"It refracts the natural habitat and expands on it," Charlie said.

"The Native Americans in that region we visited lived through the civil war. No one bothered them. But the land where we found the shield, it was populated, wasn't it? Residents and slaves hiding during their escapes?"

Bridget nodded. "Records dating back to that time and up to the modern era until the government relocated Native communities. Yes, it was populated."

"But never targeted by white troops or the government during the conflicts. There are tribes who remained in that part of Alabama alongside landowners for decades. Before, during, and after the civil war, both sides avoided that land."

Toby had listened intently, and now added his take. "You think it's more than hiding people from prying eyes?"

Tane gave a shrug and dipped his head towards the extinct volcano that appeared to be the destination. "Although you can see it, it's rare for anyone to ask about it. It's almost like something in your peripheral vision, but a voice whispers to you to ignore it. Weird, huh?"

"Like consciousness observing and altering quantum behaviors," Jules said. "We're familiar with the notion. These bangles? When I'm asleep, you can lay 'em on my skin and they'll just sit there. Hunks of rock, shaped like jewelry. If I wake up and look at them, they glow."

"What about the other application?" Charlie asked. "The ones the Americans are going to plunge us into war over?"

"Yes," Tane conceded. "We can't get it to do this for more than a few minutes, but if it is also used to deflect physical objects, if all the points activate, it can expand rapidly and destroy whatever is in its radius. To make a non-destructive dome, it has to connect to other shields at other points first, otherwise you can only shelter the immediate area—as I said, a small village or commune."

Harpal rubbed his face and leaned his elbows on his knees, chin resting on his hands. "How far can it expand? Beyond the village range. You said it might form some irregular dome over North Korea and blast the surrounding nations with its energy field."

"It's all theoretical. We haven't dared test it fully. But we do have the data from your experience in Kenya. Those orbs connected to one another all around the world. The volcanoes that were still active in some way, even if they'd been dormant for centuries, acted up. Ours didn't. The lava flow and the plates under the crust have diverted far enough away over thousands of years of continental drift. But it activated our orb. We could power the shield, not ret-conning it as we had done before."

"You're welcome," Jules said.

Tane checked out the front, the volcano looming large as they rose above the rim. There were small buildings dotted around the sides and just over the lip of the cone, the workplace for the town residents described earlier.

Tane said, "But the theory doesn't stop there. We think, if the metal plates that we see as shields are all powered at once, linked through the same neutrino particles and fed the right instructions, if it all hits the right angle at the right time, we believe all points will converge and potentially blanket the globe."

"The meteor umbrella you mentioned in Alabama?" Sally Garcia asked, speaking up for the first time since taking off.

"Or aliens," Dan said once again.

Most of them laughed. All except Sally. The Professor had been the quietest of them all. While the others were versed in factors escalating beyond what they had imagined, all Sally Garcia had wanted was to justify her outlandish theories about giants and expose the coverup. Added to that, Tane had not been entirely honest with her. Someone she had thought of as a friend as well as a bodyguard. She had seemed so upbeat about the fact she was important enough to warrant close protection from a foreign government, and now she knew they just wanted what was in her head. It must have been a real kick in the teeth for her.

"I'm serious," Dan said. "Who's to say these ancient people didn't know about aggressive aliens out there? They still haven't explained the NASCAR lines in South America."

"You mean the Nazca lines," Toby replied. "And they have explained them. It was nothing to do with aliens."

"What is it with you and aliens?" Harpal asked. "Is that why you joined Toby? Because you wanted to prove they've visited?"

Dan crossed his arms and huffed. "I'm not dumb, you know. Look up the Fermi paradox. Look up dark forest theory. You'll see this isn't a stupid idea."

"No," Charlie said. "It's just more likely they would know about meteors falling. They'd have seen the effects of it, might even have picked up some of the larger craters that it took astro-archaeology to detect. Like the one that blew away the dinosaurs."

Bridget sensed they were getting off track, and the volcano was coming up. She wanted to know as much as possible before they landed at the research station. Whatever they were studying here was plainly a big deal.

"Was there anything else here when you discovered the device?" she asked. "Books you couldn't read? Engravings?"

"No," Tane said, seemingly relieved to get back to the subject. "We only knew what our interior ministers knew, and that's only because one of them went to Eton with Colin Waterston. They'd teamed up a few times regarding odd finds, and Colin had educated a select few in return for access."

"You were on the team?" Jules said. "That undercover business with the Nationalists looking for giants. That was a cover."

"The Guardian Protocols needed me to look into stuff that the NZSIS might not cover in terms of budgets and remit. I have a science background as well as military. Which means I understand a bit of physics. But if our biggest brains can't work out why only certain people can withstand the power to control the orbs or direct it into the shield network, then I'm going to be lost." He gestured between Charlie and Bridget. "I'm hoping your engineer and your language expert can shine a light on the obstacles we faced."

"Wait a minute," Bridget said, a chill walking along her spine. "Are you suggesting you've turned it on? That it's being powered?"

"Yes." Tane pointed excitedly out of the window, a child showing his parents a certificate earned at school. "It's very much active."

All Bridget saw was the volcano, a dead mass of rock that once spewed lava and ash across ancient New Zealand. Back when the beast of a mountain lived and raged, she suspected the continent was closer together, now pulled apart by tectonic activity millennia ago. They passed over the walkways and huts familiar to anyone who had encountered volcanologists in the past, along with a miniature observatory, its telescope angled between 45 and 60 degrees.

All held their breath as the helicopter swept its tail around and halted in midair, hovering over the deep, gray caldera. Bridget doubted anyone could've expected the view that greeted them as they descended, not landing on the surface, but passing through.

It was like dunking underwater wearing scuba goggles—a clear line between above and below, a shimmering vein of air that offered no resistance to the vehicle, nor did it alter the temperature or atmosphere inside. The only things that changed were the gasps as the gray, lifeless basin transformed into a lush, green expanse. It must have been two miles from one side to the other, possibly more. Mist rose from the trees, and birds flew in small flocks. With only a few seconds to take in the scene, Bridget recognized parrots, gulls, and even a lone hawk circling.

"Is the wildlife real?" Bridget asked.

"Yes," Tane said. "We introduced them and they quite like it here. We think they sense the shield and although it wouldn't harm them, they choose not to go above it. They have everything they need in here."

"So, it's like a huge laboratory experiment?" Charlie said. "That's really dangerous. Especially when you admit you have no idea about the energy you're trying to control."

"It's amazing to look at," Toby added. "But I must agree with Charlie. In keeping the secrets of these shields and the Guardians, and even the ancient existence of giants, you've allowed this technology to come to the attention of a nation like North Korea. I assume their discovery of a similar orb within their borders led them to investigate?"

"It doesn't matter," Tane said. "What matters is the real reason I wanted to bring you here. And it wasn't anything to do with national security or getting permission from Colin Waterston or Julia Grainger."

"Then, you're working against your own people?" Harpal asked.

"I'm a Guardian. I'm working in the interests of *all* people, not a government. If we can't control this, and stop it getting into the hands of madmen like Ryom Jung-Hwan and Ah Dae Sung, we'll need more than what we've discovered so far." He was looking at Jules again.

Charlie snorted lightly, her annoyance front and center. "You want him to help you get better control over a weapon of mass destruction?"

"I don't think so," Jules said.

Charlie rounded on him. Everyone had stopped gawping at the incredible sight outside, the helicopter touching down on a helipad attached to the almost-sheer walls—one of four Bridget counted dotted around the interior.

"Easy." Jules put his hands up in surrender manner. "If they want to inject an extra element like me, I'm guessin' Tane ain't ready to take over the world yet."

"You know me so well, man," Tane said.

"What is it?" Bridget asked. "You figured out why we're here?"

"Just a guess." Jules zeroed in on Tane. "I hate guessin'. But you've brought us here because if they can't come to a diplomatic solution, it looks like the North Koreans are gonna turn on their machine, regardless. You need people with insight. People who aren't loyal to your government, or any government who might want this technology preserved."

Tane was nodding along, a big smile. He only juddered as the helicopter touched down.

Jules addressed the others. "We're not here to explore its workings. We're here in case everything else fails... In case we need to destroy the network."

CHAPTER TWENTY-TWO

Landing on what was ostensibly a volcanic research station was jarring enough for Toby's already-frayed nerves. And he wasn't the only one. After stepping down from the helicopter on the pad elevated to tower block heights over the trees, Jules stuck close to the vehicle with Bridget and Charlie, while Dan and Harpal spread out to check the perimeter out of habit. Sally removed her glasses in a daze and rubbed them with a cloth before putting them back on.

They had a matter of seconds to gaze across the lush vista before Tane urged them away from the edge. Then, they descended a staircase and followed Tane through a steel door to an unmanned, compact yet pristine processing and storage facility that smelled of sulfur. A staid, clinical interior, the polar opposite of what they just witnessed.

"Who farted?" Dan asked, wafting one hand by his nose.

"The rotten egg stench is a byproduct," Tane replied. "It's what volcanoes smell of. We keep the fake samples in here to break out and take up to the show-lab. That's where most officials get shown, along with safety inspectors and other essential visitors."

Jules said, "I thought no one knew about this place."

"It's obscure to visitors, not invisible. And defo isn't invisible to paperwork. Or to the people going in and out. And the more open we are on that front, the less we get bothered."

Toby was happy to move to the next section of the complex,

which was an elevator large enough for all of them without feeling cramped, like a goods lift or a hospital elevator.

"Where are we going first?" he asked. "I'd very much like to view any literature you have. Anything that might indicate a source or a ceremonial function."

Tane pulled the door across and scanned his thumbprint on a panel. It lit up a board, and he pressed the down button. As they descended, Tane said, "This next chamber is the business end. The energy. Where we have to be most careful."

Jules clutched his backpack on one shoulder, tightening the strap. He exchanged brief eye contact with Dan, who returned a minuscule but firm nod, then did the same with Harpal and Charlie. Bridget and Sally appeared exempt from whatever caution passed between them.

The car halted, and they stepped into a blank, steel vestibule with scanners and cameras, and grilles on the floor and ceiling. Following Tane's instruction, they all spread out, standing in place.

"Get ready," Tane said.

Toby appraised the box they were in. "For what?"

Cloudy air blasted from above and below. Cold, steamlike bursts flapped clothes and made them stagger, an odor mixing chlorine and aniseed filling the room. After ten seconds, it was over.

Bridget said, "Would have been gentlemanly to warn us."

Tane chuckled. "But not as funny."

The group let out a mix of nervous laughter and disgruntled murmurs.

Tane looked up at a camera and held out his arms. "We're disinfected and free from disease."

Silence replied.

After five seconds, Jules said, "Are you sure you're in the right place?"

"Yeah," Harpal said. "We can try a different volcano if it helps. They look kinda similar, but—"

A heavy clunk sounded. The wall slid aside with a smooth whirring noise. Beyond was a room that looked like a miniature airport control center, manned by three Maori men in dark blue uniforms.

"Security," Tane said, leading them out. The guards nodded to

Tane, the final one slapping a handshake his way as they passed. "These guys double up as technicians for the machines below and act as eyes and ears for intruders."

"Most boring job in the world," the handshake guy said.

"Glad of that," another replied.

Toby couldn't take it all in, but from his days working for Her Majesty's government in many, many fields that he still wasn't authorized to speak of, this appeared to be... "It's a listening station. Monitoring activity around the region."

"Spot on," Tane said. "As well as the immediate structural integrity and security, some of the folk in Taone Pukepuke know the real function here. Others don't. They just know they're not supposed to talk about it."

"Loose lips sink ships," Charlie said. "What's that?"

"There are two secure rooms." Tane indicated one door that looked like a vault. "In emergencies, this one can hold thirty people. The other, on the opposite side of the Ahua Basin, can take twenty. Twenty-five if everyone is polite enough to stand."

"The Ahua Basin," Jules echoed. "That's what you call the forest down there?"

"Yep. And with its rainfall per square foot, it's technically a *rain*forest. Lush, right?" Tane led them on to the exit, the room having only two ways in or out. "The Ahua Basin is a biological reserve, hidden from prying eyes by our modest experiments with a metal plate that we thought was something to do with building materials for a time. Like, an advanced bronze mold. But they unearthed it with artefacts pre-dating white settlers. Heck, it was from a time my own ancestors were just getting to grips with stone spear tips and rudimental building techniques."

"Another giant's shield," Sally said.

"We don't know that." Tane opened the door with his thumbprint but paused, holding it ajar. "The metal and the slightly domed shape are what's needed. The ones that legend says are forged from Achilles' armor are just the way they were carried by different groups. Ours is more functional. And because it's just one, we can't link it to anything else yet. It's far more modest."

"Indeed," Toby said, filling in the blanks as he went. "That makes perfect sense. It must be the physical properties and dimensions that matter."

He regarded the others, but they appeared uninterested. Perhaps they were feeling the same as him—that this wasn't archaeology, that even when circumstances escalated to dire and even deadly degrees in the past, they'd always been trying to discover hidden history because that was what mattered. Conflict and bloodshed had been a consequence. Here, they were learning much of the mystery from people who'd already uncovered it, analyzed it, and experimented with the results. Toby et al were here as advisors, and the aim was not to further humanity's knowledge but to avoid serious violence that could descend on the world if they failed.

As Charlie had said back at the hangar, they were archaeologists. Not detectives. Not spies. Not experts in quantum physics.

"Come on." Tane opened the door fully and pushed on through.

More metal stairs took the group down to a level that appeared to be carved from the volcano's interior wall on one side with ten equal panels painted a frosty white, lining the other—a modern-retconned chamber, staffed mostly by Maori men and women. Six in total, inspecting computers, handheld devices that Toby did not recognize, and each repeatedly glancing at the sphere hovering over a cradle.

Toby knew this to be opposite poles at work. Magnetism had played a part in almost all the major artefacts connected to the Witnesses and the ancient people from tens of thousands of years earlier than the humans who evolved, blinking and semi-formed from the last ice-age. The orb LORI located in Scotland had been more ornate, cupped in carved hands that didn't touch it but kept it aloft like this one. When the right connection was made, it emitted a blast of energy that knocked them out cold. Later, on a different expedition, a series of orbs around the world combined their power to threaten a plague, and only Jules could figure out how to prevent its distribution.

As Toby and the group continued around the space like some fascinated tour through an art gallery, their guide presented a towering inlet, ten feet high and four wide, like a primitive wardrobe. Above this, a concave metal plate was embedded in the roof—the approximation of a shield, but rough and non-symmetrical. Almost a clumsy hexagon.

As they all watched, awaiting an explanation, Toby offered, "The proximity of this to the orb isn't coincidental, I assume."

"Similar to the setup in Africa," Jules said. "But you enclose the person triggerin' the machine in here instead of... what I had to do."

Toby nodded agreement.

"There are a few people here who can activate things," Tane said. "But before we go on, I got someone here you need to meet."

One of the dark-haired female technicians who'd been bent over a computer tablet on the other side of the inlet said, "That's my cue, I guess." She took a deep breath, stood straight, and smoothed her lab coat before turning to the group. "Hello. Hope this isn't too awkward."

Toby had never expected to see this woman again. Having formed an uneasy truce and trusted her to do the right thing after Valerio beat LORI in the acquisition of dozens of ancient scrolls, she'd been efficient and consistent with information. Most of it useless, but she seemed to have upheld her side of the bargain.

"Prihya Sibal," Toby said, unsure how to feel. Angry that she had disappeared without a word? Relieved Valerio Conchin—the man on whom she had agreed to spy for them—hadn't killed her and disposed of the body? "You're here."

"She sure is," Bridget said bitterly.

The others gawped at her.

"Why are you here?" Sally asked.

Toby looked at the professor. "You know each other?"

"I don't think so," Prihya replied. "Maybe, though—"

"No," Sally said. "I've seen your face, though. Where have I seen your face?"

Prihya smiled. Her cheeks darkened a little. Embarrassed. "Well, if you're in the same field as me, or these guys, you might have come across some online theories. I haven't always agreed with official narratives."

"There are so many of those types of video." Sally shrugged. "That must be it."

"Glad you're not dead," Jules said. "What happened? Toby said you were helping keep tabs on Valerio."

"I was." Now Prihya's embarrassment dove deeper. Not a shy regret from a poorly researched video, but it was clear she didn't want to talk about it. "I got scared. Valerio was all withdrawn, holed up in that estate of his in India. Never went out. He was healing, able to move around in a wheelchair on his own, but he kept that big guy with him. The one with brain damage?"

"Horse," Jules said. "Never thought he'd live more than a few months. He survived?"

"Money," Charlie said. "Gets you the best care. Experimental treatments."

"Right." Prihya paced, holding everyone's attention, while the rest of the control room's inhabitants filed out at Tane's silent behest. When they were alone, she spoke more candidly. "He was manic a lot of the time. Lots of drugs keeping him going, obsessed with those scrolls that we couldn't open."

"An ancient bit of ingenuity," Toby explained to Sally. "We recovered some ourselves but, likewise, couldn't get into the cases. Like the old puzzle boxes, there was a tiny vial of acid that dissolved the contents if accessed incorrectly. We suspect some version of a lock or like a safe combination is needed to unscrew them. But they date from tens of thousands of years before we thought writing began, so I wouldn't expect to interpret them, even if we got them open. Not without—"

"Valerio managed it," Prihya said. "He used some sort of sonic device based on MRI scanning. When freezing the fluid didn't work, they had to alter the liquid some other way. They got the frequency wrong a few times, and it smashed the vials and destroyed the contents. After the third time, he ordered Horse to kill the person who messed up."

"That's not like him," Jules said. "He comes across as crazy, and murders when it's useful to him, but he ain't usually like that. Killing outa frustration."

"He's like that now," Prihya said. "Horse crushed that poor man's windpipe and watched him suffocate."

"And he wasn't some mindless thug," Dan said. "Aussie special forces. Tactical, efficient, brilliant soldier and close protection agent."

Prihya remained patient, holding herself crisply under the gaze of people who didn't trust her. Charlie had not liked the fact Toby kept in touch with her, and Harpal had floated the idea she might have been delivering planted intel. Fake reports to keep them on the back foot. Toby believed she was on the right side, though. That Valerio had manipulated her into believing LORI were the cold-hearted villains, and she'd acted accordingly. When Valerio's true nature became clear during their sojourn in Africa, she'd switched to the side she saw as closer to her own ethics and ambitions.

She said, "The next people Valerio brought in to calibrate the scanner succeeded. To a degree. An x-ray negative showed markings I couldn't make head nor tail of. I spent days trying to decode them and had access to all Valerio had gotten his hands on so far. But there was no Rosetta Stone. No key. He was getting quieter, saying less every time I reported no progress."

Toby firmed up his gaze toward her. "No wonder you fled."

"I looked up some old colleagues, somewhere off the grid."

"The guys Tane was undercover with," Jules said. "They're rural, pushing far-fetched conspiracy theories..."

"Exactly," Tane said. "We kept tabs on them, and when this unknown girl showed up—someone we'd connected to your pal Valerio—we checked her out. Recruited her. And here we are."

"Top secret." Prihya faced Toby. "It was a bummer that I dropped out with no warning. But I wasn't allowed to make contact."

Bridget said, "*She* could be working *you*."

"Feeding back to her boss," Harpal added.

Steely analysis, unblinking, from Charlie needed no words. Dan gave a sigh and pinched his lips, unwilling to voice his dissent from Toby's relief at finding her here. Only Jules appeared nonplussed by her reappearance.

Prihya said, "I'm not working anyone."

"We had her under surveillance for long enough," Tane said. "And we continuously monitor all workers here. She isn't in cahoots with anyone but us."

Prihya aimed a smile his way. "What do you need me to do here?"

"Perhaps you can explain this better than me." Tane patted the stone compartment that appeared to be linked to the orb and the plate above. "I've been out of the country for months. You've made some upgrades."

"Of course. If everyone here can get over past mistakes?" She stared at the LORI contingent one at a time, challenging anyone to voice further suspicions. "Good. Then this is what we call an 'activation suite.' It welcomes either densely muscled or DNA-rich participants who can activate the tech..." She dipped her chin toward Jules. "We have reverse engineered some of the active molecules of the meteor rock that made up those bangles and gear it to existing DNA that we keep on-site."

Charlie's eyebrows popped up. "Reverse engineer?"

"That's an oversimplification. Much cleverer people than me—physicists—took years to work out the behavior of certain particles. Now we can charge this up and keep the sphere going."

"Like a capacitor." Charlie had branched off, all business, her distaste for Prihya all but forgotten. She climbed up on the console desk and examined the array of wires and a stack of other equipment. Cables fed in and out, specs flashing up on screens that required Prihya to enter a code on her e-tablet to unlock. "This is incredible."

"And we found something else while you were away." Prihya gave Tane another shy smile and crossed to one of the frosted panels and tapped on the frame. It morphed into a display screen, black with symbols and glyphs. They were positioned in the form of an arch, like they had been inscribed around a doorway. "We used a contraption similar to the one Valerio had. I don't know why I didn't think of it when I first got here. But we scanned the casing that the Elder Race left here—"

"Sorry, 'Elder Race'?" Bridget said.

"What you call the Witnesses, the New Zealand scientists call the Elder Race. The branch of humanity that existed before ours."

All nodded slowly, getting the idea, understanding all this was connected. All led back to the people who'd disappeared just prior to the Younger Dryas epoch. What was more, Toby recognized the glyphs as the ancient language Bridget had partially decoded. And since Prihya had broken into their chateau and accessed Bridget's work, Prihya would know it, too.

Toby said, "That's the Witnesses' language. The precursor to Indus. What does it say? I see codes for power, for circuit, and for... I don't know enough. Bridget?"

"For engineer," Bridget answered, drawing closer to the screen.

"I remembered a bit of what I'd learned in the buildup to Valerio's scroll obsession," Prihya said. "I could see the dimensions of the chamber were no accident.

"It needs a 'worthy knight' to activate it," Bridget said, concentrating on the symbols. "It's been a while since I had access to this material, but it looks like a different type of DNA to Jules and the bangles, or the neutrino network."

Still frowning, Bridget turned to Prihya, who was nodding, grinning. Bridget mirrored the grin, as if the pair were best girlfriends bonding over boyfriend news.

"Isn't that extinct?" Bridget said, returning to the screen. "How can you—"

"What is it?" Jules asked, scanning the screen too. Although he'd be able to recall the meaning of any symbols he'd observed with perfect clarity, Toby had seen how Bridget's mind turned differently to Jules's. While the lad was like a wild computer, in addition to his eidetic qualities, he determined facts and drew conclusions based on available evidence, whereas Bridget's process was more creative and imaginative. "Ain't I needed? Because if that's the case, I can jump on a plane and go home."

"It's overengineered," Charlie said, hopping down from her examination of the melding of twenty-first century electronics and millennia-old mechanics. "There are machines on top of machines, redundancies that could be eradicated by stripping it back to its core purpose and setting up from scratch."

"Unfortunately, we can't do that," Prihya said. "We built one part that performed one task, but we needed to add something else to test it. Then the next piece wouldn't work without the middle one. If we turn it off to dismantle and improve the efficiency—"

"You're concerned the orb will deactivate," Charlie finished for her. "And then you'll never get it back on. Even if you plug the right person's DNA into the compartment."

Prihya gestured loosely toward the machinery. "So we can do things with it, interrogate the makeup of the rock used to house the trigger person's DNA, but we can't be sure we've covered absolutely everything. The modern world doesn't have the technology to examine the workings of it. The circuits around the world between the orbs—the neutrinos that started talking to one another and woke up this machine—works on a unique system to the one disseminating information and sending the signals. The Elder Race, your Witnesses, added to existing phenomena, which might be natural, or even yet another distinct race."

"Yes," Toby said, feeling the need to speak up after digesting as much as he could. "We learned that when Jules's mind linked to the machine in Africa. They were built or adapted by an even earlier precursor to the Witnesses, or perhaps a parallel branch on the evolutionary tree."

"I'm lost," Dan said. "Just for once, can't we pretend it's aliens?"

Harpal patted him on the shoulder. "Don't think too hard about it. It goes: us, then hop back to the Sumerians who invented language. Before that, it was the ice age and those surviving people. Centuries earlier, it's the Toba catastrophe, which is about the time the Witnesses disappeared and humans started getting cleverer. Go back, and you have our primitive ancestors living at the same time as the Witnesses for generations. Only, our Witness friends lived separately and built all these places. What our mates here are saying is, these rocks that the Witnesses used to accomplish all sorts... no one knows if they formed naturally, or if there was another, even older race who set it up."

Dan stared at Harpal, his old friend. Toby had hoped that this mission might bring them back together, that recovering their initial prize would be enough to re-employ Harpal and keep the family unit together. It didn't seem like financial recompense was on the cards, though, so maybe they would have to wait a little longer.

"What I'm hearing," Dan said, "is that there's a possibility... no matter how tiny... that these orb things talking to each other through the earth... might, possibly—"

"Still not aliens, big guy," Jules said. "More likely that solar flare and magnetic pole flip Toby mentioned back in Alabama. Right, Professor Smith?"

Toby stuttered a moment. Few people used his title, so he was unsure whether there was sarcasm present. "Yes, indeed. The magnetic poles may well have flipped due to a huge astrophysical event. This may have had other consequences, too. Perhaps... yes, they could have used the shields to deflect an extinction level event."

"You don't *know* that, though," Dan said. "Could be used to hide from hostiles, too. Not just deflect their attack."

"Show them," Bridget said.

Toby's curiosity ramped up. He wasn't usually slow on the uptake, but Bridget and Jules had plainly worked out something he'd missed. "Show us what?"

"The interconnectedness of the machines might be an accident," Bridget said.

Again, Prihya nodded. "It needs unique DNA, which is how we know it's so utterly tied to nature, to the Earth itself. The person who activates this has to be in sync with the planet."

"Not the universe?" Charlie said. "Because quantum entanglement isn't just an Earth thing."

"The only universal points relevant here are Earthbound."

"Universe?" Dan said. "It's sounding more like—"

"It's time," Tane said. "I promised you'd be amazed. I have to check now..." He'd reverted to his earlier excited manner.

"Wait," Sally said. "This isn't it? I thought an ancient race of super-brained bipeds with an impenetrable power source sounded pretty incredible."

"Pfft," Dan said. "We've seen that a dozen times."

Prihya placed her hand on the frosted screen to the side of the symbols. "Now?"

"It's time," Tane said.

Prihya placed her other hand on the glass, generating a beep on her e-tablet. She took back her hands and entered a code. The frosting faded and all the panels converted to transparent glass, revealing the volcano's interior in all its glory.

The lower angle made it look wider and more complex, with

routes furrowed through the trees, and a sparkling lake—or large pond—nearby. Above looked like a mist layer on a chilly morning, concealing this veritable Garden of Eden from the uninvited.

"Oh, my god," Bridget gasped.

"That's..." Jules leaned on the glass, one forearm horizontal, his head leaning on it as if he was out of breath.

"What?" Dan said. "We saw this from the chopper."

Toby rarely agreed with Dan when he was being dismissive of something intriguing, but in this case, it was just a new angle.

Except... it wasn't.

Harpal slung his arm around Dan and adjusted his position, pointing at something in particular. Toby followed his directions and blinked hard.

Sally, again, took off her glasses and rubbed them before putting them back on.

"That can't be," Toby said, his heart thrumming hard.

"It is," Tane replied. "The center point of the Guardian Protocols. The reason I do what I do."

"Okay, you got me," Jules said. "*Now* I'm amazed."

CHAPTER TWENTY-THREE

THE DRAGON'S PIT, NORTH KOREA

The shield, which Ah Dae-Sun delivered last night on his way to his next mission, reflected the Executive's face, distorting his fingertips as he reached for it. Hanging in the cradle that would deliver it to the matrix and seal Korea's safety forever, it was truly a marvel; a surface that shone golden at first glance, but on closer inspection it shimmered and swirled like a liquid yet was solid to the touch. Alone, surrounded by all he'd achieved, this was as close to isolation as he ever came. And he had never been closer to immortality than this moment.

Ryom Jung-Hwan had spent his life enveloped in security. Constantly. There was no telling when an enemy from abroad or a jealous rival from within the Republic might strike. The Party tolerated Executive Ryom more than accepted him, largely because he exemplified an economic success story admired in the West. This led many ultra-loyalists to believe his company should be nationalized, owned, and controlled by the ruling government. However, he'd taken precautions that made a hostile act all but futile and would serve no one.

Because of his company's sprawling nature, Ryom had sunk tentacles in every continent and in every country with a GDP sufficient to benefit his profits. He'd started with state-sanctioned partnerships via friendly Chinese companies, learning about numbered accounts and how to hide behind shell corporations. It was a facility their enemies used to fleece the rest of the world, so why shouldn't Koreans take advantage of this? Especially when it enhanced his people's lives.

Indirectly, of course.

The ruling party were clear that they didn't like Ryom Jung-Hwan operating with such impunity, in pronounced contradiction to their founding principles. But the wealth he brought in, the respect he commanded with foreign powers thanks to his under-the-radar leaps in research and development, made up for a compromise in philosophy. The only condition for allowing him to work this way was absolute secrecy; no one in the country, nor within enemy states, could know of their agreement.

Enquiries and assaults on his Antipodean holdings by Tane Wiremu and his infernal NZSIS colleagues had almost brought about Ryom Jung-Hwan's downfall. If it weren't for the Dragon's Pit and the ultimate defensive weapon he had promised the party, he would most certainly be wearing the baggy, gray coveralls of the people digging and constructing this place rather than the genuine Armani suit he sported—and which he had to present as a very good counterfeit.

This secret arrangement had one major downside: there were many brainwashed idiots out there who believed in the deification of the country's rulers and worshipped at their feet with religious zeal. Which was ironic considering religion was banned, and rightfully so. But those fools who idolized out of love and blinkered obedience rather than fraught co-existence pondered in secret if Executive Ryom held something over the party, and if doing away with him might somehow benefit the greater glory of the Republic.

They were almost as big a threat as the aggressive saber-rattling of western countries. Not as destructive or evil as the world's policemen—otherwise known as the United States and their lapdogs of Great Britain, France, and a dozen others whose pious arrogance and objective hypocrisy fueled projects like this one. But just because the mosquito was small, didn't mean it could be neglected.

In the depths of the Dragon's Pit, sheltered by the Dragon's Teeth mountain range, his safety was all-but assured. Only he and his most trusted deputy knew the abort codes to security measures that would trigger, should any harm come to him. At times like these, where he dared not invite hired bodyguards into the true heart of his empire, he activated the pulse monitor that fed through his wristwatch, a dead man's switch like no other. If one single employee or prisoner were to assassinate him or cause him sufficient damage to elevate his adrenaline-to-blood ratio above a preset limit, every man, woman, and child in the valley would perish.

He was both proud of the technological monstrosity and full of regret that it was necessary.

The section he had swept through at four a.m., after arriving unannounced by helicopter, was all but deserted. Forty feet underground and cooled by massive turbines from the dam built by Chinese contractors and engineers, the vestibule led to a vault like no other: a chamber housed in a cavern large enough for a funfair, with a private-plane-sized construction at the center. It reminded Executive Ryom of an MRI machine surrounded by scaffolding to accommodate the engineers, operatives, and for the person they were headed to New Zealand to retrieve.

A special someone whose existence had only recently come to their attention.

The phone in his pocket vibrated. Only two people had this number and Pang Pyong-Ho was only permitted to use it in the event Ah Dae-Sung became incapacitated—through capture, serious injury, or death. Here, it was Ah Dae-Sung with an update.

"We are in position," Commander Ah said. "The subjects have arrived. You were correct. There is more happening at that location than we could observe. Is the facility ready once we acquire the individual?"

"You are questioning me?"

"Not at all, Executive Ryom. But we may have to move quickly. And it is likely we will be exposed. I can see no way for subtlety."

"Do not worry about speed. Or stealth. Our extraction plan is in place. The shield will be lowered into the machine as soon as it is active. Once we can control the orb, if my calculations are correct, we will secure Korea's safety for all time."

An uncharacteristic pause made Ryom wonder if there was interference on the line, but Ah Dae-Sung asked something even less characteristic than the hesitation: "Must we spread a tsunami of energy? Would an umbrella launched from the top of the mountain not do the same job?"

The Executive had asked himself the same question. If he hadn't, he may have gotten angry with his deputy. "The risk is too great. We can demonstrate the defensive capability of our new weapon, but you know how arrogant the Americans are. Always believing they will triumph, regardless. No, unless we show that we can crush them as freely as..." He recalled how he viewed the internal enemies, those jealous at his position. "As easily as swatting a mosquito, they will launch wave after wave of attack. A war like that will lead to more loss of life than our initial launch. Have faith, my friend."

"I do not question your decision," Dae-Sung replied. "I am thankful for your clarity. We are ready to act. I will call you when we have secured the asset."

Executive Ryom hung up and once again gazed over the machine he had created. A cavern of two halves: one side for the orb and the engineering marvel, bathed in light and raised as if for an amateur stage show; the other fenced off for safety, currently dark, ready for senior military personnel, for officials he would invite to observe Korea's crowning glory, once he could be sure it was safe for them.

And also to witness Executive Ryom's inauguration as the head of the ruling party.

Who else but he could have harnessed the power of an ancient, buried technology without dissecting it first? Who else could have discerned its purpose and decoded the breadcrumbs that led from this land to Achilles' shield, and the dark purpose he could reap?

And who else possessed the iron will to do what had to be done for the glory of his people?

In less than forty-eight hours, he would be a god. And no one, not even the party leaders of the country he loved, would stand in his way.

CHAPTER TWENTY-FOUR

NEW ZEALAND

For all his adult life, Jules had struggled with emotion. To achieve what he'd felt he needed to, there had been no room in his brain. He'd battled to attain physical perfection, partly to serve him in the retrieval artefacts from deserts, mountains, deep under cities and under oceans, and also to burglarize those who had stolen without ethical boundaries and to survive the criminal networks that facilitated such trades. He'd studied for mental agility to investigate those networks and the individuals who benefited, to ascertain the locations of those artefacts based on clues penned hundreds, sometimes thousands, of years ago. Emotions interfered with his work, but he was not immune to them, he just buried them and pushed people away so ethereal notions like friendship wouldn't weigh him down.

Now, leaning on the control room's glass—more of an observation point—he struggled to name the feelings welling up inside and bursting from his chest.

Project Ahua was more than an exploration of lost architecture and construction. It was even more than the intricate examination of the orbs and their magnetically bound tech. Jules had never expected to see anything like this, presented in the deep, dead center of a volcano. Cloaking technology was one thing. This was something else.

"We've named them 'homo colossus'," Prihya said.

They looked human, roaming through the forest, its widely spaced trees allowing a view that was most definitely not an intricate fake. Four of them. Clothed in simple adornments, reminiscent of the costumes on the actors they glimpsed in the village down in the valley, but simpler, more practical. Leading the group was a ten-foot-three-inch-tall male with thick black hair on his head and face, a low brow, and a neck roughly the width of a refrigerator. The woman stood almost nine feet, her hair the same color but shorter than the man's with only wisps of it sprouting from her cheeks. Two juveniles marched alongside. Going by human growth rate, Jules ranked them as teenagers, one a little older than the other.

A churning mix of wonder and horror made Jules's head spin. Since no one else seemed able to speak, he guessed they were feeling the same.

No one, except those who'd known about it all along.

Tane said, "They were cloned from DNA retrieved from bone marrow. We found the bones—or people who worked on this before me did—in the 1980s. It wasn't until the human genome got decoded that our guys even dared think about bringing them back."

"The original intention was to study evolution," Prihya said. "This place was covered by a net, of all things. When the orb turned on, discoveries accelerated exponentially."

Jules found his voice. "You used them to activate and power your machine."

"A ten square mile commune populated entirely by giant humans," Tane said. "They have more hair, two-to-three times the size of a gorilla. Their DNA is closer to ours than a chimpanzee's—and they were our closest living relative."

"In *nature*," Charlie pointed out.

"Now we have long lost cousins," Toby said.

Of them all, Professor Garcia was the one whose face glowed brightest. She pressed her entire body against the glass, a simpering expression radiating, her arms spread as if trying to hug the family.

"Would you like to meet them?" Tane asked.

Sally peeled herself from the pane and joined the others in surrounding Prihya and Tane, like a huddle before a basketball game.

Bridget said, "They won't tear our faces off?"

Tane laughed. "Don't let their appearance fool you. They're big, and their dense muscles make them incredibly strong, but like you and I, they have the capacity for reason. They might look like apes from a distance, but they're not."

"In fact," Prihya said, "their first instinct upon meeting new people is curiosity rather than fear or suspicion. Possibly because their genes make them *so* tough."

"How tough?" Dan asked.

"We estimate they could bench a couple of school busses without breaking sweat," Tane replied. "Their skin is thicker than elephant hide, although they *can* be cut. We haven't completely tested it, but based on what we've been able to examine, their skin combined with their muscle density will absorb a .50 caliber bullet from six feet away."

Jules whistled appreciation and saw the same from Harpal and Charlie.

Dan said, "Like shooting a bullet into sand."

"Right," Prihya said. "So—time's wasting. We have work to do. Are we going to say hello first?"

Access to the forest floor was through a door on the rock-wall side of the control station, set aside from the orb and activation suite. They descended the hairpin metal staircase and emerged onto hardscrabble ground.

"Stick together," Tane said. "They're friendly but not harmless."

Jules tingled all over. Couldn't drag the smile from his face. He had no idea why this euphoria had gripped him so hard, but this was the first time in years he'd been unable to contain himself. In the past, such strong emotional waves were largely negative: grief, anger, fear. Occasionally, he found himself beaming uncontrollably when he recovered some stolen relic and returned it to its rightful place, but that was nothing like this.

Why?

And why was Bridget the only one who seemed so troubled? She had looked as impressed as Jules at first, but since descending the stairs she'd had time to think and must have snagged on something that reigned in her excitement.

As they marched in a huddle, Prihya explained, "While they are intelligent, on a par with the average homo sapien, their minds work differently. We can communicate do a degree, even co-exist, but they have little self-awareness beyond the usual animalistic need to eat, mate, and survive."

"They have a language?" Bridget asked, her voice small, tinged with caution.

"Their vocal cords can't form complex words. They do have a proto-language, and names for one another. To us, it sounds like a series of grunts and snorts, some higher-pitched syllables in there too. We've taught them some basic sign language too, so—"

"How?" Bridget was frowning now, walking more slowly as they came upon the family, their movement visible through the trees.

"Sign language isn't difficult for—"

"No, I mean, how did they discover their language? You can't retain language in your genes. You don't learn it as you grow from an infant. Project Ahua bred these creatures in a lab. If they're not able to learn English or other modern language, how did they evolve this 'proto-language' as you call it."

"I'm interested in that, too," Garcia said. "If they follow genetic imperatives to survive, that's the same a cat going feral. How is it different from abandoning a child with food and water for years, then looking in on them occasionally?"

"It's before both our times," Tane said. "The original pioneers of this were pensioners when we started. They've since passed the baton to this generation. We're the custodians. All those moral questions —"

"Conveniently sidestepped," Charlie said.

Toby raised a finger, one of his lightbulb moments. "Not side-stepped. Adopted."

Prihya held her ground, and all halted.

Toby said, "If anyone here is concerned about morality, it's me. I lost my position and my prestige in the House of Windsor precisely because of my ethical qualms about our activities. Bridget, Charlie, I share your concerns. Sally, I share your curiosity. But these creatures exist. They are alive. The moral questions were answered long before Prihya and Tane took on this... responsibility. And I'm glad it's fallen to them, not some predatory bureaucrat, or private financier. Can you imagine what would happen if someone thought to *profit* from this?"

"Thank you, Toby," Prihya said. "Took the words right out of my mouth. I have little to add, except that the welfare of our giant friends is paramount."

"It's literally in her contract," Tane said.

"Admittedly, we use them in the lab. We have little choice, given threats like Valerio. And now, the North Korean executive. But they are never harmed. We have a simulated chamber down here, and that feeds into the setup upstairs." Prihya glanced Charlie's way. "Another addition that we can't retcon to be more efficient without taking the system offline."

"You experiment on them?" Bridget said. "Like rats?"

"Bridge," Jules said. "Let's concentrate on what we can affect. What's more important? Figurin' out the ethics, or stopping Ah Dae Sung and his boss, and the death they're trying to bring?"

Bridget stared at him. "You think it's okay? Bringing these creatures to life and... enslaving them here to... to..."

Jules was about to answer when movement up ahead drew his attention. Big movement. A lumbering shadow, parting branches, plodding forward.

Prihya and Tane stepped aside, and the male giant loomed toward them.

His dimensions were not quite an ape, not quite human. Despite his ten-foot height, he looked almost squat, which Jules supposed was the musculature compensating for the body's greater mass. His form brought to mind the greater thickness of the fossilized bones in the Alabama cavern. The other three were shaped similarly, wide but muscular, with the heavy brows and extra body hair. They followed and remained behind the big man.

"This is Gilim," Prihya said, plainly amused by the apprehension radiating from the LORI contingent. "His wife is Nan, his children Noroth and Wade. Gilim and Nan see the world through an innocent's eyes, like everything is exciting and new. Noroth is a coy one, quiet, but very loving, and he likes to draw... sort of. They're markings we think represent things he's done, food he's eaten, but it's hard to tell. Wade loves frolicking in the ponds, loves being in and around water."

"Tolkien," Jules said.

Harpal held as still as he would if facing a growling junkyard dog. "I don't remember giants from those books."

Jules stepped forward. Gilim kneeled, his brow wrinkling more, shading his eyes. Jules kept going, one hand outstretched. "They didn't feature much. They're mentioned in spells, conversations, things like that. Wade isn't, though."

"That's a name in some of his more obscure literature." Sally had come alongside Jules, eager to participate. "Wade was possibly a sea giant. It's more in Germanic folklore than anywhere else."

Prihya said, "You know your stuff."

Jules extended his arm farther. He was smiling, could sense the stretch of skin around his mouth, his eyes. A deep, booming chortle rumbled inside Gilim, his own hand passing through the air. Tentatively, Jules remained on course, and so did Gilim. Jules placed his palm on Gilim's flattened fingers, the giant's hand the size of a manhole cover. He'd be able to engulf Jules's torso in his grip.

Jules pressed lightly on the skin, which felt rough and leathery, and when he turned the hand over so his fingertips pointed up, the giant clearly had fingerprints, too—dirty, ingrained whorls with filthy nails. He smelled like a wet dog, but... damnit. None of that mattered.

Jules said, "Hey, Gilim. Nice to meet you."

"Careful," Tane warned.

Jules regarded his colleagues, who had been emboldened to come forward a little hastily, now slowing.

Sally touched her hand to Gilim's too, and the enormous man before them grinned wide. His teeth were a gleaming ivory, and the breath that huffed out in another joyous laugh bore the stench of vegetation.

"No meat?" Jules said.

"They're not quite vegetarian," Prihya replied. "They can digest cooked chicken or venison—they catch their own deer sometimes—

but anything heavier makes them ill. They'll scoop up a pile of bugs in those huge hands and shovel them down, though. Crickets, cockroaches, anything crunchy. But what we think of as meat? No, they don't handle it so well."

"There'll be no grinding my bones to make bread, then," Toby said, close enough to join Jules and Sally. He placed his hand on Gilim's as Sally had done. "Oh, my."

Gilim evidently found something funny and let out another of his throaty chuckles. He eased back, grunted a few times, and then his "wife" and children ambled through. They trod lightly, only their bulk making them appear shambling as they moved. It was a kind-of nervous exploration, a nerd at a party full of popular kids, or a kitten making its first steps into a garden.

"I know you have misgivings," Prihya said, aiming her comment mainly at Bridget, but taking in all of them as she approached Nan to take her hand. "But I assure you, the only tarnish on this place is that we control their reproduction. It can't sustain a population that expands out of control. We've limited it to two family units initially, but we'll let nature take its course for the next couple of generations."

"There's another family?" Sally said, sliding her hand from Gilim's to make room for Dan and Harpal.

"Less fanciful names." Prihya smiled at the meeting of the two races, Charlie and Harpal wandering away from Gilim to say hi to Nan. The boys held back but watched carefully. "Rosso is the other male. Issa the female. Lucy and Holly the daughters. Holly was born on Christmas Day. Cheesy, but, hey."

"You control their genders, too," Bridget said, coldly. "Boys here. Girls there."

"Genetic variation is necessary. We hope to let them flourish from hereon-in, that they'll populate only this basin. But if we can't, these will be the last of their kind."

"Why?" Dan asked.

"We can't reintroduce them to the world," Tane said. "They're not the original creatures. No original culture or language. They might be susceptible to illness or pollutants in the air. We've no idea how to serve them best outside this environment. It would be cruel to bring them into a modern world. Like sending a saber tooth cat or woolly mammoth into the wild."

Bridget seemed sad as she repeated the gesture the others were employing, her tiny hand to Nan's massive one. "It's all good and well saying you're doing your best for them. What if they escaped?"

"They've shown no interest in anything outside of the shield," Prihya said.

"Could be what works outside works inside," Jules offered. "People visiting don't pry on the volcano, so why not the people living here?"

Tane sighed. "Maybe. But we clued the local Maori chiefs in. They know what we have here. They understand the need for balance. For once, the Maori and white-majority government are together."

It was so peaceful, utterly beautiful, Jules could have hung out here for hours.

"Gilim is the alpha," Prihya said. "They know who is in charge, understand we bring them food, and they've seen us medicate them when sick or hurt. They are always watching, always working things out. If they were prisoners here, if they wanted to get out, they would."

"Hence the bank vault of a panic room," Charlie said. "If they ever go berserk?"

"If that happens, we follow precautions," Tane said. "There are gas nozzles here and there, built into the floor. Tranq darts are useless, and the gas is far more humane."

Prihya stroked one of the boys and he giggled. "We used it once when they all got sick, some cold or flu thing that responded to a barrel-full of antibiotics. But it's not in widespread use."

"I have to get some pictures." Sally fumbled in her pocket for a cellphone, pulling it out in haste.

The Kiwi agent gently moved in front of her. "You know that's not going to happen."

"I have to." Sally attempted to get around him.

Her sudden, faintly aggressive move startled Gilim, his gigantic head turning her way, and his hand pulled away from Dan and Toby. The two juveniles crowded their mother.

"Protective," Jules commented.

"It's okay. Nothing to worry about." Prihya's hands fluttered in sign language, reducing the giants' concern without eradicating it. "Okay, I think visiting hours are over."

"I have to exonerate myself," Sally said. "The board think I'm a kook. They want to fire me. I have to prove this. Show them—"

"In time, maybe," Tane said, accepting the handset. "But that can only happen once we understand the tech, when we can figure out how these guys can be incorporated into academic teachings. So they won't be exploited. Then, and only then, can we consider revealing this to the world."

A persistent beeping sounded on Prihya's belt. She checked it and removed what looked to be a cellphone but wasn't any brand Jules recognized. Must have been particular to this facility, an internal comms device to prevent anything happening like Sally planned to do.

Tane moved to her, and they both listened, concern darkening their faces.

"Time to go," Tane said. "The listening station. Now."

CHAPTER TWENTY-FIVE

"How the hell did they find us?" Tane demanded.

The *how* wasn't important to Dan, though. Only what to do about it. "Defensive options," he said. "Talk to us."

Tane had led them into the security suite—the listening post, as they'd called it—where one operator reported that, "Facial recognition says a few are DPRNK civilians. No military records. But they entered the country on Chinese passports. Same with the other three that flagged up."

Tane rubbed his chin, which rasped with two days of stubble. "No Ah Dae-Sung or Pang Pyong-Ho."

"Not yet," Jules said, having read the report over the man's shoulder. "They could be hiding from the cameras."

"Or giving commands from elsewhere," Dan suggested.

Tane quickly digested the intelligence reports submitted from the dozen or so eyes in the town a couple of klicks south and hit them with the highlights. Namely, ten Chinese tourists who did not appear interested in the traditional Maori dances, local history, or the menu on offer for that evening's hangi. Two of them matched the individual likenesses of people NZSIS had asked them to look out for. It was not unusual for the village to see large Chinese tour groups, but they rarely comprised so many athletic, bleak-eyed civilians as these appeared to be. Eight men. Two women.

Jules said, "Don't sound like they're trying too hard to blend in."

"Agreed," Dan said. "Either they didn't expect you to have extra people in place, or they're coming at us soon. And probably hard."

"Then we get to them first." Tane leaned on the barrier overlooking the control room and, through that, the enclosure. Anger darkened his face. "They didn't track us. That means someone blabbed."

Dan wasn't the only one who looked toward Prihya.

"Now, hang on a second," she said. "Just because I—"

"What?" Charlie said. "Worked against us for over a year? Am employed by a billionaire psychopath who thinks nothing of slaughtering innocents?"

Dan pulled his gun and aimed it at Prihya. "Search her."

All had backed away, watching her face go slack, her mouth curling into something akin to disgust. Her eyes were wet. The curl quivered, and she bit her bottom lip. "I didn't do this. I've been here for months. They showed up when *you* did." She jabbed a finger toward Dan. "*You* brought them here, *not* me."

"Ain't got time for this," Jules said. "Toby, step in here."

"It isn't our jurisdiction," Toby agreed. "Agent Wiremu and the staff here should—"

"No." Tane moved in front of Dan's gun, facing Prihya, as if he could read her mind should he stare hard enough. "We need to deal with the threat. *Then* we work out how they got here."

Dan lowered the gun. "Fine. What are our options? Assuming that's an assault team recce, we can catch them by surprise if we move quick. Or we shore up the defenses here and wait on reinforcements."

"There are no reinforcements nearby. Just intel."

Tane pulled away from Prihya, returning to the console with the monitoring station, the weather, the dome instruments. He opened a secure channel and got straight through to the minister who was on screen with Colin Waterston.

"You heard?" Tane said.

"Yes," Julia Grainger replied. "We received the same report you did. What are your intentions?"

"We'll keep the research station submerged. But I need permission to engage them. Lethal force. I can't see a way to keep them out if we have to play nice."

Colin nodded beside her, and Dan felt an oily film on his skin at the man agreeing with his own first choice. "You have the military option, Julia. The Americans are talking directly to the North Korean authorities, but they are still denying an incursion."

"But that's what this is," Dan put in. "Foreign troops invading a top-secret research facility."

"Ma'am," Tane said. "We need your authorization for the assault weapons."

Grainger's unhappy glint showed she was uncomfortable, but she decided quickly. "Lethal force is approved but keep it quiet and away from any kids. No civilian fatalities."

"Got it. Thank you." After a couple more niceties, Tane signed off and stood tall. He faced the institute's contingent. "Action dudes and dudettes. We have a security team here to hold the perimeter. But I need people with training to take out the bad guys before they get here. Volunteers only, of course."

Dan was first to state the obvious. "I'm in."

"Me too," Harpal said.

"I'll neutralize them," Jules added. "But you know I don't kill. If that ain't good enough, I'll stay here."

"Probably best you do," Tane said. "This is not the time to get squeamish."

"I dunno." Harpal looked sideways at Jules, then back to Tane. "You want to draw them away from the civilians, he'd be the best person to do that."

Dan recalled how easily Jules moved over unfamiliar terrain, calculating complex distances, gaps, and timing. In vehicles or on foot, there was something seriously freaky about him. But... "Yeah, we take him. Charlie?"

"As much as I know you could use a sensible head, I'm staying here." Charlie shifted her kit around. "Someone has to figure out how all this connects to the site in Korea. We'll be safe with the current security measures. And if you guys can avoid that being necessary, maybe it'll mean they don't send anyone else to finish the job."

"Then we have a plan." Dan clapped Tane on the shoulder. "Lead the way."

Jules handed Bridget the backpack containing his bangles, removing a handful of gear as he said, "Your mission is more important than ours. We'll make sure you got time. But you and Charlie gotta figure this thing out. If it can be used to stop the big bad."

"I will," Bridget said, solemnly accepting the bag.

Tane hustled toward the steel staircase, calling a pair of security agents at the door. "Situation report is on your devices. Follow the protocol." He pointed toward the remaining team members, all standing aside from Prihya, who was now hugging herself, watching the jungle-like scenery below. "Stay with them. Protect them and beware of any unauthorized comms."

That last comment drew a sharp glance from Prihya before she returned to her self-imposed vigil.

"With me." Tane marched onward.

The four men proceeded in silence down the first pristine corridor, out another set of security doors, and into an elevator. The tense silence during the ride up reminded Dan of the approach to missions from his military days. All focused, all knowing this might be the last time they were all together.

It wasn't supposed to be like this. The Lost Origins Recovery Institute was an archaeology club, one that ventured into hostile territory occasionally, and often snatched artefacts from under the noses of men, women, and companies hoping to profit from certain finds. One of Dan's first projects with Toby was to beat a drilling company to the site of a petrified Crusader fort. Not valuable in itself, but it gave them the final resting place of a fabled knight, one of many on which the amalgamated character of Saint George, the patron saint of England, was thought to be based. If they hadn't taken the chance and placed themselves in danger, the company would have destroyed the fort's remains as they blasted sand and rock that had concealed it for over six centuries—all in the name of exploring for oil.

Those were the missions Dan relished. The ones they hired him for.

They were not a SpecOps unit.

The elevator opened at the top, facing into the caldera so it couldn't be seen from the valley. The wind buffeted them and the cold bit hard, and when Dan checked his surroundings, he found they could see for miles. A second helicopter pad waited twenty feet down, a camo net obscuring the equipment from anyone observing via satellite or drone. An Eagle helicopter's engines were whining to life. It was the type of aircraft used by police forces, so it would have more oomph than the chopper that brought them in.

Surrounded by what looked like natural rocks and pumice, trees, and bushes, Tane flipped open a hidden hatch and placed his hand on a scanner. A locker opened, the door sliding aside to reveal a small arsenal of firearms.

"Nice." Dan selected an MP5A3 and a belt to strap across him containing spare magazines. "And that?"

Tane handed him the Benelli M3 tactical shotgun and a case of shells. "Be my guest."

As Dan stowed the MP5A3 on his back and accepted the piece of raw firepower, Tane helped himself to a Benelli too, along with a Glock 17 and a MAG 58 machine gun.

"In case we need cover from the chopper," Tane explained, referencing the larger weapon.

Harpal selected an identical submachine gun to Dan's and a Glock 17, checking they were ready to go. "Let's hope we don't need any of this."

Jules said, "I'll stick to my own kit."

Dan picked out one of the compact Glocks and offered it to Jules, handle first. "At least take it. One magazine. In case you have to point it at someone. Who knows, maybe you can... I dunno, use it to fire over their heads. Or pop a slug in someone's thigh."

Jules stared at it. Unusually quiet for him.

"Come on." Dan put it in his hand. "You know it makes sense."

"You a cop or not?" Tane asked. "Better to have it and not need it than need it and not have it. Right?"

Jules said nothing but helped himself to a holster.

Kid must be more spooked than he let on.

Tane took them down to the pad where the Eagle was ready to launch. The net withdrew via some mechanism and they climbed on board. They strapped in two-by-two, facing one another in their seats, and donned ear defenders and mics. Their pilot was a Maori with similar face ink to Tane's.

"Bobby Arono. Meet the action dudes." Tane fired off their names, and the pilot pumped a fist at each in turn, then got back to his job. "Hold tight, folks."

Within minutes they rose high above the caldera's rim and banked to the south.

"Do we have an actual plan yet?" Dan asked through the helicopter's mics.

"I'm gonna recon," Jules said. "Are we using those?"

Tane was pulling a set of walkie-talkies from under the seat. "Not quite bone conducting subvocal ear buds, but they're small enough to go mostly unnoticed."

Dan took one of the units, a walkie the size of an iPhone that would clip to his belt, then fed an earpiece and throat microphone. They'd used similar spec in the Rangers, although these were less bulky.

"Don't freeze up," Tane told Jules. "These fellas are vouching for you, but as far as I can tell you're still a civilian."

The helicopter dropped lower than the town, its altitude falling below the lush, green hilltop that gave Kainga Pukepuke its ever-so-touristy name.

Jules said, "I don't freeze. I improvise."

"These aren't hired goons working for a paycheck." Tane glanced at Dan and Harpal, but his concern remained with Jules. "They're fundamentalists. They believe—almost like a cult—that a western invasion is inevitable, and they obviously need something other than that shield to finalize their plans. You have to be prepared." Tane pointed first to the Glock on Jules's belt, then to the left side of his chest. "Protect and serve, right, brah? You can do that here. If you got your head in the game."

Jules fixed on Tane like he was interrogating a murder suspect. "I'll do what I need to. Scout around. Get noticed. Draw them out. When we flew over earlier, I saw a track leadin' west through the trees. There's a river running beside your dead volcano. Plenty of chances for an ambush."

Again, Tane deferred to Dan.

Despite Jules's arrogance and his aversion to teamwork, Dan was confident. "Listen to the kid. He'll come good when we need him to."

Tane nodded. "Okay, Bobby, gotta find somewhere to set us down away from the town."

"Don't set down." Jules unclipped his belt and straightened his leg, accessing the baton he insisted on bringing everywhere instead of a gun. "Up ahead, that field. Get as low as you can."

"There's a rugby match on, man," Bobby Arono replied through the headphones.

Bobby flew up over the land, keeping them straight, Pukepuke coming into sight along with what resembled a football field, but the goals were shaped like a capital letter H.

Rugby. A sport Dan had never got his head around.

"Get low." Jules unclasped the hook side of his baton and made a massive step over Tane to access the sliding door. "If you don't set down, they don't know anyone got out. And you can't hide a helicopter. I just need at least thirty feet."

"We're at twenty meters," Bobby announced.

Jules cracked the door and the wind and rotor wash thundered inside. Measuring by sight and touch alone, Jules fed out a length of bungee cord, then opened the door fully.

Tane grabbed his arm. "What are you doing?"

"Relax," Harpal said. "Watch and enjoy it."

Dan had definitely not enjoyed it the first time Jules performed this trick near him. He'd landed on the wrong end of the kid's aikido flips and throws. It had proved useful in the past, although never at high speed on a moving vehicle.

"See ya." Jules jumped out.

Tane jerked forward to see what the hell this crazy kid just did.

CHAPTER TWENTY-SIX

It might have sounded ridiculous to the vast majority of Earth's population but dropping out of a moving helicopter felt natural to Jules. As the semi-conscious side of his brain snapped and crackled with definitive calculations of speed, wind shear, height, and the apparent softness of the ground, Jules saw the good he was doing. He was operating with full permission of the government, a law enforcement officer giving the orders, and a cause worth fighting for.

As his stomach looped into his throat at the sudden pull of gravity, the grappling hook section of his rapid descent line snagged the helicopter's skid and he plummeted for 1.5 seconds before the bungee rope slowed his fall. Since the drop wasn't from an immovable point, he had allowed an approximate value for how much roll the helicopter would yield and factored it in conservatively, expecting to end his journey around two feet above the grass. However, because he hadn't studied the Eagle model before, he had no baseline for its capabilities, and it proved a far sturdier bird than he'd guessed. As the elastic cord reached its apex, Jules found himself short of the ground by 6.2 feet.

Not a huge obstacle but traveling at fifty knots he wasn't confident of an injury-free landing. In the split-second in which he processed the speed, remaining drop, and taking in two teams of teenaged boys scattering from their rugby game, he let go of the baton.

Flying through the air thanks to his fierce momentum, Jules pulled his knees up to his chest, swung himself around using his body weight, and he adopted the tuck-and-roll approach as the field came up to meet him.

Better a bruised rib than torn knee cartilage.

As Jules hit the grass, he skimmed over it like a stone, popped up, expanded his legs and arms to create drag, and performed a simple somersault. He literally hit the ground running, his legs pistoning as he righted himself. But it was still too fast, and he stumbled, rolled once more, and sprang up, again at a sprint.

Finally, he was moving smoothly, able to absorb his surroundings.

It wasn't a full rugby game—ten on one side, nine on the other, all kitted out in shorts and either red or white long-sleeved shirts, mouth guards, and a sprinkling of soft helmets. Now the helicopter had swooped back into the sky, banking away from Kainga Pukepuke, all attention fell on Jules.

The biggest lad in a muddy red shirt called, "Hey!"

Jules kept running, eager to get out of the open. But rugby is a game of tackling, and these players had watched a man dressed in black drop out of the sky and interrupt their rugby match—a sport taken very seriously in this part of the world. The people working up at the lab had also made them aware that outsiders who mean to harm their sacred mountain could be in the area, so it was not an unreasonable assumption that Jules could have been one of them.

Luckily, in games of tackling, individuals hurling themselves at the target can be predictable. As Jules veered around the first, then skipped a diving tackle from the second, the two sides merged and swarmed toward him.

At one time, Jules had learned the rules of rugby, mainly because it had been a source of conversation during a job in which several British expats were involved during the Rugby World Cup. He didn't want to seem ignorant, or miss out on conversations, especially since he was gathering intelligence on a stolen bust of Alexander the Great.

This was how he knew the word for what faced him was "maul."

Usually, though, the target of the maul would have been holding the ball. A ruck happened on the floor; a maul happened when players were on their feet.

A ruck in the muck, a maul with the ball.

That this group of kids defending their village were clearly experienced players worked in Jules's favor. They seemed to be instinctively obeying the tactics from the game, one person taking point to initiate the tackle with four teammates backing him up. This allowed Jules to stutter in his sprint, leap in the air, and kick an incoming opponent in the chest. He somersaulted over the attempted maul and landed the other side.

As fast as these players were, Jules was always going to beat them in a dead sprint. He kept his head down, running free, extending the gap between him and them. Looking back, at least three players jogged toward sports bags left on the sidelines. One of them had a phone out before Jules could jump the barrier and flee around the side of the clubhouse.

They had flown over this village less than an hour earlier, so Jules had sealed the image from above in his mind. But it took concentration for him to apply it to ground-level navigation.

The manufactured village was based around a central circular point, a meeting place where they buried a pig carcass in the ground for several hours, roasting it over hot coals with herbs and vegetables, which they would serve to tourists paying a small fortune to not only enjoy a tour of Pukepuke but to dine with the guides and Maori people who lived over in Taone Pukepuke. A "hangi" as it was known.

Not that the details mattered much as he jogged through a deserted channel, arriving at a street where Maori men and women gathered in long coats, some of them open to the elements to reveal the traditional dress in which they would likely perform later. A break from rehearsals, it seemed. He hadn't run out into the group, so startled no one. Instead, he caught his breath and ensured no heroes from the rugby game had pursued.

No one.

Jules assessed himself for injuries, dusted mud from his shoulder and checked no muck had spotted his face. Once satisfied, he opened the heavy-duty jacket—the day being mild rather than outright cold—and pulled his shirt over the belt containing his throwing knives and spare mini flashbangs.

He strolled out from his spot, casual as you like, and looked around as if lost. He didn't even need to ask directions. A woman bearing a tattoo on her chin—her *moko kauae*—pointed towards the center of the village and said, "I think you took a wrong turn, mate. Your party'll be that way."

"Thanks." Jules acted suitably bashful, and speed walked away from the performers' eyes.

The village's construction reminded Jules of a western frontier town, which was unlikely to have been how an authentic village existed before white settlers descended upon the Land of the Long White Cloud. It served its purpose, though. The farther he wandered, the more facilities became clear, from a toilet block to a gift shop. Men and women of indeterminate nationalities milled around, exploring facsimiles of homes through the ages. On each dwelling, a guide delivered a quick hello and asked people if they wanted to know more about this stop on their tour. Like other staff here, like Tane, he didn't get the impression they resented any of this, as if they were proud to share their history, whilst living in the modern world. It made Jules wonder if he should look closer into his own family tree.

That was for another time.

To blend in, he looked inside one of the small houses, a round construction with a roof made from branches and leaves but did not hang around to take in the educational aspect.

He stuffed his hands in his pockets and let his shoulders drop, going for a faintly disappointed demeanor, which seemed to be what the majority of those under thirty were feeling. Or maybe they were hungry. It was still at least two hours before dinner, and they had to occupy themselves until then. He noticed a bar decked out like a caravan from the 1930s, around which several overweight men and a couple of women were enjoying beers.

Then he saw them. The Koreans. Some of them trying a little too hard to misrepresent themselves as Chinese. They overdid it with red caps featuring the golden Chinese flag symbols of a large star on the left with four stars in a crescent beside it which Jules knew citizens of that country rarely wore. An oversight, perhaps, or the agents in charge marking minions whom they regarded as pawns rather than those with meatier roles in the plan.

Jules scanned the wide street, lingering on the more interesting features, zoning in on a one-story museum entrance which extended around the back of the façades. He approached, fumbling out a phone, as most tourists here were carrying. He watched from the reflections in the museum's window as the surrounding tourists followed a set route, some accompanied by a personal guide, for which they must have paid extra.

Jules had suffered racism in the past, both overt and born of ignorance rather than hatred. One such offence that people of color encountered was the notion that "they all look the same to me." While race blindness was a real thing to a degree, usually experienced by those who lived separate from diverse communities, Chinese and Koreans shared enough DNA for the most observant analyst to confuse the two. Here, it was more than an annoyance, since Jules could not even begin to guess who might be a bad guy.

Except for those trying too hard.

He had to work with what was in front of him, so he peeled away from the museum window and moved towards a man and a woman, the man one of those wearing a Chinese branded baseball cap. Rather than approaching directly as the pair snacked on a bag of potato chips, he hung back and watched from the corner of a mocked-up blacksmith shop. Beside the blacksmith's, a pair of women wove cloth using a wooden jenny, a contraption much like a simplified spinning wheel. There was a gap between the buildings, a small alleyway which Jules used to partially conceal his presence, revealing himself to be an amateur spy.

Or that was the hope.

As soon as the woman made eye contact with Jules, he dipped his chin and scratched his face, overtly wincing and switching his attention elsewhere.

Unfortunately, *elsewhere* was a thickset man wearing a pair of sturdy boots and cargo pants, his big leather jacket concealing whatever he wore up top. He couldn't have looked more like a gangster if he tried. He also was not stupid, clocking that Jules had recognized him right away.

A quick flick of his head left and right, and the burly man charged at Jules. He acted so rapidly and with such an unremarkable gait, it was unlikely anyone would have seen him crashing Jules backwards into the four-foot-wide gap between the buildings.

The assailant was almost as wide as the thoroughfare, which lent Jules a brief advantage. He deployed a reverse hammer fist to the man's groin, but a block greeted his strike. He followed it up with an elbow uppercut which slammed home into the man's head, and for a moment Jules thought he had landed a sturdy blow. But the man had a thick skull and was touching his ear as he recovered. He spoke in rapid-fire Korean, presumably alerting his comrades. Jules took advantage of the lull and retreated around the back of the blacksmith's.

He ran at full pelt down the rough track, built for people to get around rather than enjoy a stroll with nature. The trees that had been cleared for Kainga Pukepuke were not entirely gone from this area, the stumps protruding from the ground made for a neat springboard onto a generator, then a roof. This evaded a pair of Koreans playing Chinese tourist trying to cut him off.

Summitting the building, he leaped the gap between properties, landing on a slatted roof and persisting at the same rapid pace. Over the top of this one, he slid on his backside, dropped off the edge, and reversed his course past the performers on a break. Already, four undercover agents had broken free and were chasing him without trying to hide.

Jules summoned his mental map and determined the best route away from this location was to skirt the rugby club, which he calculated was a risk, but less of a risk than causing a panic or inviting gunfire near innocents. The woods bordered this field too, so it was a decent place to find cover if needed. He also reminded himself of the gun he carried.

As he rounded the corner to the rugby club, a tree branch swung towards him. He spotted it early enough to limbo under it, and the wood only glanced his forehead. Not even sufficient to dizzy him.

The assailant was one of the Koreans, so Jules didn't hesitate in wedging a side kick to the man's knee, levering him over his hip before halting the roll halfway, then reversing direction. By this point Jules had him by the wrists and the spinning motion sprained the man's limb, releasing the tree branch, which Jules stabbed like a spear towards a shadow, ducking at the same time. The shadow's gun went off, and a bullet whizzed over his head as the improvised weapon landed in the attacker's gut. Jules used his foot to smash the man's nose, then pirouetted for extra weight, and the branch snapped as it took him out at the temple.

The other two had caught up, drawn their handguns, and Jules had to dive for cover behind the clubhouse. Three shots rang out and splintered the corner. This pair was both dressed ostentatiously in shell suits, possibly the most well-disguised of the agents, and must have kept their guns in the fanny packs which hung open.

Rather than running into open land, Jules nipped back the way he came, caught the pair by surprise, and threw the remaining stub of the branch their way. As the nearest attacker swatted at the projectile, the other hesitated before drawing down on Jules scurrying at a pre-planned angle. Unlike when he'd got the distance and timing wrong with the gunman in Alabama, Jules zigzagged and flicked one of his throwing knives. It stabbed the man in the shoulder, giving Jules time to catch up, over-rotate his opponent's wrist, and wrench the gun from his hands. Bent double, the side of his neck presented an easy target for Jules to shock his carotid with a strong knee.

Jules aimed back the way he came, finding his first assailant from the alleyway jogging in a manner he expected fat people to do. However, this man was mostly muscle and also wielded a small handgun.

Jules could take no chances here, so aimed and fired. Twice.

Pop pop.

It took the man out in the shoulder, then the hand, which surrendered the gun to the floor. But he kept coming.

Jules fired into the man's thighs. One in each.

Pop pop.

This time he fell over, face-first into the dirt. A brutal take-down, but Jules was running out of space and, potentially, time. So far, his attackers had been pawns, but there were surely more skilled fighters among them. Such as the guy he'd shot who barely grunted with the pain, just used his one uninjured hand to scoop soil into the wounds to prevent more blood loss.

Jules hurried toward the woods bordering the field. He didn't get very far. The rugby team had approached and formed a two-man deep semicircle, barring his way.

Jules said, "Okay, I know how this is gonna sound, but this ain't what it looks like."

The biggest chap on the pitch, the one who had issued the first "Hey" when Jules landed, stepped forward, his eyes on the gun in Jules's hand. "You're with Bobby, aren't you?"

"Bobby Arono, yeah." Jules looked around at the team. "We cool?"

Another youngster, as tall as Jules and at least fifty pounds heavier, gave a chuckle and said, "Sounds like you're doing a lotta good up there." He indicated the volcano. "We'll take care of this."

Murmurs of agreement followed from his teammates as they spread out towards the injured Koreans.

One of only two Caucasian boys on the team stepped forward, grinning, a role of gray electrical tape in his hands. He picked off the end and pulled out a length with a hearty *rip*. "We love us a bit of gaffer tape."

"Thanks, guys." Jules clapped the guy he assumed to be the captain on the shoulder, as he'd seen sportspeople do to one another, then ran through the middle of them. Wishing he could spend a little more time thanking them, he mimicked one of Tane's idiosyncrasies and called back, "Catch you later, brah."

And then he was navigating through the woods, listening for the heavier footfalls of pursuing gunmen as he made for the river and away from the *Kainga* population.

CHAPTER TWENTY-SEVEN

Ah Dae-Sung and Pang Pyong-Ho remained patient. On the fringes of the village, they had mingled with Americans away from those using the Chinese ruse. They'd had plenty of practice lately, even perfecting the accents and boisterous manner in which those vulgar individuals acted. They toned it down somewhat, as Americans tended to do when surrounded by their betters. Frankly, Dae-Sung was of the opinion they should act like that all the time, since there were few corners of the world where people were not better than that accursed nation.

They had an unobstructed view down the area known as Main Street, a similar reference to the supposedly wholesome area of small towns the world over. Commander Ah had watched the scramble of soldiers brought in to support them after delivering the shield to Executive Ryom's people, and it had been efficient work. Civilians back home would not have blinked at the actions of the security services chasing down someone who had, perhaps, expressed a view contrary to the welfare of the nation. However, here it drew more than a little attention.

"Goddamn it," Pyong-Ho said in his near-perfect west coast American accent. "About time there was some excitement around here."

Ah Dae-Sung joined in, adding for anyone within earshot, "Maybe they'll speed up that food now."

Americans nodded in agreement. It left them free to shift to one side for a better view.

"Why is he here?" Pyong-Ho asked.

"Our presence must have been detected."

Dae-Sung trawled his memory for how this had occurred and wondered how the New Zealanders thought he could be so stupid as to fall for such a trick. They were dangling bait, a talented and gifted specimen who could benefit the Korean people. Dae-Sung had learned only recently of the man's additional gifts, how he influenced the spheres that were powering Korea's revival, or would do once they returned.

But why do it in such an obvious manner?

Ah Dae-Sung asked, "How many have not been incapacitated?"

Pang Pyong-Ho had taken notice of those dropping off-line, although he'd admitted he couldn't see who had survived after chasing their quarry. "Aside from us, there are seven patriots."

Ah Dae-Sung considered the risk, the benefits, and decided to be bold. After all, wasn't that what Executive Ryom preached? How he had demonstrated his own superiority? It was what set him, and those who believed in his project, apart from the rank and file in the armed forces and the citizenry who sat back and enjoyed the security bestowed upon them.

Was that how they were to justify the deaths of hundreds of thousands of people? Would it even stop at hundreds of thousands? Could it go over a million?

If the defensive act planned by the Executive worked, there would be sacrifices, but how many more lives would it save?

Several million?

It all came down to how unstable the orb made the directional power of the shields. Unchecked, the only way to be sure it didn't wipe out their own population was to cast the net wide and scrape it backwards until it covered their borders.

But what if some individual with conscious control over that power was to assist them? Would that result in fewer lives lost? Could he keep it down to a few thousand instead of many thousands?

That sort of thinking was an example of weakness. All that mattered was achieving their goal.

And yet, did Dae-Sung want to be slandered with the same label afforded to famous men throughout history who were "following orders?" Nazis, Communists, savages across Africa...?

There was no need to ask that question of himself. He was certain that Executive Ryom was acting in the best interests of all Koreans, and indeed those who would be pulled into a conflict to assist the Americans. But if they showed mercy in that initial act of defiance, surely it would encourage the sympathy they needed from the international community. Surely, a less bloody conclusion would be of benefit to *all* people.

"Bring him." Ah Dae-Sung said. "He will be extremely useful."

Using a discrete microphone up his sleeve, Pyong-Ho gave the order. Ah Dae-Sung just hoped it wasn't a mistake.

CHAPTER TWENTY-EIGHT

Bridget couldn't see what was happening down in the valley, but she could hear it, as it was being patched through Project Ahua's intercom rather than the subvocal feeds they were used to. Jules's recon had gone awry, switching quickly to a mission aimed at drawing the danger away from innocents. Perhaps, with the shield's ill-defined ability to cloud curiosity, they would concentrate on Jules and on the other boys out playing soldier.

Whatever, it would buy them time. But would it be enough?

"I still don't understand how they found us," Prihya said.

"Yeah, right." Charlie was busy digesting the machine's workings. "We show up and suddenly Valerio Conchin's girl is stalling us out, giving us a tour, introducing us to her pet lab experiments—"

Prihya slapped the control desk. "You think *I* brought them here? It's *you* people who showed up out of the blue and—"

Toby stepped between them. "Now, now, rehashing that isn't helpful. Let's use our time here wisely."

The two women stared at him. Sally stared at him, glancing at Prihya.

Only Bridget kept her mind in the right gear. "Can we turn down their feed for a bit? I need to concentrate."

Charlie switched the boys' voices over to a headset so only she could hear their stilted communication between one another. She would speak up if anything important occurred.

Bridget returned to the frosted screen with the glyphs pulled from the rock and digitally restored, arranged in the exact size and pattern they would have been displayed around the entrance to the activation suite. "How long do we have?"

"Until when?" Prihya asked.

"Until anything we do here no longer matters."

"I can't answer that."

"Can't or won't?" Charlie said, checking connections on the cables.

"Can't," Prihya answered firmly. "Because we don't know their intentions, or if your 'action dudes' will be successful or not. We've evacuated all non-essential personnel, just in case. There's a security cordon on all entrances, and they've sent an alert to Julia Grainger. She has backup on standby, but this isn't a military installation. It's a science lab being attacked by foreign forces. We might have a squad of Kiwi special forces dropping in, an attack from North Korean mercenaries, or both, or none of the above."

"Too many variables," Toby agreed. "What do *we* need to accomplish? Here, in this room?"

Bridget thought that was the easiest one to answer. "Figure out how to use *our* machine to stop *their* machine."

Sally tutted and shook her head, joining Bridget to watch the screen. "Something these people haven't achieved in several months. With more resources and less time pressure."

"We just need to understand it better." Bridget fixed on each symbol one at a time. Absorbing it into herself. "We have to get into the guts of it."

Toby also came alongside, pointing out English notations on the glass. "Prihya, you've already deciphered these."

"Yes." Prihya made up the foursome, leaving Charlie to continue her inspection alone. "When I was with Valerio, we made some inroads. There's a lot of intonation, almost a... mood about certain symbols."

"Agreed," Bridget said. "The angle of an inscription can say something different to an identical numeral or hieroglyph if it's accented a different way."

"I began to think of it as a written version of spoken tongue. Like we use emojis in an email or text message to show sarcasm or an intent at humor, whereas if we didn't include that it might look insulting or give an incorrect meaning."

"Good analogy," Bridget said. "It's more subtle, though. Here." She indicated one of the *power* runes Toby had pointed out. "This is different from the ones we followed to Montrose in Scotland."

"I noticed that, too." Prihya moved closer to the symbol. She was smiling, Charlie's accusation seemingly forgotten. "It's possible each station with an orb has a modified version of this, denoting either a unique function or simply an identifier."

"There's a history lesson, too." Bridget pointed to the base of the left side of the arch. "Those parts that don't have a translation."

"I could see they were more conversational," Prihya said, crouching. "They strike me as something like a welcome. Then up over the arch itself, these largely refer to the machine itself—"

"Like an instruction manual," Toby said.

Prihya's brow pinched together briefly at being interrupted, but she shook it off. "Then farther down here..." She referred to those on the straight, vertical section of the right-hand side, of which only two were translated to English. "Basically, it's a warning. To only use it for noble purposes. And then saying..." She twirled a finger around a glyph two places down—what looked like a cross between a Celtic symbol and the Japanese writing for *peace*. "I can't tell if this means death or rest."

"It means both," Bridget said. "It's not just the angles and size that combine to give meaning. It's the symbols around it. The one above... it's denoting a choice. If you use it well, you rest easy. Use it badly, or use it wrong, you die."

"Heavy stuff."

"I can't believe this." Sally paced away from the confab. "You're all behaving like best friends."

Bridget faced her and stood tall, and Prihya got back to her feet. Toby approached but halted as Sally hunched her shoulders. Even Charlie looked up from her work.

Sally said, "I should have guessed where I knew her from. She was working with Valerio Conchin, but I forgot why I was so worried about that man. You know many people approached me about my research?"

"Yes," Toby said. "It's what drew us to you. And why Tane Wiremu was sent to watch over you. Many people were—"

"Well, that man was one of them. He was one of the first to offer me a huge sum of money to come work for him. And here's what's weird: If he'd suggested less, I might have been tempted. But that much? It sounded like a scam."

"Please," Prihya said. "I knew nothing about it. I was only there as an advisor, to help brainstorm and dig deep into this history. I was not a part of—"

"You're part of a system that says money is power. Money can buy anything. I know that better than anyone, because I can't get my tenure if the university's funding is threatened." She was on the verge of tears. Took off her glasses to get to her eyes where she stemmed any outward sign of weakness. "They have to disassociate from me. It makes me look crazy when all I was doing was exploring all possibilities. And even though I was right, because of money—which your boss, or *former* boss worships—I can't resume my work there. I have to start over. And why?"

"Sally..." Toby moved toward her.

Bridget stepped forward, too. Ready to offer words of comfort, but none came.

Sally halted them with a harsh, "No." She put her glasses back on. "And you won't let me prove to them that I'm right. Because you're scared of sharing. Scared of letting the world see what I've found. What *you* found. And used me to distract others from finding. It's not fair. But while I'm here, I demand to be included in your research. I demand to be a part of this."

Prihya said, "You are a part of this, Sally."

"It's *Professor* Garcia, actually. And why? Why am I even here? Tane thought my knowledge was useful, but you found that shield in Alabama. I have clues to other giants' sites and places I can prove they existed, but for now? Here? I'm no use to anyone."

"That's not true," Toby said. "You can be. You have so much to impart. We just have to figure this out first."

"Am I being manipulated the way she was?" Sally lifted a hand toward Prihya.

"No, of course not..." Toby began, only pausing as Prihya shifted closer.

"In a way, yes," Prihya said. "It's true, you will be able to help in the future. But for now, Tane is keeping you close for another reason: to make Ah Dae-Sung and his bosses think you are needed."

"Bait?" Sally said in a small voice.

"No, not bait. But it draws attention from the real objective. If they think we're still chasing clues, it means *they* keep chasing clues."

"That's ridiculous," Toby said. "The professor knows more about the legends, and separating myth from history, than anyone. No one here *really* knows about the giants who live down there. It's all an experiment. A massive petri dish. Sally knows the true origins, and if we need it, it can help the interpretation of—"

"*Yes.*" Bridget now paced, her feet needing to move, pressure building in her stomach and zapping around her body. "I do need help. Check this."

Sally glanced around everyone in turn.

"Doubt it's a trick," Charlie said. "Bridget wouldn't know how. Trust her."

Bridget was mildly insulted at the assumption she couldn't manipulate someone for ulterior motives, but that was a conversation for another time. "I understand the power of men influencing women, so let's be more trusting here. Prihya, this one..."

A symbol that looked like a hashtag with a circle in the middle and triangles in the boxes above and below had been decoded to say, "the chosen one." Other translated glyphs surrounded it, almost forming its own paragraph.

Bridget read the English. "When entering the god chamber, the chosen one controls the throne. The globe turns to his will."

"His," Charlie scoffed.

"Feminism aside," Prihya said, "it makes sense."

"In our narrow understanding of linear narrative," Bridget said. She pointed to the bottom left symbols. "You haven't translated these."

"No. Can you?"

"Sally, look at this." Bridget turned her head sideways. "These two symbols together... 'A king of men'... 'must be the savior'..."

"It's..." Prihya adopted the same angle. "I still don't see it."

"No, but I've worked on this language for longer. I've seen this phrase before, in a different language. 'King of men' doesn't indicate royalty."

Sally rushed forward and kneeled at the appropriate spot. "I know the phrase. 'King of men' was used to talk about giants. Like... like *Rex* in the way we talked about a tyrannosaurus rex. He isn't a literal king, he's—"

"The biggest predator," Toby said. "But if this writing is sideways, going left to right around the perimeter..."

"We got a lot of the meaning wrong," Prihya said. "Because I didn't recognize those first words, I had nothing to work on. I used what I knew. Now..." She angled her head the other way to read the previous glyphs at a new angle.

Toby plainly understood what they were doing. "What if the first assumption is wrong?"

"From an engineering perspective," Charlie said, "one bad component can have a knock-on effect. Makes it all fall down. If I understand your idea of translating this language, it holds true here. If one factor affects another, but that first one is faulty..."

Bridget turned her head the same way as Prihya, which flipped the hashtag-like figure, so the triangles were top and bottom instead of left and right. She read the English again: "Version one: 'When entering the god chamber, the chosen one controls the throne'." She forced herself to concentrate on the new formation, the writing left to right, not top to bottom. "Alternatively: 'To enter the god chamber, a man must choose to control the throne'."

"*Man* again," Charlie said. "Looks like Toby is up."

Prihya stepped back, obviously troubled. "They used the word 'man' the way we use 'mankind'. It's genderless."

"So it could also mean a human," Sally said. "Any human?"

Bridget strode across the room and opened Jules's backpack. "But only one of the kings of men—the giants—can do so without help." She took out the two bangles. "I wonder if you need special genes to use these in there." She pointed them toward the activation suite—what they had called the god chamber. "I can try."

"There's still some fierce energy flowing through there," Charlie said. "Near as I can tell, it's insulated, but there's no telling how it'll react to new variables."

"We do not know either," Prihya added. "We persuade Gilim into the reverse-engineered unit on the forest floor once a week. That powers up the machine for several days. He acts... peacefully when he's in there. Like he's... I don't know, like he's..."

"High," Bridget said, running her eyes and brain over some of the final symbols. "There are signs there of knowledge *and* pleasure. For a 'king of men' it might be quite a fun experience."

"High," Prihya echoed. "Could be. We'll have to measure his endorphins the next time he goes— Wait, where are you going?"

Before anyone could stop her, Bridget dashed over to the activation suite.

"No, wait," Toby said. "You don't know what—"

"We need more." Bridget stuffed her hands into the bangles and pulled them close, so the opposite-cut ends clamped together with strong magnetic force. "That archway essay says we get knowledge from the machine. Since Jules isn't here, there's no one better qualified to interpret what it gives us. Anyone want to argue?"

"Only from a stupidity perspective," Charlie said. "It could kill you."

"So could a nuclear-powered world erupting into war." Bridget stood at the threshold, watching her friends, her colleagues, new and old. "Safe word is 'Indus.' Pull me out if I start to smolder."

Unsure where the glibness came from—probably nerves, since her heart was racing at least double speed—she backed into the stone chamber, like an upright sarcophagus, and raised the linked bangles over her head. They clunked against the wall, as they had to each other, and...

Nothing. No flash of light, no searing pain, no images forcing their way into her brain.

"Guys? I might need a hand getting out."

But what she was seeing outside wasn't what she'd left behind. It was a rocky vista.

Her heart leaped, breath catching in her throat as she calmed almost right away. She was fascinated more than afraid.

The rocky vista was not simply boulders and rubble strewn around, but buildings *carved* from rocks, from the landscape. People roamed, tall ones, but not giants. All over six feet, some approaching seven, if the perspective was correct. She wasn't sure where she got that perspective from, but it could also have been their manner, their tall, skinny frames.

She seemed to be floating.

Then, flying.

Over the top of a mountain, she shot into the sky, trying to remember why she was here. All she knew was the floaty, tingling sensation engulfing her. The view outside the chamber encroached inside, surrounding her.

Even though she could not move, she didn't care, didn't *want* to move. She was smiling so hard, her face ached.

She plunged down, into the earth, hurtling headfirst, yet she wasn't scared. She phased through this and into a cavern where more of those tall men and women surrounded a metal orb floating over a stone cradle, dull and lifeless, until a giant stepped out of the shadows.

Where did he come from?

Didn't matter. Two tall people escorted him, but he towered over them by his head and shoulders and was at least four times as wide. Much like Gilim but clean-shaven, he showed none of the innocent wonder Gilim had upon meeting Bridget at the others. This hulking colossus knew what he was doing and spoke words Bridget could not hear.

The tall men at his side departed, and the giant advanced upon the floating metallic ball. He urged the Witnesses...

Oh my god, are these the Witnesses? The Elder Race?

The giant urged the people surrounding the orb back. When they were at a safe distance, he grabbed it with both hands. It flashed briefly, then swam with black, like oil, only made of light.

How can light be black?

And why am I even here?

The crackle of cerulean blue lightning made everyone, including

Bridget, jump, and back away. Only, Bridget wasn't really there. No one paid her any mind, nor even glanced her way. Like she was a ghost or...

A witness.

She giggled to herself.

The electrical tendrils spread, flashing and crackling throughout the cavern, but the giant appeared unfazed. He knew exactly what he was doing.

But what is that?

Bridget laughed at her confusion. She didn't know what she was doing here, watching a giant play with a massive black metal ball that shot lightning all over, and—

She flew away. Up, out of the ground, into the sky, soaring high over landmasses she recognized as tectonic plates, the divisions glowing—not literally, but in her eyes—as she passed over them. For several minutes, she dotted the land with coordinates, marking special mountains, weak spots where pressure from below granted the earth breathing room, the planet's lungs exhaling in relief at—

That's how these people think of volcanos. The planet breathing. Sucking in our lives and exhaling the spirits to live again. To live on.

And she recognized these places. Knew where they were. But the coordinates were not delivered to her in modern terms, no east-west, no longitude or latitude. This was implanted as she flew, glowing gems in the map below.

Until she saw the effects of the giant in the cavern she'd watched.

When did I get so high?

She could see almost all of this side of the planet. The continents, closer together than on today's globes, either from a time before continental drift had reached its current epoch or a visualization as imagined by a people who had not yet mastered flight and hadn't mapped the world in its precise dimensions yet. Lines of energy branched out from that one spot, a circuit board more than a spider's web, zipping not in straight lines to wrap the Earth in a protective net, but along the fault lines, the plates on which continents were based. Then, they sliced across, meeting up with the gemstone coordinates, the other orbs, hidden in the lungs of the planet.

A hand appeared before her. Then another.

"Hi," she said.

As they advanced at a snail's pace toward her, she paid them little mind, rearing up to observe more of the world, holding there, in place. Happy. Content.

She found the disembodied hands cute more than threatening. Floating toward her. She watched them, fascinated. She couldn't move her own hands from over her head, otherwise she'd have touched them. Poked them. Tickled them.

Are they going to tickle me?

They moved so slowly, though. Bridget remained where she was, enjoying the view, observing as the trails of energy met, zoning in on one focal point, a destination that glowed more intensely than anywhere else—around the Asian/Australasian plates, where a smoking mountain thumped and thrummed.

She was there an hour, amused, intrigued, even inspired by what she saw. But it was then, once she understood she was witnessing the Toba event, a catastrophic eruption that blanketed the globe and all but wiped out the early humans, that the hands reached her. They grasped her by the waist and pulled.

Then she was in a strange place with strange people all around.

"Bridget, are you okay?" the bespectacled man said.

"Talk to me, Bridge," said a woman with long dark hair.

A younger woman with brown skin and a pleasant face pulled Bridget's eye open and shone a light into it. "She's high. Like Gilim."

"How?" the man said. "She was only in there for a few seconds."

Bridget blinked, pulled away, and it all flooded back to her. The reason she was here. Toby. Charlie. Prihya.

Jules.

Dan, Harpal, Tane.

Professor Garcia.

She lurched up and leaped to her feet, startling those around her. "It's fading. It's leaving me so fast. Get me some paper. Quick. I need to write it all down."

Sally offered a legal pad and a pencil, and Bridget wrote furiously, as fast as she could whilst keeping it legible. "It's a visual trip straight into the brain. Not someone talking to me, or a direct info feed, but like an observation deck, manufactured memories, like... a dream."

"You were in there less than five seconds," Prihya said. "What could you see?"

"Plenty." She scribbled and scribbled, pouring all she could onto the page. Not in order, just at the snippets and CCTV through the ages... "Whoever built this. That's why the Elder Race was so limited. Intelligent, yes, but not inventive. It was only when the tech was removed that humans were forced to build again. How did they learn how it worked?" She was babbling and she knew it but couldn't pull it together.

Concentrate on what's important. *On what we can achieve here, in this room.*

Did she say that or did someone else? Toby, maybe.

But it was the only thing to do.

She ran out of memories, sat back, and tried to interpret her scribbles. Her account of all she saw.

"Bridget..." Prihya took the paper from her. "You wrote this."

"Yes." Bridget sensed a headache coming on. She was out of breath, needed water. Maybe a burger. Yes, she was hungry. She'd been flying for hours.

"Do you know what it says?" Toby asked.

"Of course..." But Bridget heard the slurring of her words. Like she was drunk. "Can I get a glass of water?"

"Do you know what we have to do?" Charlie said. "With this thing?"

"I think so." Bridget accepted a plastic bottle from Prihya. "We need to tell the others. This place isn't connected directly to the network. We can't stop the one at the Dragon's Pit going online from here."

"Then we go somewhere else," Toby said. "Stop it remotely from an orb that is connected."

"If we have time," Charlie said, plugging her satellite phone in to a mini laptop computer that she'd evidently stashed earlier. "We won't get to Scotland or Kenya in time."

"I have a map," Bridget said, tapping the paper on which she'd written her notes, which Prihya now held. "I can't remember it, but I think I got it all down. Let the others know."

Both Prihya and Charlie spoke at once. "We can't."

They looked at one another.

Charlie went first, working the laptop and checking the satphone. "We lost local comms when you entered the chamber. Power spike. We can't contact the action dudes that way. I'm trying to re-establish our own system."

"Oh." Bridget looked to Prihya. "What about you? What's up?"

Prihya was staring at the paper. Toby did, too, and his face paled. Sally Garcia looked and immediately glanced away, leaving Charlie to mimic Toby's shock.

"What is it?" Bridget demanded.

Prihya turned the paper to Bridget. All her notes, her writing, a comprehensive account of all she'd seen, she had scribbled not in English, but in the Witnesses' language. The same runes and glyphs they'd struggled to interpret for several months.

"Let's just hope the others can deter the Koreans," Toby said. "Or we may have a bigger problem on our hands."

And then, as if Toby had orchestrated the timing to coincide with his comment, an alarm blared.

CHAPTER TWENTY-NINE

As he ran, Jules could only make out shadows at the periphery of the tree line. Not even his keen senses and processing power could pinpoint every soul on his tail. He had no option but to keep going.

To make things hard for them, he'd left the rudimentary track and converted to cross-country. It wasn't difficult for someone who had traversed oceans of rooftops and scaled walls across modern cities, seeking the smallest handholds, reacting to shifts in the temperature and viscosity of the next surface. At least here it was consistent. The biggest danger was a thick weed or bramble escaping his attention and snagging his foot.

But Jules was nothing if not pragmatic, so his path remained as elevated as he could manage, picking up his feet in an almost comic manner when he burst across a stretch where roots, logs or rocks offered no foothold. At times it was as if he was racing through an assault course's tire section. It barely slowed him.

Barely didn't mean not at all, though, and the men and at least one woman he'd spotted stuck to trails beaten out by animals or humans, attempting to flank him. It took a mighty effort to split his concentration in two, with 75% dedicated to maintaining his course and monitoring his pursuers, while the other 25% recalled the topography he'd witnessed earlier.

The radio came to life, an exasperated Dan asking for a sit-rep. Now Jules was nearing the curve, the land sloping down into the shallow valley, they had a line of sight for the signal. He considered not replying for a few more yards, purely out of obstinance, but he was trying to leave that old self behind and be a mature member of society. A mature member of society playing catch-me-if-you-can in the forest.

"On my way," he said. "Bringing some friends."

"About time. ETA?"

"I got no idea where you're set up, so that's a kinda—" Jules cut himself off as he ducked under an unexpected branch. He rounded a trunk, sprang up to a sturdier one, swung off this, and landed on the next mound before breaking out into open ground. "I'm at the jetty."

"Grab the skiff, second from the end. It's fueled and ready."

"And a big chalk 'J' next to it, gotcha."

A steep grassy hill led down to the jetty, although twenty yards to his right there was a staircase. Jules stuck to the slick grass, lost his footing twice in three seconds, so used it to his advantage and launched himself forward onto his butt.

He lay flat, like on a water slide, and sluiced the next fifty yards before friction dented his progress and the angle evened out. Without stopping, he leaped to his feet, a glance over his shoulder showing his pursuers were well on his tail.

At sharp reports of gunfire, he started zigzagging in his run, steering clear of repeating his pattern. Bullets ripped up the turf, some pinging into the slow-moving river.

Short-range pistols.

The shooters running or aiming hastily.

The target moving away and in an unpredictable pattern.

Jules figured Dan, himself, or maybe Charlie could be a danger under those circumstances, but it'd take a lucky shot to even wing him if the six Koreans he'd pinpointed were as average as he'd seen so far.

Probability aside, they might *get lucky.*

Concentrate on getting to the boat.

The pier floated on a pooling section, where the water's path widened enough to drop its current to a trickle before picking up again downriver. There were four *waka taua*—Maori war canoes—moored at the shallowest part, lashed to the mooring first for the benefit of paying customers. Then came Jet Skis and a couple of tug-like motorized boats, and finally the two skiffs—small boats with motors on the rear.

As Jules's boots pounded the unsteady wooden platform, now unable to bob and weave due to the limited space, he asked, "You disabled the other boats here, right?"

No one replied for a moment, then Harpal said, "Actually, we were kind of in a rush."

"Needed to scatter the staff," Tane added. "Couldn't have 'em getting caught up."

Jules had noted the absence of people but hadn't given it much thought. He drew his gun and fired at the Jet Skis' fuel tanks as he passed, but a volley of shots from the land prevented him from taking them all out.

The five men and single woman were on the same level, less than twenty yards from the jetty.

I got another ten yards. That's five seconds with no cover.

Then I have to start up the motor—add on five to ten seconds.

Acceleration in these boats is non-existent, so...

Assessing his options took Jules the time between two near-miss gunshots from the shore. He would not make it to the skiff, let alone bring the Koreans with him on the other one.

Instead, he dove into the water.

The sudden drop in temperature gripped him harder than he'd expected, and he cursed his sluggish brain for not firing a warning. A consequence of relaxing into city life? Or a reminder that crossing dangerous people in pursuit of a greater purpose was a bad idea?

Whatever it was, the self-analysis would have to wait. He concentrated on not passing out in what felt like an icy tomb, found his bearings, and swam upwards.

He broke the surface, a headache hitting home while his entire body tried to shut down, urging him to curl up and shiver or seek warmth.

He denied his body that request, instead reaching up to one of the intact Jet Skis. Because they were intended for emergency use, the keys were still in the ignition, so he started it up while half-submerged.

Rounds flew, gunshots closer. The jetty wobbled with the weight of Korean agents rushing forward.

In a smooth, sloshing motion, Jules gunned the engine, which pulled him along. He used the sudden acceleration to swing his leg up and onto the vehicle like a cowboy mounting a moving horse. To use what little cover there was, he swung it around to the front, the skiffs narrowing his exposure but not concealing him as it generated a foot-high wash.

Jules watched the six agents bear down on him. The lead pair drew their beads. Even with him hunkering low and half-over the side, they surely wouldn't miss.

Come on, come on...

He'd only got the lightning-quick guesstimation wrong by a second, but it was enough to spike his adrenaline. The wave from his wash rolled beneath the attackers and destabilized the floating dock enough to send even the most skilled marksman's shots high and wide. It didn't send them tumbling, but it was sufficient to save Jules's skin and give him a hefty head start.

"Coming to you fast," Jules reported.

"How fast?" Dan asked.

"However fast a Jet Ski can go at top speed."

Through the spray and his shivering body, Jules checked behind and—as expected—they were manning crafts as he had done, doubling up. One piloting, the other to fire his way.

They'd be slower but could get close enough for a shot. If they kept in a straight line.

How long did he have until they were in range?

Ummm...

Nothing. No idea how to calculate that. His teeth simply chattered in reply. His brain seemed to be saying, *Sorry, no math today. Get me warm again and maybe we'll talk.*

"They're on me," Jules said. "How far downriver are you?"

"Half a kilometer," Tane answered.

Concerned about stray bullets, Jules assumed.

The enemies were coming, a straight line of three crafts—two Jet Skis and a slower but steadier boat, one of the six-man skiffs with the motor. The formation gave Jules less to aim at if he chose to stand and fight.

The bend in the river came up fast, which Jules leaned into, keeping central, away from shoreline hazards. He was shivering so much he found it difficult to hold on.

A couple more minutes... that's all he needed to last.

Gunshots commenced. Less frequent than before.

Low on ammo—they were carrying snub pistols to conceal them, so would struggle to pack spare rounds too. Probably enough for this job, though, if he didn't concentrate.

"Turn hard right now," Tane ordered.

Jules blinked three times, looked down at his hands and wondered why he was still going forward. Oh yeah, because he hadn't told his hands to change direction.

He did that and rode the water like a motorbike on a racetrack, his knee skimming the surface before straightening up and zoning in on his destination. Dan and Harpal were right there by an overhanging tree, manning a more luxurious motor launch than anything left at the jetty.

Dan gave him a thumbs-up, and Harpal set off toward the middle of the river.

From the other side, another engine roared, an identical craft to Dan's, holding Tane Wiremu and Bobby Arono. They arrowed into an intercept course and in seconds the concussive chatter of automatic gunfire filled the air.

Jules struggled to focus, huddling alone, before seeing he had to get moving.

Keep moving, keep going.

He rode the Jet Ski toward the action, and by the time he reached Dan and Harpal, the shooting had ended. A five-second skirmish.

The two Jet Skis were down, unmanned and floating with idling engines. Two bodies floated nearby, motionless. The pair in the skiff were now unarmed, riding toward Dan's boat, as instructed.

Tane and Dan guided the captives to the shore, and Jules followed them in, beaching all four vessels. Tane and Dan kept a tight bead on the detainees, although Jules had no clue what they were going to do with them. Only Tane spoke Korean, but what good would interrogating them do?

"Any more?" Tane asked.

Jules forced his jaw to work, suppressed the chattering teeth as best he could, but he couldn't stop hugging himself. "My recce got interrupted. Couldn't nail them all. Some are tied up at the club, some—"

"Hold on. Comms are back up." Dan nodded at Harpal to cover the supplicant agents who hadn't yet said a word. He shrugged off his coat and passed it to Jules, then frowned as he listened to his other ear. Dan was still the only one with one of LORI's subvocal ear buds, directly in touch with Charlie and Bridget. "Are you sure?"

"What's happening?" Jules asked, wearing the coat but still as cold as he'd ever been in his life.

Dan glared daggers at the pair of Koreans. "We weren't the ones creating a distraction. *They* were."

"The lab?" Tane said.

"They're at the perimeter. Tie these assholes up and leave 'em. We're needed up the mountain."

CHAPTER THIRTY

The alarm continued throughout the facility, dampened for the giants in the rainforest below, but it had been audible for several minutes. Charlie had scrambled to get the comms back up and needed to wake Phil to achieve that. She hadn't known exactly what the problem was, but Prihya said it wasn't good. There had been no time to digest the fact Bridget had written an essay in a dead language that even she didn't understand, and there was certainly no time now.

Racing up to the security hub as Phil worked his groggy magic back in England, Charlie had guessed what the alarm meant: the boys had failed, and Project Ahua was under attack. Accessing the room with two security personnel remaining confirmed it.

"I don't know how they got so close," one of them said.

The others gathered inside with Charlie, who scanned the monitors. Men were emerging from the undergrowth outside with guns, body armor, and equipment that looked like a cross between a sniper rifle and a fishing rod.

"Defenses?" Charlie said.

"Us two." The guy heading the monitoring station flipped a thumb between him and his colleague. "We have two armed personnel on each entrance and four on the rainforest level emergency exits. But how did they get so close? We monitor the entire area."

"Because we didn't think like them," Toby said. "We didn't consider what must now look like an obvious tactic."

As the ingeniously ret-conned power source reached its limit, Ah Dae-Sung ordered the men to leave the plain, battered sliver of the ancient shield in plain sight, where they could retrieve it later. They'd shaved a length off one of the metal shields they found during their initial quest, beat it out to cover one square meter, and used the portable power source with its highest yield to manipulate the energies into useful functionality. Two dozen patriots had died during the experiments, but today's successful incursion made those deaths worthwhile.

It had done its job, as had the way his people had feigned incompetence back in the village. The amateurs from this "Lost Origins" group, or whatever they called themselves, had fallen for it, and the twelve-strong strike team hidden in the forest since the previous night could move in.

"The Executive was correct," Pang Pyong-Ho said. "A uranium battery and a crescent-shaped crystal." He checked the Geiger counter. Not a sound. "Completely depleted after half an hour. What power must it take to protect a whole country?"

"The power of an entire civilization," Dae-Sung replied. "You have the layout?"

Pyong-Ho showed him the e-tablet, a crude rendering obtained from a beacon as ingenious as it was secret. Another of the Executive's prototypes that would come in handy in the new world.

"You." Ah Dae-Sung pointed at a fat man with a long, stringy mustache—an expert addition to the strike team. "Are you prepared?"

"I will need a maximum of fifteen minutes," the man said.

"Good." Dae-Sung addressed the other twelve and counted off ten of them. "Attack, now. Infiltrate if you can. Kill as many as possible. Do not stop until they are all dead, or you are."

Charlie watched the fight kick off, a bird's-eye view from cameras mounted on lattice towers that resembled radio antennae. Phil had reestablished the link with Dan, and she'd hit him with the warning and a plea for help, but she feared it would come too late. Already, the volcanologists' shack—a point that doubled as an Ahua security post—had been taken, the two men guarding it killed. The six infiltrators in body armor proceeded directly along the crater's rim and engaged a second pair—these the last line of defense before they could descend to the helipad that gave them access to the interior.

Spreading out while staying low, the team advanced with military precision, as efficient and smooth as any special forces unit Charlie had observed. This was no hastily assembled assault.

"They know where they're going," Charlie said, rounding to glare at Prihya.

Prihya shook her head, pumping her arms. "What do I have to do to prove to your people that I'm not doing this?" She looked at Toby, pleading with wide eyes. "You believe me, don't you?"

Toby swallowed. "Well, yes, I... Yes, I think so, I..."

Prihya tore herself away and turned to face the panic rooms. "I suppose I'm not allowed to hide with you either."

"What makes you think we're going to hide?" Bridget asked. "Charlie can handle herself, and I can shoot—"

"We have to hide," Charlie said, patting the two security personnel on the shoulder. "You, too."

"We can't." The head guard was tracking the battle up top. "They're coming. We can't hold them off. Our security keeps out trespassers and the occasional conspiracy theory nut. Not an army."

"All the more reason," Toby said.

The head guard stood and crossed the room to open a locker, removing a submachine gun. "Kara, this isn't your job. Sort these people out—"

"Nope." The other guard was already out of her seat, making for the weapons locker. "It's a bottleneck up there. We have the advantage."

The head guard smiled as if he'd known this would be the result. To Charlie, he said, "Help yourself to guns here. But bed down. We got a distress signal out to HQ. The cavalry is on its way. Just hold out long enough, and you'll be fine."

"What about you?" Sally said, fretting suddenly. "What about all the others?"

"The people dying?" Charlie said, sensing a shift inside herself. "It's horrible, isn't it?"

"Good luck, folks," Kara said as she and her boss exited the way they'd all entered—through what looked like a strong, secure door.

Charlie ran back through all she'd seen so far and approached Prihya where she waited until Prihya held her eye. "I'm sorry. You were never the insider."

Bridget said, "What?"

Charlie switched direction, strode up to Sally, and snatched her glasses.

Sally said, "Hey."

Charlie inspected the frame, specifically a little metallic dot on the temple stem near the hinge. "You started an odd habit when you arrived here. It looked like a nervous tic, but..." Charlie showed Prihya, who squinted at it, and realization dawned in her face, as it had Charlie. She passed them to Toby. "It's a microwave transmitter. You activate it with the heat of your fingers. Holding it there while cleaning the lens sends your location to your friends."

Toby held up the glasses, a disbelieving frown narrowing his eyes behind his own spectacles. "They were already here, though. They knew about this place."

Charlie faced Sally. "That's true. But that isn't the purpose, is it? This scans the area, giving them a layout, doesn't it? And I'm guessing the more heat you apply, or a series of vibrations in a particular pattern, that's their target. They know exactly where they need to be."

Sally was standing straight, arms to her side. "Why on earth would I do that?"

Toby lowered the glasses and stared at her. "Because if your friendly contact from New Zealand won't help you prove your theories correct, then you'll have to rely on the North Koreans to do it."

"Oh my," Bridget said. "It was you who alerted them in California. You let them track you to the cave in Alabama, and that phone call you made to the museum..."

Sally slapped her sides, sighing partly in relief, partly in exasperation. "Okay, Sherlock Holmes, you got me. Fine. Yes. I have a microwave transmitter in my glasses. But look at it from my point of view. I've always worked with them, to a degree, so it'd be silly not to continue."

"I knew it," Prihya said. "I knew I knew you from somewhere. Not your face or voice, but the description Valerio gave. He said one of his peers was part of the same journey we were on, but they had to rely on some crazy American woman. I didn't think it could be you if Toby vouched for you. How did you evade the intelligence services?"

"Ah, that's a doozy." Sally appeared amused, peppering her words with the occasional laugh, as if embarrassed at a home video blooper. "Executive Ryom's technology also conceals privacy, including mine. I'd accepted their funding in different parts of the world, but I hoped to get free of them by hanging out with Tane for a while. But, you know, it turned out he was part of the same conspiracy. Tane pretended to be my friend, while he was really helping the establishment covering things up."

The skin on Toby's face seemed to slacken. He'd appeared affectionate toward the woman, but Charlie doubted it'd be anything romantic given Toby's blanket reluctance to pursue that area of his life. Yet, it must have been hard. He'd defended Prihya with decreasing firmness, and now this had turned him 180 degrees.

He said, "You betrayed us all."

Sally nodded sadly. Then, suddenly, she ran for the weapons locker and snatched a pistol. She heaved it up, pointing it at Charlie, then waved it back and forth. "I know how to use this."

"Use it?" Charlie said. "You can barely hold it."

Sally's grim expression firmed up for about two seconds, before sliding into a simpering, almost pained scowl. "I know. It's so heavy, isn't it?"

Charlie stepped forward.

Sally skittered farther back. "I'll shoot."

"You won't." She rushed at Sally.

The professor pulled the trigger. Nothing happened. No click, no bang, nothing.

Charlie slapped it from her hands and caught it with ease. "You think they keep these loaded? The slide isn't even engaged."

"Oh... bother." Sally sat floppily on the stair leading to the internal door. "Fine, I surrender, whatever."

That she showed no awareness of what she'd done must have stung Toby hard. He marched as far as Charlie and could manage one blustering word: "*Why?*"

Sally rolled her eyes, as if he was stupid for even asking. "Because I was right. I knew I was right. They cornered me by releasing that material, so I had nowhere else to go. I had to cooperate with them. It wasn't like you people were going to help me expose the big lie."

"That's what this is all about?" Bridget said. "All this death, all the death that's gonna come...? To prove you were right?"

Sally stared at her for a long beat, then blinked and nodded. "Well, yes. You can sympathize, can't you, dear? Of these crazy cover-up people, you want the truth. Don't you? That's all you've ever wanted."

Bridget inhaled, about to reply, but bit back whatever she was going to say.

"What do we do with her?" Prihya asked.

"Panic room," Charlie said. "Phil, you there?" She listened for a second, but with no reply she figured they'd killed the comms again. She was almost glad. "I'll hang out here with the armory. Shoot anything that comes through that door. I'll join you if I can't hold them."

"Not by yourself," Bridget said.

About to argue quite firmly, Charlie staggered as the floor shook. A concussive blast roared up from below, shaking the fittings and flickering the lights.

Bridget held herself up on the control desk. "What the hell was that?"

"They're here," Prihya said. "They blew the external hatches."

Charlie ran toward the door leading down to the observation lab. "You have external hatches?"

"We release animals in here, bring supplies. You can't have helicopters zipping in and out three times a week."

Charlie saw the logic. "We have to stop them."

Sally heaved herself to her feet. "Oh, stop being such drama queens. It'll be fine. They're all quite sweet guys, really."

Charlie said, "Bring her along. Keep an eye on her."

She pulled open the door and headed down to the deck. She had to see the damage for herself. However this turned out, the tranquil life the giants had led to date was shattered forever.

CHAPTER THIRTY-ONE

In the control room overlooking the rainforest floor, two guards were rearming themselves, prepping to delve back into the fray. Charlie could only watch as ten men in black tactical gear streamed through the breach into the forest level, the blown loading dock door having scattered the inhabitants with loud, fear-drenched hoots and screams. The team pushed on, half of them wielding carbines, the others armed with cattle prod-like probes and one with a hefty rifle that had to be a tranq gun.

Tane and his people had acted as consummate professionals to date, and their ability to insert a man into an American university, summon the resources they witnessed in Alabama, and whisk them halfway around the world at a moment's notice testified to that. So how had an entire military unit snuck up on a government laboratory-come-wildlife reserve without detection?

The obvious answer was that there was more than one insider. Either that, or Toby's theory was correct: they'd somehow used one of the Guardians' shields to cloak their presence and sneak up to the perimeter. The rest of the attack up top was a diversion for the main strike team setting the charges.

"It's not working!" Prihya cried, slapping the red button for the emergency knockout gas.

"They disabled the entire system," Toby said. He and Bridget operated other panels, ones they'd only observed others using, but it was clear nothing worked as it should. "I suggest we hole up in the panic room and wait for reinforcements."

Below, two masked men broke off from the primary group pursuing the family, pushing through the thick foliage, aiming for the monitoring station's access hatch.

"Can you cut them off?" Charlie asked the two guards, both reaffirming their grasps on their weapons. "We'll secure the prisoner and—"

"I'm not a prisoner," Sally said in the most reasonable tone in the world. "I have to finish what I started. Thanks for understanding."

Bridget marched over and socked her in the face—a full-on right hook that splayed Sally's hair and sent her tumbling.

The guards paused to see if more fighting would crop up here. When it didn't, the one who appeared to be senior wished the group luck, made for the access door, and disappeared down the staircase.

"Well, I..." But Sally was lost for words.

"You're a prisoner," Bridget said.

Prihya laughed. "Beat me to it there."

Charlie checked on the duo's progress coming this way, then urged everyone toward the metal staircase heading up to the security station. "I'm sorry, Prihya. You understand why—"

"No time for apologies." Prihya manhandled Sally to her feet and shoved her the way Charlie was headed. "Let's regroup."

"Indeed, ladies." Toby extended an arm, indicating they should follow Charlie's lead—a cop directing traffic. "Let's move to the back room, and barricade ourselves in, and—"

Gunfire cut him off. Charlie was already wondering if she should say something later about his condescending "ladies" remark, but then a howl added to the racket.

"That's Nan." Prihya halted on the stairs and pushed past Bridget and Sally, running right up to the observation glass. "I can't see her."

Charlie sighed and hurried to join her, calling back, "Go, get upstairs. Activate the panic room."

"What about you?"

Charlie surveyed the scene below. The gaps left by the attendants were empty, so it was all happening under the canopy.

"They don't have any fear of humans," Prihya said. "We feed

them, and we medicate them. The only time we do anything invasive, we knock them out, so they don't know it's us. Now..."

The woman looked forlorn, a child who'd lost their favorite pet. More gunfire directly below snapped her out of it. Both she and Charlie tried to see underneath.

Had she sent those two men to their deaths?

Ah Dae-Sung slinked behind a tree, evading gunfire from the doorway up to the control room. He had memorized the schematics and also had a backup GPS, accurate to ten feet, on his wrist. The two men guarding the entrance would have to die, of course, but he was juggling more than one set of balls.

"Do you have the asset?"

"We have it cornered," was the reply from Pang Pyong-Ho.

Dae-Sung left the security personnel to the private he'd commandeered to accompany him on this side-mission. He did not want to commit to leaving the fray without first knowing they had achieved their main goal. Using a riflescope, he peered to the area Pyong-Ho had pursued the beasts and snagged on movement. Yes, they'd cornered the big one. The alpha.

Gilim.

From the moment they'd entered, the creatures standing almost ten feet tall had scattered at the explosions. The nano camera and microphone embedded in Professor Garcia's glasses had sent the images and sound via low-frequency microwave bursts and also mapped the complex for their raid. Thanks to this Ah Dae-Sung and his team knew everything Garcia had learned, but she still had more knowledge than the sum of the Executive's men combined. She would be another asset if they could extract her. Others, too, those who had manned this magnificent feat of technology.

From down here, the sky was blue, open to the elements, but their satellites had filmed only a dead volcano. It was a watered-down version of what they would unleash in Korea. Putting technicians to work who'd had experience of a similar machine would be advantageous.

But not essential.

They had hoped to snare one of the giants as soon as they breached, but the lumbering brutes Garcia had filmed turned out to be nimbler on their feet when spooked. The female and its offspring went on ahead while the male slowed, then drew the squad away.

It was remarkable, almost sentient, behavior.

Yet, no matter how they might have looked like bigger-than-usual humans, Ah Dae-Sung reminded himself to think of them as cattle. As beasts groomed for the service of humans. This was no more murderous than farming. He was ready to pitch in and abandon the retrieval of personnel if he had to.

"Secured," Pyong-Ho said. "We have it."

"Good." Dae-Sung unclipped a grenade from his belt. "Complete the mission. I will retrieve our other package."

Prihya Sibal had led a life of instinct, which resulted in many regrets. One such regret was trusting Valerio Conchin over the Lost Origins Recovery Institute, having at one time assumed them greedy grave robbers rather than—like her—purveyors of the truth. After seeing through Valerio's schemes and his quest for power, she'd fled, ending up in the employ of Colin Waterston, before receiving the offer to sequester herself here. Off the grid and doing some good in the world she'd searched for all her life.

She had just watched all that unravel. It had taken less than three minutes.

Three minutes to blast their way in. To chase those graceful, magnificent creatures into the heart of their habitat. And, eventually, she'd watched as they cornered Gilim in a clearing.

He fought the cattle prods, the electricity crackling and sparking, the blue lightning visible from the observation deck marking it as a powerful charge. But he couldn't hold them off forever. At least he'd kept them away from his children and wife. Technically, she was his mate, Prihya supposed, but they showed such tenderness toward each other, it was like watching an old, happily married couple. The scientists here threw some good-natured mockery her way whenever she slipped and used the term in their presence.

It had been so nice.

They had done such a lot of *good.*

Her fresh start, leaving behind her mistakes, was underway.

Now, poor, gentle Gilim had been shocked numerous times, bringing him to one knee. He barged aside the nearest invader who'd ventured too close with the tranquilizer gun, but the others had not been so foolish. He slapped the darts as they embedded in his skin, but he couldn't fight the drugs as they entered his system. What must have been skin-absorbent chemicals took several seconds to render him unconscious.

"Got 'em," Charlie said, returning from the security level. "Can you use one of these?"

The Welshwoman presented Prihya with a Glock 17, the standard issue sidearm for the New Zealand police and other law enforcement. She'd run up there after Toby herded everyone else to the panic room, determined to hang on to their freedom and lives. Charlie wanted Prihya to follow, but she'd refused.

This was Prihya's *life*. Even if she couldn't save them all, she had to try *something.*

"I can shoot," Prihya said, accepting the gun and checking the breech for a round.

Then an explosion thundered beneath—a sharp crack and rumble all in one. Smoke billowed from the door down which the guards had disappeared to hold off anyone trying to get up here.

"We're out of time." Charlie steadied herself.

Prihya dragged a chair to the door leading down and jammed it under the handle. "We have a few minutes. What now?"

"Is there another way into the rainforest?"

Prihya wasn't sure why Charlie asked the question. "You'll risk that?"

"If they want Gilim, it's not for anything good. If we let them get out, there's no stopping them."

Prihya hit more buttons on the panel, seeking one—any single knob or lever at all—that worked. Nothing did.

"The glass?" Charlie said.

"It's designed to stop a rampaging giant with three times the brute strength of a silverback gorilla." She indicated her Glock. "This won't touch it."

"Then—"

Gunfire shredded the barricaded door.

The two women retreated into the shelter of the chamber Bridget had activated, the recess enough for both. Charlie crouched low, aiming, while Prihya did the same whilst standing.

Under a second hail of bullets, the chair splintered, and the handle blew off. The door crashed open.

"Hold," Charlie said.

Prihya waited. It was true that she could shoot, but she was no marksman. Plus, wooden targets and tin cans didn't fight back.

Two men glided out of the smoking doorway, clad in black, with full face masks that filtered out the particulate from the explosion below.

Prihya guessed the guards were dead but couldn't think too much about that right now. They had one chance, and the clock was ticking fast.

"Now." Charlie fired.

Prihya fired.

The two men staggered backwards.

Prihya and Charlie rushed out of the chamber. Charlie fired twice more, one in each chest, center mass, and Prihya again shot the one who was struggling the most.

"Deep breath," Charlie said, leading her into the stairwell.

Prihya inhaled and, ignoring the two bodies, delved in through the door, hoping they weren't too late.

Bridget had almost boiled over with fury. That bitch Garcia was lucky to get away with a single punch. Heck, if it hadn't hurt her wrist, Bridget couldn't swear she wouldn't have hit her again.

Now, trying to figure out how to lock the panic room door, she was tempted to take her frustration out on the woman who had led the bad guys here. But it was just the three of them, unable to close the magnetized locks on a featureless, gray area with only a monitor and an internal comms unit.

"It's all part of the plan," Sally said, sitting cross-legged on the floor. "I know, I know, it looks bad. But try to see it from my point of view."

"*Your* point of view?" The tone Toby used dripped with the same anger as Bridget felt. "You led a hostile enemy to take over this commune. A place man has meddled with nature and tried to make amends for it. To give these gentle creatures a home, to... to..." Spittle dotted Toby's lips as he tried to get his words out.

"To do the right thing," Bridget finished for him. "All this mysterious tech, and all the people here—security services, military, even politicians—they just want to do what's best. Which is to keep it from becoming a weapon. And you've handed it to them."

Sally looked up at her from the corner of the room. "You still haven't understood yet, have you?"

"Understood what?" Bridget scooted over to her, crouched at her eye level, ready to hit her once more.

The professor smiled, her eye having swelled a little. "That I was *right*. Isn't that worth at least a little kudos?"

"You really are crazy." Bridget returned to the door which Toby was holding closed. "Any luck?"

"Power to the security grid is out of our control," Toby said. "Normally, it's power that keeps it open. When that gets cut, a room like this is sealed. No one can get in. Of course, a key would have been simpler."

"That's what Charlie meant by 'overengineered'."

Charlie had departed with two guns that were in a box within this room, hoping to slow down the Koreans enough for reinforcements to arrive. She'd taken one look at the complicated setup and despaired.

"It looks like a panel in the wall," Toby said. "And soundproof. If we keep it closed, they have no reason to come poking around."

"Maybe Charlie will take them out before they get here," Bridget said.

"Oh, that would be awful, dear," Sally said. "That way, I'll never get to visit Korea."

. . .

In the now-deserted control room, Ah Dae-Sung gasped for breath. He'd been sloppy, and his aching chest served as punishment. The vest had saved him, but he had to rip it off, sucking air into his lungs as he lay on the floor. Had they used a higher caliber weapon, been a couple of meters closer, or one more shot through the weakened plates in the vest, and he could have died.

The soldier beside him had not been as fortunate. The grouping of the witches' bullets was tighter, penetrating the armor thanks to the weakening of the protection by the first two slugs, then the third punched through. The near vicinity and the accuracy of the shots combined to finish him.

Shame. He'd been a fine soldier. Ah Dae-Sung would find out his name later and address the man's family with tales of his heroism.

He rolled over and pushed to his hands and knees. Had someone under him made such an error, he may have shot the idiot on the spot. He would not be so slack again.

He stripped his fallen comrade of spare ammo and moved on, checking the display on his forearm that the microwave transmitter was still working. The American professor appeared to be located up the stairs in a security center. Or at least, her glasses were.

Assume nothing, he reminded himself.

"Commander Ah, we are ready for transport." The words from Pang Pyong-Ho were loud and unexpected, but welcome.

Dae-Sung blinked away his grogginess and focused on his target. He was a professional, yet here he was concentrating on his own well-being. Perhaps he'd spent too much time in the west, associating with the enemy.

No, just because something was hard, because it came at a personal cost and exhausted the body and mind, it did not excuse selfishness. Nor did it excuse leaving an advantage on the table when it lurked within one's grasp.

"Good," he said. "I am bringing additional assets. Stand by."

Charlie had no doubt what the enormous gurney was for. Resembling the type of wheeled stretchers used by paramedics, it was manned by four soldiers and bore more straps than civilian equipment and a harness. It was also three times larger with eight wheels and sprung suspension.

"What do we do?" Prihya asked.

They were hidden in foliage twenty yards from the access hatch.

"Hold," Charlie replied.

There wasn't much they could do given the firepower in opposition. When the headcount had halved, Charlie thought they stood a chance. But the four departed troops had returned, all they could do was shadow their progress and hope for an opening.

A howl filled the air, followed by two lower trills, a keening of grief and fear.

Prihya said, "We have to *do* something."

Charlie didn't verbalize an answer, but she moved sideways, following the route of the four men who'd had to take a circuitous path to make it over the ground. The layout had been carefully designed, mimicking nature but offering channels where equipment could be wheeled and carried. Although she and Prihya kept well hidden, that didn't take into consideration the wilder areas that actually were natural.

The howl eased, but Prihya sped up. "Come on."

"Not so fast," Charlie urged. "We have to be smart."

Prihya pulled ahead of Charlie. As Charlie grabbed her arm, Prihya rounded on her, hissing her words. "If they are this agitated, there is no telling what they will do."

"What do you mean? They're docile. Peaceful."

"With a strong survival instinct. And inhuman strength. How can you not get this yet? Our friends engineered the bodies, but not the minds. In times past, Gilim would have been born into a tribe, not a lab full of scientists. He'd have learned their language, not cobbled one together. They'd have had societal rules, emotions, friendships, families. These look like the giants of the past, even have many of the same instincts, but they are not what we think of as *civilized*."

"What are you saying? Summarize. We don't have time for the lecture."

"That they are instinctive animals. Like a domestic cat whose owner dies, and no one comes by to find the corpse. It will stay a domestic cat until the second it realizes it has to fend for itself, and then it will never curl up on a human's lap again."

"You're saying they're feral? Reduced to their lowest form?"

Prihya shook her head. "I would not say *lowest*. But basest, perhaps, yes. They are socialized, not domesticated. Nan's mate is in danger, and that might mean her children are in danger too. The other family unit will find safety, but if they perceive a threat, we cannot stop them."

Charlie envisioned a gang of apes rampaging through the undergrowth, desperation driving them toward what would quickly become prey.

"Okay," Charlie said. "I have an idea."

Ah Dae-Sung edged the door open, scanning the security room: a series of monitors, lockers, with cameras watching those watching the monitors. A locked door at the end gave off a certain submarine vibe, a circular handle sealing the exit with electronic locks as well as what would likely be bolts. It would take several attempts with conventional explosives to make even a dent from outside.

He'd taken the correct decision earlier, blowing a hole in the structure itself rather than infiltrating via the human access points.

But there was something else.

He'd tracked Professor Garcia's signal to this room. The room she passed through earlier, transmitting the complex and reverse mapping the schematics to allow Dae-Sung and Pyong-Ho intimate knowledge of the layout. He'd cautioned himself to not assume things were as they appeared.

They'd thought the young black man, Jules, might be useful, but it would require a greater detour to bring him to heel than it would Professor Garcia. And since they were on the verge of acquiring their primary goal, with their secondary individual seemingly in touching distance, a third side quest was an unacceptable risk at this stage. Jules was a bonus to snatch if the opportunity presented itself, nothing more.

He dusted his hand over the flat screens, brushing over the instruments and testing the padlocks on the lockers, listening, alert for movement nearby. He could shoot the padlocks off, but what would be the point? And all he heard was the battle petering out up top. Even if those defending the facility overpowered his forces, they had accomplished their mission.

Or as good as.

Then Dae-Sung's patience found him brushing a panel which felt solid, followed by the tiniest imperfection between this one and the next. He pressed the raised slice of metal with his thumb.

It gave, pressing it flush with the other.

In such a precise, expertly constructed room, it struck him as odd. Gradually, the thought of it warmed him from within. At the same time, it sent a jolt to his extremities, a clarity to his mind and eyes. His ears tuned out the sporadic gunfire and shrank their radius to this area alone.

He let the panel go and the imperfection, the millimeters of difference, was gone. It was level. Flat.

He unsheathed a short-bladed tactical knife and set it between the panels. Twisted. The blade bit and levered the second sheet out slightly.

Something pulled it back.

There was no doubt.

Ah Dae-Sung prepared his sidearm in one hand, the knife in the other. He jammed the blade's point into the gap and pushed, achieving another small measure of give. Whoever was hiding there pulled it again, but this time he was ready. He pushed the knife in farther, crowbarring the hidden door so a gap appeared.

The door sprung open, and three people piled out. On the bottom of the brawl was professor Toby Smith, who'd been clamped to the interior handle, while the girl had her hand on Professor Garcia's mouth. Garcia had tackled Smith, and the three were now at Ah Dae-Sung's mercy.

He stepped back and aimed his gun. "Professor, step aside."

Garcia waited for the girl—Bridget Carson according to Executive Ryom's intelligence sources—to let her go, then stood slowly, first getting to one knee then pressing upwards.

"Okay," she said. "Thanks for that. Can we leave?"

Dae-Sung sidestepped, keeping Bridget in sight as she also rose to her feet. "Just let me finish—"

"Oh, no, mister." Garcia wagged her finger. "No killing, no siree. That's not part of the deal."

"They serve no purpose. We can take no chances."

"Except, if you do, I won't cooperate."

"Then we leave you here." He turned his gun on Garcia. "And shoot you too."

Garcia squinted at him, one eye on either side of the barrel. "Are you mad? I have more knowledge about those *things* and this technology than these people combined. And definitely more than you."

Ah Dae-Sung reminded himself of the briefing regarding this woman. Corrupted by mainstream American influences of social media, conspiracy suppression, and the general malaise suffered by all decadent societies.

One bullet.

Three.

Then it was over.

But that would be easy. And prove his deviation from the plan was a waste of time.

"You could torture me, and I'd probably do what you wanted anyway, but wouldn't it be so much cleaner and, frankly, a less hostile working environment if I actually *wanted* to help figure this all out with you?"

Ah Dae-Sung had switched to fifty-fifty about shooting her. Then an update came through.

"They're attacking! Flank them. Defend the transport."

There was no point going for the men. Charlie figured with Dan and Jules around they'd have had a chance to pick them off one at a time, but with Prihya an inexperienced shooter and Charlie having trained only intermittently over the past few years, they were not exactly an elite fighting force.

"Shoot the cart," she'd told Prihya.

The plan bloomed to life fully formed and had felt like a revelation. But, as Prihya shot at the tires from an angle ten feet from

Charlie's position, the bullets thunked home into the rubber. Nothing burst.

Nothing, except Charlie's sense of cleverness. It was like firing a BB gun at a tractor tire.

As the men with firearms swung toward her, Charlie picked off the first two.

The meathead they knew as Pang Pyong-Ho barked orders, forcing Prihya down behind the tree she was using for cover and to steady her aim. They reconvened their assault on Charlie, who was similarly ensconced. Wood tore off as the defensive group pushed her back.

Charlie had already accounted for this, though. She ducked and crawled behind a boulder to the next tree, where she popped up and drew down on the big guy.

Take out one of their leaders. That will hobble 'em almost as much as losing the gurney.

But Pyong-Ho dove aside, fleeing another couple of potshots fired by Prihya. He used the unconscious Gilim as cover.

While Charlie was aware it took more than a 9mm slug to penetrate the colossus's hide, that didn't mean she wouldn't find a weak spot, a wound already inflicted by the assault team. She fired on the gurney instead.

While the thick, possibly solid, rubber tires simply absorbed the bullets, she aimed for the mechanism at the center of the top rail. This was where the bed would slide backward, pivot down on a gimble, and allow the men to scoop the giant up like the back of a truck transporting cars to a showroom. Her rounds sent metal flying, sheering segments from the joint, but she couldn't tell if it did any permanent damage.

"Excuse me."

A man's voice. Behind her.

She kept her aim but ceased firing. Turned her head.

Ah Dae-Sung led Prihya with her hands on her head, alongside Professor Sally Garcia.

Caught cold, Charlie flashed on the faces of her children, of her husband, furious at her for placing herself in danger, for risking her life yet again. Anger and grief tumbled through her head, nausea churning as she awaited the final blackness of a bullet in the head.

It didn't come.

With what she prayed was a stay of execution, Charlie placed her gun on the ground, using wide, obvious movements. Couldn't give him a reason to think she was going to try anything. Not that she had much faith in him taking them prisoner. It was far more efficient to drop them where they stood. She wondered why she was still alive.

"Professor," Ah Dae-Sung said. "Help my men with the creature. I have to finish things here."

"No killing," Sally warned him.

"Oh, of course not." But as soon as the traitorous woman swanned out to the clearing, all-but swooning to behold the ten-foot Gilim, Ah Dae-Sung cut the faint smile and ushered the women away from the professor's eyeline. "Breaking my word is always awkward. But in this case, sadly, it is necessary."

CHAPTER THIRTY-TWO

Jules didn't gamble. It wasn't in his nature. He took data—visual, audio, tactile—and processed it faster than most human beings on the planet. It was a quirk. An advantage most of the time. The only downside was his inability to switch it off without spending weeks retraining himself to ignore that segment of his psyche. When on patrol, he was glad of it. When not, he'd compartmentalized it.

Unfortunately, compartmentalizing it had made him rusty.

No longer did he simply "know" things. His mistakes on this expedition proved it. When he was down in Pukepuke, surfing the rooftops, evading capture, it seemed like it was coming back to him. Melding his duty through Tane Wiremu and his loyalty through Dan and Harpal, fighting back against the men infiltrating the village almost felt... good.

Now, though, after seeing what Charlie was up to, unable to warn her that the commander was approaching, a gamble was all he could think about. He didn't know enough to carry out his idea effectively.

Okay, all the variables were there, from the air density to each giant's location based on the noises emanating from them and the time it took to echo back off the volcano's sides. What he hadn't had time to study was the nature of Gilim and his family.

Alpha down—*check.*

His mate distraught—*check.*

A natural replacement for the alpha—*nowhere to be seen.*

If they were anything like animals in the wild, they would not respond well to Jules's interference. The other male giant, Rosso, might take his attempts to communicate as a direct challenge, and nothing could stop a homo colossus from tearing him apart.

Perhaps Dan and Tane would cheer him on.

On the way back here, speeding upriver on a jet ski having changed into one of the captured soldiers' uniforms, Jules had even rehearsed the argument that was sure to evolve once they were all together... if he survived.

- *I don't take orders from you.*

- *It's not about taking orders, it's about listening to people more experienced than you.*

- *The only person with more experience than me worth a damn is Tane, and that's just because he's known about these creatures longer than me.*

- *Wait on back up. It's incoming...*

None of that was said, though. Not out loud. There was some swearing, some shouting of orders, demands to return and not be so stupid, but it wasn't stupid to Jules. It was the way he'd done things all his life. How he'd survived. How he'd taken on people more powerful than him and won, how he'd escaped the cops on five continents, how he'd missed living for the past year and now wondered if New York was a mistake.

Was Brittany a better option? He'd made enough money through his earlier cuts from LORI's finds that he didn't need wages, at least not for a decade or more.

No time for second guessing, though. Now was a time for gambling.

Thirty-five seconds after concluding he couldn't help Charlie from his ingress point—the hole blasted in the mountain—Jules had located Nan and her two children, Wade and Noroth. She squatted, like a cat about to pounce on a sparrow, only nine and a quarter foot tall and stockier than the Hulk. Her clothing hung loosely, and she'd pulled her hair back over her ears, eyes pointing directly through the path leading to the central pavilion where Gilim had fallen. And where Charlie and Prihya were about to fall afoul of a rear attack.

During the thirty-five seconds it took for him to get here, Jules formed this loosest of plans, second-guessed himself over and over, and here he was about to chicken out.

The two children snorted with frustration, padding around behind their mother. The shaggy-haired one, Wade, occasionally stomped forward, clearly trying to return to his father, but Nan held out a thick arm and shoved him back. There was plainly a hierarchy that the youngsters respected.

Jules watched them, counting in his head. Forty seconds had passed, and he predicted Ah Dae-Sung would only need another thirty to be in range of Prihya and Charlie.

He revealed himself and stood still, arms by his side.

Nan's massive head whipped around. The two boys clocked him too, and reared up, chests out, like men squaring off in the street outside a bar. They held back, though, waiting for permission. Nostrils flared. Lips peeled back.

Prihya had insisted they spoke a kind-of protolanguage. From what Jules had heard earlier, it was more advanced than anything in the modern animal kingdom, including dolphins, but it was more tonal than actual words. Guttural and basic.

He bowed his head and averted his eyes, showing supplication.

Another ten seconds had passed.

Prihya.

Charlie.

Heck, Gilim. No one knew what awaited that poor guy if they didn't stop this extraction.

Nan lowered herself onto a fist and leaned in to Jules. He kept his head down, unsure how long he'd have after Ah Dae-Sung reached Charlie and Prihya. It could be she wouldn't need his help, but the sheer numbers were too much for him.

Nan snorted, spraying him with a fine mist of nasal particulate. No boogers, but he hoped the big gal didn't have a cold. She then brought one hand around, a fist. Jules tapped the female giant's hand with his own, eyes down, demonstrating supplication—a common gesture in animals. She and the two boys relaxed somewhat.

Jules lifted one eye, enough to see all, finding the trio watching him. The mother remained a sentinel, immovable, the boys skittish despite holding their ground. Jules risked lifting an arm, a greeting gesture he gambled—there was that word again—that they'd recognize as friendly.

The younger sibling—Noroth—tilted his head. Frowned. Then lifted his own hand. He waved in a childish manner, a smile creeping into being.

His big brother saw what he was doing and lowered himself on his haunches, as if about to charge at Jules. But Nan grunted to calm him, made a few clicking sounds followed by a low *f-f-f-f* noise. She was attempting to communicate with Jules, leaning in closer to hear his response.

But Ah Dae-Sung was probably within range. Jules was out of time. He'd hoped to gain some insight, some Bridget-like moment of clarity as she frequently had when stressing over a problem—a code or deciphering a key to a previously undiscovered language. That wasn't going to happen.

So, he flicked Nan on the nose. Nothing violent, not like a slap. Still, she jerked in shock. Wade and Noroth growled. Jules laughed.

As soon as Nan's eyes widened and her shoulders tensed, Jules took off running. He didn't need to look back to know all three had twisted, set their muscular tree-trunk legs, and bounded after him. The shaking ground and howls of anger were plenty.

Charlie sank to her knees, staring up at her captor. "You can't get away with this."

"I *am* getting away with this." Ah Dae-Sung used his free hand to make Prihya join Charlie.

"You promised you would not kill us," Prihya said.

The commander glanced toward the clearing, through the foliage, and back to the women. He leveled his gun at them. Finger on the trigger. "What she doesn't know will not hurt. And if she finds out—"

A primeval howl pealed out of the forest, startling Ah Dae-Sung from his task. He didn't immediately return, either, his brow furrowing at the *thoom-thoom-thoom* of heavy footfalls, like a meteor shower striking the earth.

It was the opening she needed.

Charlie threw herself at Ah Dae-Sung. If he'd been pointing the gun at her, she'd have had no chance, but the commotion surrounding the prone Gilim had startled him.

Mistake.

She went for the gun first, but he was faster, pulling it away from her reach as he sidestepped and threw a ridge-hand strike. It connected with the back of her neck. Shards of pain split her head and her shoulders, sending her tumbling forward. She staggered sideways before the ground came up to meet her. She twisted to land on her back, seeing Dae-Sung restore his calm and swing his gun up.

Prihya tackled him at the knees, pinning the joint together and shouldering into the backs of his thighs. A classic rugby tackle. It looked like she'd indulged in the local sports. Ah Dae-Sung couldn't stay upright but held onto his weapon as he keeled over.

Despite the pain, which felt like a trapped nerve, Charlie rolled forward and pinned the commander's gun hand. While Prihya struggled to hold on, Charlie slammed the man's arm against the ground, but the weapon would not come free.

He pulled a knife.

Charlie shouted, "Prihya, move!"

Prihya let go and rolled, just as Dae-Sung slashed downwards. The blade drew blood, a gash across her upper arm.

Charlie attempted a final twist of the submachine gun, but it wasn't going anywhere. The knife was, though, so all she could do was relinquish her grip and scramble backwards. Not before the blade cut into her leg, though.

It embedded itself in her calf, drawing a yelp and forcing her to stutter in her escape.

The commander was up on one knee. Charlie sensed this was the end. No more fighting, no more chances.

Except...

Three giants burst into the clearing—Gilim's mate and their two sons. They spread out, as if being directed by some unseen force. The soldiers who'd been strapping Gilim onto the gurney that Charlie had tried to sabotage fanned out, arming themselves. Pointing their weapons at the newcomers.

Ah Dae-Sung was no longer aiming at her. He yelled in Korean, and the workers with the prods and what looked like ropes and pulleys darted around, shouting into radios. Regrouping, fanning out, forming a perimeter.

But they were too slow.

Nan smashed the nearest enemy sideways, contorting his body into angles a human skeleton should not bend. He was dead before the first time he bounced. Guns fired, drawing blood, but penetrated no organs. The two juveniles spread out, both charging toward their father. Wade barely glanced at the gunman who was firing on auto, just kneed him at full speed as he plowed through.

Noroth gave two men his attention, though. He reached out and slammed them together, mashing them into one another with a sickening crunch.

Guns chattered, bullets flew, but—as LORI had been briefed—7.62mm rounds drew blood but could not penetrate the super-dense muscles of homo colossus. And they were angry. Fighting mad and determined to protect Gilim.

Charlie then spotted the human accompanying them.

Jules.

Of course it was Jules.

Jules had used the rampaging giants as cover, drawn them here having lit the fuse with the insulting flick, then let the keg explode as the threat to their kin became clear. His gamble had paid off.

Sprinting on, he only paused once to scoop up a rock and fling it at a gunman who drew down on him. It hit the man square in the forehead, giving Jules the half-second he needed to barge into him. He lifted the guy off his feet, redirected his target's momentum into a midair spin, and thrust his heel through the guy's jaw before he landed. Jules ran onward, having lost a step.

The abduction was continuing, though. They'd discarded the gurney and instead hooked a clamp to the straps holding Gilim in place.

Even darting from the most dangerous section of the fray, Jules absorbed multiple inputs: left and right, ahead, up and down. And now he saw Charlie and Prihya recovering, heading for what he hoped was cover. Charlie was limping, trailing blood.

Having realized their bullets just angered them, a couple of the attackers opted to use the electric shocks to fend off the incoming giants, while others fussed over Gilim. The commander was nowhere to be seen. Another man appeared to be giving orders on the ground. The man with the muscles. The one Tane had told them was Ah Dae-Sung's trusted lieutenant, his second in command. If Dae-Sung had disappeared, he was heading for the final extraction. And if none of the armed minions were paying Jules much attention, that meant they had bigger things to address.

Like repeating their trick with the shield back in Alabama.

As if on cue, the wind picked up, a radial whirl of a tornado that Jules recognized as downdraft. The helicopter positioning overhead was a heavy-duty transport with engine mufflers. Although not silent, the battle had masked its approach. Any aerial defenses must have been defeated, and they were relying on Tane drumming up support.

It would be too late.

Jules ditched his escape plan and redirected himself to the sleeping Gilim. The men were still prepping him, but the extraction would now be more precarious. No time to mount him on secure equipment.

It could kill him. Then where would it leave this colony?

Already beyond Gilim, fleeing toward Charlie, Jules switched direction. He took an arc behind the prone creature, keeping low as the troops guided the helicopter's harness toward an accumulation of straps, the center of gravity for the big guy. He struck the first of four men in the back of the head with his elbow. It wasn't strong enough to cause brain damage, but he'd be too dazed to fight for the next minute or so.

Which was all Jules expected he'd need.

He scrambled up onto Gilim, saw how the Koreans were fending off the family with their oversized cattle prods, and the high-pitched keening from Nan, veering away as she called into the forest. More vibrations thundered toward them.

Forget Tane's backup. All Jules needed was to buy enough time for the other alpha to find them.

Jules dropped the other side, to where the three remaining troops were tugging clasps tight—two grunts and Pang Pyong-Ho. He took the first one at the knee, a horrible injury but the guy would have avoided if he wasn't involved in this affair. Jules felt no guilt as he put a flat hand through his throat to disable him further.

The next one abandoned his job and raised his knee in preparation for a round kick. But in the fraction of a second between initiating the move and shifting to its second phase, Jules read the intent —a swift taekwondo attack. He countered it with a pivot into the joint to nullify its range, swept the standing leg, and brought his own knee into the man's ribs. It flung him sideways, clearing the way for Jules and Pyong-Ho to face off.

The Korean lieutenant patted the thick, solid form beside him, and faced Jules with a look of glee as he adopted a backward fighting stance.

Taekwondo was a national sport in both Korean states, as synonymous with their cultures as krav maga was in Israel and rugby in New Zealand. In most of the world, Taekwondo teaching focused on the sporting aspect, but when learned to a military standard—which Jules guessed Pyong-Ho would have achieved—it was a fast, deadly fighting style. Most practitioners were smaller than his prospective opponent here, though, as the real masters relied on speed and strength.

In his teens, Jules was a world champion in krav maga, and could best his wing chun teachers just two years after commencing. But his chosen go-to fighting art remained aikido. It used an opponent's strength against them, emitted an almost balletic manner with which he could dispatch attackers, and the hard, fast, and direct strikes from his other fighting styles had left many a bodyguard, mercenary and thief wishing they hadn't gotten physical with the skinny looking kid.

Jules adopted a casual stance to Pyong-Ho's formal one. He found he could move faster, springing forward and back. This would not be as simple as taking out a random merc.

Pyong-Ho made the first move, a shuffle and a dummy kick. Jules hopped to the side, still getting the measure of him.

But that was what the lieutenant wanted. It shifted Jules out of range and allowed Pyong-Ho to wrap his arm around one of the central straps containing Gilim. He winked, gave a sarcastic salute, and in a terrible American drawl said, "Another time, pard'ner." He sounded like a child doing a cowboy impression.

With a handful of soldiers abandoning the perimeter to leap on and cling there, the helicopter hoisted Gilim into the air. Pang Pyong-Ho and those with the strong enough grips rose out of the forest.

Nan charged forward, her skin blemished by bullet holes and electrical burns. She sprang up, after her mate, swiping at him as he receded out of reach. She landed with an almighty thump.

The trees shook and a new giant emerged. Rosso—full of primeval survivalist rage—crashed out of the canopy, branches the size of human limb splintering off. With his run up, he had better distance, better height, than Nan. His fingers gripped the main cable holding Gilim, slapping aside the nearest soldier, who fell over fifteen feet. Teeth bared, drool slopping, he swung again, this time toward Pyong-Ho.

A mechanical *chug-chug-chug* began, louder than the rotors, flashes from the helicopter's body. Tracer rounds tore through Rosso, a rail gun providing the firepower needed to penetrate.

He howled as his body jiggled, then released his grip before plummeting to the earth.

Jules had to run to avoid being squashed.

The giant slapped to the ground with an earthquake-like thump. He lay there, bleeding, staring at the sky.

They *all* stared. Nothing anyone could do but watch. Even Nan was too heartbroken to remember why she'd started chasing Jules, and all Jules wanted to do was comfort her.

Instead, he backed away, in case she looked to other humans for vengeance. Jules had done all he could. And it wasn't enough.

CHAPTER THIRTY-THREE

It was all over. Jules had never felt so empty, so worthless. He'd followed Tane, and he'd followed his instincts, and neither had borne fruit. A North Korean fighting force had invaded New Zealand's sovereign land and stolen a creature to power a weapon that could destroy cities, if not countries. When Jules set out a few days ago, taking leave from his role as an officer of the law, he'd expected a somewhat exciting archeological puzzle and maybe even a dig. If he'd known that it'd escalate to full-blown massacres and hauling the world to the brink of war, he'd have stayed home and done yoga.

Home.

That was an odd concept to him.

Could he even be a cop now? After his failures here? Not protecting Gilim, not serving the people.

All together again, the remaining group occupied the observation deck, battered and bruised. The only addition to their troupe was Julia Grainger, who had arrived in person with the too late reinforcements and began the debriefing by spitting fire. After absorbing the horrific news of fourteen dead and seven badly injured, she quickly morphed into a more diplomatic approach.

"How long until they can activate their weapon?" she asked.

Tane said, "We don't know how they'll get out of New Zealand. Probably cloaked the same way they approached Ahua. Let's say four hours. If they then take between ten and twelve hours to reach the

Korean peninsula, add a day to get set up with Gilim and the shields…"

"A day?" Jules said, staring out at the forest and the distraught giants consoling one another. Two families in grief. "How do you figure?"

Prihya answered for him, sounding as tired as Jules felt. "To charge up the activation suite, it's at least an hour with Gilim compliant. Then, we need several hours for the shield to absorb that energy. Multiplying the same factors, using three more shields, and redirecting it through whatever setup they have there… Yes, a day, day and a half max." She folded her arms across her body. "If they want to control the energy spike and resulting dome, they'll need Gilim conscious and willing."

"They can't just strap him in and wake him up?" Toby said.

"No, we tried it," Tane said. "It has to be a conscious act. Entering the machine and activating it."

Bridget presented the page she'd written on, the glyphs and symbols of the people known by LORI as the Witnesses and by their hosts as the Elder Race. "Perhaps there's a clue here. I can see more patterns now, and there's some continuity to it."

No one had discussed this in any depth. Yes, Jules was shocked when Bridget told him what happened, but it was similar to his own experiences when plugged into the network: vivid, clear images, knowledge pouring in. But when the subject disconnected, their recollection of the event faded. Less like a dream, more like the way bright white dots fade from sight after staring at a candle for a while. You know you've done it, but the actual events have disappeared. Surprising that it had happened to Bridget when she was not genetically tuned to elements like the meteor rocks and powerful spheres, but her account of the experience made a certain sense.

Jules said, "This section isn't connected to the main network."

"It can send information to the other orbs, but it can't *control* anything," Bridget said.

"Neutrinos have no mass," Charlie elaborated. "So they can still pass between points. Just not through the fractures in the Earth's crust. Because we're not on one anymore."

Prihya tapped a pen on her chin, a look of concentration as she glanced between the activation suite Bridget had used and the agitated giants below, then to the orb and the machinery surrounding it. "If that's the case, and we wire it to one of our guys down there, it might tap a different chamber. Somewhere else."

Dan perked up. "Somewhere else like Korea?"

"That wouldn't work," Bridget said. "But you could send it through virtually any other point on the planet. A different orb that can still be activated. If we can work out the commands..." She rustled the paper she'd written on.

Jules said, "We don't know anything for certain."

"It's the best we can do, though," Toby insisted.

"It's more likely the executive'll have thought of that. If we send conflicting signals, it'll either do nothing or it'll do something we don't want. Something bad."

"Like a feedback loop?" Charlie suggested.

"Yeah, like a feedback loop. I'm thinkin' that'll either destroy or disable every machine in the network."

Harpal said, "There has to be another way."

"Why?" Jules asked.

Dan stood and scanned the faces. "What do you mean, 'why?' Because there has to be."

"No there doesn't."

Dan scowled and was about to do something macho-looking or aggressive, but Bridget intervened.

"He's right," she said. "People always say, 'there has to be another way,' and we've always found an alternative to the worst-case scenario in the past. But that doesn't mean there *is* one. Destroying it now, before the American Navy fires a bunch of cruise missiles at a Korean mountain range... maybe that's the best bad option."

All considered it. No one was happy.

Julia Grainger broke the silence. "What's our timeframe for coming up with alternatives?"

"Negligible," Tane replied. "Hours to choose, hours to enact it."

Toby puffed up his chest and spoke in a firm, measured tone. "Then we must destroy the network before Ryom Jung-Hwan can activate the wider machine. Prihya can manage it, I'm sure."

"Then there's Gilim," Jules said. "And his people down there." He watched the two families mooching around, picking through the detritus left behind. They had moved the bodies of their slain enemies to the side, laid them respectfully on their backs, and retreated to a spot where they could not view the dead. "They miss him. They don't understand why he isn't there. Where he could have gone."

"No concept of a world outside theirs," Prihya said. "And they've never experienced death among their own kind."

"One other point we haven't discussed," Dan put in. "This so-called network. This defensive shield. What if we dismantle it, and one day we need it?"

Tane and Julia studied him before the minister's phone trilled. She answered it and adjourned to a corner to take the call.

Tane twigged what Dan meant. "The ability to deflect a meteor strike?"

Dan nodded. Then shrugged. "Or, you know, alien invaders. A magnetic flip thanks to a solar flare. Something like that."

For once, no one laughed at Dan's notion of aliens visiting the planet—for good or ill. Jules had nothing left in him that constituted amusement. He was empty, ready to pull the trigger and destroy this whole thing, return to New York and... Then what? Dismiss all he'd seen and be a cop? Quit and teach yoga? Race around the world delivering black market artefact hoarders a lesson they'll never forget?

He said, "Can we contain the knowledge? With internal failsafes?"

"What do you mean?" Prihya asked.

"What happens to the giants here if we destroy the mechanism worldwide?"

"They grow old, maybe breed, then die like everyone else."

"Yet the Koreans are preparing to launch their own version, to isolate themselves further. Won't they need more like Gilim to keep things going? They ain't immortal."

"It's failed," Julia Grainger said, rejoining them as she hung up on the caller. "That was Colin Waterston. The Koreans won't even take the US President's call. Nor the UN's, or the British or New Zealand Prime Ministers. No world leaders, no military communications of any kind. That whole country is a bunker. They're cutting themselves off."

"And the fleet?" Dan said.

"US Navy is a day and a half away from effective range."

"Isn't there a response from the North Korean fleet?" Harpal asked.

"Not as far as we can see. And they don't have enough subs to sink those battleships."

Toby said, "The Chinese? How are they taking it?"

"By not objecting to the US presence. They are considering their position regarding military action. If Ryom's project threatens them, they'll act."

"The Russians?" Dan said.

"No comment except that they're 'standing by.'" Grainger straightened her back. "We take that to mean they'll see which way the wind blows before taking a side. Officially, they see no evidence of aggression from their allies in the North Korean government. I expect they will side with them against the US."

Tane said, "It can't be contained now. No one can stop the machine from activating. The US will fire their cruise missiles at that location, and I guess we'll see. Either the war will have fewer casualties than the shield ripping across the continent, or the human race is in serious trouble."

Jules made a *Hmmm* noise.

Bridget said, "What was that?"

"Just Jules murmuring," Toby answered. "But it was an interesting murmur, I think you'll agree."

Jules quashed his annoyance by pivoting away and staring into the forest below. He needed to gather his thoughts.

"When Jules makes a noise like that," Bridget explained, "it means he's thinking."

Toby agreed. "And for a lad whose brain calculates a dozen factors in the blink of an eye, it's always something worth thinking about."

"Hate to admit it," Dan said, "but he might be about to disprove his own point about the lack of an alternative."

"Well?" Grainger said, stepping toward Jules. "If you're as bright as they say..."

"Give me a break." Jules spun and set his jaw, taking in the group, all waiting on him as if he was about to turn water into wine. "This is a dumb idea. Can't work."

Tane said, "We'll take dumb over nothing."

"I haven't got it straight myself yet. But can you access all your intelligence on the Dragon's Pit? Can we view it here?"

"Sure, but—"

"Then do it. And stand back. I need a few minutes of silence."

CHAPTER THIRTY-FOUR

The connections weren't there yet, but something that had been said more than once stuck with Jules. That was the key that kept turning in the lock. Unfortunately, the lock was rusted and difficult to turn, the answer hidden. But the NZSIS intelligence on the Dragon's Teeth mountain range and the prison camp ensconced in the valley might serve as a squirt of oil. As Jules digested it in merciful silence—silence except for the shuffling of shoes and tense nose-breathing, but he could cope with that—he eased the lock aside, and door cracked open.

He was ready for an audience.

"The Dragon's Pit is officially a mine," he said. "It's a labor camp for the sake of labor. They were minin' gold by the thimbleful until Ryom Jung-Hwan bought it from the government ten years ago. It's situated where the valley turns in a dogleg, where the walls are almost sheer. Paths lead up the sides to guard stations and a massive garbage dump. Beyond this is five hundred square miles of rock and scrub-land. Very little water away from the reservoir, and it's freezing."

"No need for big walls," Tane said. "The land is deterrent enough."

"And you don't get many satellite photos 'cause it's near-constant cloud cover."

Toby said, "The breath from a dragon running over its teeth."

"Yeah, let's leave the myth stuff for now. Unless you got something important." When no one else interrupted, Jules went on. "But we know the mine's more than a gulag, and the gulag's gotten bigger the last few years. More people got shipped in, and suddenly, they were building something."

He pulled up the latest surveillance picture from a few months earlier.

"Now it's a dam. According to the government, it's a hydroelectric facility that bunged up a small river. It don't power anything inside the country, but shared intelligence reports say it appears to be online."

"Meaning it's powering something," Charlie said.

"Probably the machine they're usin' to activate the shields. They just can't control it to cover their prison camp."

"So they know enough to know their limits," Prihya said.

Tane nodded, understanding. "That's why they took Gilim. Because they need him as an anchor."

Jules said, "With that final component, they have no limits. But they can limit themselves."

"Or expand the destruction," Grainger said.

Toby slapped the desk he was leaning on. "And they got that knowledge through Sally Garcia."

"Much of it will be legend and hearsay," Bridget pointed out. "How much use can she be?"

"Depends what else they're hidin'," Jules answered. "And there's only one way we can find out."

"Parachute an SAS unit in," Harpal said.

"Or Army Rangers," Dan said, the former Ranger getting territorial.

"Whatever." Harpal appraised the screen with the blown-up gulag and dam displayed. "They'd see anyone coming."

"He's right." Dan had closed the frosty distance between himself and Harpal, and they were on the same wavelength that Jules remembered. "Can't just drop in on somewhere like that. Soon as they break cloud cover, they're screwed."

"They might be," Jules said, "but *we* might stand a chance."

It was like a Mexican wave of furrowed brows, starting with Toby, then rippling across the group.

This was the part Jules didn't want to express but saw little option. "The Americans are using bombs. Not enough time to send up a drone to take out the place, no time to plan an assault. Same with the Brits. The Chinese and Russians ain't gettin' involved in case they need Ryom and his government as allies. You know any other country willing to go in, ready to improv?"

"The Aussies might," Dan replied. "They're underrated and really badass."

Charlie said, "You want *us* to mount an assault?"

"We're archaeologists," Toby said.

"Me, Dan, Harpal, and Tane." Jules made a grim canvass of the guys he'd named. "At the risk of being a bit sexist, the ladies are better placed here, with the machine, ready to blow it if we miss."

Charlie showed off her bandaged leg and the aluminum cane she'd been given. "I'll allow it. Just this once."

Toby coughed. "Ahem."

Jules said, "You're a big brain too."

"You can make the tea," Harpal said.

Toby rounded on him. A younger man might have flipped him the bird, but as an honorable professor, Toby resorted to a pointed sigh.

"Back to this." Jules picked up a tablet and performed a quick search. "We're in New Zealand. Famous for its extreme sports, right?" He eyed Tane a moment, received a nod in reply, and revealed his result. "So this equipment is readily available. And ain't exactly standard issue for Special Forces."

His three would-be teammates inspected his proposal.

Harpal's eyes flared with excitement. "I've been meaning to get you guys to play with one of those for years."

"So..." Jules placed it aside. "How do we travel there? Tane?"

"We can source a plane," Tane said.

Grainger shook her head. "You'd never get clearance. They'll shoot it down if you go over North Korea, and the Chinese won't allow us to use their airspace."

"Alfonse?" Charlie suggested.

"I'll try him," Toby said, taking out his phone.

"Let me." Bridget relieved him of the handset. "I think he'll be sweeter if it comes from me." She retreated to a quiet spot.

"Who's Alfonse?" Grainger asked.

"A chap with a lot of contacts," Toby replied. "He could get a plane and maybe even approval to use their airspace. He's very resourceful."

Jules was still working through it. Toby's other comment—*we're archaeologists*—rang true, and it was possibly the most outrageous aspect of all this. "I got moves. I can fight. I can shoot. I can get in that valley unseen, if Tane gets me the equipment we need."

"I will," Tane said.

"Good. Thing is, I trained to go up against the bad people I was robbing. Evading capture by cops. Takin' out bad guys' security. Yeah, I do okay against the special forces dudes one-on-one, but that's 'cause I got the advantage up here."

Jules tapped his head. Didn't even glance at Dan as he knew there'd be an objection. But he'd bested Dan without hurting him too badly and had only seriously hurt a handful of people in the past—those who'd given him little choice.

"Point is, I never experienced combat. I keep a logical head. When I got a few seconds to work out an escape or how to take someone down, I can do it. I ain't a commando. This isn't the... what's it called? The A-Team? Going up against some ragtag group of wannabe gangsters? This is us invadin' a military installation. I'm way outta my comfort zone here. It's the toughest fight I ever had."

Jules realized he was monologuing, something that annoyed him in other people. Filling dead air until a piece fell into place.

Bridget returned to them, having concluded a phone call. "Alfonse sends his regrets."

"No go?" Harpal said.

"Some things, he said, are beyond even him."

"Then we're done." Dan bowed his head. "It's war."

"I might have one idea," Bridget said. "But I'll need a little time."

Jules didn't ask permission. He simply accessed the forest level and wandered out to the clearing where Gilim's mate and two sons were idling. They saw him and Noroth snorted, leaned on a fist much like a gorilla, but his mother came alongside him and stared at Jules.

"Hey," Jules said, lifting a weak hand into a wave.

No response.

The other family was close by, too. Jules could hear them, but they were on the other side of a dip in the land where trees had grown thickly. He had approached with as much open ground as he could, hoping he wouldn't startle them. He had assaulted them after all. The fact his actions had prompted these peaceful beasts to use their strength to defend their home was irrelevant if all they remembered was him flicking his finger at the female colossus.

Nan had seemingly forgiven him. Either she'd worked out why he did it, or it was such an insignificant act she didn't hold a grudge.

"I'm sorry I got here too late," he said.

Nan's head tilted. Listening.

Did she hear and understand? Or was it noises to her? Like a cat meowing at a human?

A heavy *crunch* sounded. Foliage parted to Jules's left. The other patriarch, Rosso, lumbered through, four feet taller and wider than Jules. Wounded but functioning, he placed himself between Jules and Nan, and glared at Jules.

Time to run?

Nan made a keening sound, followed by a throaty huff and some short, sharp grunts.

Rosso narrowed his eyes and backed up, wincing in pain. They couldn't tell how deep the bullets from the helicopter's machine gun had penetrated, but one arm hung loose, and those to his torso and stomach caused him obvious discomfort. Prihya had told them a medical team would knock them all out and perform surgery once the area could be secured, the systems controlling the gas brought back online, and the personnel restored. Even injured, he never took his attention off Jules, handing Nan a corpse. It was a deer that he'd carried easily under his good arm.

Dinner.

When his parents were murdered, the fourteen-year-old Jules had stayed with an elderly neighbor. She had insisted, and he'd helped around the house for a few days. He'd kind of expected to remain, but then Child Protective Services had intervened and slotted him into a system not designed to cope with the numbers it was charged with, nor seemed to care enough to change. During that time, other neighbors from their building had brought food: pies, brisket, desert, and sandwiches. He'd thought it odd but learned in time that it was something friends did for grieving families. No one wanted to think about preparing meals whilst crippled with sadness. And the bereaved still needed their strength.

"You're carrying on," Jules said. "It's the worst moment of your lives and you're keeping goin' somehow. Keeping the kids in line. Friends bringing food..."

"We're in business," Bridget said from behind him.

Jules turned to find all of them holding position at a beaten path twenty feet away so as not to startle the grieving families. Charlie, Dan, Harpal, Tane, Prihya and Toby. Ready to risk it all. Ready to play at more than archaeology.

"When this is over," Jules said, approaching his friends, "let's go find a new dinosaur or something."

"You got it," Dan said.

Toby offered a paternal smile, his eyes wandering briefly to the giants. "It'll be next on the list, I promise."

"First, though," Charlie said, "you have a flight to catch. Bridget came through."

"Okay." Jules moved up close to Bridget. "I'll thank you if we come home alive."

Bridget's smile was wide but tinged with worry and sadness. "I'll be waiting."

PART FOUR

CHAPTER THIRTY-FIVE

Although Bridget had never concealed her family's wealth, she frequently came across as somewhat embarrassed by it. Not entirely *embarrassed*, Jules supposed, but she certainly avoided advertising it. Today, however, she was more than happy to share the "unlimited resources" her father had placed at her disposal.

The Cessna private jet, collected after a brief layover in Canberra, Australia, was far more luxurious than LORI's, which they'd mothballed in Brittany thanks to the cost of fueling it. This plane was part of the Carson fleet acquired last year and was in the process of being rebranded when the call came to loan it to the rough-looking men who'd arrived from New Zealand.

With the plane already fueled and checked, the Action Dudes flew it north, having negotiated safe passage over Indonesia, before looping down south of Japan and around the west coast of South Korea, before driving on north over the Yellow Sea. Alternating between sleep and prep, the journey was faster than a commercial airline, and they soon skirted Korea Bay and flew over the Chinese mainland between Jinzhou and Dandong. As arranged through officials friendly to the Carson Corporation, they proceeded unimpeded farther north, over Yalu province and into Tumen, before turning a slow 180-degrees to arrow into North Korea.

Approaching North Korean airspace, Dan and Harpal set the plane on autopilot, changed into their operational gear, and joined

Tane and Jules, who had been going over the sketchy satellite photos of the Dragon's Pit since Korea Bay.

Officially a mine, the clouds parted rarely, but on one such occasion a German satellite captured the lines of "workers" and the armed guards who seldom graced the face of many strip mines. It was undoubtedly a gulag, a prison where inmates were worked to the bone before either being reeducated to make them better citizens upon release or their ashes scattered after their death.

"The intel is months old, though," Tane cautioned. "Compare it to flyovers two years before, and it looks like the Dragon's Pit inmates've constructed an entire dam in the valley during that time."

Harpal whistled in appreciation. "That's a heck of a construction project."

"It cuts off this river," Jules said, showing them a line out of China's Tumen province, which split into several smaller rivers. "Stretches across this narrow section of valley and creates a reservoir, with the main residential section of the Dragon's Pit below the water level. It drains into streams and leaves a lot of channels branching off south and east."

"From what we can tell," Tane added, "it doesn't feed into the national grid. It's powering nothing except itself."

"Or whatever they need Gilim for," Dan said.

All understood what was at stake here.

"This is the best LZ." Tane pointed at a landing zone a half-mile the other side of a hill and would take them thirty minutes of hiking to reach the Pit. "It was a garbage dump during the gulag's early days, but they switched to filling in a disused quarry above the valley once the dam started going up."

"And there's no other way in?" Harpal asked. "I mean, I'm cool with a HALO, but how long since the rest of you did one?"

"Rangers had us practice four times a year," Dan said. "It's been a while, but assuming the kit doesn't fail, I won't either."

"I'm cool." Jules hadn't performed a jump like this for five years, and that was one of three. And never from 20,000 feet—well above the maximum cruising height for most planes of this spec. He had gone through the checklist, so his near-eidetic memory was intact. He just had to hope his muscle memory clung to the same level of detail as it had done in his martial arts, shooting, and parkour.

They'd all donned the jumpsuits over their SWAT-style attire, sealed to survive the freezing temperature and lack of oxygen during a high-altitude, low-opening (HALO) jump. It was the only fast way to infiltrate a country this well defended. They'd need breathers and helmets, in addition to wing suits to fly them accurately toward the exact location. Not that they were full wing suits, not like the flying squirrel ones, just some extra webbing under the arms to help steer and slow their descent. It allowed the Cessna to venture close but not so close it would alert the authorities. A few tiny humans were unlikely to trouble even the most advanced radar.

Tane recapped as they synced their watches. "Once we're down, we'll have two hours to disable the machine and retrieve Gilim, or Bridget and Charlie will try to blow the network. Every section on earth will implode, and no one in the vicinity will survive. If we fail, and they can't make that feedback loop work, the Americans will launch their cruise missiles, and the world is at war."

Jules heard beeping from the cockpit, but shot back, "Hey, if our own Professor Toby 'state the obvious' Smith decides to retire, you should take over. "

Tane laughed. "I don't apologize for being thorough. I'm gonna repeat myself again before the jump, and you can't stop me."

"Nah, but I can grab another nap." Jules checked inside the cockpit and found a red light flashing in time with the beep. "What's this?"

Harpal came over. "Damn, it's a warning light. Someone's hailing us." He sat in the pilot's chair and put on a headset. "This is Neo Zulu Oz; can we help with something?"

Dan crowded in, too, while Tane paid attention as he pulled the reports and photos together.

Harpal's brow furrowed, and he answered in a hurry, "We're in Chinese airspace on an approved vector—" He stopped talking, shook his head, and removed the headphones. "It's Korean."

Tane rushed over, took the cans, and listened. "They want to shoot us down." Into the mic, he said, "Negative. We are..." He switched to Korean. Far from fluent, but he'd stated earlier he could get by. He snorted in frustration and threw the headset into the co-pilot's chair. "He's a fighter pilot. Says we're in a disputed area. A neutral zone. He's on an intercept course. We have to change direction, or he'll blow us out of the sky."

"We can't," Jules said. "If we do, we'll miss our window. The wing suits won't get us there."

"What if we jump now?" Dan asked.

"Maybe."

"Maybe is all we have." Tane barged past and gathered the gear they'd got ready. "We have thirty seconds. Yes, or no?"

Jules was the first to join him, taking up the GPS unit they would use to guide them in, followed by a helmet that covered his entire head. "This plane was supposed to ditch in the ocean. I guess a rocket up the butt won't change much."

Dan and Harpal donned their rebreathers and helmets, and helped each other seal them in. The oxygen tanks—one-liter canisters strapped to their sides—were already in place, and the parachutes slipped on easily.

It was actually forty-two seconds before the scream of a MIG's jet engines shook the plane. The Cessna undulated like a surfboard on a wave.

"Warning pass," Tane said, muffled through his oxygen mask. "There won't be another."

"Punch it," Harpal said, mouth equally shut in.

Without time for a second check over, Dan made for the door. "We need to get out before the MIG turns. A visual of us bailing out'll give the game away."

"Then stop talking and open her up," Jules said, feeling like a Spitfire pilot with the mask strapped over his mouth and nose.

Dan gripped the lever and heaved it aside. The door gave a tight squeak. Everyone held onto the overhead rail. Dan thumped it open. Wind howled in, sucking at them as the cabin depressurized. The onboard computer compensated, but the altitude began dropping right away.

Dan jumped.

"You go next," Tane said.

As Jules was the next closest, he didn't argue. He moved hand over hand, stabilized himself, then dropped out, arms pinned to his side.

The sensation was always the same, his stomach shooting up into his throat. He monitored his own speed, jumping to 50MPH within a second, before passing the belly-to-earth maximum velocity of 120MPH three seconds later. But since he was in a head down, arms-pinned position, he carried less drag and continued to accelerate.

An explosion lit up the sky, then the MIG's wake buffeted him as it plowed overhead.

Jules's velocity prevented him from looking back. This had become a total gamble whether the Dragon's Pit knew they were coming. They needed to drop at least ten thousand feet before engaging the wings, which would take the edge off the snap of the final parachute opening—less risky than a typical HALO jump, but they'd still be traveling far faster than was safe, especially so close to the ground. They just had to get there first, which was easier said than done.

G-forces pressed on his face, his eyeballs, making his eyes water. His neck ached, so he repositioned his head to take the pressure off. He sensed his velocity approach 150MPH and getting faster still. His head felt like it was squeezing his brain. No ability to speak, no way to check on the others. The altimeter beeped in his ear; the beep-beep-beep more rapid as he approached 10,000 feet.

The continuous beacon sounded.

Jules remained head down and spread his arms an inch at a time. He felt the air resistance bite the webbing under his arms. He craned his neck up and stretched his shoulders back. Too fast and he'd flip backwards into an uncontrollable spin, rocketing head over heels where not even deploying the 'chute would save him.

Gradually, he came up, perhaps at 8,000 feet, but he'd lost count. He pulled almost horizontal, the classic belly-down position. He dropped far slower than a regular skydiver, and it took all his strength and concentration to remain stable. He risked a glance at the GPS on his forearm.

His location flashed green, his target red.

It was too dark to even try spotting anyone else, so he dipped his right shoulder, eased his torso into a downward angle, and steered back on course.

Able to see the contours of the ground, the mountains below stretching into the distance, Jules realized the beeping had ceased and someone was talking. His ears had popped at some point, and now he'd tuned in to the radio.

"Repeat, Bangle Boy, are you with us?" came Dan's voice.

Jules's throat croaked with the exertion of the past two minutes, but he found enough breath to speak. "I don't remember agreeing call signs. And definitely not that one."

"Bangle Boy is with us," Dan said with a whoop. "Asian Mr. Bean, Kiwi Bird, we are good for landing."

"He totally made those up this second," Harpal answered.

"I think he's drunk," Tane said. "Or altitude sickness."

"Guessin' Dan's is a bit cooler?" Jules asked.

"I'm Golden Harpoon," Dan said.

"Not anymore," Harpal replied. "You're the Pink Cowboy."

"Not a chance."

"Hey, Pink Cowboy," Jules said, "what's your altitude? I'm at 6,000."

"Three. Target in sight." Dan snorted. "And I'm Golden Harpoon."

"Got that, Pink Cowboy," Tane said. "Kiwi Bird is at 4,500. Bangle Boy, you need to drop faster."

"Copy that." Jules referred to his GPS and saw Tane was correct. He descended between two peaks, recognizing the landscape from the satellite photos. "On the final approach."

Because the Dragon's Teeth mountain range was pretty high, the valley was way above sea level, so coming in at 3,000 feet, Dan must have been almost on the water or the ground. At 4,000 feet, Jules leveled out, letting the small wings and his speed glide him onwards. The more experienced pair of Tane and Harpal had overtaken him.

"Got a visual," Jules said.

"Golden Harpoon is down safely," Dan reported.

"On my six," Tane said. "I see the LZ."

The dots on Jules's GPS were closer, almost touching. All they had to do was guide themselves around a peak to the left and pull to a halt at 100MPH.

Simple.

Jules tailed them, following their path, counting down with the coordinates. They approached the mountainside as planned, eased upward until they saw the landing zone—a garbage dump below the dam but hidden from view and allowed to fester, where it had rotted down to an uneven mass of junk. It was a small target at such a high speed.

They also couldn't deploy the chutes hurtling almost horizontally, so Jules switched position again. Arms to his side, feet down this time. It increased his speed. When he achieved the high position, he hit the parachute.

The *whoomph* of canvass overhead decelerated him so fast he half-expected an airbag to slam into his face. He'd forgotten something for once: the toll this kind of incursion took on the body.

"Kiwi Bird down safe," Tane said. "Asian Bean, what are you *doing*?"

Below, Tane was there, beside Dan, Jules on target too. However, while Harpal had deployed his parachute, he was much higher than Jules. And he was flying off-course.

"It's Asian *Mister* Bean," Dan said.

"We can argue later," Harpal replied. "But I caught a thermal. I'm correcting... I'm—"

He was well off-course, rising awkwardly like an injured hawk buffeted in a storm. Even as Jules was only watching shadows, he could see Harpal struggling to correct, drifting beyond the garbage field. He was turning, twisting into a stunt parachutist's spin, heading for the hillside too fast.

He steered away, taking him out... out... past the hillside where he'd be exposed to the Dragon's Pit dam and anyone watching the area.

Jules touched down hard, but without damaging his knees, and rolled, snarling himself in his lines. Dan cut through the tangle and the soft ground allowed him to stuff the chute into the muck without it flying away.

"Asian Mr. Bean, report," Dan said.

No answer.

The three guys ran silently to the dump's edge, looking out on a valley less than a mile across, a sheer wall off to their right, the dam itself towering over them, spectacular against the night sky. Something fluttered atop the dam, billowing hard.

"I'm here," Harpal said. "I've landed. Sort of."

The object ceased fluttering, Harpal gathering his canvass and stashing it to hide it from view.

"I'm on a balcony, a lookout point, I think. But I don't hear anything."

"Can you get down here?" Tane asked.

"Negative. Not right away. I'll try to join you soon, but there's a whole network of scaffolding going on."

"New plan," Dan said. "Look down there."

Jules and Tane followed his finger. They were a little over halfway up the dam, granting them a view of the scene below. The prison camp stretched for a half-mile down the valley and seemed to fill it with huts, buildings, and machinery.

Jules retrieved night vision binoculars from his pack and brought them to his eyes, adjusting for the flares of illumination. People shuffled around in the lights of flickering fires and low-wattage artificial bulbs. They all wore the same boiler suits, their heads shaved. Some carried tools, others slumped on the ground.

This was the Dragon's Pit gulag.

Jules lowered the glasses.

"Asian Mr. Bean stays up top," Dan said, who still had his own binoculars to his face. "We were always gonna need eyes and ears up top, so this is just a change of location. He can help us get down there and find a route into the main complex. Agreed?"

"Agreed," Tane said.

Jules said nothing. He set off, tramping his way to what he was sure would be a living hell.

CHAPTER THIRTY-SIX

Winding down from the former garbage dump, an overgrown road hooked back on itself in a series of hairpins, raised sides hewn out of the valley walls concealing their approach from eyes below. They had to be on the lookout for cameras and patrols, although Harpal would —hopefully—spot movement before they did.

Jules made a quick inventory of the gear they'd brought, Tane and Dan doing the same alongside. Because of the HALO jump, they'd used small packs—wide against their backs but as flat as possible to accommodate the 'chutes, air tanks, and thermals. At the top, in a pouch designed for it, Jules found the snub-nosed Glock 17 which Tane had insisted upon, then snug against this was one of his batons with the grappling hook and a bungee cord wrapped inside. Two multi-tools of differing sizes often came in handy, and each of them had packed a full-strength flashbang grenade. Jules pulled out a belt which he'd stocked up with his preferred selections of throwing knives and mini flashbangs and secured it around his waist.

Finally, encased in bubble wrap since the foam rubber was too bulky, he checked on the two stone bangles. Jules didn't want to be left high and dry if it turned out they were needed. It was a risk, though. If they fell into the Executive's hands, they might prove even more dangerous than if Valerio Conchin had succeeded back when Jules first hooked up with Toby and the Institute.

Seems like an age ago. Another life.

They reached the bottom without incident, scanning the camp and the surrounding land which was a hundred-yard dash from the lane entrance across a forked road, the other prong leading back down the valley. The perimeter fence appeared flimsy by prison standards, and a tower in the center held a single man, two unlit spot lamps, and two mounted machine guns. Each weapon had a 180-degree sweep of the complex. Huts served as accommodation, lining the grid of lanes and "streets" and were lit only by wan lanterns.

The residential section reminded Jules of Second World War-era prisoner of war camps, complete with prisoners in coveralls, the only addition to the black-and-white footage in his memory being gray fleece hoodies, which struck him as an odd act of mercy. But then, workers freezing to death was bad for business.

"How many are there?" Dan asked.

"The barracks will easily hold eight, so probably sixteen to a hut," Tane said.

Harpal added, "I count twenty prisoners out and about. Exercising or can't sleep, but no one seems to be troubling them. One guard in the tower. More prisoners in a yard below me, and they're coming in and out of the main building. You have a patrol on the perimeter—two two-men units making a circuit. Goose-stepping all the way. I assume for appearance's sake."

Jules was still taking in the setup. He'd seen what Harpal just called the main building from up top. It appeared to be a blocky concrete structure with antennae and stronger electrical lighting than the rest of the camp. From here, it was taller than it had first seemed, and now they could view the road at the opposite end which—like the one they came down—used a hairpin route, although only one, which led to a flat outcrop.

Jules said, "Helipad. That's their primary way in and out. The exercise yard is a barrel for shooting fish, so the prisoners can't storm the castle. But that facility is our target." Jules lowered his binoculars. "I'm guessin' it goes a lot deeper than we can see. And it's takin' a huge amount of energy."

"Two helipads," Dan said, pointing. "There's another on top of the primary facility too."

"Makes sense." Tane packed his binoculars away. "More than just one way traffic. Harpal, how's our approach?"

"Surprisingly lax," Harpal answered. "There's no one on the door. Two lookout towers, plus a couple of guys up here guarding the dam access."

"They don't need much," Dan said. "It's inaccessible. Like the old Siberian gulags. There's a fence, sure, but the most effective security is prisoners knowing they'll die from nature if they make it past the guard tower and the machine gun."

"Still," Tane said, "they're having a big night, launching the shield. You'd have thought they'd step up."

"The main building has more guards," Harpal reported. "And there's something weird on the dam itself. Those things that looked like they were carrying out repairs? I want to get a closer look."

"Not yet." Dan packed everything away except his Glock with the silencer attachment. He also had a submachine gun strapped to him, along with a K-bar knife on his belt. "Harpal, we clear for a run?"

"Patrol's coming," Harpal said. "Give them two minutes. Stay out of sight."

An icy wind howled down the valley, drawing out the wait. With Harpal narrating the troops' progress, no one needed to peek up from the natural barrier and risk an eagle-eyed soldier spotting them.

Eventually, Harpal said, "Clear. The tower guard is looking the other way. You have a straight run at the gate."

The three action dudes didn't wait on a countdown, instead sprinting through the dark to the wood-framed chicken wire perimeter. The lock was a simple but massive padlock, which Tane got through in seconds using a key scrubber.

Dan eased the gate open, and they all slipped through, replacing the padlock without engaging the mechanism. They progressed to the nearest hut and pinned themselves to the blindside.

Harpal said, "Good, you're clear. You need to cover the ground carefully. But there's no telling what the prisoners will do if they see you."

Jules risked an eyeball down the next lane, viewing a couple of filthy, emaciated bald men shuffling with cups of water drawn from a rainwater butt. Their eyes remained on their drinks, plodding along, concentrating on getting through the loose dirt of the floor.

He came back to the guys. "I think we're good. These people are empty. Traumatized. Can't hurt to keep a low profile, though."

"What are you thinking?" Tane asked. "Grabbing a hoodie?"

"Exactly. Wait here."

Before anyone could object, Jules slipped around the corner and into the dorm. It was pitch black and stank of body odor and mold, with an after-whiff of disinfectant. His eyes took a moment to adjust, then he made out triple bunks full of human forms. His ears picked out the deep breaths of sleeping people.

He advanced inside, placing his feet deliberately, unsure what he was looking for, but came across it with a quick scan: shelves containing the ubiquitous clothing the other prisoners had been wearing. In the dark, he identified the largest two boiler suits he could find, plus one in his own size, and three hoodies.

Sorry for stealing your stuff. But if we win this, you'll be free tomorrow.

A floorboard creaked. Two people stirred. A young woman on a bottom bunk rolled over to face Jules. She blinked her eyes open, raised her hands to rub them, but Jules fled before she completed the movement. Although not before snatching a pair of crusty work gloves from the sill by the door.

He silently closed the door and scrammed back to where he'd left Dan and Tane.

The boiler suits were too small for them, but Jules managed to change fully into his. Dan and Tane squeezed into the bottoms and tied the arms around their waists, the gray fleece hoodies covering the knots and their weapons. Jules also stuffed his hands into the gloves, the dirt on the outside baked on. While Tane's skin tone might pass for Asian in this light, his facial tattoo was a dead give-away. Dan might circumvent only passing interest, but Jules's was a bigger risk than either. They'd seen no black people here, meaning he needed to conceal himself as much as possible. The work gloves would arouse less suspicion than the high-tech tactical gloves he'd flown in with.

Once they all closely resembled the other inmates—shrouded in hoods—they wandered out into the site.

"That's so cool, guys," Harpal said. "Slow down, though. No one moves that quickly. And you all need to slump a bit. No one is as tall or healthy looking as you."

As they progressed deeper into the camp, knees bent and shoulders pulled in, it became clear that it wasn't only the terrain outside the camp that kept order. The squalid conditions left many prisoners sobbing, some virtually comatose. Guards were not needed to the extent they would be in a US penitentiary, but they existed. With Harpal's help, they circumvented a couple of random soldiers cutting through the camp, and they remained on the blindside of the tower guard wherever possible. The weak lights also helped, mobile generator-powered, the chugging machines positioned on every fourth corner alongside cans of fuel to top up as needed. No nice, clean hydroelectricity for these lowly humans.

Jules said, "If they need generators for power out here, they're usin' even more power from the dam than we realized."

At the exercise yard, which resembled more a basketball court than something from a WWII camp, they took stock, lounging in a way they'd seen the inmates doing. Jules even slumped on his backside against the wall, head in his hands.

It wasn't entirely put on. The sights were crippling to him. A lifetime of suppressing his emotions in terms of friendship, romance, and consumerist desires hadn't prepared him for the agony he was witnessing here. Thwarting evil, fighting off terrorists, preventing a plague—it all seemed so distant compared to roaming amidst the dehumanizing treatment of these people.

Concentrate.

Despite his position, Jules had a clear line of sight across the ground, the courtyard sloping up toward the base of the dam where not one, but two facilities protruded. On the right, it stretched three-quarters of the dam's width, the left less than a quarter.

He said, "That's weird."

"What is?" Dan asked.

"The two structures. Look at the bigger one."

The two military vets appraised the span of the buildings.

Dan said, "I don't see it."

"One's newer?" Tane suggested.

Jules didn't have the energy to get annoyed at their lack of observational prowess, and time was wasting. "The left one is a modern build. The bigger one on the right is carved out of the land."

Tane squinted that way. "You sure?"

"Don't ask," Dan said. "If he's not sure, he doesn't say."

So he listens sometimes.

Jules said, "The right side could be what the mining operation discovered. Buried under hundreds of millennia of geological shift."

It had been cleaned up, restored to something that—from above—would look like a concrete bunker or bland two-story office building. But Jules recognized the flowing, natural lines, the way it melded into the ground and the far side of the valley.

"Like the tomb in India," Dan said.

"Right. And here's where I start guessin', but it's an educated guess. The big, ancient structure is where they'll have the orb and all the dangerous stuff."

"It's also the most heavily guarded," Tane said.

Jules had already concluded that. "Then we'll have to be sneaky. Harpal, you good?"

"When you're inside, we might lose comms," Harpal replied. "But I'll keep myself amused. There's something I need to check out. Might be important."

"Okay, then." Dan checked his pistol was in place, tucked under the hoodie. "Time to be sneaky."

CHAPTER THIRTY-SEVEN

PROJECT AHUA, NEW ZEALAND

"I don't know how much help this will be," Phil said over the speakers Charlie had set up while working the lab's computers.

"Whatever you've got," Charlie said. "I have to do *something* while the language twins are holding their private party."

Charlie noticed Bridget glance at her with a faintly amused eye roll, but she and Prihya concentrated on the screen and the blown-up writing that Bridget had jotted down in the Witnesses' language. They knew certain phrases and some letters and symbols—which Bridget had explained didn't translate directly to English—but they hadn't cracked it yet.

Phil said, "Sally Garcia has been a busy girl. She's stayed off most people's radar, flying low as what looks like an eccentric kook."

"I think she *is* an eccentric kook," Charlie said, watching the screen that Phil was sharing with her. "She's not pretending. But she knows more than it seems. Maybe more than even she realized."

"Yes, probably. Based on how many people have been courting her, I'd say she's very valuable. Russia, China, North Korea, of course."

"Of course."

"But New Zealand is in there, plus the UK—"

"Which explains Colin's expert knowledge of all this."

"The Indian government sent someone to meet her, the Striovians, the Canadians. Pretty much everyone except the Americans."

Charlie considered that.

Toby, who'd been listening to both conversations, said, "The USA is a young nation. Obsessed with mythologizing their own brief history and maintaining the status quo. If well-respected academics, who bend the ear of politicians up the chain, are saying Sally is cuckoo, it stands to reason they'd ignore other options."

Charlie nodded. "Like her being right about giants living in the recent past."

Phil said, "America wasn't the only country to dismiss her. She met with all those who were looking into her work, and it seems only Striovia and North Korea kept tabs on her. From the emails I can intercept on the servers she's used, they chatted a lot more on some unrelated issues. Striovia's interest dried up sometime last year, when the seals went hot, and you guys disrupted their country's international relations. But certain private individuals from North Korea remained in touch."

Toby ran a hand over his face. "But why side with them?"

Charlie could see the names popping up on the dense text-filled dataset Phil was working from. "Those are companies owned by Ryom Jung-Hwan, I assume?"

"On paper, they're scientific research firms," Phil answered. "Drugs companies looking at mental health treatments. But the premises they list..." Phil brought up a montage of a mapping software's street view. "Either hardly occupied or abandoned. They're shells."

"Good lord," Toby said. "So Professor Garcia thought she was being courted by serious scientific establishments, which she had to keep secret from her university until they granted her tenure. Her other work, her deep academic research that didn't go near the existence of giants and the like, must have been immense."

"Then we came along," Charlie said, zoning in on something Phil had unearthed and switching to a different computer. "Validated her early work. Ah Dae-Sung tried to snatch her and tempt her here, but she wanted to hold out a bit longer, get that tenure, and do it the right way."

"Exposing her to the catacombs in Alabama made her realize the end was nigh." Toby watched Bridget's screen for a moment, but—as Charlie expected—there was little progress. He stood at Charlie's shoulder. "Ah Dae-Sung revealing her real theories to the world pushed her into a corner. She believed she had no choice but to cooperate. The only people who could achieve what she needed were employed by this Executive character. What are you doing?"

"What *is* she doing?" Phil asked.

"Executive Ryom is a careful man," Charlie said, uploading her own specially written malware to the server that had hosted Sally's research and most incendiary videos. "But there's a back-link to Ryom's servers. Where they invited her to share her findings last year."

She clicked the go button, and her digital worms spread out, searching for crevasses and ingresses, anything that might aid the boys or Bridget and Prihya.

Charlie sat back. "This might take a while."

Toby sighed. "Okay, then. Cup of tea, anyone?"

Everyone raised their hands.

DRAGON'S PIT GULAG, NORTH KOREA

The looming cave of an entrance was like accessing a concert or convention center, two lanes of foot traffic accommodating a trickle of men and women. More were coming out than going in, suggesting to Jules a shift was ending, the tasks inside requiring fewer workers.

Meaning Executive Ryom and his people were close to their goal.

Jules and Tane approached the "in" lane using the same shambling gait at the workers-come-prisoners, but there would be no hiding their faces once they arrived at the checkpoint.

"This had better work," Tane muttered.

Jules's tolerance for inane chitchat had never been high, and Tane's clichéd declaration set the hairs on the back of his neck on end. He'd come to expect better from the big Kiwi, so said nothing.

Must have been nerves. They were less than ten yards from the two soldiers.

This close, though, Jules could see these were not proper Korean uniforms, just designed to look like them. Enough to inject a healthy portion of fear into the inmates.

Jules said, "Harpal, you still with us?"

"I'm here," came the reply. "Still need to check out that scaffolding, but I'm watching the guard tower."

"Anything else we need to know about?"

"I can't see much else. I assume there'll be cameras."

That was one part of the plan they could do little about. They'd spied two cameras pointing out of the building and two pointing in and could only gamble with their range. Were they fish-eyes or conventional lenses?

Impossible to tell.

They followed one figure with a limp, the pair of guards alert enough to exit their hut beside the yawning entrance.

"They're armed," Jules said.

"AKMs," Tane replied, meaning the submachine guns strapped to them. "An updated AK-47, but the Russians aren't keen on them. You can get them cheap as surplus."

One checked a clipboard while the other left his AKM in place and put a hand on the butt of his holstered pistol. With so many departing and few going in, it might have looked suspicious.

Jules and Tane kept a half-dozen yards back, watching the routine play out as it had the previous arrival. There was no check for those filthy, tired souls leaving.

The limping figure then clenched its stomach in pain, grunted, and keeled to the side, staggering, before falling flat on their face. The guard with the clipboard watched it with disinterested annoyance, as if it was an everyday occurrence. It probably was.

The other guard, younger and clearly junior, went over and crouched beside the fallen prisoner. His face moved closer, then he called to the superior.

The senior guard sighed and tramped to the pair.

By the time he noticed that the fallen man was a former US Army

Ranger who was holding the junior soldier by the scruff of his neck and pointing a K-bar knife at his exposed flesh, Tane had already reached the scene and pressed a gun into the senior guard's back. He muttered in Korean, and they carried on out of sight to the side of their shed.

Once concealed, Dan stabbed his guy, deftly diverting the blood away from his clothing, while Tane pulled his into a choke hold before snapping his neck. The pair stashed the fresh bodies behind the hut before limping back down the path and rejoining it for an approach that—hopefully—raised little suspicion.

Jules usually felt sick at a loss of life. *Any* life. Even bad guys who'd been happy to kill him. His philosophy that everyone could redeem themselves if given the chance typically sat at the forefront in his mind. Not today, though. Today, he was complicit. He'd given approval to this plan, when normally he'd object and seek a non-lethal solution.

Had he been hollowed out by what he'd seen and judged those men unworthy of life? Or was it that he needed to feel less in order to do his job back home? When Sergeant Massey's life was threatened, Jules could have shot and killed the assailants, but he didn't. He chose another way.

This time, it barely registered. They hadn't died at his hands, so it wasn't on him.

The trio continued inside with no further resistance, the mouth gobbling them up with one bite. Darkness surrounded them, only a faint light up ahead showing them the way and occasional footsteps heading in the opposite direction.

Around the first bend, dim bulbs on the floor illuminated the way. Like emergency strips on a plane, they gave off only essential light. Dust filled the air, this roughhewn passage through the stone wall having been dug rather than discovered. Jules picked out the telltale marks of machine-tooled carving around the walls. They had found the place, but not the entrance... or they'd built this one to make access easier.

They came to a corner, manned by a prisoner who looked so tired he might have been drugged. He was giving out masks like those found on a building site and accepting dirty ones back from those departing to soak in a barrel of grimy water. Tane asked for three. The man stared, his eyes lifeless, but he lacked the energy to enquire as to Tane's presence. He just handed over the garments.

Wearing the masks, Dan and Tane were better disguised than Jules, so he had to remain careful, although it was a little easier with the bottom half of his face covered.

Moving on, they found themselves in a smoother, better lit corridor. It expanded, double the width, enough for two family cars side-by-side. The stone walls, floor, and ceiling were gray and solid, with the occasional masked inmate passing them by in the opposite direction.

Dan said, "Where do you think they're going?"

"Home," Jules said. "They're being dismissed."

To their right, another passage branched off, this one more modern—polished smooth and paved, with poured concrete walls. The end was open, with more intense lighting.

"That's our target," Dan said.

"Okay." Jules turned that way.

Someone shouted, "*Oh*!"

They all turned to the sound to find a female guard waving at them from down the original corridor. She shouted something else.

Tane translated. "We don't go this way."

The three of them kept their heads low, their masks and the shadows of their hoods giving only limited camouflage as they obeyed the woman's gesture to move along. Jules lingered a second longer, letting the guys lead and keeping his face averted, conscious of triggering the alert if the woman examined them too closely. He self-consciously tugged at the cuff of his gloves.

As they traveled deeper, the warren again grew more modern, like the corridor leading to the bright room moments earlier. Jules assessed they progressed under the lakebed. They passed through a chilly cavern that opened into what looked like a natural cavity but was being treated like a warehouse, with boxes, shelves, racks, and tall cupboards. It was smooth. No stalactites, no uneven ground.

It was like an entire campus underground.

"Good job that guard didn't look too hard at us," Dan said. Another irrelevant and obvious comment.

"They're all in a hurry," Jules said. "This isn't a military facility. It's a minimally staffed corporate project. They don't want anyone here who shouldn't be. And if they're putting on extra workers, it's to prepare for something else."

Tane said, "Dignitaries? Once they have their shield up and running?"

"Don't know. And we're not going to any supervisor. This way."

Jules led them to the right, the direction seeming to go back on themselves. He recalled the curve of the passageway near the corridor the woman had directed them away from, and added it to the angle into this warehouse-type section. Sure enough, it led to a closed door with an armed soldier outside. He spotted them when they were twenty yards away and shouted.

"He says we can't be here," Tane reported, his head down. "We must leave."

Although he lacked the gift for language that Bridget had, Jules picked up a lot and worked things out faster than anyone he'd known. He'd already digested a few phrases since listening to Tane translate several times, but he was far from understanding Korean yet. However, he'd figured out what the soldier was trying to convey from the tone. And he'd already slipped his baton from up his sleeve where he'd stashed it.

With a sharp jerk of his arm, Jules flung the baton straight and hard, striking the guard in the forehead. The man in uniform staggered, fumbled for his gun, but Jules was already on him. A blow to his gut, a jab to his windpipe, and a swiftly applied choke hold followed.

He was down.

Not dead. But down.

The door wasn't locked and led to a vestibule and a second door. This one *was* locked. It resembled something on a ship, with deadlocks and a seal, handles to turn rather than a knob to twist. Jules could see in through two small panes at the top, both as thick as his hand. Dan and Tane crowded behind him, taking it in turns to watch their backs.

It was an odd setup. A machine similar to the one back in Project Ahua dominated the far wall but was somehow simpler in design. The shield taken from Alabama hung in place high above the panel, the orb to the side was currently dead and gray, and it was attached to a crude chamber, the same dimensions as Ahua's. Jules only then realized the Ahua folks had made theirs more comfortable, while this was just stone with a reconstructed front door of what looked like opaque glass, yet Jules somehow believed it was something else, a natural crystal, perhaps. It was all connected. All ready to go.

Awaiting the orders of the people entering from a wide-open doorway at the head of the room—it led from the modern corridor down which the female soldier had forbidden them from wandering.

"It's them," Tane hissed, this being his turn to watch.

"Who?" Dan asked from his position, slumped like an exhausted worker a few feet inside the storage depot.

"Ah Dae-Sung, Ryom Jung-Hwan and—"

"Sally Garcia," Jules said, surprised at the venom he injected into the words. "They're getting ready."

Accompanying them, three men in lab coats scurried to the panel beneath the orb. Movement higher up caught Jules's eye, and he craned to see. There was a catwalk covering three quarters of the lab with a heavy machine gun mounted at one end, like something taken from a helicopter gunship. Someone checked the weapon over, as the techs were sorting the ground level controls.

Jules concentrated on the panel, the few buttons, including a comically large red one. An abort switch. It wasn't like the complex setup of modern computers tapping into the ancient. This was more stop-start.

He angled his view to find more items embedded in the roof. Two more shields but different shapes to the Alabama one, and he guessed there was another out of his sight. To his left he could see a fence, a sturdy chain-link model, with only darkness beyond this.

"What are they doing?" Dan asked.

Jules focused on the main trio who observed the technicians from a distance. Those in lab coats must have studied this on Ryom's behalf, prepared all the cables, melding old and new, and applied their knowledge to Ah Dae-Sung's ability in the field.

First Sally Garcia. Then Gilim.

"It's the epicenter of their experiments," Jules said. "The shields are in place, the orb looks ready, and the activation chamber—all connected. All ready to go. Just needs a—"

A flash filled the small window, dying as fast as it bloomed, its only remnants the dots and swirls dancing in Jules's vision.

"Someone taking photos in there?" Dan said, coming forward to swap with Tane.

Jules blinked until he could see more than he couldn't and resumed his vantage. The lights were on now, the orb a spinning mass —somehow multicolored yet black at the same time, like an oil slick suppressing a rainbow in strong sunlight. Ah Dae-Sung, Ryom Jung-Hwan and Sally Garcia lowered darkened goggles, having plainly expected the burst of light. Then they all chatted briefly before the Executive shook Dae-Sung's hand and clapped him on the shoulder. Sally received a firm nod.

Jules said, "Whatever they're doin', it's gonna be soon."

"She's leaving," Dan said from the window.

Tane asked, "Who?"

"There was only one 'she' in there," Jules said. "The mad prof." He beckoned Dan over. "Okay, I've got our bearings. We know they can't do anything without the big guy, and since Sally ain't stickin' around, she must be going somewhere important, right?"

Dan said, "Probably, yeah."

"We stop that, we might stop the whole thing."

Tane thought for a moment. "Take away the component they need rather than take down all of it."

Jules said, "They could still do a lot of damage if they don't have Gilim. But will they risk it?"

"No way to tell. But let's try this first, then circle back if necessary."

Jules glanced at Dan, who nodded. Jules nodded, too. "Stay together, or split up?"

"Harpal, you read?" Tane tried. No answer. "Okay, let's follow her. We learn what we need to learn, then act on it. But one rule: if one of us gets caught, the others carry on. No negotiating, no hostages."

Jules kept his lips tight together.

Dan gave another nod, this one hesitant. "This is too important to worry about one person. Or two."

"Okay." Jules suppressed the hot acid in his gut, seeing the logic, knowing both were correct. "We carry on until it's over. No matter what."

Now they were all inside, Harpal was no use to them perched up on the hillside next to the dam. He was still curious about what the people were doing on the face that would require scaffolding. It couldn't simply be to facilitate repairs, nor the makeup of the construction. It descended from above, as if hooked on over the top and dropped low over the sweeping, almost sheer wall. They were equidistant from one another, too, another indicator this wasn't for maintenance.

Of course, it might've been for something that needed tending to periodically, like cleaning air vents. It was just that Harpal had seen nothing quite like it before.

Could be a defensive measure we didn't pick up on.

He needed to see, but two men who looked bored as hell guarded the closest access. They hadn't spotted him land on their blindside, nor as he scrambled for a better view of the landscape. He figured they'd grown complacent after months or even years of not much happening and couldn't have been alerted to any problems below.

With no artificial light except the yellow phosphorus bulbs around the dam itself, Harpal moved slickly over the arid escarpment, natural troughs and rocks giving him sufficient cover to reach the gate unseen.

Closer, he made out a path winding from the guard station down the side of the structure, widening to a single-track road—presumably to get supplies and equipment up there when needed. The path over the top of the dam was wide enough for two buses side-by-side, although the fence was more for show.

Harpal drew closer, recalling the drills Dan had forced him to endure over the years, training he'd accepted might be useful one day. But Special Forces tactics were imprinted on Dan, whereas Harpal was more about stealth and deception. In an urban setting he might have been able to pose as a lost tourist, but here it wasn't an option.

Patience was key in such approaches. Harpal had crawled as far as he dared.

From the kit brought with them he took a snub-nosed Walther and fitted the suppressor. It wouldn't altogether silence the gunshots, but if he was fast enough, they wouldn't echo around the valley like firecrackers at New Year. He checked the slide, chambered a round, set himself, and scanned the target area once more.

Two men. Non-military uniform. AKMs, holstered pistols, radios clipped to their shoulders.

Okay. Just go for it.

Harpal glided out and speed-walked directly toward the pair. Two-handed grip. Aiming at one of them. His feet landed side-first, rolling his boot sole all the way to the toe before lifting the foot again—a technique closer to silent than tiptoes. But not completely silent.

One guard looked directly at him.

Harpal squeezed the trigger, snapping the man's head back and dropping him in place. The other watched his comrade fall, so shocked he probably didn't quite believe it was real. By the time he brought a second hand to his AK, Harpal had shot him too. He checked the pair were dead, then scaled the two-meter fence, landing scruffily on the other side.

The dam curved away from him, the walls on either side coming up to his chest, so he kept himself low. If anyone was monitoring cameras up here, it seemed unlikely he'd go unnoticed, but the lights were dim and there were no eyewitnesses, so he had a chance. Hopefully, he'd be gone before anyone came to investigate.

Scurrying fast, gun at the ready, he arrived at the first of six scaffolds. It reminded him of booths he'd seen at concerts where lighting and sound mixers were stationed. At least the top of the section was. Harpal climbed up, checked for movement and sound, found none, and continued to the edge.

The latticework of thick steel poles and wooden platforms swayed an inch or two, but with nothing but five hundred feet of thin air between himself and the gulag below, a couple of inches of give was like riding a roller coaster. He withdrew from the edge and lay flat on his belly, pointing his gun into a hole through which the top of a bamboo ladder protruded.

The next level down was empty.

Again, he listened before venturing on, taking the ladder, and arriving one floor below. A cold breeze picked up, rattling the planks as if it had waited for him to get here.

All he could see was open air on one side and a smooth, sheer wall the other. Now he wondered if they designed this structure to support the weight of a human adult. He'd kept his backup 'chute, but if the poles and planks disassembled without warning, he'd have no chance to leap free. And yet, he descended the ladder—lashed together with something resembling grass but was a strong material akin to twine—to another level.

On this next floor, the wobble was more pronounced, his mass destabilizing it further. Looking on the bright side, he had only one more level before he ran out of room.

The ladder jiggled, the bottom of the scaffolding hanging together by swaying joints. Wooden floors, steel structure, bamboo ladders. What a combination.

As he touched down onto the final network of planks, his own knees trembled.

"I'm fine. I'm okay."

The wind whistled as if in reply, a haunted house eeriness leaving him very lonely indeed. If an angry, restless spirit popped up beside him and ordered him BEGONE, he would obey and not look back. When no ghost showed itself, Harpal returned to the matter at hand, searching for what function these uniformly spaced drop-off points could serve. It didn't take him long. And what he discovered made him wish for a haunted house.

"Bridget, Charlie, you there?"

Charlie answered, "Thought you were on radio silence."

"Emergencies only. This counts."

"What's up?" Bridget asked. "Is everyone okay?"

"At the moment, yeah. But this whole dam is wired." Harpal kept his hands behind his back as he peered at a five-foot-square block set into the brickwork, with wires entering and leaving a sealed metal box, leading along the dam's face to the next hooked-on scaffold. "It's daisy-chained too. Like your comms nodes. If one blows, they all blow."

"What does that mean?" Charlie asked. "They've sabotaged the place?"

"I don't know what the trigger is. But if it gets pulled, the gulag disappears along with everyone in there. And it wipes out everything in its path for miles."

CHAPTER THIRTY-EIGHT

They still don't trust me.

Sally Garcia kept a shadow in the form of a stocky Korean man in a too-tight khaki-green uniform who carried a gun on his hip and seemed incapable of smiling. He spoke no English except for the occasionally monosyllabic word like, *No, Go, You, Here*, and *Please*. By far, his most common utterance was *Please*, which may have been an attempt to mollify her but just came across as passive-aggressive, each *Please* being accompanied by a curt gesture, making it more of an instruction than a polite request.

Point at the door: *Please*.

Gesture to halt: *Please*.

Smile, checks her pockets for the tenth time: *Please*.

Besides, no amount of manners alleviated the threat of the firearm.

Was it a mistake? Going all in with the people most closely aligned to her goal instead of those most closely aligned to her ethics? They'd forced her into it, after all.

No. The people she'd trusted back in California were as bad, just in a different way. They had seemed okay, but had used her for their own ends, prepared to discard and silence her at the first opportunity. Her work would be forgotten or—as the breach of her private files attested—she'd be buried under the same debris as the plethora of tin-foil-hat-wearing nut jobs out there.

Except she wasn't crazy. The past few days proved it. And over the coming hours, she'd show why all those people—her peers, her so-called friends, thousands of faceless keyboard warriors on the internet—should have believed in her.

Having switched the machine on, all they needed was the final component, hence her departure from what they'd called the Conduit Chamber. She'd picked up her shadow on the way and navigated the passageways outside before crossing the short path to the science annex. Although it was built in the same style as the ancient structure in which the orb was housed, it was as up to date as a person could imagine, like stepping through a time portal from the past to the future. White walls, disinfectant pods, a double-thick sealed door to be opened by authorized personnel only—one of the few security measures they'd allowed her to access.

The guard stood to the side and gestured to the palm-reader. "Please."

Sally placed her hand on the flat glass and waited. The scanner beeped happily, a green light flashed on above her, and a hiss signaled the first door sliding open, louder than she remembered from last time. More of a *pop*.

Her minder then leaned against the side, his arm barring her way.

She put her hands on her hip and said, "Oh, heavens, what's the problem?"

The stocky soldier's lean turned into a slump with his eyes half-closed. Blood dribbled from his mouth as he slid down the wall, his uniform stained red.

A scream jettisoned up her throat, but a gloved hand over her mouth silenced it. Her assailant pinned her arms to her sides and turned her to face the opposite direction.

Two prisoners approached, one with a smoking gun that had a large addition to the barrel. The louder than usual hiss—the *pop*—from the door had been the suppressed sound of a bullet, which struck her minder in the chest, killing him outright. But where did these poor, unfortunate people get a gun? And what did they hope to achieve if—

"It's okay, Professor," said the person holding her from behind. "Just show us inside."

She nodded, recognizing the voice. When the hand left her face, she said, "Tane? Is that you? What are you doing here?"

"Inside," said one of the others, his hood still up, clearly Jules Sibeko.

Sally led them into the anteroom, Dan Vincent dragging the guard's corpse with him. Like the entrance to the facility in New Zealand, the sliding door closed behind them, then nozzles sprayed them with disinfectant, misting the entire unit. She was trying to work out if they were now working with the Executive or if this was some sort of raid. She guessed the latter but wasn't worried.

Shielding her eyes and mouth from the spray, she said, "It's too far along."

"What's on the other side of here?" Dan asked.

"The laboratory."

"He means security," Tane said.

"Oh, I can't say. They'd be very upset with me."

Dan poked her with the gun he'd used to kill the guard. "Quickly, before this opens. Or you get to head out first."

Sally couldn't understand his harsh tone. It wasn't like she'd done anything to him personally. Perhaps he was a sore loser.

The spray ended, having coated them with a fine film. Dryers kicked in.

She said, "Okay. Last time, there were two guys."

"Cameras?" Tane enquired.

"Only the ones on the outer door."

The dryers cut out and the men all tensed. Dan bent over slightly, taking a position behind her.

She said, "Oh, dear. Am I a human shield?"

As the door slid open and the other boys pinned themselves to the walls, Dan said, "Something like that."

"Ironic, considering it was shields that brought us all together."

With the door open, Dan pushed her out. The guard station was empty. Actually, calling it a station was a bit of an exaggeration. It was a desk where people were searched leaving more often than when entering. Ah Dae-Sung had told her they were confident no one could breach the camp undetected, so the bigger risk was losing secrets should anyone try to reveal what the laboratories here were doing. He surely meant her when he said *anyone.*

Now, it wasn't manned.

"Tea break?" Sally suggested.

"Show us," Jules said.

"Show you what?"

"You know what," Tane said. "Take us. Now."

"Okay, but do keep an open mind, won't you?"

An open mind.

How many times had people used that phrase to justify beliefs that appeared unusual or extreme? Jules had seen all walks of life express that phrase in one form or another. He'd seen progressive politicians ask for open minds with regards to healthcare, gun regulation, the concept of a universal basic income. Fundamental Christians often attempted to prove the King James Bible was the actual word of God, irrespective of the thousands of translations, lost books, and a host of other aspects that cast doubt on that, and they'd be able to do that... if sinners and atheists *kept an open mind.* He'd even heard both sides of civil rights protests—cops and conservatives, black allies, and liberals—ask audiences to *keep an open mind* before espousing one opinion or another.

I know it might sound odd at first, but keep an open mind here...

...These riots prove "some people" don't deserve to be treated like "decent" folk...

...Change never happens without civil disobedience; uprisings are necessary to achieve equality...

...Free money to everyone means a bottom-up economy, so even the rich win!

...Free money to everyone means a bottom-feeding nation descending into anarchy...

All provable by all sides if you just... *keep an open mind.*

It was a mystery to Jules why the world had tilted that way, where pre-existing opinions were more important to some than facts that might disrupt their opinion. Why go mining for disingenuous reasoning when a fact was staring at you and begging to be absorbed and assimilated into your critical thinking?

But there were some very rare occasions, situations where he didn't think an open mind was necessary: Neo-Nazis seeking to unleash a plague, nations arming themselves to annihilate another, billionaires murdering innocents in order to seek a cure for his own terminal illness. They all fell under the same heading as dead fetuses floating in jars.

Sally had escorted them to a laboratory. It was smaller than it appeared from the outside, meaning there must be more out back, but it was state-of-the art. Pristine. All glass dividers and metal surfaces. They entered the half that was decked out with an array of equipment from test tube centrifuges to electrolyte analyzers, and passed a whole bench dedicated to DNA analysis. Jules had only read about much of this stuff, but he recognized a CRISPR/Cas9 setup; part of it looked like a microscope, other bits had automated pipetting tools, a system for calibrating electric scissors... all to splice and rewrite genetic code.

Jules said, "You were growing your own homo colossus."

"Not quite," Sally replied as they got up close with the glass containers. "*They* attempted to grow *their* own but failed."

"So they took ours," Tane said.

Jules approached a barrel-sized glass vessel holding a humanoid specimen curled up as if asleep. It had a large forehead, and its ribs and spine were visible under its gray, translucent skin.

He said, "They're not yours, Tane. They're their own people." He looked up at Tane. "You just give them somewhere to live."

"I meant..." Tane appeared to be searching for something to say, but there were no words.

Sally continued in her chipper tone. "I have to say, this isn't my work. I'm not a biologist. Or a geneticist. Or whatever this is."

"And *what* is it?" Tane said.

"You can see. They use genetic splicing to recreate the giants from bone marrow they found."

"Found? They just found it lying around?"

"No, no, no. They found it because my research led them to certain migratory routes, and they dug the DNA out of frost that had covered it during the last ice age. They got all excited, but it was too degraded. They tried to fill the gaps with human DNA, primates, lots of things. But none of it worked. They don't know why."

"Because they evolved along a unique route," Jules said. "Modern homo sapiens, chimpanzees, hominids, Neanderthals… all had a common ancestor. But the giants must have had a different one, going back even further in time. Probably the same genetic branch as the Witnesses, or whatever came before them. We're too different."

Dan said, "How do you know that?"

"I kept an open mind. I listen. I can… sorta remember stuff from when I plugged into the machine. It's not a memory like I remember what I had for breakfast, but I know when I guess right." Jules eyed Sally Garcia. "Your Executive friend is an animal. He's worse. Animals don't do this. And you're culpable for helping him."

"People need to know," Sally insisted. "They need to know we share our heritage with more than hairy little hobbits."

"Why?"

"What do you mean, why? *Because*."

Jules pressed his eyes, stemming the rage inside him. He'd never been so ready to harm another human being, but if Ah Dae-Sung or Ryom Jung-Hwan were in front of him at that moment, he'd have broken his no-killing code in an instant.

Is it really more obscene than the plague you stopped?

Using these prisoners, the giants, the plan to kill so many… yes, it's worse.

"No one *has* to know anything," Jules said. "That's nonsensical academic entitlement. This ain't about truth or helpin' people understand. It's about *you*. Provin' you were right. So you decided to shortcut it and side with some of the worst people on the planet."

Jules noticed Tane and Dan tense up, more concerned at him than with Sally.

"I got an important question," he said. "Why were you coming here?"

"Here?" Sally said. "It's where I work."

"No, *specifically*. Why were you leaving that place and coming here at this precise moment?"

"Mainly for the blood work." Sally headed for a separate bench beside the CRISPR section, where a closed unit that resembled a microwave oven stood. The clear frontage showed a petri dish rotating. "It's checking all the chemicals have been flushed. We don't want to leave anything to chance."

"Flushed." Jules couldn't summon enough bile in his voice to express what he was feeling. It came out flat and empty. He crouched by another glass barrel, the occupant smaller but even more malformed. "This isn't your work, Professor. This is next-level mad scientist evil—"

"Are you okay?" Bridget asked in his ear.

They'd reestablished comms once they got out of the underground bunker, tailing Sally at a distance before taking the chance on following her in here.

Jules said, "I'll be fine."

"Are you sure?" Bridget said.

"Yeah." Jules stood and pulled his Glock and marched toward the exit, the way they'd come.

Dan said, "Hey, wait up, where are you going?"

Jules dipped his chin, every limb jazzed with electricity, with the impending fight. "To destroy everything."

He rarely cut loose, couldn't afford to. He was aware of his abilities and his limitations and knew that he could kill if he had to. And if these people—these wealthy, entitled men willing to slaughter tens, maybe hundreds, of thousands of innocents—needed to die to prevent more suffering, he'd have to suck it up and do it.

Bridget said, "Jules... Just think a second."

He was at the edge of the lab, ready to turn into the exit and retrace his steps into the chamber when he halted dead.

A faint but definite sound.

He turned to Sally, her and the guys waiting for him across the lab. "You said you came here *mainly* for the blood work. What was the other reason?"

Sally smiled. "To see if anyone would follow me, of course." She smirked, chuckling as Dan and Tane reestablished their shooting grips. "Did you think you could sneak in here unnoticed? That's so silly."

People were coming. Jules had only seconds to decide: hide or fight?

PROJECT AHUA, NEW ZEALAND

The boys in North Korea went silent. Not always a terrible sign. Often, they just needed to be quiet for a spell, and Bridget held onto that hope as it became clear no one was going to reply to repeated requests regarding what was happening. As Charlie pointed out, all they could do here was keep working, get ready to act if the deadline approached, and do whatever they needed to prevent the US launching a preemptive strike against a power they didn't fully understand. If that wasn't enough, there were the explosives on the dam to worry about.

Toby was the last of the group in the Ahua lab to cease asking them to respond, his lined face betraying how stressed he was. Bridget felt sorry for him, not least because his usual role in their task was redundant. There was no better researcher, in her mind, no one who could dig out a historical ambiguity, compare it to known, provable fact, and draw a new hypothesis. It had been his mining of myths, legends, and the writings of people present for such events that led them first to Mexico, then to Alabama.

Now, he was a bystander. And Bridget could do nothing to help beyond stare at her own handwriting and compare the glyphs and symbols she'd penned during a freak-out of a barely remembered dream, and hope to glean something that could help, when the action dudes came back online. Or even if they didn't.

She said, "It's no use. I'll have to go back in the pod."

"Not a chance," Charlie answered.

She was also at a loose end. The difference was, she didn't let it show as obviously as Toby. She tinkered. She checked the setups, the factors they had translated to date, and theorized by jotting notes. She'd already commented on the prospect of killing the entire network and outlined the risks.

Better than the alternative, though.

"Four shields," Toby said, pacing. "Four functions. Bridget, do you have anything at all there yet?"

Bridget exchanged a glance with Prihya, who had made even less progress. What they had established was Bridget's doing, syncing what she'd written with the bare bones of a translation they had available.

She said, "I have references to the energy, along with either a holy person or a special one. The shield, of course. That matches Prihya's on the wall." Bridget wafted her paper toward the image of the glyphs lifted from the activation suite. "And there's the usual phrases and tones we found on previous artefacts. The warning."

"Of misuse?" Toby said.

"Of the ignorant using it. Look..." She was about to demonstrate using the scribblings she'd made, but that was pointless. No visuals needed. "I've dug in the language we already know about, and that accounts for about a third of the writing relating to the shield. Like you just said, Toby. One function—although they call it a 'reward'—is protection and shelter using one device. Another 'reward' is protection using four or six in a ring around a larger mass, say a city or small country. Then there's the planet-circling cocoon to protect from meteors and, to keep from hurting Dan's feelings, unfriendly alien invaders."

Bridget paused to allow a mild but inappropriate laugh. The others smiled, containing their mirth, like a ripple of giggles at a funeral.

"Or its fourth function... a weapon. It can be used offensively."

"To attack?" Toby said. "I have seen no evidence of such a function. Unless..."

"Unless what?" Charlie said.

Toby put a finger in the air. "What if it *was* used offensively? In the story where all this started for me. They way Mr. Dae-Sung used it to approach this place?"

"The Trojan Horse," Prihya said, pivoting away from her screen. She appeared inordinately happy. Understandable, since that was what had brought her to Valerio's attention, and subsequently into the LORI fold: her ability to do what Toby did, but on a more out-of-the-box level. "It might not have been a literal statue full of men..."

"But a unit of excellent fighters," Toby finished. "Sent in without being seen, then attacking them from within."

Bridget snagged on something then. "Trojan Horse..."

Charlie said, "What is it?"

Bridget chewed it over in her mind. "That phrase, Trojan Horse, it's made its way into modern vernacular. Whether it's sleeper terror cells or computer viruses... it's a modern phrase. What if..."

Her thoughts raced, turbo boosted by something inches out of reach. She put her foot to the floor and pumped the accelerator.

What is it...?

"We use a phase, an idiom, to say what we mean. That's in English. Other dialects have other phrases, other words. Fox in the henhouse. Wolf in sheep's clothing. A poison apple..."

"Yes," Toby said. "They all mean the same thing. Harm hiding in an innocent form."

"So, what if that weapon...?" Still, Bridget racked her brain, but it wasn't there. She placed the paper flat and beckoned Prihya over. "Here, it talks about a 'mist warrior', like on your door to the activation suite."

Prihya checked what Bridget was asking her. "Yes, a fighter who cannot be touched. We assume, because of the shield's protection. But the context... next to the warning..."

"I don't get it," Charlie said.

"Think about it," Bridget said. "The Trojan Horse, the wolf in sheep's clothing. What if you had a warrior, or thought you did, but it turned to mist? What might the consequences be?"

"You'd lose," Toby answered.

"Right."

Bridget calmed her breathing, closed her eyes, and focused on this alternative approach. Not an exaggeration, not a myth or nickname, but a metaphor. A warning.

She opened her eyes and pulled the paper up in front of her, taking it in all at once, including the mist warrior passage. It all fell into place.

"If used correctly," she said, "the shield starts small, and expands outward, giving the bearer protection. But it if doesn't, it digs in, expanding like an explosive, wiping out everything from a few meters into the earth and above."

"A tsunami," Toby said. "From one single device, or four."

Bridget nodded. "Expanding out to the next active ring."

"But there isn't another active ring," Prihya said.

Bridget swallowed, her lips dry. "It's a failsafe. If it falls into the wrong hands and isn't controlled by a 'worthy' candidate—the giant—it'll grind out over the south-Asian landmass. It'll wipe out Pyongyang, South Korea, all over China, possibly all the way across to Eastern Europe."

"That's madness," Toby said. "Why build something like that?"

"They didn't, remember? They just figured out how to use it." Bridget ran over the later glyphs, guessing at them from the earlier context. "If the earth is worthy... others will step in to prevent disaster."

"You translated that?" Charlie asked.

"No, but... it's kinda here." Bridget pointed to the back of her head. "I don't know why, but I know it. They made this like... The way we built nuclear stockpiles."

Toby frowned, even more lined than he was when the guys fell silent. "Mutually assured destruction."

"It forced people to work together. In peace. With only a select few able to regulate the power."

"*Billions* could die," Charlie said.

"It should only have been those who misused it," Bridget said. "At least that was the plan way back when. The others—us if we were there—were supposed to stop it."

"But didn't." Prihya stared at the activation suite. "And we're too far out of the loop to be the ones to stop it."

"We can only destroy it. Using that feedback loop theory."

"We should do it now," Charlie said.

"Agreed," Toby said.

Bridget was about to ask for more time, for a chance to let the guys shut it down from their end, when a gunshot cut her off. It took her a second to realize it wasn't nearby but had occurred over comms.

The boys in Korea...

"Dan? Jules?" Bridget said. "Are you okay?"

But yet again, there was no answer.

CHAPTER THIRTY-NINE

DRAGON'S PIT GULAG, NORTH KOREA

Dan Vincent wasn't dumb. At least, not in the way that most people were. *Think about how stupid the average person you meet is*, his first Rangers CO had told him, *and consider that half the population is dumber than that*.

You didn't make the grade in the US Army Rangers, or any military Special Forces unit, by being stupid. Physical fitness, fighting arts, firearms, blades, explosives, tactical awareness... all that and far, far more went into crafting a Spec Ops soldier, and every step was as intensive and mind-sucking as any PHD.

A doctorate in combat.

He might not have had the academic pedigree of Toby or Bridget, but he had sense. He'd learned, and he'd experienced far too many dangerous situations to not listen to his gut. So, when Jules darted out of sight, dropping low rather than moving in a straight line, he knew something was wrong even before he said the words.

"Company. Take cover."

They were caught within the lab section, with no back door. Clearly, health and safety inside this giant energy-field-generator-slash-*Island-of-Dr.-Moreau*-knock-off wasn't a huge concern.

By the time two soldiers rounded the door jamb and adopted shooting posts, Tane had positioned himself behind the biggest, sturdiest-looking machine in the place and Dan took Sally Garcia hostage. She was significantly smaller than him, so he used a bench as partial cover and bladed himself side-on, so she covered more of his body, leaving only the elbow of his gun hand exposed, along with the arm snaking around the professor. There may have been an inch or so of his head open to a shot from an expert marksman, but even he would struggle to make a kill like that.

Ah Dae-Sung joined the pair who'd taken point, keeping low himself, his gun at the ready—what looked like a Russian SR-1 Vektor. "Surrender now. We can put you to work instead of killing you."

Dan half-expected Jules to come steamrollering over, but the two grunts remained at their post, AKMs prepped to spray, while their commander ventured forward.

Where was the other? The big guy?

For a moment, Dan worried Pang Pyong-Ho could flank them with a second unit, but the lab was sealed. They were stuck in here.

"Nowhere to go," Dae-Sung said. "We can wait you out. Our plans will go ahead with you barricaded in here or locked in a cell. I do not care."

Tane said, "Sally coming here really was a distraction, wasn't it?"

Dae-Sung scoffed. "Of course. Did you seriously think you could infiltrate our most important facility without detection? I admit we were set up for a larger invasion. In fact, I am still unsure how you got so close. But you will tell me. In time."

Dan felt ridiculous even before he said it, but he had to ask, "When? When did you pick us up?"

"When you crossed open land and broke in through the gate. Very brave. Foolish, but brave. This place might look like some Cold War relic, but we monitor everything. We lost you a few times but killing our guards at the bunker entrance did not go unnoticed."

"Why not take us out there?" Tane demanded.

"We were interested in your plan. Perhaps your colored friend could offer something extra."

It had been a while since Dan heard a term like "colored" to describe a black person. He supposed a country that was 99% indigenous wouldn't be across all the preferred vernacular.

Dae-Sung went on. "We know he can manipulate certain elements that might be useful. Is he under one of these benches? Perhaps he'd like to join us. Certainly, he'd be of more use than—"

"He left," Sally said. "Right before you got here."

"Hmm." Dae-Sung took a second to pull out a miniature walkie-talkie and speak rapid-fire Korean into it, before firming his grip on the Vektor. "He cannot stop what is to come."

"And what is that?" Tane asked, gliding sideways to hamper the commander's angle on him. "Crazy terrorists are still crazy terrorists, regardless of the scale."

Smart, Dan saw. *Keep him talking. Give the kid a head start.*

"We will liberate all Koreans," Dae-Sung said, holding his ground.

Tane steadied himself, lowering his stance, improving his sight of the soldier on the door to Dan's left. Dan shifted left with Sally in place, keeping several pieces of equipment between them and Dae-Sung. On the surface he'd look like he was hiding deeper, but in reality, he had a clean shot at the guard on the right if he needed it. Once Dae-Sung left himself open, Dan and Tane could take down the two armed soldiers and cut down the commander in the crossfire.

Tane said, "Really? That's your big vision? Take over the South and force them into the same isolation as this hellhole?"

"Not at all." Dae-Sung peppered his tone with amusement. "The South will no longer be a vassal state of the USA. They will rise, independent and strong, and we will set our Northern Republic free from the grip of a dynasty that has held onto these people for decades. All people will share in the single, unified state. All people will work to bring glory and wealth to a unified Korea."

"All people?" Dan said. "That sounds like maxed-out socialism. Hasn't worked so well for you so far."

"Americans." Dae-Sung's utterance dripped with disdain, as he'd heard people refer to the dumber side of the nation's citizens. "You always mix up these political ideals. No, what the Republic of Korea has is not true socialism. There is no true socialist country anywhere in the world. No true communist country, either. And America is not some capitalist utopia. Absolutism is the enemy of progress, don't you know?"

Dan couldn't place the quote. Figured it didn't matter. "What do you know about capitalism?"

"Enough. I know your politicians hate helping your people because this means those in power no longer look down upon them, like kings. But they embrace socialism when those kings are threatened. Your handouts to billionaire companies and banks when they are failing inside your stupid economic system... how is this different from the Russian government handing oil contracts to those who swear fealty to the powerful? How is cutting tax for the wealthiest so they can buy back their own stock options in any way creating jobs for the downtrodden?"

He laughed in the same condescending way Dan had heard many times in recent years as if those outside his country knew better than he did.

"You live in the world's biggest oligarchy, my deluded friend. A system designed to keep the lowest castes in their place while being happy to remain there under the lie you call 'freedom.' We, on the other hand, live in the world's biggest concentration camp. Our commandants are power-mad kings by any other name, and we suffer. Because, like you have been brainwashed to believe your king-run 'capitalism' is the bastion of freedom, our all-powerful kings have indoctrinated us to see them as protectors, as saviors. They need to hoard the wealth, the resources, and not share them with the people."

Dan was itching to shoot this prick. He just needed one opening.

But Dae-Sung wasn't done monologuing. Wasn't done with what was clearly an attempt to stall them here. He said, "Two countries. Different lies—one a lie of freedom, the other of protection. The people are compliant here for two reasons: first, they know what I know... that the Americans would rather destroy our country than allow us a level playing field in international commerce, so we must protect ourselves. Second, if they endanger our country by dissenting, they will end up in a place like this. Protection first, then power. But under Executive Ryom's leadership, they will fear nothing. They will work toward the greater good, shielded from America's imperialist agenda, until the world comes to us and begs *us* to join *them*."

"Ryom's companies," Tane said. "They're embedded everywhere."

"And this will give our people true freedom. Power to prevent invasion from the west, and leverage to engage diplomatically. Offer new and future allies protection from the Americans. All without a nuclear arms race that would destroy the world. We are *saving* the world."

"Through death? Isolation? Don't you see this puts your people in more danger?"

Dae-Sung ducked lower, silent for a moment, then returned to the men. "Enough. I believe they are ready to start."

"Oh, that's great," Sally said. "Can we watch?"

"That's what your nonsense speech was about?" Dan asked. "Delaying tactic?"

"Better than risking a shootout," Dae-Sung said. "And it is not nonsense. I had hoped you would at least try to understand."

Sally pawed at Dan's tightening arm. "I asked them to keep an open mind."

"But yes," Dae-Sung said. "Keeping you contained is more important than killing you. And we'll pick up your friend soon enough. So... enjoy your time with us. It's going to last a while."

"We'll stop you," Dan said.

Dae-Sung retreated, keeping solid objects between him and the guys. "Even if you succeed, you kill everyone here. So choose carefully."

Sally said, "Wait, what about me?"

"Thank you for reminding me. Now we have what we need, her knowledge is more useful to you than to us." Dae-Sung checked where Tane was, then whipped up his pistol and fired three times.

Sally jerked with each slug. Dan felt a sharp tug at the side of his ribcage as one bullet cleaved through her, winging him. He dropped her and dove aside, ducking the hail of gunfire that followed.

At least Jules made it out. Hopefully, he was going with the promise they made earlier.

...if one of us gets caught, the others carry on...

Jules had been about to leave when the word "colored" fell from Dae-Sung's lips. He'd promised, after all.

...if one of us gets caught, the others carry on...

He wasn't one that was easy to rile when it came to racial slurs.

Often, the point of the language was to get a rise out of the target of the abuse, so there was a line to walk between standing up for oneself and depriving the abuser of power. In Ah Dae-Sung's case, Jules suspected it was more of an ignorance thing. Less common today, but he'd heard predominantly old people use racially charged terms when they meant "black" or "African-American."

This instance had been a good thing, in a way. It forced Jules to reconsider his egress. Besides, there were far more important things to be angry about right now. Like the threat to his friends' lives.

Moments before Ah Dae-Sung came in with his guards, Jules had predicted the danger and hid under the desk that manned the regular checkpoint. The boots then marched past, and Jules expected the shooting to begin quickly. He would hit the emergency release button on this side of the decontamination unit and the gunfire would conceal his escape for a few minutes at least.

It didn't happen. They talked instead.

Damn it, and I thought Valerio Conchin liked the sound of his own voice.

It became apparent that they were stalling.

Why?

With the sentries on the door focused inside, and with Dae-Sung occupied within, Jules risked checking through the anteroom's glass for backup. None appeared.

This wasn't some never-ending army. They were limited in terms of personnel—either through secretive paranoia or through funds. Perhaps funneling arms and ex-military types here would draw too much attention, or...

None of that mattered.

The priority was obviously the orb, and that cavern with the shields positioned inside. Jules needed to get to it, and quickly.

They talked for longer than seemed practical with Jules wondering if anyone was going to start shooting. Then someone did, finally, discharge their weapon. Someone returned fire, and the pair of guards unleashed their barrage. Jules saw his chance...

...if one of us gets caught, the others carry on...

Jules had a bead on the two gunmen. He could kill them and allow Dan and Tane the drop on Ah Dae-Sung.

No. I'm not killing like that.

But, as ever, he had no problem wounding them. He fired four times—two for each guard, one in each thigh. They fell, probably didn't even know where the shots came from. They simply couldn't stand up anymore.

After that Jules didn't hang around. He sprinted for the disinfectant unit, slammed the release button, and threw open the first door, then the second, checking back briefly.

No one followed. No one was shooting his way. The fight was contained with the pair on the floor and whatever was going down inside the lab.

Good.

He used more caution as the outside air hit him. The two-lane thoroughfare was still in place, but busier. Prisoners were being funneled from the camp toward the main building.

Something was happening.

Jules pinned himself to the wall, trying to read the situation.

It was a handful—a couple of dozen, maybe—using both lanes. The last person to pass was only yards from where Jules had taken cover. And Jules couldn't see where the guards who were plainly directing this group were located.

Now or never.

Go on or go back to check on the others.

Guessing time.

This was more important...

A gamble.

Jules flipped up his hood, stretched up his mask, checked his gloves were in place, and adopted a hunched, shuffling posture as he followed the crowd. No one stopped him. No one pulled him over. He was just another lost soul amid the rabble. And they delved back in toward the staging area. Except... not.

A handful of soldiers herded them over to the right and through a dark passageway. Stern faces, the threatening pointing of weapons—clubs as well as firearms.

Jules kept his head down, struggling to keep up while maintaining his shambling ruse. But in the darker tunnel, he grew more confident and eased up on it a bit. Up ahead, a lighter room turned the wandering inmates into hazy silhouettes, a destination he had no choice but to join.

Once inside, Jules didn't understand at first. An oddity to be sure, but it focused him. He had little choice about what he did next. The only question was how he would achieve it.

And if his friends had any chance of helping him.

It happened so fast Dan barely had time to consider his options. First, Sally went down, dead before she hit the floor. No quirky last words, no redemption as she realized the errors of her ways. Just an airy-fairy beatific look of confusion as she slipped from his arms. The woman had believed this was the right course, up until she was no longer of use.

Perhaps it was better that way. She'd have no regrets.

The AKMs rattled in earsplitting unison and all around the lab erupted, blasted to pieces by a near-indiscriminate spray. Ah Dae-Sung had ducked out of the line of fire, so there was little they could do.

At least the lab benches were metal, and the skirts reached to the floor, providing adequate cover for now. From direct attacks, that was. They didn't stop half a dozen ricochets pinging too close for comfort, though. That, and the jars containing the failed cloning experiments were shattering, spilling liquid over him and Tane, and soaking the floor.

"What is this stuff?" Dan called.

"Formaldehyde," Tane said. "We going for it?"

"Against AKs?"

"Wait for the reload."

That was obvious, but then what would they face?

Suddenly, the automatic fire ceased, replaced by a dual cry of pain. Dan and Tane locked eyes, as if daring each other to believe something that was almost too good to be true.

Dan said, "That kid."

Assuming nothing, he poked his gun and half an eye over the bench. The two men with the AKMs lay sprawled on their backs, upended turtles wrestling with heavy weaponry. Dan drew a bead and fired. Once, twice. A headshot apiece.

"Now where are you, you—"

As if responding to him directly, Ah Dae-Sung fired his Vektor from around the door frame. Dan read this as the commander springing into action as his men fell, going after Jules, then ended up torn between pursuing him and delaying the two predators who were sure to descend.

"Not wrong about that." With room to maneuver, Dan levered the MP5A from under his hoodie. Rather than disrobe, he unclipped the strap and set to work.

Tane had done the same.

They alternated, bursts of three battering the wall and door that Dae-Sung was using. He returned fire, spending his mag. In the pause to reload, they shifted position, advancing on their enemy: one burst from Dan as Tane moved, then Tane returned the favor, performing the standard tactic twice to reach an angle into the entryway.

Nothing.

Dan communicated using hand signals: *I'll take a look.*

Tane: *I'll cover you.*

With Tane aiming into the corridor, Dan positioned himself on the opposite side from where Ah Dae-Sung had fired. Although he couldn't check for a pulse, he was sure the men he'd shot in the head were gone—no freak grazing of the skull from those bullets. It was worth taking a chance on leaving their weapons at their side, especially as the commander posed a greater danger.

Dan counted down in his head, nodding so Tane could read his intent.

Then he was out, into the corridor, scanning wildly with his gun, covering every corner and possible ambush point he could see.

Tane glided out behind. They cleared the guard's empty desk, the disinfectant chamber, even a cupboard full of stationery.

"He's gone," Tane said.

"Yeah, but so's Jules." Dan hustled through the wide-open unit, emerging to the shade of the lab's entrance, where he pinned himself to the wall, suspicious at the quiet, almost deserted thoroughfare from the building to the camp. "Even if we stop them, we'll kill everyone here. That's what he said."

"So, choose right," Tane finished. "The explosives. They're the failsafe."

"Harpal, you there?"

Harpal replied in a scratchy, stuttering signal. "Go for Asian Mr. Bean. Or are we ditching the call signs?"

"That commander guy seemed pretty confident no one could touch them," Dan said. "They got a failsafe in place to prevent anyone leaving if they fail."

"So, if we win, everyone in the camp loses?"

"Bridget, Charlie, you online?" Dan asked.

"Barely," Bridget replied in the same scratchy stop-start way.

The interference must have been from the power source inside, not quite cutting them off but capturing them in the current halo of static.

Dan said, "Do you know how to stop it?"

"Yes, but it's risky."

"We have no good options," Tane said. "Less than an hour until the US Navy launches. Jules is inside, looking for a way to dismantle it, which will blow the dam and kill everyone here. Or our guys back home are ready to take down the network. Or... we let Ryom do his thing."

"What do we do?" Harpal asked.

No one answered.

Then a cough. Then a stutter. Then Toby said, "Trust that Jules will find a way. Harpal, attempt to defuse the bombs. Dan, Tane, you find a way to evacuate the camp. We will stand by here, ready to act if Jules cannot succeed before the missiles start flying. Julia Grainger will keep us updated on that front. Everyone?"

Charlie said, "Agreed."

"Sounds good," Tane said.

"Okay, we got it," Dan said. "Let's go to work."

CHAPTER FORTY

Even more than when they first discovered the staging area, the stark contrast between the space's pristine surfaces and the filth and squalor endured by the prisoners struck Jules as obscene. It was pure and light, although its purpose was, arguably, worse. Only now he was viewing it from a new angle—from behind the chain-link fence he'd seen through the lab's door, a seven-foot barrier connected to a portable generator with a barbed overhang angled to make scaling it more difficult—if they weren't electrocuted first.

Jules kept his surgical mask on, his hood up, and his hands in his pockets, merging with the prisoners at the rear. All of them slouched, streaked with dirt, and draped in the hooded rags endemic in the gulag. Their eyes were wide, almost hopeful as the activity ahead of them commenced.

Making his way through the crowd for a better look, Jules pushed the thought of what might be happening back in the lab to the deepest recesses of his mind. They'd all understood the risk: that capture meant death. The mission before him was too important. It ached to think that way, all but stabbing through his abdomen, but he'd expect the same of them were the circumstances reversed.

Concentrate.

The mission was in front of him, not behind.

The smooth, half-egg-shaped workspace looked like a stage, set on the same level as the odd zombie-like audience. It was lit and busy with a mixture of soldiers and scientists, but the circle of trust appeared small: Executive Ryom was the guy in charge, watching all with his arms folded. Accompanying him, Pang Pyong-Ho acted as either a bodyguard or personal assistant while two men in lab coats tended to the human-shaped chamber, checking plugs and power levels, another two monitored the blackened sphere that would activate the shield, and four guards with those cattle prod devices but no guns stood by, plainly awaiting orders.

All this, watched from ground level by the stunned, bedraggled mass, and from the balcony above by a black-clad private security officer, manning the railgun Jules spotted through the small window earlier, a weapon of war taken from a helicopter gunship or similar vehicle. It was riveted to the balcony floor, too heavy, too powerful for a man to wield it like a typical machine gun.

The other big addition to the room since Jules and the others passed through earlier was a coffin-shaped metal box on wheels. Twice as long as Jules was tall and about four times as wide, it didn't take a genius to work out that it contained Gilim.

The hinged lid opened, revealing the giant himself. The audience managed a gasp, but even that sounded tired, as if performing a physical feat. Solid clasps pinned Gilim down—two on each arm, two on each leg, one across his stomach, and another at his neck. He was awake. Groggy, but conscious.

The men around the workspace spoke in Korean so their words went largely over Jules's head, although his sponge of a brain had absorbed some of the language during the past few days, so he picked up, "Careful," and, "No mistakes," and something along the lines of a threat that ended with, "Dying." The final bit could have been, "all will die."

Jules tapped his ear, and—at the back, out of earshot—said, "Anyone copy? It's now or never."

No one replied. The comms still couldn't penetrate.

Damn.

More orders flew. The soldiers with the charged sticks formed a barrier between Gilim and the Executive. Ryom pointed and shouted something. One guard thrust the prod at Gilim's stomach and hit the trigger. The prongs crackled and Gilim tried to buck, yet only strained against his bindings and howled in pain.

The first man backed off. Ryom barked another order. A second man moved forward with the electrocution implement. Gilim tried to cower, to pull away, but he was stuck fast. The Executive murmured something, and the approaching guard did not stab Gilim.

They'd shown him what they could do, how they could hurt him.

Ryom nodded sharply to one technician in a lab coat—scientists or engineers, it was hard to tell. The tech typed a command on an e-tablet and pecked a "go" key. One of Gilim's wrist clasps disengaged.

The giant lifted his hand, bending his arm at the elbow. He snarled, but as soon as a set of prongs crackled with blue sparks, he lowered the hand and relaxed his face.

The second part of his arm binding gave way. Gilim did nothing. then the other arm came free. He flexed.

The guy manning the railgun steadied himself, adjusting his aim.

When Gilim untensed, they released one leg, then the other, leaving only the metal loop over his stomach and one at his neck.

Jules kept his head down, but he was sweating. He let the gloves slip from his hands and fall to the floor, needing his fists ready, tactile. He didn't think anyone would spot his skin color under the circumstances. Their eyes remained glued to the stage show.

Would they turn him in anyway?

They all looked so emaciated, so tired. Yet also fascinated. This was the accumulation of their backbreaking labor, why they'd suffered so much, why they'd lost friends and loved ones along the way. This... was the *torture* of an innocent creature presented as a spectator sport.

And they hit Gilim again. He cried out, arching his back, his arms splayed aside so the man who'd shocked him had to duck.

Shame he didn't take your head off.

Jules had never been so close to killing. Perhaps his philosophy was as flawed as Dan said. What purpose did allowing someone like Executive Ryom live on serve?

A clear conscience for Jules, sure. But what else?

This was a man willing to kill dozens in acquiring their target and in the name of paranoia and racial superiority. Only his achievement mattered to him. Only Korean lives mattered to Ah Dae-Sung and Pang Pyong-Ho.

How could Jules justify letting these men live? Perhaps a muddy conscience was a price worth paying.

He shouldered through the small audience. The barrier's electrification made climbing over all but impossible, and although it was only seven feet high, the barbed overhang made a leap akin to a high jumper beyond Jules's athletic ability.

The tech released the final bindings.

At Gilim's slow but deliberate movement, pushing up onto one elbow with narrowed eyes and a low brow, it was clear the giant was taking in his surroundings. Planning, thinking about what to do. A sentient creature, capable of thought and logic, of knowing what was going on around him.

A rod crackled, then the other three did too. Gilim pressed himself backwards.

He was a gentle beast, for sure. Other than spats between themselves, these giants had never experienced true violence before the incursion. It took Jules's direct threat to Nan to force them to act, to revert to a massive show of force.

Gilim would have no capacity to plan a fight.

It was up to Jules to show him the way. But if he unlocked Gilim's primal, survive-at-all-costs urge, it'd be difficult to wedge that cork back in the bottle—as Nan, Wade, and Noroth had shown. If it was the only way to prevent a catastrophe, Jules was duty bound to enact it.

One of the techs gestured for Gilim to sit upright, his arm horizontal then bending his elbow to a right angle. Nothing happened. The tech referred to his tablet and then the subject. He repeated the movement, slower this time.

Gilim's head eased around, his gaze shifting from the guy trying to communicate with him to those with the painful weapons, lingering on Executive Ryom, before ending back on the man in the lab coat. The man seemed to smile, although it was difficult to see from behind the chain-link fence.

Gilim pressed his knuckles into the bed on which he was lying and pushed himself into the requested position, gradually and cautiously, like a partygoer with a stinking hangover trying to limit the nausea of their overindulgence.

More sign language, and Gilim eventually stood, towering over his captors. With every command translated from the computer tablet, he glanced at Ryom with undisguised hatred. The intelligence behind Gilim's brutish exterior shone through, pinpointing the man giving the orders, the human being responsible for his pain and confusion, for ripping him from his home and family and pressing him into servitude here. In this strange place.

Jules had weaved his path. With the dazed inmates paying him little mind, he assessed his options beside the noisy generator.

A generator.

In a hydroelectric dam?

They'd seen these dotted around, powering the wan spotlights outside, the alarm system, and now the lights in here and the fence keeping this rapt audience at bay.

They were concerned this activity would blow the transformers, taking out the main grid and unleashing the masses on the few. Here, they'd been shepherded in, presumably so they could spread the word about the authorities' ultimate power, but they must pose a danger. If this fence were not an obstacle, would they chance exposing the scientists and the Executive to such unwilling yet subdued prisoners?

They guided Gilim toward the sarcophagus-shaped compartment, upright and open. Its dimensions appeared a touch small to Jules's eyes, and judging distance, speed, and the size of objects were all factors his brain chewed up and spat out with the ease of 2+2. A rare gift that had served him well.

Sure enough, once they got the message to Gilim, the giant needed to duck to get inside. He resisted, though. This was nothing he'd encountered before, not consciously, and bending into a place like this visibly frightened him. A jab from an electrical prod forced him to jerk and arch his back. No howl this time. Just a grunt and a glare Ryom's way.

The soldier manning the railgun up top had tailed Gilim throughout, keeping him in sight, ready to unleash the 90mm rounds should he threaten to escape.

Then, compliance.

Jules had no more time. No one was coming to join him. No power outage, no last-minute explosion to distract security. His friends had been caught, and Ah Dae-Sung was probably prepping to execute them. Once they were clear of the lab. Perhaps Sally was resisting again, demanding no harm come to them.

He could only hope. But hoping did no good right now.

In the dark corner, where the exhausted men and women hid him from the guards at the rear, Jules lowered himself to the ground, removed the hooded fleece, and slipped his equipment from the compact pack: a snub-nosed Glock 17, one of his batons with the grappling hook and bungee cord, two multi-tools of differing sizes, and a full-strength flashbang grenade. He was kitted out like a SWAT commando, missing only a submachine gun, which they couldn't risk fitting onto him for the HALO jump. Sergeant Massey back home would get a kick out of this.

Jules thumbed his belt. He'd insisted on his usual array of throwing knives and mini flashbangs, too. Although the knives inflicted dreadful wounds, they were never fatal. Better someone walked with a limp or suffered an aching shoulder each winter than ending up six feet under. To date, he'd been successful in never *needing* to kill, with only one unintentional blip on his ledger.

Would today change this?

Gilim backed into the enclosure. Jules closed his eyes, hating every moment that he hesitated. If he'd launched into action sooner, he could have spared Gilim what he expected was to come, but if he didn't wait, he predicted a far worse outcome. No straightforward answers here.

The door closed over Gilim. From one sealed box to another. Except this box had a translucent door of something crystal-like, the enormous man inside touching the interior, hunched over at the top. It sealed with a clunk.

And that was Jules's cue.

He ran up onto the generator and, having fed out the right amount of bungee cord, threw the grappling hook over the balcony railing. He dropped to the floor, the elastic stretching taut, which snapped back and whipped Jules high into the air. He tucked into a ball and flipped over the fence, throwing the larger flashbang grenade toward the men ringing the giants' chamber as he snagged a handhold on the upper tier.

The flashbang went off below, a massive crack assaulting Jules's ears even this far away. Plenty to disorient the people surrounding the chamber and the black, dangerous orb within the power coupling.

In a smooth swing, Jules lifted himself over the balustrade and drew his sidearm.

Also a safe distance from the worst of the effects, the gunman with the huge caliber weapon was already heaving it toward Jules. Too slowly, though.

Before the first bullet could fire, Jules blasted his Glock twice—one slug through each shoulder. As soon as the gunman jerked aside, seeking non-existent cover, and pressing his palms over the wounds, Jules fired twice more. The man's hands spat blood, terror contouring his face.

Then Jules's mind turned. It wasn't so much that time slowed down for him, but the decisions came fast. Like he couldn't forget the techniques of shooting, throwing knives, or generating the most power from a side-kick, nor could he prevent logic and pragmatism from guiding his decisions. Before his fourth bullet shattered the man's second hand, Jules had already assessed the angles necessary for two more shots. After immobilizing the gunner's hands, he loosed off two more, taking him in the meat of his thighs.

While Dan would have planted one in the man's head, Jules opted for years of physiotherapy. If the guy survived what was to come. Which was debatable.

Jules retrieved his baton, leaped over the railing, and descended to the staging area, where the men were scrambling to recover from the ringing in their heads—the four technicians, the four guards, and Executive Ryom were all goggle-eyed and holding their skulls together. Only Pang Pyong-Ho was on the verge of picking himself up fully, shielding his boss and diving behind the metal coffin in a stuttering motion. Gilim growled and pounded from inside the compartment, protected from much of the blast, but must have been hit by the light flash.

Meanwhile, the audience had cowered but not fled. All curled up on the floor, a Pavlovian response to gunfire and violence, some only now daring to peek out from their tangled limbs. They must have thought they were being mowed down by some attack.

What the hell had the authorities here put them through?

Jules touched down with a cushioned landing and charged. Gun up. He fired into the men who'd prodded and shocked Gilim. He targeted the most painful zones—the knees, hip bones, the feet, and hands. Blood flew, bodies fell, unable to fight, and the gun's slide snapped open when it was empty.

He didn't slow down. Two scientists, Ryom Jung-Hwan, and Pang Pyong-Ho remained unharmed. Jules tossed the mini-flashbangs—only a tenth as powerful as the real deal, but plenty to confuse and scare an enemy.

They popped as planned, and Jules palmed two throwing knives before dispatching the pair of techs who'd hurried away from his attack, lunging for the control panel beneath the spinning sphere. He flung the blades into their backs, embedding in the muscle between shoulder blades—again, painful without penetrating essential organs. As he ran by, angling for Pyong-Ho and his master, Jules fired his heel into the knee of the guy closest to the controls. The joint snapped, preventing him from completing whatever task he was attempting.

Then the air blew out of Jules. He slammed against the cradle holding the orb and the black surface rippled with color. Not that Jules had time to appreciate it. He rolled instinctively aside as another ferocious kick came in.

Pyong-Ho had switched from defense to attack. No firearms, no blade, just him.

Jules ducked and swept at the incoming opponent but missed, still not at full capacity after being winded. He sucked air into his lungs, fast and sharp, jumping onto the console and pushing off to summit the chamber in which Gilim was imprisoned. He slid down the opposite side, evading Pyong-Ho's grabbing hand, and sprang up onto the coffin where Gilim had slept. It gave him time to drop to the other side and force his lungs to work properly again.

Pyong-Ho moseyed around the side to face him. Yeah—*moseyed* was what he did. And then he stood there like a gunslinger prepping for a quick-draw duel. Only neither of them were armed.

Okay, Jules had kept three throwing blades and one mini-flashbang. But the cruelty he'd witnessed, the glee with which they wielded power and held it over the subjugated masses of the Dragon's Pit, overrode the factors that gave him a bigger advantage in this fight.

Perhaps those Hollywood tough guys were onto something after all.

Pyong-Ho opened with a dummy kick and two feints with his fist, then followed up with the real deal of a snap kick to the knee. Jules skipped over it and thrust an open hand at the dummied punch. He turned his own bodyweight backwards, then used the raised arm as a lever along with the kick's momentum to toss Pyong-Ho over his hip, releasing him as he fell a good four feet away.

But he was up in half a breath. A snort and a tense pump of the fists said he wouldn't fall for that again.

And so it was. The thrusts and parries came fast, and Jules couldn't block them all, resorting to a retreat tactic to evade an almighty upper cut. He landed on Gilim's compartment and sprang back with a close-in kick to Pyong-Ho's groin—a move the muscle-head was ready for.

He secured Jules in a bear hug and slammed his forehead down repeatedly. Jules's brow flared, his nose numbed without breaking. His brain clanged around. All he could do was slip a knife out of his belt and jam it into Pyong-Ho's tricep. It didn't disable him, but the damaged muscle was weaker. Jules shifted position, lowering his shoulder, then jabbed the wound with stiff fingers.

He refused to feel bad about "cheating" as the monster of a man released him.

Just enough time to breathe. To check his situation and the surrounding threats. The men he'd taken out were still poleaxed; the black orb vibrated harder; Gilim hammered on his box, desperate to escape, his fear an angry bloodlust as drool fell from his lips; more guards had arrived behind the fence, corralling the audience, trying to get them to leave, but most were watching proceedings, back on their feet, more of a spark to their eyes than Jules had seen since they landed. Executive Ryom was nowhere to be seen...

Losing time, Jules then fired a volley of strikes at Pyong-Ho's vulnerable spots—where all human beings are weakest. The neck to stun, the groin, the kidneys. He jabbed a finger at the man's eye, but it Pyong-Ho blocked it. Jules's next big attack, aiming for the knee, missed too, as his opponent got his act together.

He didn't see the back-hander fly.

It caught Jules in the temple, rattling his brain and sending him tumbling. A fist flew by as he ducked, but Pyong-Ho's taekwondo was note-perfect, landing a sweet round-kick in Jules's ribs, followed by a sweep that took his ankle. Jules would have landed hard, but Pyong-Ho's meaty hand—the one not encumbered by a blade in the tricep—clamped onto his neck. Fingers closed around him, all but meeting on the other side. Pyong-Ho lifted Jules and slammed him against Gilim's prison. Again, the air whooshed out of him.

Being winded for the second time in as many minutes would take a toll on even the fittest athlete. And although Jules had at one point approached professional levels, he'd eased up of late.

There was nothing he could do.

Too weak to defend, too rattled to think his way free, Jules lay against the polymer, with a giant pounding away beneath, and waited to black out for the final time.

CHAPTER FORTY-ONE

"Okay, it's time," Harpal said, the scaffold swaying as he shifted his weight. "Let's step this up."

"I'd love to pretend I know what you mean," Charlie replied. "But can you be more specific?"

"I'm not sure I can. This whole setup..."

Harpal tried to summon the vocabulary to describe the device, but it wasn't easy.

Phil came on the line. "Right, then, give it to me step by step."

"Hi, babe," Charlie said. "Glad you could join us."

"*I'm* just glad you're not in the firing line for once."

"You know I've been stabbed in the leg, right, *honey*?"

If Phil heard her, he gave nothing away. "Harps, give it to me. You got a video you can send?"

Harpal shook his head as if anyone could see him. "We didn't bring phones, and cameras were too much bulk. Didn't think we'd need them."

"Phones wouldn't work in that location," Charlie added. "And the Executive heads an advanced tech company. Could have compromised our network."

Phil said, "Then let's hear what you see."

"A box." Harpal examined the setup more closely without touching the bricks of plastic. "There are..." He counted each side of bricks. Seven by seven. "Forty-nine bricks of explosives in a metal case."

"Wires?"

"Cables. There's a thick, black one connecting this to the one near the middle of the wall. I can only see a few inside. On top is a black box with a green light next to three more that aren't lit."

Phil sighed, thinking. "Can you cut the cable and see what's inside?"

Harpal took out a folding knife and sliced a shallow groove in the thick, black rubber. He checked how deep it went and cut a little more. "I'm a centimeter in. This is some serious insulation."

He deepened the gash until a train of color showed. "Okay, I see wires."

"How many?" Phil asked.

Harpal's hands were numb, his pulse pounding in his neck. He was sweating as he widened the gap and his stomach hollowed out at what he saw. He didn't need a munition or demolition expert to convey what it meant.

He said, "Too many. Dozens."

It was like a fibrous muscle, a multitude of red, green, yellow, and blue wires woven together so it was impossible to see which were active and which were redundancies.

"You can't deactivate it," Phil said. "Our options just got a lot thinner."

Harpal left the booby trap to the elements and returned halfway to the platform's edge, where he could view the prison camp without making the whole world sway.

"Sounds bad," Charlie said.

"How long until the Americans launch?" Harpal asked.

"Last update from Ms. Grainger," Toby said, "leaves us twenty minutes."

"Dan, you heard that. We have to wait on Jules, but you need to clear this place, get them all above the water level. If Bridget and Charlie take down the system, this whole site is gonna blow."

. . .

Jules's world closed in, black circling the edges of his narrowing vision. He'd lost his strength and his advantage, a year and change of civilian life having robbed him of his edge. Adhering to common rules written and unwritten, learning their ways, overwriting his instincts, had led to this moment—an enraged Pang Pyong-Ho pinning him to Gilim's compartment, hand around his neck, squeezing the life out of him. If only he'd taken control of that railgun and slaughter everyone below him... This would have been over in seconds.

Pyong-Ho's free hand, with the blade embedded in it, served to block off Jules's feeble attempts to fight back. It must have been painful to move it, but this fight would be done soon enough.

Twenty seconds before Jules's brain could send no more messages to his body, thirty-five-to-forty seconds until he fell unconscious, and maybe ninety seconds until death if Pyong-Ho chose to finish him.

It was his own fault. Getting angry. Allowing his rage at the men before him to define his actions. He could just go to sleep here, and all would end as it should. In fire. In death. As it had throughout human history.

Fifteen seconds until he could no longer move.

A vibration made his senses seek out its source. Something he couldn't ignore. Something he'd never have ignored a year ago. And here, at the end, he recalled the reasons he'd never ended up this way in the past.

It wasn't only his constant training that raised his fighting prowess above military champions and psychotic thugs. His internal approach was different, too. Aware of all. Of his own body, his mind, his surroundings.

Calm. Measured. Unemotional.

And his senses were reporting back that Gilim's ferocious hammering, his panicked desperation to get out of the manmade chamber, was trembling the structure. The control panel.

He couldn't see it from here. Couldn't reach it, even if his vision extended that far.

Calm. Measured.

He pictured the scene. His eidetic recall 20:20 in optimum circumstances, tainted here by a lack of air.

Ten seconds to paralysis. Twenty-five until blackout.

Perfect recall: The orb spun black yet bright above head height; the shields hung in their cages, with cables spreading out like tentacles; the control panel like something out of a 1970s sci-fi TV show, the bridge of a starship on a budget.

But simple.

Simpl*ified.*

That was what had struck Jules as so odd—how it wasn't a ton of computer screens and buttons. It was the twenty-first century. Of course it was all run by tablets and laptops away from the principal center. Only a few buttons remained.

Including the one he needed.

Five seconds until Pyong-Ho rendered him immobile.

The darkness closed in, only Pyong-Ho's face in view. He sweated with the effort of pinning Jules, strangling him, and dealing with a blade jammed into a very tender spot.

Jules thumbed his remaining flashbang, the marble-sized smoke bomb-come-firecracker that he'd used for years to distract an opponent in a non-lethal way. It was his only chance. The only chance this region had, the only way to prevent a conflict in which millions would perish. One tiny little explosive.

And Jules's hope that he remembered the layout correctly.

He set the fuse and flicked it to his left, under Pang Pyong-Ho's armpit, toward the big red button. In a typical factory or power plant, or even a treadmill in a gym, it would serve as an easily accessible abort switch.

Jules pictured the flashbang flying, first up to its apex, then down, down toward the panel. If he'd calculated the distance and height correctly, the tiny device would detonate five feet away from him, an inch or two above the button and—

Pop!

The timing was spot on. The only question was whether the mini bomb's concussive force was enough.

Pyong-Ho laughed. "What is this, American? Distraction?"

The vibration beneath Jules increased. Not a trembling, but a shove. A surge of tectonic plates. Jules gagged as Pyong-Ho jolted backward.

Jules rose into the air and slumped aside as the door opened beneath him. He slid sideways, out of the way of the heavy, polymer-crystal door crashing over as Gilim freed himself. No cry of fear, no growl, no grunt.

What followed was a *roar*. Like a grizzly bear defending its young.

Gilim surged out of his prison with catlike agility. His musculature was tough, but sleek, efficient. Although he looked like a brute, he exhibited the speed of the great apes, combined with a human understanding of the world around him. And he had identified his enemy.

Pang Pyong-Ho stood no chance. Without a hint of gloating or grandstanding, Gilim thrust out an arm at the fleeing bodyguard, curled his fingers over the man's head. His other hand snatched Pyong-Ho's torso, not easing up on the pressure, and ripped off his head.

Jules still wasn't able to stand, gasping for breath as his pulse pounded through his skull, reacquainting itself with the oxygen it so desperately needed. He was nothing but a passive observer, wishing he could turn away.

The men on the ground who Jules had disabled all started crawling or shuffling toward the exits. They'd scattered in limps and lollops to allow Jules and Pyong-Ho to fight. Evidently, they'd stuck around to witness their man finish Jules off, but now they couldn't scatter fast enough.

Gilim recognized them as his tormenters, though, and plowed into them. Bones broke, blood flew. Some of the jailers tried to escape via the anteroom, where the audience was crying and whimpering, only to be repelled by the electrified fence. The abort button hadn't dropped the current.

The people on the other side were filtering out, withdrawing under orders, stopping only to glance back as another of their tormentors met a grisly end at Gilim's hand. Jules couldn't see all of them but, on a few faces, he picked up a smile or two. The first he'd encountered in this place.

Did they sense freedom approaching?

But there was an addition to the mix here, in the lab. Three armed men racing in from the rear, firing en-mass at Gilim. Ah Dae-Sung one of them, the commander on the front line.

When did he get here?

Orders flew, guns fired. Bullets penetrated Gilim's skin, but not the muscles, not the bones. Painful. But he was so enraged it was like throwing stones at King Kong.

The carnage turned Jules's stomach. He had known, on some level, that this would be the result. That this was what freeing Gilim meant. That the blood was literally on someone else's hands made him feel less guilty, but as Jules pushed to his feet, sensing his extremities returning to functional capacity, he faced the simple fact.

I am responsible for this.

When Gilim finished the final technician, he rounded on the gunmen as they defended the wide double doorway through which they must have brought Gilim. Jules guessed that was the escape route Executive Ryom had taken, where arrangements would be made for his safety.

His legs were a little shaky, but he could move. He tested his balance.

All good.

And as Gilim charged, smashed through the first gunman, and bounded headlong toward the final guy and Ah Dae-Sung, Jules careered forward on an intercept course. He'd have no chance to stop the ten-foot behemoth, not even trip him up, but he had to try.

"Gilim!" he cried.

The giant's head turned to Jules, veered that way for a second, but pulled up short. All gunfire ceased, all screaming muted.

"Go," Jules said.

"I cannot." Ah Dae-Sung sidestepped, taking the last soldier with him, both aiming their peashooter weapons at Gilim. They covered the double doors leading to the passageway which, in turn, led to the exit.

Gilim growled and dove forward.

Jules got in his way. "No!" He held his arms up, halting the giant.

Gilim braced, fists either side of Jules. He clearly recognized him. If not a friend, then an enemy of his enemy. How long that would last, Jules couldn't guess. He only knew that in this moment, Gilim didn't want to kill him.

Jules said, "Just go."

"We must hold the creature here," Dae-Sung said.

"Your boss ain't worth it. This guy will kill you."

Gilim's breath clouded hot on Jules's face. Sour and meaty, it made Jules gag, but he remained in the giant's path. A snort, a growl. His patience was wearing thin. But Jules couldn't let this go without trying. He couldn't stand aside.

"Jules!" Dan shouted, entering against the flow of prisoners leaving the anteroom. "How'd you get comms up?"

Jules heard it in his earbud as well as in person. Tane backed Dan up, both alive but on the wrong side of the fence.

"*You* got comms back up," Jules said. "Useful. And I don't know how."

They came up to the perimeter but must have seen the electrocution warnings despite what they were watching: Jules in front of the ten-foot Gilim, blood and limbs spread all over, and Ah Dae-Sung waiting to die, should Jules allow it.

"Probably close vicinity," Tane said. "Later for that. Right now, we need to get you out. We can't stop the dam blowing, so it's now an evac. Leave them."

But Jules had allowed his emotions, his anger, to cloud his judgement too much already. This was his way. *Preserve human life*. There was always another way. Except where Pang Pyong-Ho was concerned. Jules would be dead if he hadn't unleashed Gilim.

Did that make Jules a killer? Pointing a loaded weapon at an enemy?

"Let the big guy past," Dan shouted. "It's not you finishing them. It's him. It's—"

Gilim rounded on Dan and roared at him. Both Dan and Tane backed away, despite the fence between them, before Gilim lumbered to the side.

"I can't stop him much longer," Jules said. "You wanna live, you leave, and close those doors quietly behind you."

Ah Dae-Sung foolishly stepped forward one pace, agitating Gilim.

He held position but spoke loudly enough for his words to carry to Dan and Tane. "You do not understand. None of you."

Dan hefted his gun but had no clear shot at Dae-Sung. "I understand you're cooked. We stopped your ass-shield, and if we don't report in that it's decommissioned, you got fifteen cruise missiles heading this way."

"It is not decommissioned." Ah Dae-Sung flapped his hand, shaking his head in despair. "This creature wasn't there to power it, or act as a conduit. It was there to *stabilize* it."

Something Bridget had said before came back to Jules. That it was part of a phalanx of other points on the globe. A shielding device, not simply for individual use—although that was how the Guardians used it—but potentially a global shield. To defend against rocks falling from the sky, like the one that wiped out the dinosaurs or smaller, localized disasters that could have been witnessed.

Witnessed.

The Witnesses.

Who would have been around at the time of the Earth's last magnetic flip. *42,000 years ago.*

This was always about cocooning the planet. From pre-history through to the Guardians concealing its legacy, to discovering the DNA needed to control the unstable elements, present in the race of giants they'd protected from certain death. The slave race who helped build the magnificent structures of the ancient world, who fought as comrades to the Guardians, who came to the United States long before that country even existed, and lived alongside the Natives, found peace, and a life outside of servitude.

"They didn't hide giants' existence from the world for some arbitrary reason," Jules said, having processed his conclusion in a couple of blinks of the eye. "They couldn't risk activating this shield without the proper knowledge. And that was lost."

Damn, Bridget. Your obsession with knowing everything might pay off.

Gilim's breaths came deeper, slower, seemingly sensing a shift in the danger, in the mood of the room.

"We got this," Jules told Ah Dae-Sung.

"You do not." Dae-Sung patted the other soldier on the chest. Both aimed up at Gilim. "If we can buy more time, we will. You must call off your air strike, or the world will suffer. We must save executive Ryom."

"What's so important?" Tane demanded. "He lied to you, used you, made you think what you were doing was noble. But it's just a power grab. For him. Not your people. Like this concentration camp. An army of prisoners and workers, all in place to make him the most powerful man on Earth. How can you stay loyal to him?"

"*Because...*" Through gritted teeth, Ah Dae-Sung stared at Gilim. "Executive Ryom's life readings are linked to a series of explosive charges. If he dies, or his heart rate increases to dangerous levels, the detonators will trigger, this dam will be destroyed, and all will die here. And this machine? No one knows how it will react."

"It'll blow like a neutron bomb," Jules said. He directed a firm eye at Dan. "Remember Scotland? How that pulse knocked us all out? Well, imagine that with an energy blast on top, spreading out across the country. Across every country linked to the orb."

"What do we do?" Dan called back.

"Evacuate. I gotta shut this down."

"We must protect the Executive," Dae-Sung said.

He then gave an order in Korean. The soldier looked terrified for a moment, then opened fire on Gilim.

The giant roared, lunged forward, and would have swiped Jules aside had he not read the intent and threw himself flat to the floor.

While Gilim smashed his way through the pawn of a soldier, Ah Dae-Sung ran out the half-open double doors. Once Gilim was satisfied his immediate threat was dead, it took him a moment of rattling and yanking and pounding on the doors to wrench them open, then he ducked under to pursue.

Jules leaped up and made for the same door.

"Where are you going?" Dan yelled. "Get out of here."

"Evacuate," Jules replied, pausing in his exit. "Trust me, I got this. I understand it all. I understand *me*. I understand the machine. Just gotta get Gilim back here. You get the people out, and make sure Bridget and Charlie can shut the network down."

CHAPTER FORTY-TWO

Closed in, they couldn't use heavy artillery, so it was sensible that Ah Dae-Sung trailed the breadcrumbs outside. Jules would have done the same. If he were a cold, calculating soldier.

Gilim knew no better than to follow his nose. He had a target, the man who'd ripped him from his family, hurt him, forced him into confined spaces, and then hid until he could hide no more. The massive form lumbered, hunched over, through the corridor, ignoring anyone who didn't fire on him. His pace was impressive, the equivalent of Jules at 90% speed.

But Jules was operating at maybe 50 to 60% capacity. The exertion of the past few days, the jump, the fight with Pyong-Ho... he was sapped but not finished. He struggled to maintain the chase, but wouldn't give it up, not yet.

The fact Ah Dae-Sung was luring Gilim outside, to where he would have more room to fight, suggested they didn't want to take that chance. They needed Gilim neutralized. And for that, they had to subdue him.

Maybe even kill him.

Activating the meteor rocks and the elements in the Ruby Rock and Aradia bangles required Jules to be conscious. That melding of human observation and the mix of neutrinos and gluons and all the other facets that made quantum mechanics so unknowable, so different from most of the physical world, could hold true here.

If Gilim died, they all died.

And the best chance for him to survive—along with the millions threatened by the device if Bridget and Charlie blew the network—was to leave the Executive alone.

"You got it, Bridget?" Jules asked as he charged through the next large door. He gasped as he found himself outside.

He knew what the plan was. And it was clever. Brutal but clever.

"Nearly." Bridget was nothing if not fastidious. She'd make guesses, but where a certain outcome was available, she'd strive for it, even under pressure.

"Hurry."

They'd lured Gilim to the yard above the barracks where prisoners would exercise. The tower equipped with high-caliber machine guns protected it. They were not as powerful as the railgun in the lab or on the gunships that raided the volcano facility, but Jules figured they'd pierce the giant's armor-like muscle.

Kill him?

Maybe.

With Ah Dae-Sung in sight, shepherding the Executive and a cadre of five more goons toward a sturdy-looking gate on wheels, Gilim ran across the yard.

Jules yelled, "*Gilim, no, wait!*"

The guard towers lit up. The central one, plus a second embedded in the valley wall which they hadn't spotted earlier—camouflaged against the night-draped landscape. Two machine guns blasted away, aiming for Gilim in a crossfire. Bullets cut up the frozen dirt, tracers flashing as they impacted. His flesh tore, making him stumble and scream. He landed hard, shaking the ground—an impact that stuttered the barrage.

Jules assessed the open space between the facility and the towers. Even if he could run the half-football-pitch of land, he could only scale one tower. By that time, they'd pepper Gilim and likely kill him.

The giant, hobbled and bleeding, turned himself over and pushed halfway to his knees.

Jules said, "I need air support."

"You got it," Harpal answered.

As the machine-gunners recovered and opened fire, part of the first tower blew inward, halting the shooting. Then a smattering of bullets impacted the second, and the yard fell silent. Returning to the first, more bullets from up high slammed home, and the guard manning that tower fell out, tumbling to the floor without even a shout. He was dead already. No one emerged from the other, but no gunfire blasted either.

Both were dead.

"You're welcome," Harpal said.

He'd come armed with the same weapons as Dan, but so high, he'd been able to spot the commotion, so Jules had known he'd have an angle, even at the very edge of the submachine gun's effective range. Again, he'd known the outcome would be death, even though he hadn't pulled the trigger himself.

Gilim lumbered away, shouldering through the solid gate where Ah Dae-Sung and the Executive's party had fled, gambling the towers would give them time to evac the main man. The giant growled and huffed, favoring his right side, but there was no doubt he was still powerful. The larger rounds, as far as Jules could tell, had inflicted damage, but weren't life threatening.

Jules gathered his breath and set out after them all. "Bridget, where are we?"

"Two minutes," she replied.

"Patience, Sibeko," Charlie added, presumably from Bridget's side.

Jules skirted the yard's edge, sticking to the shadows. No telling who else was watching. "Patience ain't my strong suit. And we're on a clock, but I can't tell you the deadline."

"Eleven minutes," Prihya said. "They launch in eleven minutes. You must declare the place neutralized by then, or we're all at war."

"Yeah, so... Bridget? You got something for me?"

No reply. He knew she was on it, so didn't push it. All he could do was press on, after the injured creature whose instinct told him to kill his enemy, to stop these men from hurting him further, from going after his family. Gilim did not know they were an entire ocean away.

Only one thing stuttered Jules's approach, and only briefly.

Beyond the fence, the dark expanse of the gulag's residences teemed with motion. Hundreds of adults in various stages of fitness swarmed around. None of them knew where to go, what to do, just that danger had come calling in a form worse than the guards who controlled their daily lives.

"Dan, you gotta get a grip on the prisoners," Jules said, hoping they hadn't ventured into another blind spot.

"These bombs aren't going anywhere," Harpal answered, even though Jules hadn't addressed him. "The valley will flood, and we'll lose the machine."

"Okay, Asian Mr. Bean, you call it." Dan was back online, unseen, but must have been nearby. "Gimme some eyes."

Dan listened for Harpal's reply and tried to see more of the gulag, but it was difficult with such dull light.

"I think we can ease up on the call signs," Harpal said. "And 'gimme some eyes' isn't the best instruction ever."

Dan and Tane cut around the base of the dam, up onto the edges where it seemed the camp had attempted some limited farming. All he could determine was the dam itself, the prison yard, the entrance to the facility embedded in the mountain, and the vague edge of the mile-wide barracks, which reminded him of a prisoner of war camp. The people were swarming, but there wasn't much in the way of direction.

Dan said, "Where do we need to frighten 'em?"

"Frighten?" Tane echoed.

"Only way we can evac 'em is to get them up high. And I don't have a bullhorn. Or a clue where the PA system is controlled from. Do you?"

"No, but..."

"Asian Mister— Harpal, you read? I need a route up to our LZ that the inmates can manage."

"Not above the dam?" Harpal said.

"Just high enough so they don't get washed away. You do that?"

"Sure, one minute."

. . .

"Bridget, I'm switching channels," Jules said, tapping the bud twice. He waited a moment. "You there?"

"Yes, and I have what you need." Bridget lacked the usual spark of excitement present whenever she worked out a code or deciphered a hieroglyph. This was too important, not a mystery, not a treasure trove, but life and death for millions. "Are you with Gilim?"

"Not yet."

The path spiraled, and Jules maintained a line of sight on Gilim, a single twist leading to an outcrop on the western hillside, a clear run to a helicopter pad that—when Jules scanned the dam looming hundreds of feet above—would have been hidden from Harpal's view. No way to tell it was there.

On the pad, a sleek helicopter warmed up, with the five goons pushing the executive toward it. Ah Dae-Sung ran backwards, his submachine gun's stock mounted on his shoulder, probably wishing he'd opted for something heavier—perhaps a grenade launcher. Yet, LORI's one advantage on this mission was the hubris displayed by their enemy, an assumed superiority in all areas of life. Be it militarily or political, moral or philosophical, it was going to be their downfall.

The squad of men lined up, forming a last defense at the perimeter of the rotor wash. Dae-Sung ushered his boss toward the helicopter with the whining engines, its rotor speeding up for takeoff. The tower-led machine guns had given them less time than expected.

If they killed Gilim, though, there'd be nothing to mitigate the shield's critical mass. If the Executive got away, there'd be nothing to stop him activating it remotely, the controls being mobile rather than engineered into a panel.

If Jules allowed Gilim to kill the Executive, the dam would blow, and trigger a chain reaction stretching across the globe.

Perhaps he'd grown inured to the violence, to the carnage, but as Gilim tore into the goons, who must surely have known they were giving up their lives for a few seconds' grace, Jules felt nothing. He viewed it with the same cold detachment as calculating a jump between buildings, the angle of a throwing knife, or the pressure required to snap a lock. It was a matter of timing.

And the men had slowed the rampaging giant enough for Jules to overtake. To ignore the bone-crunching skirmish between Gilim and five under-prepared bodyguards as they used their pistols to defend themselves. This time, Jules succeeded, running up the incline to their left, like a cyclist zipping up the steepest part of an indoor track, and tapped a reserve of energy to sprint on, taking Ah Dae-Sung by surprise.

He launched himself at the commander who was concentrating on Gilim's position, disarming him with a swift over-rotation before unleashing a furious volley of elbows, knees, and fists. Executive Ryom staggered on toward the helicopter, but as Jules fought with Dae-Sung, Gilim had finished with the last stand of goons, and hurtled forward.

Dae-Sung pulled a knife, which Jules parried. He gripped the commander's forearm, missing his chance to apply a lock on the joint, his opponent too experienced despite the sudden beating Jules had dished out, and went for a sweep of the leg. Dae-Sung stepped over it, but that wasn't Jules's intent. Jules instead held the man up, levered him over, and extended one fist to the sky.

The speeding rotor lopped off his hand and the knife and limb sailed high overhead and away to safety.

Jules threw the stunned Dae-Sung to the ground and ran after Ryom. "Move to your left!"

The Executive glared back at Jules, then boggle eyed as Gilim thundered towards them. The rotor blade, although plenty to slice through Dae-Sung's wrist, was not quite at full speed, and stood no chance against the giant's super-hard muscle.

Jules—perhaps having retained some measure of what he'd witnessed in Kainga Pukepuke—dropped his head, ran as fast as he could at Ryom, and slammed into his waist. He wrapped an arm around the man's thighs, hoisted him up, and continued charging aside.

The rotor cut into Gilim, breaking skin as the bullets had, but shattered at the stem. The engine burst out in smoke. A squall of gears and cranks and a hundred moving parts filled the air, and the helicopter's tail spun, propelling it sideways. It lifted off the ground a few inches, whipped around into Gilim, who punched the main body. This sent it hurtling over the platform's edge, tipping end over end, before exploding in a massive, orange fireball.

. . .

Harpal came good, issuing instructions which Dan trusted he'd based on more than a hunch. With the residential sector set out in a grid, bending to the contours of the land, he and Tane placed themselves at points that plotted two stages of a curve. He imagined the line started at the corner where the dam met the mountainside, arcing over to the bottom of the road that wound up to the very top.

"Herd them up that path," Harpal said. "I'll redirect them to the dump."

"Let's hope it's just a precaution." Tane took off toward the outer position, ignored by the handful of prisoners milling aimlessly around.

Dan's experience was much the same, following Harpal's directions toward the coordinates closer to the dam, until he found himself at a huge water butt where three men and a woman queued with metal pots. All four were wearing filthy overalls and although each huddled a blanket around them, they were rail thin and shaking. They saw his gun, and all averted their eyes.

"No, no, it's okay," Dan said, pointing down the lane toward the access road. "That way. You have to leave."

No one spoke.

Dan jabbed his finger harder and spoke more slowly. "Go. You. Have. To. Go."

Because intoning words helps translate them, right?

No, dumbass. It doesn't.

"Tane, how do I tell these people to run for their lives?"

"You can't learn Korean that way," Tane replied.

"Just give it to me. I'll say it. One word at a time."

Tane did so, and Dan repeated it.

"Salgo. Sipdam...ye...on." He pointed again. This time the people took notice. "Jin...ibloleul. Dallyeo."

"That was atrocious," Tane said. "But I guess it'd have gotten the gist across."

While Dan thought he'd rocked the line, the men and woman bore the same expression—part confusion, part fear. A Caucasian man stuttering words at them in the middle of the night. Why wouldn't they believe him?

"Okay, screw this." Dan jogged a few yards away, set his carbine to single shots, and fired into the floor near their feet.

They jumped, then huddled together.

"No, you idiots." Dan pointed yet again at the route he wanted them to take. "Run. Leave!" He fired again into the mud nearby.

This time, they got the message and—again, as a huddled mass—hobbled along the row in the right direction.

"That's what I'm talking about," Dan said, resuming his path to where he needed to be.

"They ducked into a different barracks," Harpal said. "They're hiding from you."

"Damn it, don't these people want to be saved?"

"They're conditioned to behave," Tane put in. "Even when a big brave 'Meri-cun shows up to deliver some freedom."

"I suppose the crusading Kiwi's had better luck?" Dan replied. "Hey, Crusading Kiwi is a really cool call sign."

"I got a handful heading the right way. But it's not enough. We can't reach everyone."

"Well, give me a couple of minutes. I got an idea." Dan sped up his jog, eager to put his plan into action. It was going to work, for sure.

Jules and Ryom untangled themselves from one another. The Korean was not a fighting man. He opened his shirt to reveal the wires attached to his chest, then pointed to his watch. The only surprise to Jules was that the wires appeared to be surgically embedded in his skin.

Can't transfer them to someone else.

"Make your animal stop," the Executive said.

Gilim lay on his side, propping himself up on one fist. Although the blade hadn't cut him in half, it had severely wounded him. Worse than the guns from the prison yard. And now here was Jules, standing between Gilim and the man he clearly saw as a mortal enemy. As the one responsible for all his hurt, his loss. That was why he leaned forward, poised to strike at Jules, the protector of the man Gilim simply *had* to kill.

"Ready, Bridget," Jules said. "Any time now."

She relayed what he needed. What, deep down, he didn't want to give out, didn't want to do, but there was little choice. At the same time, he knew it was right. His core instinct—to preserve even the worst of human life—bloomed within him. It made his chest warm and his limbs relax. This was what made him... *him*. How he'd lived well for so long, how he'd contributed to the Lost Origins cause. Denying it, forcing it away, and living a life of other people's rules and regulations. Be it society's norms of friendly interaction or the NYPD's endless laws and procedures, he was never happier, never more fulfilled than following his own path. And Bridget had helped him find that path, as she helped him find it now.

Jules repeated the guttural series of syllables transmitted into his earpiece.

Gilim froze. His massive brow wrinkled and his ear twitched.

"Not quite like that," Bridget said. "Elongate the sound. *Grrrrrff*. Not *grrff*. Listen again."

Jules held up a palm to Gilim, a universal gesture for *wait a minute*, and concentrated on the recorded huffs and grunts that Bridget had determined meant the words he needed to say. And it wasn't as dumb as it had sounded back at their home. The giants were descended from the same common ancestor as humans, shared much in the genes, including the vocal range, but lacked the capacity for retaining alpha-numerical language the way homo sapiens did.

"The intonation is important, too," she added.

Jules repeated the longer grunt, gesturing to Executive Ryom, cowering on the ground.

Must help, Jules was telling Gilim. Or trying to. *Many dead.*

"Try 'friend'," Bridget said, and played another sound. "Put a fist on your chest when you say it."

Jules repeated the short, low snuff of a noise and made the gesture as directed.

Gilim lifted his injured arm, a fist to his own chest, and said the same thing to Jules. Then he turned the fist over and made a louder, throatier sound, his eyes narrowed toward Executive Ryom.

"I'm guessing that means the opposite of friend," Jules said.

Ah Dae-Sung remained with them, too, dragging himself across the platform with the helicopter debris strewn about. He'd used a belt as a tourniquet but was still bleeding. He was making for a gun. Still, here, at the end, he had to do his duty. Even if it doomed them all.

"Try this," Prihya said, cutting in. "I cut it together from the audio Bridget recorded. It's rough, but I think it'll work. I'll tell you the hand signals as you speak. Okay?"

"Bridget?" Jules said.

"Do it," Bridget replied. "I don't know what it is, but she seems certain."

The audio played.

Jules did his best to repeat it.

Gilim listened. Watched.

The hand gestures were tough to translate, but it seemed Jules was getting through. Like listening hard to someone speaking with a thick foreign accent. As Jules conveyed the complex language of throat and hand, Gilim switched his attention between Jules and Ryom, glancing to the building, to the people in the distance far below. He lingered on Dae-Sung for a moment, before listening to Jules's final syllables.

Gilim backed away. One hand cradled the wound from the helicopter blade, while the other supported his weight as he lumbered aside. Even Ah Dae-Sung lay still. Watching.

"What did I tell him?" Jules asked.

Gilim eased himself onto one hand, lowered his backside to the ground, and creaked back against the hillside with a massive sigh—an old man reclining in bed after a long day. He watched, breathed, his nostrils flaring but no longer fighting, no longer in fear for his life. Trusting again. In Jules, if not in the men who'd hurt him.

"You told him he can help the people who are suffering," Prihya replied. "If he goes to sleep, no more violence, other people will live."

"So, he's just going off for a nap?"

"No, but he'll leave you alone while he rests. He's hurt. And you told him the enemy was not a threat. His family is safe."

"You got all that from a bunch of grunts?" Jules said.

"Bridget worked out the key to it all. The base code."

"Like some primates," Bridget said. "Combined with the simplest human traits of—"

"Save the lecture." Jules was standing between Executive Ryom and Dae-Sung, with an additional factor about to become a problem. "How long we got until the missiles fire?"

"Eight minutes," Charlie said. "Which means twelve minutes until the orb blows, leaving you—"

"Yeah, yeah, I got seven minutes to cut the power and confirm it. Which should be plenty, except..." Jules followed Dae-Sung's concerned frown. "Except that's easier said than done."

It was a crowd. Dozens of inmates, trekking up the slope down which the helicopter had plummeted, with another group winding up the path Jules had chased them from the yard. They must have passed Gilim on the way here, but—undeterred—they'd pressed onward, coming to face the men who'd imprisoned them.

At least fifteen trudged up the hillside, the first few rising to the platform level as those from the other direction—Jules counted twenty-three at first glance, but there may have been others still following—filled the approach path. Some paused by the bodies left after the fight, but most seemed determined to face their tormentors.

Jules said, "We got some people here who just chose the worst possible moment to exercise their human right to free assembly."

There was no other way out. And Jules wasn't sure he should try to find one.

"What are you doing?" Harpal asked.

Dan was tempted to shut him out. He wasn't sure if it'd give him greater pleasure to listen to him bitching away, or to ignore him. Unusually for him, he chose a middle way. "Watch and learn."

"What does that mean?" Tane asked, his voice rising. "Harpal, what does he mean by that? Because it sounded like something I won't like."

"Oh, man," Harpal said. "You won't like it. But there's a few people I can see who'll hate it that bit more."

Despite the lives on the line, including his own, and the wider fate of Korea and—yeah, okay, despite how unreal and cheesy it sounded to his inner monologue—the impending specter of World War III, Dan fought to keep a giddy sensation down. He supposed it must have been the multitude of life-or-death scenarios he'd experienced, both as a serving soldier and in the employ of Toby Smith, but when things like this paid off, he tingled all over.

Not that anyone would know it from his grim face.

Dan said, "Ready?"

"For what?" Tane asked.

"Doesn't matter. I'm doing it, anyway."

Dan had punctured one of the generator fuel cans and trailed the stream along the lane which almost resembled a medieval street. The one-story huts that doubled as bunks were at risk, might even burn, but he hoped to make enough noise to startle the inmates from their sleep.

The first thing he did was fire a volley of bullets in the air and yelled, "Up! Get up!"

A few heads peered out, terrified, unwilling to venture into the open. As Tane said, they were conditioned to remain where they were supposed to be.

Then Dan tossed three flashbangs all in different directions. Including one at the pooling gas. He dove inside one of the barracks, fingers in his ears.

Even outside, even with his ears covered, the concussion was still painful. Not enough to deafen him behind the wall, though.

Back in the lane, Dan found it had done its trick. Three fuel cans were ablaze, and inmates were dashing out of their beds, their "homes", and into the maze of buildings.

Dan fired again into the air and snagged the growing throng's attention. "Anyone speak English. Anyone? Even a little bit?"

Tane said, "Seriously?"

"Anyone? Speak English? Anyone here?"

A feeble hand rose—a woman of around sixty. Okay, maybe she was forty, but this place would rob anyone of twenty years. No matter.

"English?" Dan said.

"Little," she replied, holding her thumb and forefinger an inch apart.

Dan pointed the half-mile toward Tane. "Lead them that way. Up the mountain. You are free. Go."

"Free?" She looked frightened at the prospect.

"Free. But..." He chopped a hand at the dam face, towering over everything. "That. Might explode. Go boom. Understand?"

She turned all the way around, speaking to the people nearest her, translating.

"Suck it, Agent Wiremu," Dan said. "It's working."

"Boom," the woman said.

That was when an almighty crash rang across the valley. All eyes drew that way, including Dan's. The direction Jules had chased the big boss man and the giant. Where a helicopter waited.

And which now tumbled end over end down the side, exploding halfway to the ground.

Then figures channeled themselves that way. The effect Dan had hoped for with his flashbangs and gas fires was successful—but elsewhere. And people were funneling themselves in the wrong direction.

"No, no." Dan touched the old woman on the arm, waving desperately at anyone who saw him. "This way. Go this way. Or you die. Understand?"

The woman translated, and it got through to some. But the flow of evacuees he'd hoped for was more of a trickle.

Jules came back on the line, breathless and—for a change—unsure in his tone. "We got some people here who just chose the worst possible moment to exercise their human right to free assembly."

Whatever that meant, it didn't sound good.

The crowd formed a circle. Even politer than a British gathering of tea aficionados waiting for the host to pour. They were so used to being ordered around, it was as if the guards' authority had transferred to Jules. It might also have had to do with those at the head of the pack witnessing Jules speaking to the giant, and this creature—the first they must have seen outside of a fairytale—obeying him.

To say he "controlled" Gilim was inaccurate. But they had come to an understanding. And now this horde of exhausted, frightened men and women were waiting for... something.

Gilim pulled his feet under himself, about to stand. The people nearest him cowed away, while some jittered on the spot, a move Jules identified as being prepared to fight. They pushed weaker people behind them, a puny flesh barrier between Gilim and the dozens who'd endured hell. But to Gilim they were more humans, strangers, and it was strangers who'd hurt him, who'd wrenched him from his home, from his family.

"Friends," Jules said to Gilim. He signed what he thought was appropriate.

Prihya came on the line with another mix of soft huffs and grunts. Jules imitated her the best he could.

Gilim exhaled a deep breath and although he maintained an air of caution, he sat back down, showing the inmates he was no threat to them.

Unfortunately, that spike of adrenaline seemed to have injected more urgency into them. Those who'd been ready to defend their friends against a creature who could tear them limb from limb zeroed in on Executive Ryom and Commander Ah.

"Tane, you got any idea what I do with a bunch of gulag inmates who don't speak English? Or—I'm assuming—Spanish, Latin, or any of the Arabic languages I got stored away."

Tane said, "You want them to murder the human dead man's switch?"

"How about trying the 'friends' ploy again?"

Dae-Sung beat them to it, calling out to the crowd. With the camp emptying below and up here, Tane clearly had enough concentration to report what was being said here.

"He's begging them to spare Ryom. Says his heartbeat is linked to the explosives. Everyone will die if they kill him."

The crowd was silent. Mostly male, but some of the more able-bodied women were here, too. One man at the head of the pack stepped forward, a stronger looking guy, likely a new arrival. He eyed Jules, but his focus was on the men who'd abused so many.

Tane translated what the prisoner said: "You do not deserve to live. This place should not exist."

Then Dae-Sung's reply: "I speak the truth."

"Remind me what happens if the dam blows," Jules said.

"The camp is obliterated. The valley floods."

"Towns? Settlements?"

"There were none on our last flyover, but no telling for sure. Why?"

"I need to know some words. You good with that?"

"Sure," Tane said. "Although your man there said the prisoners would vote on what happens next."

"Okay." Jules told him what he wanted to say to the man, this self-appointed leader.

"Are you sure you wanna say that?"

"It's their business, not ours."

Tane gave Jules the words, and Jules got the man's attention.

In Korean, slowly and phonetically, he said, "If you kill these men, the dam will collapse. You will die here."

The man's jaw tensed. A glance to Ryom showed the Executive nod and point, words whose intonation suggested he was advising the mob to listen to Jules.

But Jules wasn't done. He continued Tane's words: "The giant is our friend. He was abused the way you were. I have to leave now. What happens to these two..." Jules gestured to Dae-Sung and the Executive, "... is your choice. But if you end their lives... take them above the water level first. There, you will be safe."

The pack's leader turned to the people closest to him. All nodded.

Jules said, "Our timeframe got smaller. But they all need this. And I think I can do it. I just need Gilim to follow me."

As the crowd murmured among themselves, deciding what to do next, Jules approached Gilim. Prihya was already making the sounds he needed to convey.

I need help. To save lives. Come with me.

It took almost no time at all to convince Gilim. He rolled to one side, scattering the people nearest, and he and Jules started out, scrambling directly down the incline toward the access road. And as they began their journey downward, the last Jules saw of Ah Dae-Sung and Ryom Jung-Hwan was a mob of prisoners—*former* prisoners—closing in around them.

CHAPTER FORTY-THREE

Jules didn't even try to speak as he ran to the main building that was now empty. They met no resistance, at least from the gulag security.

"Did he just kill everyone?" Toby said.

"They needed that," Jules said as he entered the compound, expecting to lose comms. "Needed some measure of revenge. To build their own future, take control of their lives."

"But—"

"I got this."

Jules heard nothing more as he delved inside, comms cut off again. Still obviously in pain, Gilim supported himself on a hand as he lolloped on, alongside Jules, back into the cavern where the bad people had all but tortured him. He had to duck in the final passage-way, then paused in the mouth of the staging area.

The orb was still black, its dark rainbow-tinged spin continuing despite Jules cutting it off from the activation suite. The door Gilim escaped from hung wide open on its hinges, and the big metal coffin he'd arrived in lay on its side. The floor remained littered with bodies, which Gilim looked over with a faraway expression. He prodded a couple, but Jules had to urge him onward.

Namely, to the chamber.

Jules held the huge hand, but Gilim stalled. He shook his head and stepped back—a horse refusing to jump a hedge.

"Please," Jules said. He had no access to the language, cut off as he was. He'd recited the noises but hadn't grasped what they meant, and he couldn't repeat all that.

But he had one thing.

The backpack. He pulled off his fleece and rolled the pack off his back, then removed the two bangles. He tugged off his gloves and touched the stone artifacts with his bare skin. They glowed dully, but it was enough to fascinate Gilim.

The giant's face creased, pointing his finger closer to the bangles. He gave a short, sharp laugh.

Jules had hoped there might be something here. If he was genetically tuned to them, and homo colossus were used as conduits for the same technology, it made sense that some echo in Gilim's subconscious heritage would resonate.

Jules placed the items on the console next to the big red button he'd activated through his mini flashbang. The tiny metal flecks in the bangles lost their light. Now, he needed to stop the worst of all options coming to pass.

Gilim made a small groan and pulled a disappointed face.

Jules gestured for him to lift the bangles.

Gilim obeyed. At the touch of his finger, the two artefacts glowed. It might have been a trick of the light or because Gilim was casting a gigantic shadow, but they seemed to glow more brightly than when Jules held them. Gilim grinned at the effect.

Jules nodded.

Gilim met his eyes and offered the bangles.

Jules accepted them and slipped them on his wrists. He walked to the chamber and stood beside it with one arm extended toward the interior.

Gilim took a breath. Stared at the machine. Then he exhaled and marched forward. He barely hesitated. He halted beside Jules and backed inside the stone box with the crystal-looking door.

As Gilim settled into it, squirming as if trying to make himself comfortable, Jules smiled. "Thanks for trusting me."

Jules closed the door, sealing Gilim inside, then hopped up onto the control desk. With limited buttons and levers, most of the functions running from an e-tablet, he could traverse the panel and stand directly in front of the orb.

Static surrounded him. Invisible little fingers picked at the hairs on his arm, his legs, the back of his neck. As he lifted his hands, the bangles heavy on his wrists, he repeated himself.

"Thanks for trusting me. Let's hope I don't let you down."

"Are you outside?" Bridget said.

Jules looked around the room, as if it was more likely she'd teleported here than spoken to him via the subvocal earpiece.

"How'd you do that?" he asked.

"Me? We just heard you talking about trust."

Jules observed the orb, and how it appeared to shimmer when Bridget spoke. "It's the network. Somehow, our comms is passin' through there."

"What are you doing?" Toby said. "We have to give Grainger the nod. Are we safe yet?"

"Not yet. Gimme a minute, will you?" Jules shrugged the bangles down so his skin was touching them, waited for the flecks to illuminate, then plunged both hands into the orb.

He howled like he never had before. It was like skinny-dipping in acid. Burning raged up his hands, to the point he thought they'd shear off.

But he somehow knew the answer.

He pushed on, ignoring frantic cries in his ear, asking if he was okay, was he in danger, was he hurt...

When the bangles touched the orb, all pain ceased. If anything, it was serene, a light vibration tickling his skin. He shuddered, half-laughing at the dispersing of all that agony.

"Jules?" Bridget pressed. "Answer us!"

"I'm fine," Jules said.

He glanced aside, noting the activation suite containing Gilim was doing funky things, too. It had glowed at first, but now appeared to frost over.

No, not *appeared* to frost... it *was* frost. Ice. A car windscreen on a winter's night.

"It's compensating for the energy overload," Jules said, unsure how he knew that. A knowledge transfer directly from whatever quantum energies he was accessing.

"Are we done?" Toby asked.

"Give the word." Jules extended his fingers, partly testing they were still there, but also to inform the particles swimming and crashing around the bangles that he was ready to proceed. With what? He couldn't put it in to words right then, but he knew one thing. "Tell Grainger to call off the Americans. I can do this."

"Do what, exactly?"

Jules was about to answer, but a low bass *thoom* cut him off. The structure shook. The orb wobbled.

"Sounds like the inmates made their choice," Jules said. "But don't sweat it, folks. This is gonna be *so* cool."

The cage-like scaffold swayed and juddered as the dam wall shook. It was like riding a bull during an earthquake.

"Just as I'd got used to the place," Harpal muttered.

He'd listened as Jules explained what he was doing, but as the power below ramped up, the interference grew, and he had a better view of the prison from here. To get out, he had to scale the rickety bamboo ladder, which was, oddly, the most stable aspect of the platform.

Up one level, he held tight to a vertical steel pole on the outside to keep from throwing his stomach into the crossbar.

The first explosive detonated on the far side, popping a clump of brickwork like a champagne cork. Water discharged as powerful as a fire hose, blasting far and long, raining down on the gulag below.

"Oh, that's not good."

Harpal shoved back and took the next ladder even faster, knowing they'd failed to stop the chain reaction. The prisoners had risen up, taken their masters to task, and passed judgment. Now they were running—*about time*—from the danger of the collapsing dam.

The scaffold beside the first booby trap collapsed and plunged down faster than the new waterfall. A second later, the next one blew, then the next, and—finally—the one right below Harpal.

He was at the top. His fingers clutched the wall's lip with his fingertips. And the floor fell away.

With morbid fascination, he twisted to watch as the structure practically folded in on itself before spidering out as it tumbled down.

He dug his toes into the rough face and pushed upward, pulling and straining, wishing he'd done more pull-ups during his downtime. Yet, with his muscles aching and his fingers raw, he swung a leg up and rolled to safety.

Only, as he gathered his breath and looked over the edge, he saw what he'd feared most.

Thousands of gallons of water sprayed hundreds of feet, drenching the population, four rivers already forming, washing away anything not nailed down. Panic drove the hundreds of humans away from the dam, but all that stood between them and death was Dan, Tane, and some very frantic gestures, instructing them the right way.

Harpal just hoped getting enough of them going in the right direction would mean the majority followed them up the path before it was too late.

Was it too late already? Cracks spidered up from the four holes and more masonry burst free, causing more hazards.

Harpal didn't even have time to curse. He leaped up and ran. Arms pumping, the ground beneath his feet swaying. He was running on a surfboard, floating on a tumultuous sea.

The end was in sight, the gate he arrived through. But all below were set to perish. They'd stabilized the shields, avoided World War III but failed the inmates, the people who'd suffered directly at the hands of a power-mad—

A more powerful jerk of the floor sent Harpal flying. Mere yards from the end, from the salvation of powering up the hillside above the water level, he splayed forward onto his stomach, hitting his chin on the concrete.

He wasn't giving up, though. And even as the walkway pitched sideways, the superstructure collapsing beneath him, he clutched the rail and stumbled onward. A vain hope but hope all the same.

Then, out of the corner of his eye, Harpal caught a flash. A big one. And the results of Jules's manipulation became visible.

Instead of expanding up into the ionosphere and dropping like a faulty umbrella to crush a country at the border, a controlled, crystallized sheet of light burst out of the ground at the dam's base and expanded directly upwards, past Harpal, and over the reservoir's level. It curled over him like fingers closing into a fist but stopped short of balling fully and crushing all in its grasp.

Harpal made it to the guard station, vaulted the fence, and staggered to a halt. As much as his body called to him to rest, he couldn't simply drop and close his eyes. He had to see what the shield was doing.

The crystal-colored energy radiated from the shields embedded in the ground, rising upward, more a frozen wave than a half-fist. It sealed against the two sides of the valley, ascended over the reservoir's former level, and caught the tons of bricks, mortar, and water pressing from behind. The dam had folded and collapsed like Lego and would have crushed everything below without the control generated from the orb and the giant's stabilizing DNA.

And, of course, Jules, doing what he does.

"Whoa, guys, this is..." He then saw the stutter. The blip in the shimmering force blanketing the area.

"It's temporary," Dan said over comms. "But we're getting there."

Sure enough, through the undulating light of the Guardians' great feat, of the Witnesses' genius in uniting the two forms of energy, the barrier held, and the people below funneled to the west. A human caravan flowed upwards, out of their prison, a stream of injured and weak people, helping one another, rising from hell to safety.

Tane called it in. "All clear, people. Mission accomplished."

No missiles fell. Maintaining communication with Charlie, Bridget and Prihya meant Jules knew he'd been successful, the Action Dudes up top signaling that the water had stalled, and the inmates were climbing to safety.

He maintained his vigil over the machine, though, his hands sunk deep into the orb, covering the Aradia and Ruby Rock bangles.

Gilim's chamber remained iced over. Movement inside had halted.

"I can't keep this thing here forever," he said.

"The valley can take the flood," Prihya replied. "Just not all at once. Can you reduce the shield instead of crashing it down outright?"

Jules didn't know where he ended and the orb began. He was bonded to it. It flowed through him and him through it but voicing that would make him sound insane. He had complete control over it. And what Prihya said made sense. Executive Ryom dammed a river, so returning it to its natural state would wash away the gulag and establish a new river. But dumping millions of tons of water through the tight aperture of this corner of the valley, would create a tidal wave that would destroy any towns or villages close to the former route.

It should have been hard. Should have been complicated. Were it designed by modern man, it would have been password protected, probably a two-stage authorization setup. Not here. Not melding person with object, fusing molecules and consciousness.

Here, he just did it.

"Are the guys clear?" he asked.

"It's as clear as it can be," Bridget said. "Harpal says he can't see any more movement."

Charlie came on the line. "Tane and Dan are following the last of the evacuees. It's okay."

"Are you sure you know how?" Prihya asked.

Jules resisted a facetious reply, his contact with the network robbing him of any sense of ego, petty irritants, and a need to shift all discussion directly to the point. He liked this. A calmness. Peace he'd never known before.

"Jules?" Bridget said.

"Yeah, I'm here."

"You zoned out there."

"I did?"

"For, like, half a minute. Are you okay?"

"This is... it's like swimming for my brain." Jules wanted to float, to see everything these spherical wonders had seen. To ask it everything. He was sure it would reply, too. He needed to ask

"Are you *high*?" Charlie asked harshly.

Way harsh, in Jules's opinion. Plus, he'd never been high, so wouldn't know what it felt like. Faintly drunk, yes, but he hadn't enjoyed that. He enjoyed this, though.

"I am part of the universe," Jules explained. "I'm flowing into it, and back out, and it's part of me. The shields are a conduit, and—"

"He is *so* high," Prihya said. "*Jules*. Snap out of it. Concentrate. You have to lower the energy shield and get Gilim out of the chamber before he dies."

"Dies?"

A spike drove through Jules, from his chest to his brain.

Yes, Gilim. The ice compensated for the heat, and the corrupted DNA that that been grafted to his original race's genome had made it more difficult to force the machine to operational capacity. He was dying before from the heat and power surging through him, and now he was dying from the cold.

"I can't do it slowly *and* save Gilim," Jules said, dredging his mind up, out of the water. "I gotta cut it out dead."

Bridget spoke fast, computer keys clacking in the background. "Wait, Jules, if you do that..."

"Not if." Jules retracted his hands and stepped on the abort button. "It's done."

Immediately, the lights went out and the generators kicked in with the emergency backups. Gilim's compartment popped open, steaming as freezing air met room temperature. Gilim, frosted over, opened his mouth, and groaned. His fingers opened as he saw Jules coming toward him.

Jules used his sign language and the grunt he'd picked up to say, "Wait."

He climbed up and disconnected the cables at the top. No power. It was now separated from the orb, which returned to its blackened state.

"Okay." Jules stayed up there, but beckoned Gilim out.

The giant moved stiffly, shivering, his entire body giving off steam. He gazed up at Jules, who mimed an instruction. Gilim thought about it, then gripped the chamber.

"Holy crap, Jules," Bridget said. "What did you do?"

Dan raced up the hillside. Although the road hairpinned around back and forth like the Hollywood Hills, it was still steep, and his lungs burned with the effort. It was a relief, though, an end to all they'd been through. Yet, it wasn't the millions of lives saved from an unnecessary war that lifted his spirits, it was the ones he could put a face to. Those liberated from the horrific prison below, fleeing under the guardianship of the shield of Achilles.

Yeah, okay, he vowed never to say anything that lame out loud.

But it was spectacular. The crystal-like barrier translucent, almost transparent, with diamonds glittering and refracting the moonlight, and—

Then it wasn't there anymore. Nothing to keep the waters at bay.

"Bridget, the shield's down!" He sped up. "Tane, get a move on!"

Although they were nearly at the right level, there was no telling how hard that torrent would hit, or what it'd do to the land it crashed into.

They needed to get higher.

The downside of lightning-quick calculations and ignoring the prattling of other people worried about an outcome which he'd already ascertained was a dead cert, was that sometimes the pieces didn't fall into place as quickly as Jules would like.

As the water pounded down from above, crashing through the valley, the circular underground subdivision would never withstand such pressure.

"Jules?" came another voice. He thought it was Charlie, but now he'd disconnected from the Witnesses' grid, they were relying on regular comms. And that wasn't enough.

"Stand by," Jules said.

A broken response replied, indecipherable as a thousand cannonballs rained down above them. The bedrock, as strong as it was, couldn't possibly hold it back. The room shook so violently, Jules couldn't stay on his feet. Gilim kneeled on all fours.

"NO!" Jules cried. He slapped the machine, kicked the chamber. "This! Do as I said. Watch!"

But it was too late. Jules heard it first, then felt the shock wave, the damp in the air. The water had penetrated the installation. A wall of it blasted by the anteroom, torrents exploded out of both the smaller door and the double-wide corridor, drenching all.

At least I saw it all working as it was supposed to. At least I saw the truth.

Then the lights went out, and Jules could die... at peace with himself at last.

Dan stood shoulder-to-shoulder with Tane, watching as the enormous wall of concrete disintegrated, and billions of tons of water expanded in seconds, dropping into the valley—partly a waterfall to rival Niagara, partly an upturned bathtub, spilling with nothing to hold it back.

The gulag's population had spread out along the garbage dump, finding places to rest and gather together for warmth. Although it was overgrown thanks to nature's partial revival, they would start a few fires shortly.

"Hey, what's up, guys?" Harpal said, half-jogging toward them.

"Good, thanks." Dan threw himself into bro-hug that lasted three seconds before both instigated the obligatory backslap that broke it up before returning to the view. "You?"

"Yeah, I'm okay." He grinned. "You've been busy."

"You can say that again, brah." Tane stepped in and they shared a thumb-linked handshake before bumping shoulders. "Where's your man? You see him come up?"

"I don't think he's coming," Bridget said, her voice cracking with each word.

Dan felt his face stretch into disbelief. "What? He's gotta come up, he's—"

"The network went blank," Charlie said. "Our orb here looks like a rock. It's dead."

Dan stared out over the cascading water. "But he let it all go."

"He figured it out," Bridget said. "Letting it go like that—he could get free, and... and..."

Charlie stepped in. "The dogleg half a kilometer down the valley will stem the mass for a few seconds. You saw it back up slightly."

"Yeah, like a big wave coming back at us," Tane said, describing the sudden rise in the surface.

"It reduces the power, slows the flow, before releasing it onward. None of us are experts here, but we guess it's taken the sting out of the volume of water. It'll settle down into a major flow instead of a massive flash flood."

"What about Jules?" Harpal said. "And our giant friend?"

No answer.

"Charlie?" Dan said. "Are you there? Bridget?"

"He couldn't get out," Toby said somberly. "There was no way for him to escape."

Dan closed his eyes. He'd lost comrades before. Brothers-in-arms. Too many to think about. Some he was close with, others less so. But even those he chose not to joke around with or drink with during downtime, those he avoided because he found them objectionable, he respected their sacrifices.

This was different.

He opened his eyes to watch the waters churn. Another surge reversed track having struck the valley wall half a click downstream and met the current flowing forward. A whirlpool formed, swirling as the opposing forces battered one another, then merged, before dispersing.

"What's that noise?" Harpal asked.

Dan listened, tuning his ears beyond the crashing of waves and the chatter of survivors.

Whump-whump-whump-whump.

"Helicopters," Tane said.

Engine mufflers, rotors, overlapping reverberations.

"More than one," Dan said. "And it's gunships. *Everybody down*!"

Harpal just wanted to rest. Was that too much to ask? First, he got blown off course, then he hung off the edge of a dam on the world's worst building site, then had to climb back up before it disintegrated, before finally negotiating the collapsing structure itself.

"Gunships now?" he moaned, swinging to position the gun he'd stashed on his back.

Tane and Dan prepped in the same way, although ammo was low, and there was nothing to stop the North Korean authorities from lighting them all up before razing their haven to the ground.

"Wait," Bridget said. "Don't do anything."

"Huh?" Dan was checking the sky with his binoculars. "We gotta—"

"It's the Chinese," Toby said. "Bridget asked her father to put her in touch with someone in the government. They must have got through."

Four WZ-10 medium attack helicopters rounded the bend up ahead, followed by a massive transport helo. It was at least a fifteen tonner, probably a new Z-8L—almost the length of a public swimming pool, it'd house dozens of people. The most injured, the most in need. Even from this distance, as it rose above the scene, the wash blew like a hurricane.

The inmates scattered again, but Tane waved his arms and shouted in Korean, plainly saying it was fine, it was a rescue.

The war-machine helicopters circled, likely scanning the territory for threats, while the Z-8L transporter heaved itself around for another pass. Harpal expected them to hover, for medical personnel or military to descend and secure the area, but instead it continued out, over the roiling remnants of the water draining from its former status as a lake.

The levels kept going up and down, the dogleg Charlie spoke of returning the flow to meet the main volume emptying into it, opposing currents forming whirlpools.

And it was over one of these whirlpools that the massive Z-8L descended. A cable and harness dropped fast, along with two people on their separate lines.

"What the hell are they doing?" Dan asked, still not relaxed as he lifted his binoculars again. He and Tane clearly weren't convinced the Chinese gunships were friendly, despite Toby's assurances.

"Looks like they're trying to..." Harpal took Dan's binoculars and sought out the helicopter's target.

Dan was already laughing. He slapped Harpal on the back.

There was something floating in the water. Churning in the circular current, a huge metal box with a clear front bobbed like a cork. It spun on its vertical axis, only halting when one of the rescuers attached a line.

"What *is* that thing?" Harpal said, lowering the glasses.

"That," Tane said, "is an airtight wardrobe designed to withstand the pressure of an indestructible energy weapon, capable of housing something the size of a giant."

The people on the lines secured the straps from the third cable to the rectangular cuboid, set it horizontal, and the helicopter rose. The "wardrobe's" door opened, and Gilim sat up inside.

He lurched to find himself up in the air, the container swaying violently and threatening to tip him out. Yet, just as suddenly, he calmed. Turned his head.

Harpal watched through the binoculars.

And Jules was there, in the flying vessel, holding the giant's face in both hands. He placed his forehead against Gilim's, and two enormous arms wrapped around Jules. Gilim's eyes closed, and Jules slowly disengaged. He held on, wind billowing at him, and waved thanks to the two men on either side of him.

Harpal said, "Hey, Bridget. Toby. Charlie. Guess what?"

Jules was searching the landscape, clinging to the open door. He halted on Harpal and the others and swung his arm in an outsized gesture.

"What?" Bridget managed. "What is it?"

"He's alive." Harpal could barely contain himself. He hooted with laughter, relief, joy. "Both of them made it and... Dan, take a look at this."

Dan retrieved the binoculars. "What am I looking for?"

"Is he... laughing?"

Dan chuckled. "Yeah. That's a sight. Bridget, I think you did the impossible. Jules Sibeko is alive and laughing his ass off."

PROJECT AHUA, NEW ZEALAND

Hundreds of miles to the south, across an ocean, in a volcano repurposed to house a branch of humanity that died out hundreds of years earlier, Bridget Carson slumped in her seat. A draining of tension and anxiety, relief at all the things she'd feared would happen having been sated.

Beside her, Toby leaned on the dead console, his head bowed. Charlie remained upright, beaming as wide as Bridget had ever seen her, and Prihya approached the glass, touched it, and spoke to the unseen families below.

"We're bringing him home, guys. He'll be here soon."

It was also sad for Bridget, though. Her deal with her parents was for this one expedition. An expedition that escalated, admittedly, and she'd never have guessed how far it would expand. But there was no denying it was over.

Out loud, not caring if anyone heard, she said, "Thanks, Daddy. Thank you for the helicopters. For helping me save my friends. I'll be home soon. I promise. I'll make you proud."

CHAPTER FORTY-FOUR

After the dam burst, they all flew directly to New Zealand, while the UN, along with NATO, China, the United States, and whoever else held a stake in what had occurred over the past week dealt with the fallout from the threat, now neutralized. They also offered support for the Dragon's Teeth Dam disaster, but the North Korean authorities declined, stating the flood was an "internal matter." Satellite data backed up their intelligence that the region was largely unpopulated, and although the landscape was changed forever, human settlements suffered only minor flooding. While it was impossible to be 100% certain, the intelligence services for the UK, New Zealand, and—as far as anyone could discern—the USA were satisfied it did not constitute a humanitarian crisis. The nations involved quietly granted the former prisoners asylum in their chosen countries—mostly in South Korea and China—and the North didn't mention their existence once.

Don't ask, don't tell.

In the days that followed, recuperation was key. Project Ahua assigned the team a couple of houses to share in Kainga Pukepuke, rubbing shoulders with the staff from the tourist attraction and the scientists who populated the labs. After returning Gilim to his volcano home, he was patched up as best they could, and he was healing fast. Jules wasn't sure—and nor were the biologists and doctors who examined him—if it was something natural within homo colossus DNA or if his time in the capsule, linked to the network, had helped regenerate his energy and damaged tissue.

With little more than a wash and a change of clothes, Jules, Dan, Harpal, and Tane had been permitted to see Gilim off, back to his forest home. Protocol had demanded they sedate him before the flight, with several hours of checks before readmitting him to his home environment. But once all the poking and prodding was over with, they revived Gilim on the repaired loading dock overlooking the lush mountain valley. Jules helped ease him back to consciousness, the rest of the team holding back at a safe distance.

The pair needed no words. Jules recognized the gestures, the facial turns and tics, and he returned the affectionate notes with his own exaggerated expressions and hand movement. There was no knowledge as such, no definitive translation from gestures to words, but it worked, like long-term lovers who understood each other in near-psychic synchronicity.

"Get a room," Dan said.

A ripple of laughter followed. Including Jules. Gilim might not have got the joke, but he smiled at Jules's happiness.

Finally, the door lowered, and Gilim recognized the forest within. The technicians and scientists, including Prihya, had left the families where they were, in case they bounded over to greet Gilim, and they all ended up rolling around out in the open. Jules ushered him inside.

Gilim ambled in, hesitating when Jules remained in place. He tilted his head, an almost worried expression.

Jules stepped toward him and, without thinking about it, told the big guy via gestures, *Don't worry. I'll be back. Time for you to go home.*

Gilim gave a good-natured huff and turned back to his destination. He reached inside, then his feet followed. They were tentative steps, but once he ventured under the enclosure, surrounded by foliage and his familiar surroundings, he showed no nerves. No concern that, maybe, these humans were tricking him. He sped up, bellowing into the forest, a greeting call announcing his return.

Honey, I'm home!

A thunderous keening replied, and that would be the last Jules heard of them for a while. The dock's shutter descended and the outer skin that looked like the landscapes rolled across. Gilim was home, and the team had business to attend to.

Intervals between medical checks allowed Julia Grainger and several serious men and women from unnamed countries—out of uniform but obviously high-ranking military officers—to ask questions, listen, and for some of the puffier-chested cynics to accuse LORI of lies. Mostly, though, Jules and the rest of the team settled in for the long haul. They'd been questioned about matters of international diplomacy before and knew how this went. As expected, Jules had his "secondment" to the DoD extended, which he supposed his captain would be unhappy about but had little choice to agree with.

Not that it mattered. He'd already drafted his resignation letter.

Once the questioning was over, Julia Grainger remained their NZ government liaison. There was no formal medal ceremony, no dignitaries to shake hands or offer a debt of gratitude. And that was fine. Jules didn't want any of that. Nor did Tane. It was his job, after all. Dan and Harpal grumbled a bit, Dan in particular being used to medals in the event of "near-inhuman military feats of derring-do," as Toby put it. Jules could tell Toby would have appreciated a little recognition, but Colin nixed that by hinting that Toby was the one who'd led the Koreans to the giants' trail in the first place.

And Colin Waterston was the final installment in this debriefing extravaganza.

At Tane's request, they held their farewell dinner in Kainga Pukepuke, he and some close friends from the project using the oven pit laid out for tourists paying to experience an "authentic" hangi. Tane promised them his version would be closer to the truth and not sanitized for the sake of mass-consumption.

The meat was cooked perfectly, the vegetables likewise, and Jules could tell Toby was enjoying Colin's impatience with the wait. They played music, retold aspects of the adventure they'd shared, and lit bonfires as the sun went down. There was even a little half-hearted dancing, but that was one skill Jules had never gained, so when Bridget attempted to pull him up for a boogie, he held fast.

She lingered with him a moment longer. A barely detectable

sparkle in her eyes was something Jules had previously written off as a trick of the light, but it was brighter here, in the fire's glow. He now believed it must be some tiny imperfection in the iris, a mutation that enhanced her countenance that needed attention to spot.

But he continued to hold fast, and with a couple of drinks in her, Bridget danced with Charlie, Harpal, and Tane, shaking off the stresses and fears that had burdened them, at least for a little while.

Beers came and went, and Jules again attempted to enjoy the frothy concoction, but it just wasn't for him. He'd succumb later to a whisky, but for now stuck with water.

Soon, they sat around two picnic tables pushed together and indulged in toasted bread, much like a pita, with a variety of dips that served as a starter. While they waited on the main course and their stomachs thanked them for the carbs and dips, Colin started his predicted opening, steering clear of any accusations that Toby was partly responsible for the Koreans' actions. They were already on the case. If not for Toby speeding up their plans and forcing them into the open, the Executive might have taken his time and snuck in under the radar, decimating cities in the process.

Colin raised a wine glass containing a beverage that he'd apparently found distasteful but made more palatable by adding a slug of sparkling water. "This successful operation could not have been possible without the cooperation of so many governments and... other groups... banding together for the good of the world. That the world may never know what we did here, that does not matter to me, and nor should it you."

Both Dan and Charlie mouthed the word "we," plainly perturbed at Colin insinuating himself into proceedings as anything other than a bystander.

"This multi-nation ambassadorial mission should be hailed as the first of its kind. The first of many, if we can come together in a common cause, should the need arise again."

"I can think of one or two common causes," Jules said.

"Quite. But never have so many people of different nations stood up to be counted as one." Colin adopted a more pompous demeanor, a feat Jules hadn't thought possible, perhaps hearing an orchestra swelling on the soundtrack playing in his mind. "New Zealand. Britain. China. The United States—"

Toby held up a piece of bread and said, "Colin, my old friend. No offence to our cousins, but I'm pretty sure the ambassadorial side wasn't their prime concern."

"Not the government, no. But there were others at work." Colin held out a hand, a cue for a man and woman to step out of the shadows.

Bridget said, "Mom? Dad?"

"Hello, Bridget," Roger Carson said.

"Hello, dear," Audrey Carson said.

Both wore casual clothing. It was the first time Jules had seen Roger without a suit.

"As you know, Bridget," Colin said, "your father was instrumental in securing Chinese cooperation."

Bridget untangled herself from the table and stood still for a moment. She cast her gaze over her friends, coming back to Jules, before smoothing herself down and crossing the space to embrace her parents. Her dad kissed the top of her head, her mother her cheek. Bridget beamed up at them as she withdrew and held hands with them over to the table where a place awaited them.

"Thank you, everyone," Roger said as his wife took a seat.

Another speech, Jules thought.

Bridget apparently sensed the same and fixed him with a mirthless frown mixed with a faintly incorrigible smile. She dipped her gaze to the bench seat.

Roger got the message but halted halfway to a seated position and straightened upright. "Can I ask something of you all? Is the briefing I received true? As someone with a major stake in the operation, and now charitable funding for Ahua, I gained access to what sounds... I don't know what it sounds like." He concentrated on Bridget. "This is what you do?"

"Not exclusively," Bridget said.

"Sometimes," Jules said, "it's really dangerous stuff."

"Not helping." Bridget placed a hand on his arm, which both Roger and Audrey followed until she spoke again. "The Lost Origins Recovery Institute takes what we see and acts upon it. We know there is more to the Earth's history than modern science teaches, like we know there's more to the universe and the oceans. Dark matter is an unknown, something they can't detect or see, but it's definitely there. We've explored less than half of the deep oceans, and who knows what's lurking under lakes sealed in ice for millennia?"

Bridget let her eyes wander to everyone in turn around the tables.

"Toby pulls together the best experts, so we don't have a big staff. People passionate about the work. We find clues to track down interesting artefacts and places that might offer insight into the gaps in human history. Sometimes it pays well. Sometimes it doesn't."

"Yeah," Dan said, "Alfonse isn't gonna be happy."

Toby gave an amused shrug. "We've spoken. The church will receive one of the shields we recovered. The rest of them will be distributed around the nations involved in liberating the camp."

"And the prisoners granted asylum in their chosen country," Colin said. "Courtesy of some intense negotiations by yours truly."

"Round of applause?" Harpal said sarcastically.

Colin bristled and opened his mouth to respond, but Roger asked another question.

"And this evidence of a race before ours, intelligent, organized..."

"All true," Bridget said. "We were digging deeper when..." She cut herself off.

"When we recalled you," Audrey Carson said.

"Yes."

The only sound for several seconds was that of glasses being picked up and sipped from.

Roger said, "These... Witnesses. The Elder Race. It sounds like madness. Why build something like that machine? When it could destroy as much as it could protect?"

"They didn't build it." Bridget had completed most of her translation of the glyphs she'd jotted down following her trip into the machine. *Most*, she'd explained to Jules a day earlier, because she wasn't sure of the intonation, her scribbling going too fast to discern a slanted character from a hastily drawn one. "They evolved along a different path than us. In isolation. We think there were several pockets of humans like this, and they birthed many of our modern myths and legends. From Olympus to Atlantis. But they didn't build the machine that the Executive wanted to exploit. They just figured out how to use it."

Roger frowned, finally taking his seat. "So... there was another generation? The ones who put these powerful objects in place?"

Dan said, "My money's on—"

"Aliens," said everyone who was clued-in to Dan's theory.

Dan grinned. "You'll be sorry you mocked me."

Roger let the moment pass, then pressed on. "This other race... the one you know nothing about... how do you know they existed?"

Charlie said, "The same way astrophysicists know dark matter exists. Because they see its effects."

Toby nodded and put his finger in the air, his *ah-ha* pose that Jules had grown familiar with. "After the discovery of Uranus, a French mathematician called Urban Le Verrier predicted Neptune's existence based purely on fluctuations in Uranus's orbit. This was in November 1845. In 1846, John Couch Adams made similar predictions and sent his calculations to George Airy at the Royal Observatory—"

Roger had a hand up, nodding. "I get it. But what I don't get is how they died. Why they left all this."

Jules said, "If the earth is worthy... others'll step in to prevent disaster." He sipped his water. "Bridget figured that out."

"You just translated that?" Charlie asked.

"No, but... it's kind of here." Bridget pointed to the back of her head. "I don't know why, but I know it. That, and what I wrote... They made this like... the way we stockpile nuclear missiles."

Toby frowned, even more deeply than Roger had, his face more lined than ever. "Mutually assured destruction."

"But with no war. It prompted action, not direct conflict. It forced people to work together. In peace. With only a select few able to regulate the power."

"Billions could die," Charlie said.

"Only those who misuse it," Bridget said. "At least that was the plan way back when. The others were supposed to stop it."

Jules tried to clear his mind. Accessing knowledge imparted during his own trip into the network during their encounter in Africa. "Sounds like the mutually assured destruction wiped 'em out, along with much of life on earth. One of the big extinction events, prior to homo sapiens' ancestors evolving."

"You have a letter from these guys we don't know about?" Dan asked.

"I took a similar trip to Bridget over a year ago."

"Yeah, under the mountain in Kenya. Thought you didn't remember anything."

"The experience doesn't give the traveler memories the way a vacation does. Bridget felt the same. It's more like a lesson, some kinda knowledge sharing thing. But there's an obvious reason. Or a possible reason."

All were staring at him.

He said, "Their brains worked different from ours."

"Of course." Toby snapped his fingers. "We're a separate branch of the evolutionary tree. More in common than what separates us, but still. We use tools, but so do chimps and octopuses. We use language, but so do the Witnesses and their forebears."

"Meaning," Bridget said, "that we don't need a Rosetta Stone for their written language, but to work out what they thought. Their philosophies, their culture..." Her speech sped up. "Once we understand the idiosyncrasies of their ways, how they lived, we can do more than interpret their language."

"We can really know them." It was the first time Prihya had spoken, and everyone turned her way.

They'd been cautious about inviting her, given their past, but she'd never killed an innocent to their knowledge, and she appeared genuine in her disavowing of Valerio. Jules had always hoped that would be the case, that she'd come around, eventually. He couldn't criticize her for taking her time, either. It had taken him longer to accept these people as his true friends, that he had a home with them were he to choose that option.

She said, "I'd like to help. I mean, I'm going to continue our work here, but... if you want an extra pair of eyes, or someone to help with a dig... give me a call, okay?"

"We will," Toby said.

"Be glad to have you," Dan added.

Charlie simply nodded and appeared to mean it.

Bridget said, "But I probably won't be a part of it. Will I?" She focused on her father. "I don't have a preference, Dad. Just choose somewhere for me. I'll go wherever you want, and I'll do my best, as long as you let Toby and whoever joins him continue working. The chateau, the airstrip... they'll pay their way, but—"

"I'm glad you said that," Roger interrupted, "because your mother and I have found a suitable college for you."

"Oh."

The table hushed. The fire crackled. Tane's friends were plating up on a separate table—good friends to have, and they seemed happy to do him the favor. They'd foregone the traditional Maori outfits, of course, and they would join the team to eat rather than put on a touristy show.

Roger said, "You agreed you would study a proper subject. Something in business, science, or law or... something practical. No arts or humanity."

"And I'll stand by that," Bridget said stiffly.

Jules watched on, forcing himself to disconnect from it. He didn't like that Bridget kowtowed to the man this way, nor that Toby would let it happen. Frankly, he'd been surprised Toby hadn't sought a better HQ, but Bridget had insisted on them staying in Brittany. All the work they'd put into the place, Charlie's server that almost matched the spec of a supercomputer alone would cost hundreds of thousands to replicate or transport.

Roger said, "Given what we have seen of your resourcefulness this week, and the passion you clearly hold... not to mention that this may well grow into something of global significance, we have decided you should attend the Université Paris-Saclay. They do an excellent Bachelor of Science degree as well as a master's option. In archaeology. To compliment the languages and history you took in England."

All looked at them sharply.

Bridget again sped up her usual words. "You want me to... do a degree in the career I want?"

Audrey patted Roger's hand. "All we've ever hoped for you is that you find something useful to do in the world. And with what we've seen so far, who better than a Carson to lead the way?"

"And," Roger said, "I have offered them a funding proposal. Remember the dig in China that has delayed a different project?"

"The new warrior statue find?" Toby said, excitedly. "Bridget, that would be perfect for you, it—"

"Yes, exactly." Roger smiled at Bridget. "What do you say? Not a top ten college, but a good one. With a science degree that you can fall back on if this whole Witnesses thing comes to an end and you need a career."

"It's a few hours from the chateau," Audrey said. "When you're done studying, you can go to see your friends, or they can drop in on you in Paris."

"If..." Roger pointed... "If you're not in China interning or helping manage the finds."

Bridget gasped. She was too happy to speak. Jules put his arm around her, felt her grin against his chest.

He said, "Guess you get to go home after all."

Before departing New Zealand, Jules insisted on saying goodbye to Gilim. It didn't last long. It seemed neither of them were big on farewells.

"I'll come visit," Jules told him.

He couldn't pinpoint when, exactly, this bond sealed tight between them. His recollection was that it grew out of trust, of understanding what needed to be done, and how to do it. At the end, when he thrust his hands into the orb, Jules simply knew it was the right thing, that he was the only one who could do it, and that Gilim's presence allowed him to do it without risking destruction on a previously unheard-of scale or burning up himself.

He didn't accept that he was "special" or that there was any such thing as "fate," but he could not avoid the fact he was a pivotal part of the running of these machines. His mother must have been like him, a guardian in her own right rather than a direct part of the Guardians movement as Tane had declared himself to be... but custodian of the Aradia bangle rather than a shield. Add to that the education she'd imbued him with—her pushing to immerse himself in critical thinking and history, and even the martial arts in which he'd become so adept...

Yes, his father was also an expert in krav maga, but it was Jules's mother who'd encouraged him to compete, to better himself. If it hadn't been for her death—so painfully random, and the culprits already punished—Jules might have grown up in a healthier environment. But circumstances set him on this path.

As he departed Ahua and boarded the plane with Toby, Bridget, Dan, Charlie, and Harpal, with no intention of returning to New York for any reason other than packing a few items, he settled into one notion. Something he'd never felt before or, if he had, he'd pushed it away.

He was on his way home.

Gold of the Lost Empire

The Lost Origins team returns for their most epic adventure yet, searching for a lost city and finding the key to unlocking one of humanity's oldest, most enduring legends.

Search your online retailer for "Gold of the Lost Empire"
Or scan the QR code to buy from Amazon

NOVELS BY A. D. DAVIES

Lost Origins Novels:

Tomb of the First Priest

Secret of the Reaper Seal

Curse of the Eagle Plague

Guardians of the Four Shields

Gold of the Lost Empire

Adam Park Thrillers:

The Dead and the Missing

A Desperate Paradise

The Shadows of Empty men

Night at the George Washington Diner

Master the Flame

Under the Long White Cloud

Alicia Friend Investigations:

His First His Second

In Black In White

With Courage With Fear

A Friend in Spirit

To Hide To Seek

A Flood of Bones

To Begin The End

Moses and Rock Novels:

Fractured Shadows

No New Purpose

Persecution of Lunacy

Standalone:

Three Years Dead

Rite to Justice

The Sublime Freedom

Co-Authored:

Project Return Fire – with Joe Dinicola

The Dead and the Missing

A missing girl. A PI out of his depth. A criminal network that won't hesitate to kill them both.

Adam Park is an ex-private investigator, now too wealthy to need a job. But when his old mentor's niece rips off a ruthless criminal and flees the UK, Adam tracks the young woman and her violent, manipulative boyfriend through the Parisian underground. Here, and onward in Asia, he learns of a brutal enterprise for whom people are just a business commodity.

To return the girl safely and protect the ones he loves, Adam will need to burn down his concepts of right and wrong, at any cost to his soul.

The 1st book in the Adam Park series is out now!

His First His Second

Meet Detective Sergeant Alicia Friend. She's nice. Too nice to be a police officer, if she's honest.

She is also one of the most respected criminal analysts in the country, now assigned to a cold northern town, investigating the kidnap-murders of two young women. Now a third has been taken. But Richard—the father of the latest victim—launches a parallel investigation, utilising skills honed in a dark past that is about to catch up with him. As Richard's secret actions hinder the police, Alicia is forced into choices that will impact the rest of her life.

The 1st book in the Alicia Friend series is out now!

Fractured Shadows
A Moses and Rock Novel

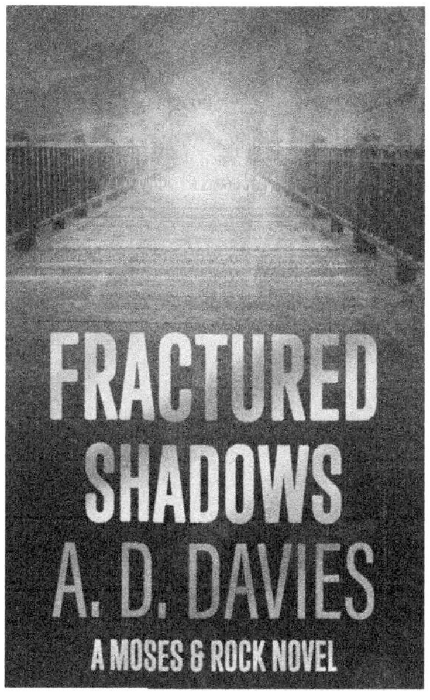

Will his last chance with the police become the final nail in his coffin?

Paired together in the secretive intelligence unit Division 43, Moses and Rock think they've landed an open-and-shut murder case, quickly arresting the son of a brutal criminal. But when detectives from another station furnish the killer with an alibi, it is clear something deeply sinister is afoot.

As Moses and Rock delve into the worlds of organised crime and police corruption, they must survive an underworld expanding its reach, colleagues willing to commit murder to protect themselves, and a history that Moses strives to conceal from everyone, including his new partner.

Project Return Fire - By Antony Davies & Joe Dinicola

An inadvertent trip through time...

A battle to decide the fate of mankind...

One chance to set things right...

Deep in the Juras Mountains, Johnathan Santarelli's team of Army Rangers investigates a radioactive anomaly. Suddenly Santarelli and his men are transported to 1945 in German-occupied territory!

Far from their loved ones, the Rangers want nothing more than to preserve the timeline and get home, but when an elite Nazi unit captures future technology, and the Rangers are confronted with younger versions of important people from their present, they question if this trip was a coincidence after all. Before long, the U.S. team realizes it has a higher duty: stopping the Third Reich from turning the war in Germany's favor.

Before they return home, the team must battle the Nazis for the future of time itself...

Project Return Fire is a military time travel action adventure novel set during World War II. If you like bloody battles, soldiers in action, combined with the shock of being ripped through time, then you'll love this action-packed thrill ride.

Printed in Great Britain
by Amazon

39330483R00253